LAURIE GRAHAM is a former J
contributing editor of *She* ma
writing fiction and radio dra
include *The Future Homemakers of America*, *The Unfortunates*
and, most recently, *Gone With the Windsors*. Visit her website at
www.lauriegraham.com

Visit www.AuthorTracker.co.uk for exclusive information
on your favourite HarperCollins authors.

From the reviews of *Mr Starlight*:

'A wonderfully effervescent history of mid-twentieth century
showbusiness and a rich portrait of a British working-class
family with more intrigues and secrets than a Renaissance court
... A touching, convincing, and uplifting book'   *Daily Mail*

'A marvel. Graham's style is riveting; hilarious one-liners fall in
quick succession'   ANTHEA LAWSON, *The Times*

'Funny and energetic right to the end, and a must for anyone
who can remember Liberace'   JOANNA TROLLOPE

'Like Mr Starlight himself, this novel is pure entertainment'
                                                    Sunday Times

'She has wit and insight to match Nick Hornby, and the entertainment value of Helen Fielding'   *Independent*

'As fresh and even more ambitious than Graham's previous best-
sellers ... she creates a Dickensian cast of absurd entertainers'
                                                    Guardian

'Funny doesn't come much sharper than Laurie Graham'
Mail on Sunday

'Laurie Graham's skill in constructing a story which is both sensational and thought-provoking is impressive' *TLS*

'If you haven't yet discovered Laurie Graham's warm-hearted and hilarious novels, we can't recommend them highly enough'
Glamour

By the same author

FICTION
The Man for the Job
The Ten O'Clock Horses
Perfect Meringues
The Dress Circle
Dog Days, Glenn Miller Nights
The Future Homemakers of America
The Unfortunates
Gone with the Windsors

NON-FICTION
The Parents' Survival Guide
The Marriage Survival Guide
Teenagers

LAURIE GRAHAM

Mr Starlight

HARPER PERENNIAL

London, New York, Toronto and Sydney

Harper Perennial
An imprint of HarperCollins*Publishers*
77–85 Fulham Palace Road
Hammersmith
London W6 8JB

www.harperperennial.co.uk
www.lauriegraham.com

This edition published by Harper Perennial 2006

First published in paperback by Harper Perennial 2005
First published in Great Britain by Fourth Estate 2004

A catalogue record for this book
is available from the British Library

ISBN 978-0-00-730648-0

Typeset in Fournier MT with Folio Display by
Palimpsest Book Production Ltd, Polmont, Stirlingshire

Dedicated to

Caryl Avery and Les Zuke,
my A to Z friendship,

and

to my best boys,
Tony Bird and Charles Darwent

Give my regards to Broadway
Remember me to Herald Square
Tell all the gang at Forty-Second Street
That I will soon be there

COHAN

MR
STARLIGHT

ONE

He had six bathrooms at the finish, every one of them done up to a different scheme, although most of them were never used. There was his, with a heart-shaped tub and a mirror on the ceiling, and the monogrammed towels folded just so, and nobody else supposed to go in there, only Pearl who looked after him. And then there was my favourite with a glass block floor and gold-plated dolphin taps, and a whole wall filled with water and tropical fish. Not that bathrooms interest me that much. Still, it's funny to think how we started out in Ninevah Street, with a lav down the yard and a jerry under the bed, in case you needed to go in the night, and a tin bath dragged indoors and put on the hearthrug, but only for special occasions.

We all had baths when our Dilys was getting married, so that was quite a production, and I had another one, I remember, when I was bad with the measles and the doctor had been sent for. But generally speaking, you could go all year in our house and never see that tin tub. Until Sel started getting top billing and Mam got stars in her eyes. Ever after that, if it was club night, it was bath night.

I was in the trimming shop at Greely's Motors in those days, working six in the morning till two in the afternoon. You could earn more doing a night shift but after I got jilted, the size of my pay packet didn't seem to matter any more. Renée and I had been saving up, getting our little bits and pieces together for when we were married, but when she called it off, well, I lost heart. And if I worked the early shift it meant I had my evenings. I could do the clubs with our Selwyn, as his accompanist.

When we started out they billed us as the Boff Brothers but that soon changed. Soon it was Selwyn Boff, the Saltley Songster, with Cledwyn Boff on piano, only in smaller letters. It has been my experience that once your letters get smaller they're unlikely to get bigger again. Then, as he developed a following he dropped the Boff and tried being just plain Selwyn.

'Your own, your very own Selwyn,' the emcee would say and by then nobody cared who was playing. As long as Sel was out front, holding the ladies' hands, looking into their eyes, making out he was singing for nobody in the world but them, he could have had a chimpanzee on the piano stool. Mam used to say, 'Did you play nicely last night, Cledwyn?'

I'd say, 'I could have played bare-arsed with my elbows for all anybody would have noticed.'

And I'd duck before she could clout me.

Our mam's profession was teaching pianoforte so we were all expected to learn when we were nippers. But Dilys apparently would never sit still and pay attention, so she was sent to tap dancing instead, and when Mam decided Sel had the makings of a singer he was sent to Miss Jaycock in Paradise Street, for voice and elocution. After that I got the piano to myself and when I joined the Boys' Brigade I learned the trumpet too.

Mam believed everybody should be able to do a turn, even if it was only play 'God Save the King' with a comb and tissue paper, but Dilys never liked performing. She'd sidle off outside and hide down the yard if we had company, if she thought Mam was going to make her climb up on the table and do 'You are my honey, Honeysuckle', and then, later on, she did put up a lot of weight due to married life and you can't dance if you're heavy. It's harmful to the knees.

I was the true musician of the family, but my brother did have another kind of talent and I never begrudged him that, not even for all the times he got written up in the Sunday papers and told a load

2

of fibs or never even mentioned me. He may not have had the best voice in the world, and he never did learn to sight-sing, but he had the knack of showmanship. He could lift people out of themselves and send them home happy. That's why he got bookings while trained musicians went hungry. But you can't argue against box office takings. I suppose that's what Uncle Teilo recognised in him.

Teilo wasn't our real uncle, but he was bookings secretary at the Nechells Non-Political Club and he wasn't without influence at the Birmingham Welsh and the Rover Sports and Social, and he'd shown a friendly interest in us from when we were young lads. Also, he was very fond of our mam. I believe he may have made her certain offers, over the years, only she was a bit hazy as to the whereabouts of Dad.

We had our debut at the Birmingham Welsh before the war. Sel was only ten. We were the first act of the evening, doing 'Gilbert the Filbert' and 'I Don't Want to Play in Your Yard', and whatever we were paid, I don't remember seeing any money. It must have gone straight into Mam's purse. She only ever let us do Friday nights because Sel had school and I had work to get up for, but the Boff Brothers became quite a name, and when I came back after the war we picked up where we'd left off. Of course, by then Sel wasn't a boy soprano any more. By then he'd been going to the pictures and getting some big ideas. 'I'll be appearing in a dinner suit from now on,' he said.

Uncle Teilo said, 'Oh yes? What did you do? Knock somebody over for their clothing coupons?'

But he'd been to Horace's, the house clearance people, and bought a dead man's suit.

'I want the lights down,' he said. 'I want total darkness before I come on, then Cled'll play a glissando and when the lights go up, there I'll be.'

'Oh, I don't know,' Uncle Teilo said. 'How will folks see to drink?'

But he did agree to a few things. We moved up the billing to close the first half and we were allowed a lacy cloth on the top of the piano and a potted palm. Bloody thing had to be lugged on the bus

3

every time, but Sel said it raised the tone. He wanted the audience to give proper order too and not walk in front of him with glasses of ale while he was singing, but that's the kind of respect that has to be earned. Still, by the beginning of 1948 we were getting top billing and Sel announced he was handing in his notice at the Milk Maid ice cream factory and turning semi-professional.

Dilys said, 'Oh, do be careful, Sel. The Milk Maid's a good place to work.'

Mam said, 'Well, there are only twenty-four hours in the day and he has to groom himself for stardom.'

Dilys said, 'What about his benefits? What about the retirement scheme?'

Mam said, 'Where he's going he won't need a Milk Maid pension.'

I said, 'What I want to know is where does this leave me? We're supposed to be a duo.'

He said, 'We still can be, for the time being. Until things really take off. There comes a time when you have to decide what you want. A Milk Maid pension or fame? A long-service medal from Greely's or a life?'

I said, 'Why can't you ever be satisfied?'

Mam said, 'You're a good little pianist, Cledwyn, but that's all you'll ever amount to. Selwyn's a true performer. He gives his all.'

I suppose he started giving his all after he got his first shiny jacket. He'd decided the potted palm and the penguin suit weren't enough, and he wanted to make himself more memorable, so he went off to London on a day return and came back with some glittery stuff that was meant for ladies' evening gowns. Mrs Grimley, next door, ran it up for him on her sewing machine and the first time he wore it, at the Non-Political, there was nearly a riot. All those women pushing to get up front and touch it, Nechells not being a place where you saw a lot of gold lamé.

The next Saturday he went back down to Oxford Street for more supplies. Mrs Grimley said she couldn't be doing with any more of it because of the fraying and the mess on her carpet, so he took it all to a tailor called Funkleman and had two more jackets made, one in silver lamé, one in rainbow glistenette. Funkleman thought our Sel was loopy but he took his money anyway.

After that he spent all his time thinking about suits and relied on me to do the musical groundwork, picking out new songs, trying out new arrangements. If we were doing both halves he'd change his whole outfit before the second set. He'd come running on and twirl around, so they could get a good look at his outfit. And the ladies appeared to like it. They didn't seem to care if he was out of puff and his singing was affected. Sometimes we'd only do half of the second set because they kept calling to him, egging him on to dance around some more and come down to the front, and make goo-goo eyes at them and ask them their names. Married women with their husbands looking on. He was lucky one of them didn't come over and thump him, but it never happened. Sel always got away with murder.

So the routine was, if we had a booking I'd go straight to bed when I got home from Greely's, to try and get some sleep, although I hardly ever did, what with the daylight streaming in and Sel upstairs practising his twirling, like an elephant with clogs on. Then, about five o'clock Mam would start filling the tin tub, so he could have a soak before tea. She'd put towels on the clothes horse and arrange it round him like a screen so he could be private. I don't know why she bothered because she was in and out every minute, topping up the water and scrubbing his back. 'Don't mind me,' she'd say. 'You haven't got anything I haven't seen.'

And he didn't mind. He'd just sit there smiling like a great pink bab, steaming and smelling of white heather bath salts.

'Why don't you get in after him, Cled?' she'd say. 'It's a pity to waste the hot water.'

But I wouldn't. A stand-up wash in the kitchen suited me and I wouldn't have put it past him to do a jimmy riddle in the tub, just to spite me.

As it was, I'd had to move out of our bedroom. 'He needs a room to himself,' Mam said, 'so he can work on his presentation and conserve himself for his public.'

She got him a full-length mirror and made a star out of a silver cake board and stuck it to the door, and I had to move downstairs and have a zed bed in the front room.

I said, 'Why can't he have the front room? He could hang his stuff from the picture rail.'

We never used that front room. Nobody did in those days. It was kept for funeral teas, but luckily we never seemed to have any.

'And have everybody peering in,' she said, 'spying on his costumes? No, no. That wouldn't do. You have to understand, Cledwyn. A star has to keep his air of mystiquerie.'

So everybody peered in at me instead, especially Mrs E from next door, because the front-room curtains were the kind that only looked like curtains. You couldn't actually close them. I always waited till I was under the covers before I took my trousers off.

We were getting three or four bookings a week, travelling as far as Wolverhampton or Castle Bromwich sometimes, struggling on the bus with his shiny jacket on a special hanger and him with his collar up and sunglasses on at seven o'clock on a January night so as not to be recognised.

'I'll have to get a car,' he kept saying. 'I'll buy it and you can drive me.'

I wouldn't have minded.

'We'll have tartan rugs in the back,' he said. 'And a personalised number plate. SEL 1.'

We were doing all right for money by then but Sel could spend it faster than they could mint it. Day trips to London. Cuff links and fancy shirts and high-heeled boots from Drury Lane. He kept a log of what he'd worn where, so he wouldn't repeat himself. He bought silly things as well. Knick-knacks for his bedroom. A suitcase with his initials on it.

Mam encouraged him, of course. 'Beautiful,' she'd say. 'You've got very good taste, Selwyn, like me.'

But it would have been nice if he'd put a few quid aside every week, like I did. There were things needed doing around the house. The roof needed re-tiling and the gas stove was from the year dot. And then there were the sanitary arrangements. The council were bringing in home improvement grants and not before time.

I said, 'I think this is something we should look into. Get this place brought up to standard. We should do it for Mam.'

The way it worked was you paid half and the council paid half, and you could get a proper bathroom put in, next to the kitchen. Mrs Grimley had signed up for it and the Edkinses at number 15, but Sel wasn't interested.

He said, 'Mam, do you want the upheaval of getting a bathroom?'

'No, I don't think so,' she said. 'Where would we keep the coal? And how would we go on without our convenience?'

That was what they did. Took your coal house and the outside lav and converted them into all mod cons.

I said, 'That's easy. We can get a bunker for the coal and we won't need an outside lav any more because we'll have an inside one. And lovely hot baths whenever you want them. We can put a shelf up, for your Amami and your talc. You'll be like Cleopatra.'

'I don't know,' she said. She was wavering, I could tell.

I said to Sel, 'Tell her how nice it'd be. No more lugging in bathwater for you every club night.'

'Cled,' he said, 'frankly I'm thinking bigger than Ninevah Street. Bigger and better, onward and ever upward. I'll be moving on soon so what's the point of spending money on this dump?'

I said, 'Oh, well, then, you'll be moving on so *you're* all right. What about the rest of us? How about a few comforts for Mam in her old age?'

'You plum duff,' he said. 'When I move on, she'll move on. And so will you, unless you intend trimming car seats the rest of your life. I'm on my way to the big time, our kid, and you and Mam are invited along.'

But his first move out of Ninevah Street was nearly his last. He came close to moving on somewhere nobody else can follow.

TWO

It was September of 1949 when it happened. It had been so hot the tar was melting on the roads and there wasn't a breath of air. You didn't feel like doing anything, only sitting still in your vest and pants and having a glass of lemonade, but we had club appearances three nights in a row so we had to stir ourselves, and of course we got a very poor turnout. People were staying at home, sitting out on their front steps, hoping for a cooling breeze. Things were so half-hearted the night we played the Alma Street Liberal I said we should cancel the rest of our bookings till the weather broke, but His Numps wouldn't hear of it.

'Sel Boff never cancels,' he said. 'The show goes on.'

So the show did go on. We were appearing at the Birmingham Welsh, with a novelty gargler who did the William Tell overture, Chucky Crawford doing his old card tricks and a vocalist called Avril who was just starting out, dark honey blonde with a nice frontage and a big voice for such a pint pot. She was making a play for Sel, straightening her stocking seams in front of him, getting him to fasten her necklace. I could have saved her the trouble. When it was show-time he had a one-track mind.

He seemed all right in the first half. We did 'Start the Day With a Smile', 'Where or When' and 'You Rascal You', and he'd acted the giddy goat as usual, running around, showing the ladies his new cummerbund, getting into a sweat.

I said, 'I don't know why you insist on wearing a jacket in this heat. Why don't you get yourself a short-sleeved shirt like me?'

8

'Because I don't want to look like a PT instructor,' he said. 'Because I'm tonight's star turn and my public has expectations.'

Then, just before we were due back on, he said, 'Cled, I don't feel too clever.'

I said, 'Is it your guts?'

'No,' he said, 'I keep coming over dizzy. Ask Mostyn to give us another five minutes.'

Mostyn was the emcee. He said, 'It is stifling tonight. I'll open another window.'

I fetched a glass of water and carried it through, and there was Sel, collapsed on the floor, turning blue around the mouth. I thought it was his heart. You do hear of it happening in young men. His eyes were open but he appeared not to hear me. We needed to phone for an ambulance but the telephone was in Mostyn's office and he had to find the key.

Avril was shouting, 'Hurry up, you silly old sod. There's a boy dying while you're going through your pockets.'

'I am hurrying,' he said. 'You go out front and keep the punters happy.'

'Send the gargler on,' she said. 'I'm not leaving Selwyn.'

Chucky Crawford said, 'Don't worry, I'll go back on.'

By the time Mostyn came back from the telephone Sel's eyes had rolled back in their sockets.

Avril said, 'Did you tell them to hurry?'

Mostyn said, 'Ambulances always hurry. And you've got a few things to learn about show business, my girl. Rule number one, whatever's going on backstage, you look after your audience.'

'Mostyn,' she said, 'there's hardly anybody in and as long as the beer keeps flowing they won't complain.'

And it's true. It's been my experience that people would rather take part in a heart attack than watch card tricks any day.

That ambulance had no great distance to come but it seemed to take hours. We were in a cubbyhole that passed for a dressing room, boxes of Christmas trimmings piled up on the shelves, mops and buckets in the corner, wondering if Sel was going to last the night.

Avril had his head cradled on her lap, stroking his hair. 'Beautiful curls,' she said.

I could have told her where those curls came from: a Toni home perm done in our Dilys's living room.

When they arrived they gave him oxygen and asked me a lot of questions. All I knew was he'd had a ham salad and a glass of orange squash for his tea, the same as I had except I'd let him have my spring onions. I didn't like to eat anything like that on a club night, in case I got lucky with the ladies. Also, he'd had brown pickle instead of salad cream, and three rock cakes. He'd seemed right enough during the first set apart from missing a line or two, but he did that some-times, when he ran out of wind. He never breathed properly, for a singer. They said they were rushing him to the General Hospital and I might want to notify his next of kin.

Then Uncle Teilo turned up, alerted by Mostyn. 'Oh dear,' he kept saying. 'My star turn. Oh dear, oh dear.'

By rights I should have ridden in the ambulance. I was family. But Teilo whispered something to the ambulance people, elbowed his way in.

'You go and fetch your mam,' he said. 'Don't worry about Sel. I'll make sure he gets a top doctor.'

I'd have had to wait for a bus only a very nice couple called Jean and Dennis offered to run me home in their Hillman Minx.

'We couldn't bear for anything to happen to him,' Jean said. 'We follow him all over, don't we, Dennis?'

He had fans like that even in those days. The husband didn't say a lot. It always was the ladies he appealed to, but still, that Dennis drove like the clappers to get me back to Ninevah Street.

Jean said, 'And then we'll run you to the hospital, won't we, Dennis? Who'd have thought it! Selwyn Boff's brother riding in our motor!'

'Did you loosen his cummerbund?' That was the first thing Mam wanted to know. 'Did you tell them he was invalided out of the RAF?'

I could have strangled her. Three times she ran back into the house, fetching things to take to the hospital. Indigestion pills and his hairbrush and then the evening paper, for the crossword puzzle, and all the while the car was ticking over, burning juice.

I said, 'Leave that! He's in no state for crosswords.'

'He will be,' she said. 'He'll perk up once he knows I'm there. Did you tell them he can only drink sterilised milk?'

I said, 'He's unconscious, Mam. He won't be drinking any milk tonight.'

She said, 'Well, if they give him the wrong milk and he comes out in hives we'll have you to thank.'

I said, 'I'm not his keeper.'

'Yes you are,' she said. 'That's exactly what you are. He's only a bab.'

They allowed us to see him for five minutes but he was in a big machine, to help him with his breathing so we couldn't really see him at all. They said they hoped to be able to tell us more in the morning.

Mam said, 'I'll just brush his hair. Tell him I'm here.'

'Not tonight,' they said. 'He's too ill.'

That's when it hit her. 'Oh, Cledwyn,' she sobbed. 'Whatever can it be? Don't let me lose him. I couldn't bear to lose him.'

She wouldn't come home, insisted on waiting there all night though there was nothing to be done.

I said, 'Should I ask Dilys to come? She could wait with you.'

'No,' she said, 'Dilys is neither use nor ornament at this time of night. She can't manage without her sleep the way I can.'

I said, 'Well, if I'm going to be up all night, I'd better phone Greely's, tell them I shan't be in tomorrow morning.'

'Just go home,' she said. 'I don't need anybody to sit with me. It's a mother's job to keep watch. And it'll be me he asks for when he wakes up.'

So Jean and Dennis kindly drove me home and when I offered them something for their trouble and their petrol, Jean said, 'You keep your hand in your pocket. We don't want your money, do we, Dennis? Of course, what we'd really love is an autograph.'

'Happy to oblige,' I said. 'Where's your autograph book?'

'Oh no,' she said. 'This wouldn't be the right time. He's a sick boy. But when he's on the mend, if you think to mention it to him, a signed photo would be lovely.'

I expect she lived to regret not letting me sign her book, especially after I'd had my hit single.

Sel got worse before he got better. He was on the critical list for several days and Mam instructed us on what we were to say to the reporters.

Dilys said, 'There aren't any reporters, Mam.'

Mam said, 'That's because you keep using the front entrance. They'll be round the back, thinking to catch you out. That's what they did when Judy Garland was in hospital.'

Avril tried to visit too, just the once, but Mam soon saw her off. 'Family only,' she said. 'Doctor's orders.'

This wasn't quite true because Uncle Teilo was buzzing around every day, looking for progress reports, wondering how many more bookings he'd have to cancel. Sel was unconscious for a whole day and when he came to we had a bit of a fright. 'I've gone blind,' he said. He was clinging to Mam. 'I can't see anything. I'm too young to go blind.'

Mam said, 'Don't worry, Selwyn, Mam's here. Mam'll send for a specialist. Cledwyn, tell your Uncle Teilo to get a specialist. Whatever it costs.'

But it was only blurred vision. Gradually it cleared, then his eyeballs turned yellow and his belly swelled up like a balloon, and he itched so much he scratched himself nearly raw. It had all been caused by his jacket, they said. He'd been poisoned by the stuff that had been used to clean it. Carbon tetrachloride. Mam said, 'It was no such thing. It was DabAway. And I only freshened it up. What was I supposed to do? Leave the sweat to rot the seams? Costly fabric like that?'

They said Mam wasn't to have known. It was in very tiny print about using the product in moderation and airing the garment thoroughly after it had been cleaned. They said four bottles was a lot, but she still shouldn't blame herself. She said, 'I'm not blaming myself.' But I think she did, on the quiet.

At the end of the first week they asked me to step into the doctor's office.

I said, 'Are you sending him home?'

'No,' he said, 'far from it. Your brother isn't out of the woods yet. There could be kidney damage. We have to wait and see.'

I said, 'How long?'

'Two to three weeks,' he said. 'If there is damage . . . you might want to consider whether your mother should be warned.'

I said, 'She'll do whatever it takes. She'll cash in a policy if it's a case of going private.'

'It isn't,' he said. 'It's a case of a possible sudden deterioration.'

Dilys was visiting when I looked in on him. She was trimming his hair and they were laughing and joking, no idea he might be on death row. 'Cheer up, our kid,' he said, when he saw me. 'You look like you just saw a ghost. Come and sit down. I've got quite a story to tell the pair of you. I've had an amazing experience. A vision.'

Dilys said, 'Well, you are on a lot of medication.'

'Nothing to do with medication,' he said. 'A beautiful lady came to me, in the middle of the night. She was dressed in long white robes.'

I said, 'It was probably that little staff nurse with the nice ankles.' I had my eye on her myself, always crackling her apron, pretending to be busy.

'No,' he said. 'It wasn't any nurse. It was a visitation. She stood as near to me as you are and she was bathed in a heavenly glow.'

Dilys said, 'You must have been dreaming. Had they given you a jab?'

'No,' he said. 'I was as wide awake as I am now. Something made me sit up all of a sudden and there she was, smiling at me. But here's the best bit: she knew all about me, all about my singing career and everything.'

I said, 'Did she tell you Industrial Brush Social Club want to charge us for a no-show?'

'Bugger Industrial Brush,' he said. 'This lady laid out my whole life before me. She said my days singing on the clubs are finished. She said I have a Higher Purpose.'

Dilys said, 'What, like Dewi Elias?' Dewi was one of Aunty Gwenny's in-laws, worked as a roofer for years until he slipped and had a bang on the head. Then he went for a deacon. Reckoned he'd heard celestial voices.

'Never mind Dewi Elias,' he said. 'I'm on the threshold of a momentous change in my life.'

It made my blood run cold to hear him making plans, after what I'd been told.

'See?' he said. 'That's why I was spared from DabAway poisoning. She told me I'm meant to go to America and there I shall make my fortune.'

Dilys said, 'Could it have been the lady with the library trolley?'

I said, 'Not in the middle of the night.' I was hoping he had seen a vision, in a way. He was too young to die.

He said, 'She was sent from above. I know she was. One minute she was here, clear as I see you, next minute she was gone.'

I said, 'Did she glide away?'

'Not so much glide as fade,' he said.

Dilys said, 'You haven't told Mam?'

'No,' he said. 'I didn't think she'd like it.'

He was right about that. Mam didn't even like Joan Wagstaff visiting, who had been one of his best pals in school, and she was a married woman.

I've often wondered if it was caused by the pills or if he made it all up, but he stuck to the same story all his days. Then again, Sel never saw any harm in being approximate with the facts.

I walked with Dilys to the bus stop.

She said, 'Are you going to say anything to Mam?'

I said, 'I think I might. If America's on the agenda she ought to be warned.'

I was inclined to leave well alone with the other business. If Sel

14

started to go downhill I could always get the doctor to explain things to her. No sense in running to meet trouble.

I said, 'It could kill her.'

Dilys said, 'What? Him going to America? I don't think so. She's made like a Sherman tank. As long as Sel's in the limelight she'll keep rolling.'

So I brought the matter up with Mam that same evening.

'Visions!' she said. 'I'll give them visions. They've been letting nuns in to bother helpless invalids. I shall make a complaint to the matron in the morning.'

Mam hated nuns. We were chapel. Well, we weren't anything, really, but if we'd had to be something we'd have been Ebenezer Congregational.

'Well, that settles it,' she said. She'd got a right old cob on her and I hadn't even got as far as the details of Sel's Higher Purpose in America. 'I'm getting him out of there,' she said. 'I'll have him moved somewhere nice and quiet where he's not troubled by intruders.'

And she did. As soon as he got the all clear on his kidneys he was on his way to a convalescent home in Abergele, thanks to the generosity of well-wishers from the Birmingham Welsh, and then on to Aunty Gwenny's, for fresh air and home-made currant bread. It made no difference, though. He may have been sitting in the Land of our Fathers with a rug round his knees, but in his heart he was already on his way to America.

THREE

I was six when Sel came on the scene. I'll never forget the day. We'd had team games that afternoon, out in the yard at Bright Street Infants because it was such a nice day and I'd been called out to the front to show the class good ball control. I was feeling very pleased with myself and then when I got to the corner of Ninevah Street I bumped into Mrs Edkins.

'Cledwyn,' she said. 'You've got a new bab at your house so you'd better come to me for your tea tonight.'

I ran home so fast, to see if it was true about the bab and beg Mam not to send me to Mrs E's. Normally my sister Dilys could have given me my tea. She was fourteen. Only she was on holiday at Aunty Gwenny's, getting over tonsillitis. But when I ran in the door there she was, back from the country, and Mam was on the couch in her nightie and His Numps lay in a drawer out of the sideboard, all wrapped up in blankets and a woolly bonnet.

First thing I said was, 'Can Dilys give me my tea? I'll be good.'

Mam said, 'Look at you, in a muck sweat. What have I told you about running? See what's in the crib?'

'Is it a bab?' I said. I'd never really seen one close up. 'Where did it come from?'

'Under a gooseberry bush,' Mam said. 'Now go and wash your face and then you can give him a kiss.'

I said, 'How long is he stopping?' and Mam and Dilys both laughed. The main thing was, I didn't have to go to the Edkinses for my tea, as long as I went about on tiptoe and didn't wake the baby.

I hated going next door. There was nothing to play with and Mrs E smelled of fried bread and sometimes she didn't button up her blouse properly, so you could see things, unless you closed your eyes tight. Dilys wanted to name the bab Skippy, like in the cartoons, and I wanted him to be called Billy Walker, like the Aston Villa captain, but Mam said neither of those were proper names and he'd to be called Selwyn. Selwyn Amos, like I was Cledwyn Amos, after her brother Amos who'd died in the Battle of the Somme. Dad wasn't around at that time so he didn't get a say. Even in 1928 it could be hard finding the right kind of work. A man had to be willing to travel. By the time he turned up again the new bab had opened his eyes properly and was all signed up as Selwyn Amos. It was official. Dad didn't seem to mind.

According to Mam, our dad had had a college education, though where he'd had it we never knew, and it didn't appear to have done him much good because he was always getting laid off, or having a falling out that wasn't his fault and being sent on his way. It was a good thing for us that Mam had a profession.

Mam met our dad when she came to Birmingham before the First World War. She'd been in Oswestry in service, and then she'd come to a big house in Edgbaston, to be a governess to somebody's kiddies, teaching them their ABC and piano and manners. She was Anne Roberts, from Pentrefoelas, and she was quite the traveller of the Roberts family. Her sister Gwenny married Rhys Elias and never went any further than Denbigh.

Aunty Gwenny and Uncle Rhys had three sons, all named John because only the youngest one lived, and he did pretty well for himself. He ended up in Chester, in wholesale fruit and veg.

Dad's people were the Boffs and they came from the Shrewsbury area. I don't think we ever met any of them.

Aunty Gwenny didn't approve of Dad. 'You could have done better, Annie,' she always said and she nicknamed him 'Gypsy', which stuck.

But I never heard Mam say a word against him. 'Gwenny doesn't understand,' she'd say. 'She's not seen the world the way I have.

Your father's overqualified for the work that's on offer around here.'
As to why we didn't all move somewhere nearer to work that was
up to his high level of aptitude, that was never gone into. Actually,
it quite suited us, his not often being there. It was only a small house
and he was a big man. And Mam kept cheerful enough. She had her
piano pupils and there was always Uncle Teilo if she needed a new
light bulb screwing in.

I've often wondered if our dad's problem was drink. We were
teetotal so we never had alcohol in the house, but money did seem
to run through his fingers and he used to weep sometimes, too, which
might have been brought on by the demon drink.

But Mam always stayed calm. 'Go down to Sturdy's,' she'd say.
'Mr Edkins says they're setting men on. Go and ask at the gate.'
She'd give him the bus fare and a bit extra, to help him feel like a
man, but she never let him see where she'd fetched it from. Mam
had hiding places all over. In her shoe sometimes. In her brassiere.
'And remember not to mention your college education,' she'd say.

But he'd usually come back with a long face and a story. He was
too old. Or the powers that be had it in for him. I question whether
he even went to Sturdy's gate and asked.

I liked having a bab in the family. After Sel arrived I didn't get
so much attention paid to me, which meant I could stay out in the
street later, practising my ball control. And with Dilys helping in
the kitchen I could get away with things Mam didn't allow, like not
eating my crusts. Then, just before Sel's first Christmas, Dilys got
a start as a jam tart packer at Oven Fresh, which meant Mam had
all the housework to do again and I could get more time on the
piano.

I loved my music. Mam had children sent to her for lessons who
had to be threatened with the stick before they'd practise, but not
me. And I caught on fast, too. Mam wasn't a great one for dishing
out praise but she did tell me once I had natural ability.

Sel was a wakeful type of baby and he only had to see me lift the
lid of the piano to start smiling. That's how I picture us then: him
propped up in the corner of the couch, big and bonny, blowing

bubbles and dribbling down his bib, and me playing him my little pieces, still too short to reach the pedals.

After he learned to walk he'd tag along behind me everywhere and on school mornings, when I had to go and leave him, he'd cry as though his heart was broken.

Mam'd say, 'You're too soft, Cledwyn. Just walk out of the door and don't be so daft. Babies are meant to cry.'

I never really understood the wisdom of that.

So me and Sel were close from the beginning although, of course, as the years went by we had our ups and downs. By the time he started at Bright Street I was nearly ready to move on to the big school. I didn't want him trailing behind me, expecting me to play with him like I did at home, but one thing about Sel, wherever he went people liked him. He made some little friends of his own that first week and that was how he carried on. He was no footballer and I don't even remember him joining in a game of conkers, but he got along with the girls, like Vera Muddimer and Joan Wagstaff, skipping with a rope and playing Kings and Queens and getting up little concerts. He joined the Cub Scouts but he only went once. He said, 'I'm not going back.'

And Mam said, 'You don't have to, darling, not if you don't like it.'

I said, 'You made me go. You said I had to persevere.'

'Selwyn's cut from a different cloth,' she said. 'He's not tough, like you.'

So he was allowed to stay at home and develop what Mam called 'the domestic arts'. Stitching an S on all his hankies. Rearranging Mam's ornaments. Decorating biscuits. Dilys used to bring bags of mis-shapes home from Oven Fresh and he loved titivating them with coloured icing and silver balls. He could be quite artistic. I was already working at Greely's by the time he passed for the Grammar School. I said to Mam, 'I hope he'll get on all right there.'

'Why wouldn't he?' she said.

I was worried about him because the Grammar School was boys only. I said, 'He's going to miss Joan and Vera.'

19

'Selwyn makes friends wherever he goes,' she said. 'And there's time enough for girls later.'

And it was true, he did have the knack of playing the fool and winning folks over, even the ones who called him a sissy. It was as though he was daring the whole world not to like him.

When Dilys was eighteen she started walking out with Arthur Persons. Mam never let them out of her sight. They had to keep the door open while they said goodnight out on the front step, even if there was a gale blowing, and if she couldn't be in the room supervising them, I had to keep watch.

'Play your new piece for Arthur,' Mam'd say, which meant she needed to go outside and pay a penny and I was supposed to guard our Dilys's virtue.

Poor Arthur. He endured two years of that while they saved up for a bed and some easy chairs, and then they got married, in the spring of 1933. The wedding took place at Miller Street Congregational. Dilys wore a blue suit made for her by Mrs Grimley and Uncle Teilo walked her up the aisle, our dad having had to rush away to Gloucester to follow up a business opportunity. Me and Selwyn were attendants. I wasn't keen but Dilys begged me. I was twelve years old by then and I'd seen some of the get-ups attendants were expected to wear. There were often weddings round the corner at St Botolph's and I'd seen boys dressed in velveteen and lacy collars. But Mam said there'd be nothing like that, just a bath the night before and a nice clean shirt and tie, so I agreed. Sel had long white socks and new shoes, and he carried a lucky cardboard horseshoe to give to the happy couple as they came out of the chapel, and the reason I remember that is he was so pleased with his white socks he spent the whole time looking at them and worrying in case they got smudged. If you look at Dilys's wedding photo all you can see of him is the top of his head because he's busy gazing down at his legs.

Dilys and Arthur started off in one room at Arthur's parents' house in Tysely, and then they got a flat with shared kitchen and bathroom on the Pershore Road, and all the while Arthur was climbing the ladder at Aldridge's Machine Tools and doing very well for himself. By the time Dilys was in the family way they were buying a house at Great Barr with a garden front and back, so much down and then so much per month.

Every so often Dad would turn up with a bag of laundry and holes in his socks, and I'd be sent to Jewks's for a skein of darning wool. 'And while you're out,' Mam'd whisper, 'run round to Uncle Teilo's and tell him your father's home.'

It was one of Dad's homecomings that led to a big falling out between Mam and Dilys.

'Tell Arthur your father's available for work,' Mam said.

'No need,' Dilys said. 'I expect they'll be giving it out on the wireless. But Arthur can't get him work.'

'Of course he can,' Mam said. 'If he's any kind of son-in-law. If he's as high up at Aldridge's as he cracks on.'

Dilys said, 'If Arthur sullied his hands setting Dad on he soon wouldn't be anything at Aldridge's. I'm not asking him.'

Mam said, 'Then I'll get him a start. I'll go to Aldridge's myself and tell them who I am.'

'Don't you bloody dare,' Dilys was shouting. 'Don't you bloody bloody dare.' I could see her point of view. There were always complications where Dad was involved, complications and recriminations. It was just as well Dilys stood her ground because Arthur was too mild to have done it for himself.

Then Dad went off to the Labour Exchange one morning and didn't come back. It was the usual pattern.

Mam said, 'I expect he was offered something. He'd heard there might be an opening in the Potteries. That's how it is. If an opportunity presents itself you have to jump in quick, before someone else does. You don't have time for goodbyes.' But I noticed his spare shirt was gone and so was my Brylcreem.

I went over to Dilys's to tell her Gypsy was gone. I said, 'So you and Mam can patch things up now.'

'I don't know,' she said. 'It's quite a relief not having to see her.'

I said, 'Sel misses you.'

'Bring him over on the bus,' she said. 'I'd like that. And Mam doesn't need to know.'

But however much Sel missed Dilys it wasn't enough for him to go behind Mam's back. 'No,' he said. 'Mam's the mam and Dilys is the girl, so what Mam says goes. And if you go to Dilys's again, I'm telling.'

So we were incommunicado until Arthur came round one night and said Dilys had had two lovely baby girls and it was time to let bygones be bygones. And as it was Dad they'd quarrelled over and he himself was a bygone just then, Mam relented and we all went to see the new arrivals. They'd named them Betsan and Gaynor.

I was fifteen and Sel was nine, which seemed young to be uncles, but we were both pretty chuffed about it.

Dilys said, 'Sit on those kitchen chairs, the pair of you, and each of you hold one of the babies.'

I was up for it, but Sel wouldn't. 'Their legs are too thin,' he said. 'And they've got funny skin.'

There were certain things he never liked to touch and there was no persuading him. He could be very funny that way.

'Well, Dilys,' Mam said. 'Now you've got your work cut out.'

'Don't worry,' Dilys said. 'I've got a good man to help me.'

After that peace broke out and we saw Dilys most weeks. If Villa were playing at home she'd bring the girls over to see Mam while me and Arthur went to the match. I always liked Arthur. He was as gentle as a lamb. Then sometimes we'd go over there, to Great Barr, on a Sunday afternoon and we'd have tinned salmon and salad and pears in syrup or fruit cocktail, and then walnut cake, with white icing and glacé cherries. Happy days.

Then, of course, along came the war and I decided to jump before I was pushed. I tried for the Engineers and when they realised I could get a tune out of a cornet they made me a bandsman, which meant being a medical orderly too in case we saw action. I was at home, on embarkation leave, when Dad turned up. His face suddenly appeared at the kitchen window, cigarette behind his ear, silly grin on his face, as if he'd just come home from work, not been missing, whereabouts unknown, for more than twelve months. 'Put the kettle on,' he said. 'Where's your mam?'

She was at Spooner's, fetching gammon for my send-off tea.

'Bloody wars,' he said. 'I did my bit in the last lot. And you'll be all right at Greely's. Reserved occupation.'

I said, 'I volunteered.'

'Oh yes?' he said. 'More fool you. And what are you doing, half-pint?'

Sel was snipping holes in a piece of paper, making a doily for the cake stand. 'Helping my mam,' he said. 'And there won't be enough gammon for you. You weren't expected.'

But of course Mam gave up her rasher for Gypsy and when Uncle Teilo called in she came over very light-hearted. Whatever Dad said, she laughed, whatever Teilo said, she laughed, although he didn't seem to be in a very humorous mood. 'I'll be seeing you, Annie,' he said, as he was leaving. 'You know where to find me.'

'Home is the hunter, Teilo,' she said. 'So I won't have to trouble you for any more light bulbs.'

We didn't sleep much that night. I was wondering what war was going to be like and Sel wasn't happy about the new arrangements. 'Don't go in the army, Cled,' he said. 'What if you get shot?'

I said, 'I have to go, our kid. It's my duty. And it's your job to look after Mam.'

'I always look after her,' he said. 'But why did he have to come back and upset everything?'

I said, 'You know Dad. He probably won't stay long.'

'Yes he will,' he said. 'He told Mam he's going to build her an air raid shelter.'

But Sel didn't know Gypsy Boff as well as I did. By the next time I came home on leave he was history. Mam had volunteered him for the Miller Street Home Guard but he only lasted a week or two and then he'd disappeared for the duration.

I said, 'I suppose he was too brainy for the Home Guard?'

But Mam wouldn't be drawn on the subject. 'People lose touch when there's a war on,' she said. 'As you'll find out.'

I reckon he must have had a woman somewhere. Some lonely widow who was glad to have his ration book. We did see him again after the war, though, so whatever else had transpired, the *Luftwaffe* hadn't flattened him.

I didn't have a bad war, compared with some. I saw some terrible sights but at least I came home. There were quite a few I'd known at Bright Street who didn't make it, and then there was Mr Grimley from next door. He was believed to have copped it when they bombed the cannon factory in Armoury Road. They never found anything of him. He just never came home again.

I was demobbed early in 1946 and not long after I arrived home Sel got called up to do his National Service. He had to report to a recruitment station in Acocks Green.

Mam said, 'This government seems determined to rob me of a son.'

I said, 'They'll never take Sel. One look at him and they'll send him home.'

'What do you mean?' she said. 'He's a fine-looking boy.'

He was tall and well-built, but there was that soft girlie side to him too. I couldn't see him clambering up and over a cargo net. He didn't have the musculature for it. I couldn't see him getting stuck in to bayonet practice. And neither could he. 'I'm not letting them cut my hair,' he said. 'I'm going to tell them I'm a pacifist.' So he went off to Acocks Green, whistling and smelling of talc and expecting to be back in five minutes, but he was gone all day and when he did turn up he looked like a bulldog chewing on a wasp. 'Fat lot you know,' he said. 'I've only gone and got into the RAF.'

Now, there was a lot of competition for the air force. Nobody just walked, especially not a boy who didn't have the right attitude.

I said, 'You can't have done. You've misunderstood.'

'No I haven't,' he said. 'They asked for anybody who'd passed their School Certificate and there was only me and one other, so they said we were both in. Now what am I going to do? I don't want to fly aeroplanes. I want to work on my singing career.'

Mam said, 'Go back and tell them you're musical. Tell them you're willing to serve in a concert party.'

I said, 'This is National Service, Mam, not *Take Your Pick*.'

'Then he can be a bandsman,' she said, 'like you. I'll write to them.'

I said, 'He can't play anything.'

She said, 'He can play the triangle. You don't need to be Paderewski to be an air force bandsman.'

He said, 'But I don't want to be a bandsman. I'm going to be a singer.'

Dilys said, 'The RAF does have a nice uniform, Sel. Anyway, perhaps it won't come to it.'

But it did come to it. Well, it did and it didn't. He got his papers to go to RAF Padgate for basic training. He left on the Friday while I was at work and by Tuesday night he was back home, medically exempt due to 'Weak Back and Nervous Temperament' and whistling again. He walked straight back into his job in the payroll office at the ice cream factory, Uncle Teilo got us some club bookings and we all settled down again.

Sel practised his singing in front of the dressing-table mirror and I kept up to date with the hit parade. A song didn't have to be aired many times before I had it committed to memory, and we were known around the circuit for offering a good mix of old and new. I began trying my hand at composition too and, although I didn't receive a lot of encouragement, I'd say many of my early efforts have stood the test of time: 'Gnat on the Windscreen of Life', 'Knee Deep in Love', which I wrote for Renée when we started courting, 'You Pulled the Chain on Me', written after she called things off.

Renée had a look of Rita Hayworth about her and she was my first experience with the fair sex. Mam didn't like her, but Mam never got along with other ladies. She'd chat for hours with Mr Edkins next door, laughing and joking, but the minute Mrs E poked her head out she'd turn frosty. And she was the same with any girl I looked at. 'Too full of herself,' she'd say. Or, 'All kid gloves and no drawers.'

Me and Renée had to do what courting we could in the back row of the Gaumont, so after six months I asked her to marry me, in the hope of moving things along in the bedroom department. After we got engaged Mam had to allow her in the house, begrudging as she was. It looked like being a long haul, saving up for our bits and pieces, but at least we could be in out of the cold. At least we didn't always have to have fish and chips and a cuddle in the bus shelter. We even had full-scale relations, just the once, when Mam was getting over pleurisy and went to stay at Aunty Gwenny's.

But then Sel had to open his mouth and ruin everything. 'Mam,' he said. 'I reckon there's a spring gone in the front-room couch.'

'Why?' she said. 'Have you been going in there, wearing it out?'

'Not me,' he said. 'But Cled did, and when he lay on top of Renée it didn't half make a noise.'

It was all very well for him. He hadn't matured to that degree yet. His idea of having a good time with a girl was meeting Vera Muddimer for the Shoppers' Lunch in Lewis's. He thought it was highly amusing when Mam said I'd have to move out if I was going to treat the place as a knocking shop. But I couldn't move out. We didn't have enough in our savings account, and after that Renée wouldn't show her face in Ninevah Street. 'I've got needs, Cled,' she said. 'So you'll have to decide. Is it me or your mam?'

I said, 'If you'll just be patient. Another twelve months and we'll be set up.'

But she suddenly got it into her head to leave Greely's and be a bus conductress, five pounds a week, free uniform and half-price travel. And then, well, the writing was on the wall. A bus conductress has men hopping on and off all day long. It was really no job for an engaged person who was having second thoughts.

FOUR

After Sel had recuperated from his suit poisoning Uncle Teilo was keen to get us bookings for our comeback season, but His Numps wouldn't apply himself to it. 'Time to move on,' he said.

Uncle Teilo said, 'Oh yes? Where to? Has Norman Hewitt been talking to you?' Norman was another big fixer in Birmingham. Sel just laughed.

I said, 'Well, I think I should be kept in the picture.'

'Look, Cled,' he said. 'We've been a good team, but we've got different plans. I'm a pro and you're playing for pin money. And you can't say I didn't warn you.' It was that business with the lady in white.

I said, 'You don't have to go to America to branch out, you know. We could travel further afield, do some private functions. Sutton. Lichfield. We could get a little motor.'

'No,' he said. 'I'm going to America. I've outgrown this place.'

I said, 'Please yourself. I'll go solo. You're not the only one with a following, you know. I'll always find a welcome at the Birmingham Welsh.'

'Good,' he said. 'In that case you won't get your knickers in a knot if I go my own way, under new management.'

Dilys said, 'Don't worry, Cled. Perhaps it won't come to it. America might not want him.'

But when Sel set his heart on something he always got it. Like that painting by numbers kit he pestered Mam for when he was nine.

Like that old clock covered with cherubs he outbid everybody for at a big auction. Ugly bloody thing, supposed to have belonged to some French nob and he paid thousands for it.

So he went off on one of his jaunts to London and came home with a pair of patent leather boots and a promise of work through the Ted Sibley Agency, Representation for International Artistes.

Uncle Teilo had popped round to put a new flex on Mam's iron and we were all sitting having tea when Sel walked in. 'I've done it!' he said. 'Ted Sibley signed me on the spot. He had to admit it wasn't every day an act like me walked through his door.'

I said, 'When are you leaving?'

'When the right opportunity opens up,' he said. 'See, Cled, you don't just leap at the first thing you're offered. You have to know where you want to get to, and then you have to have a plan and everything you do has to fit in with it. It's no use jumping on a bus going to Walsall and then complaining it never took you to Kidderminster.'

I said, 'Thanks for the tip, big shot. So what's it to be? Broadway? Hollywood?'

'The top,' he said. 'That's the only destination that interests me.'

'That's the ticket, Selwyn!' Mam said. 'I always knew you'd go far.' She didn't show any signs of being grief-stricken.

Uncle Teilo said, 'Some tin hut in Africa, that's where he'll end up. Concert parties in Umbongo Land. Ted Sibley! After all I've done for you. You could be playing the Aston Hippodrome in a year or two if you stick with me.'

'No, Teilo,' Mam said. 'He has to move on, same as I did from Pentrefoelas. People who've got any gumption always do. You're never appreciated in your own backyard.'

I said, 'Well, I'll be staying on your books, Teilo. As a matter of fact I've got a few ideas of my own. I might look around for a bass player and a drummer. Maybe a little vocalist too. A nice little songstress who's easy on the eye. The Cled Boff Combo. We'll be playing some of my own material.'

'Oh yes?' he said.

A bit of enthusiasm would have been nice.

Dilys didn't like the sound of Sel's plans. She said, 'Who is this Ted Sibley anyway? Sel's too young and trusting to sign papers for going overseas.'

Of course, Sel always brought out the protective side in women. They always worried about him and ruffled his hair and cut his toast into soldiers. I put a lot of it down to his dimples.

She said, 'Will you go with him, Cled? Make sure he doesn't get double crossed?'

I said, 'I'm not giving up my prospects to play nursemaid to him.'

Mam said, 'You don't have any prospects.'

Sel said, 'I'll be all right, Dilys. I'm twenty-one. I've got my wits about me. And I've got talent. All I have to do now is share the good news with the rest of the world, specially those Americans. They're going to wonder what hit them.'

I watched Mam's face. 'And there's the difference', she said to Uncle Teilo, 'between an artiste who starts on the clubs and an artiste who stays on the clubs.'

Dilys said, 'Well, I still think Cled should go with him.'

'Cled won't go anywhere,' Mam said. 'He's a stay-at-home.'

Sel said, 'Look, if you want to try your luck too, Cled, I've no objections. Go and see Ted Sibley. If you've got what it takes he'll sign you, if you haven't he won't. And you're well thought of at Greely's. Let's face it, stardom isn't for everybody. But whatever you do, don't any of you worry about me. I'm on my way and I don't need a babysitter.'

He was so full of himself and all he had was a pack of promises, not a single paying engagement in the book. *I* was the one getting enquiries from Wednesbury Oddfellows and the Sluice and Penstock Social. I thought, 'I'll show the ruddy lot of you.'

I took a day's holiday and went down to London to see this Ted Sibley. It caused quite a flutter in the Trimming Shop. I had to promise to send them a picture postcard, even though I was only gone for the day. Sel insisted on coming with me.

I said, 'You're the one supposed to need nannying.' I'd been to London before. I'd been through on a troop train. I said, 'Got you worried, have I? Think Ted Sibley might recognise who's the real musician in the family?'

'Ah, come on, Cled,' he said. 'Don't be like that. Don't let's fall out. We've both got something to offer. You're a good steady instrumentalist. I've got that added vital ingredient.'

We went to a cafeteria and he put away two eggs on toast and a pot of tea. I couldn't manage a thing; I was so churned up with nerves. I'd never had to audition for strangers very much, with Uncle Teilo having so much pull.

Sel said, 'Here's my advice. Forget you're trying out for Ted Sibley. Pretend you're at home. Enjoy yourself. Pretend you're playing for Dilys and Arthur. And look at it this way, if it doesn't pan out, at least you're a skilled car seat finisher. You'll never starve.'

I played 'Lazy Bones' and 'Nice Work'. It was a good piano, but I wasn't up to my usual mark. Ted Sibley had the habit of narrowing his eyes while he was listening, giving the impression he was in pain, or falling asleep.

I said, 'I'm better with an audience.'

'You should be so lucky,' he said. Then he threw me a play list and told me to show him what I could do on trumpet. That was when I hit my stride. I gave him 'Blue Orchids' and 'Night and Day' and my own arrangement of 'Little Brown Jug', mood perfect, note perfect, even though I was in a bit of a haze. I think it had been caused by a beverage called a Rusty Nail, bought me by Sel to help settle my stomach. Anyway, Sibley stubbed out his cigarette and said, 'Yeah, you'll do. I'll put you on my books. You understand what's involved? You'll have to have a medical. You have to be willing to travel. You single, Cled? No encumbrances?'

I was between romances as it happened. I said, 'Is that it, then? When do I start?'

'As soon as I need a trumpeter,' he said. 'Are there any more of you at home? Any other Boff talent I should know about? No chorus girls? Sax players?'

Ted Sibley did a lot of business with the shipping lines and he was looking for a tenor sax for a sailing to Ceylon and some high-kickers for a variety show going to South Africa. There was no telling where an international entertainer could end up. 'And Sel,' he said, 'I'm still waiting for a photo of you in a normal suit. Single vent, no spangles, remember? I can't sell you as a supporting vocalist if you look like something off a flying trapeze.'

'I'll get it done tomorrow, Ted,' he said, and then he winked at me. 'I'll wear something from Hepworth's Mr Normal Collection and just let my natural incandescence shine through.'

He didn't appear to notice he'd had a ticking off. He'd received so little criticism in life I'm not sure he always recognised it when he heard it. And it never crossed his mind that things might not go his way. All he could see was that house with the swimming pool waiting for him at the end of the rainbow.

We went back to the cafeteria and I had my first breakfast of the day and Sel had his second.

I said, 'I'll have to give Greely's a week's notice.'

'Yeah?' he said.

I said, 'Renée used to say I didn't have enough get-up-and-go. I've a good mind to go round to the Midland Red depot tonight and see what she's got to say for herself now.'

'Yeah?' he said.

I said, 'Where is Ceylon, exactly?'

'Don't know,' he said, 'and don't care. The only boat I'm getting on is one going to New York.'

I said, 'It might be nice to see some other places first. World travel is bound to give a man a certain something. It can't help but give you more pull with the ladies.'

'Yeah?' he said.

He had several girls keen on him at that time, including his old school pal Vera Muddimer, but he didn't seem inclined to make the kind of move they were hoping for. He knew the facts of life. I'd filled him in on all that. You pick up those kinds of things when you do military service, but of course that was an experience that had passed him by.

I said, 'Don't you like Vera?'

'I love Vera,' he said.

I said, 'Then how come you haven't got round to kissing her yet?'

He said, 'I kiss her all the time.'

I said, 'I don't mean on the hand. That's just fooling around. I mean *kissing*. On the lips.'

'Bleeah!' he said. 'Germs!'

He was an oddity.

'Cled,' he said, 'I hope you're not expecting us to get booked for the same engagements? Just because we're family doesn't mean we're joined at the neck. Ted's business is getting the best he can for his artistes. He can't be ruled by sentiment.'

I didn't have any expectations. Once we were back in Ninevah Street it all seemed like a dream and anyway, I didn't want to prejudice my position at Greely's. I said to Mam, 'Nothing may come of it. Sel talks as though it's in the bag, but it's not.'

But Mam said, 'Of course it is. You'll probably get a letter tomorrow.'

Uncle Teilo wasn't so impressed. 'Chugging back and forth on some tub,' he said. 'What if you get seasick?'

Mam said, 'They won't get seasick. They went on pleasure pedalos in Cannon Hill Park and they were as right as ninepence.'

Sel said, 'Yes. And anyway, I might only have to chug forth. Some millionaire impresario might come aboard and discover me. Then I'll be down that gangplank and on my way, first trip.'

No letter came the next day, nor even the next week, even though Sel had sent in a plain vanilla photo as instructed.

I said, 'Looks like Ted Sibley was all talk. How about going back with Teilo? Put a bit of jingle in our pockets?'

'Not me,' he said. '*You* go back with Teilo.'

But Uncle Teilo had got the hump.

When I asked him if he had anything for me he said, 'Back from your world travels already? That didn't last long. Well, I've got all the solo pianists I need just now, Cledwyn. I've got Winnie Skerritt and a nice steady boy from Coleshill, who knows which side his bread is buttered. So I'm afraid I can't help you at the moment.'

I said to Sel, 'Brilliant. We appear to have lost our shirts on Ted Sibley and now Teilo's turned funny.'

'Ask me,' he said, 'you're better off staying at Greely's. Clock in, clock out, pick up your wages every Friday. See if Norman Hewitt can get you something. But let's face it, Cled, you haven't got the balls for real show business.'

Then I came home from work the following Monday and there was a letter waiting for me, propped up in front of the mantelpiece.

Mam was banging about in the kitchen.

I said, 'Well?'

'Well what?' she said.

I said, 'Did Sel get New York?'

'He'll get his tomorrow,' she said. 'They send notices to bandsmen first, then the soloists' letters get posted the day after.'

Sel was out, eating Kunzel cakes with Vera Muddimer and pretending not to be bothered that he hadn't heard anything.

When I was on the early shift Mam always kept my dinner for me till I came in, hot enough to take the roof off your mouth, but it was stone cold by the time I'd finished looking at that letter. Six transatlantic sailings with Cunard, subject to a medical examination. Contract renewable subject to my giving satisfaction. Terms of employment enclosed.

I said, 'I've done it, Mam. I've got a job playing trumpet on the *Queen Mary*. I've ruddy well done it!'

'Now, Cledwyn,' she said. 'I don't want you crowing and upsetting your brother. It's very hard on his nerves, all this waiting.'

'I'm not bothered,' he said, when he eventually turned up. 'You need nerves of steel in this business and I've got them.'

Mam said, 'You've got a very generous spirit, Selwyn. You deserve every success.'

Of course, he made sure she was out of earshot before he said anything else to me, whispering, trying to needle me. 'You'll only be

33

a bandsman,' he said. 'You won't get your name on the programme. And you'll be kipping down in the depths,' he said, 'Down with the rats. If the boat sinks you won't stand a chance. You'd better start practising "Nearer My God to Thee".'

Then Mrs Edkins came in to borrow a shilling for the gas meter.

I said, 'I'm sailing to New York, Mrs E.'

'Subject to medical examination,' Mam said.

Mrs E said, 'I didn't know you had it in you, Cledwyn. Now won't it be a caution if Selwyn never gets a letter and you have to go without him?'

'No,' Mam said, 'it won't be a caution, it'll be a clerical error. Now take your shilling, Connie Edkins, and stop bringing on Selwyn's nervous tension.'

Of course, he did get a letter. It came the next day, offering him the same sailings I was on, as intermission singer. By the time I got home he'd been to the post office to draw money out and gone to Man about Birmingham to buy a blazer and two pairs of strides. 'Hello, sailor,' he said, when he saw me. 'Splice the mainbrace!'

He was back in a good humour. 'What did they say at Greely's?'

I hadn't actually got round to telling them. It was a big step, giving up my security and when it came to it, that morning, I'd had some doubts about going through with it. I'd proved I was a match for Sel and that was what mattered to me.

We had seven days to consider and send the papers back, and it was a funny thing made me do it in the end. They'd just brought something in at Greely's called time and motion studies, which was a man with a clipboard, writing down every move you made including when you went to answer a call of nature. It was in the interests of greater efficiency and nobody liked it. Stan Walley, our shop steward, reckoned it was a Trojan horse got up by management, looking for ways to lay people off. I wasn't a big union man myself but Stan turned out to be right and I've often wondered whether I'd have got the chop, if I'd stayed long enough to find out. As it was, something in me snapped that morning. Clicking his ballpoint pen, getting under my feet.

34

I said, 'I've been offered work on a transatlantic luxury liner so you can stick that stopwatch up your arse.'

And that was that. I signed on the dotted line and then we waited to get our medicals. Arthur and Dilys thought I'd been hasty, giving my notice at Greely's. Dilys said, 'Sel failed for the RAF. What if he fails this time? You surely won't go without him?'

'I don't know,' I said. 'Maybe I will.'

But Sel's weak back was of no concern to the Cunard doctor. We both passed A1 and when we came out on to the Marylebone Road it was still only half past twelve. We had the rest of the day ahead of us. The rest of our lives.

He said, 'I'm going round the shops. Are you coming?' He wanted to buy some sparkling cuff links and once Sel started shopping you could be there till they were cashing up and putting the lights out.

I said, 'No. I think I'll wend my way to a Corner House for cod and chips. I might go to the pictures.'

'That's the spirit,' he said. 'You go your way and I'll go mine. I'll see you at home.'

I saw William Holden and Broderick Crawford in something and then I went on to a very saucy peepshow, so it was nearly nine o'clock before I got back to Ninevah Street.

'Where's Selwyn?' Mam wanted to know.

It was past midnight when he came creeping past my door, new shoes squeaking.

I said, 'You're in trouble with Mam.'

'No he's not,' she shouted. '*You're* in trouble, for losing your brother.'

'It's all right, Mam,' he said. 'I made myself scarce so Cled could go to an opium den.'

'As long as you're safe,' she said. 'Now get up to bed.'

He was hanging about in my doorway.

I said, 'Get your cuff links?'

'Yeah,' he said. 'And I had sex.'

I said, 'You did not.'

'Yes, I did,' he said. 'Did you?'

I said, 'No. I didn't feel like it. Where did you have it?'

'Not saying,' he said.

Not saying because it hadn't happened.

I said, 'You're a bloody liar, Boff.'

He went off to bed laughing.

'I'm in the mood for love' – I could hear him whistling while he was putting his pyjamas on.

FIVE

I had a right royal send-off from Greely's. They'd had a whip round and they presented me with a travelling shaving compendium and a card signed by everyone in the Trimming Shop. One of the bosses even came down from the top floor to shake me by the hand.

I said to Stan, 'See, they are human after all.'

'That's because you're leaving,' he said. 'Think what you're saving them in severance pay.'

Our first sailing was mid-April and we had to be aboard twenty-four hours before departure. There was a lot to do, packing our valises, saying our farewells, and we were quite the celebrities in Saltley those last few days. Mam sent me round to Jewkes's to buy her a hairnet and Mr Jewkes got so carried away, surmising how much money we'd be earning, after stoppages, he took the last hairnet off the card and then put it back in the window, empty. I always remembered that.

And then Mrs Edkins yoo-hooed me from the doorway of Spooner's the butchers, wanting me to go in so she could show me off to all the ladies who were queuing for their meat. 'This is Annie Boff's other boy,' she said. 'I've known them both since they were babs, and now young Selwyn's going to America to be a star, and he's taking Cledwyn here along with him. Isn't that nice?'

The morning we left, people gathered on the corner of Ninevah Street to wave us off. Mam was coming with us, to see us on to the train, but Dilys never liked goodbyes. She said she'd stay behind and make a start on stripping the old wallpaper off Sel's bedroom wall.

'You won't know it when you get back,' she said. Dilys loved paperhanging.

He said, 'I'm not coming back.'

Dilys said, 'Oh, don't say that.'

Sel said, 'Don't worry. It won't go to waste. Cled might be glad to move back upstairs.'

He'd insisted on riding to the station in a taxi. 'Stars don't wait at bus stops,' he said. And he was wearing sunglasses.

Mam said, 'I'll leave you here, then,' when we got to the barrier. 'I won't hang about.'

She'd spotted Vera Muddimer and Joan Wagstaff. They were down on the platform with a big sign that said 'Bon Voyage' and Mam never liked competition. Still, it was hard to watch her walk away, all on her own. Sel was smiling and bouncing around, but I was having a few qualms myself.

Vera said, 'Cheer up, Cled. Or shall I go in your place? I can play "Good King Wenceslas" on the mouth organ.'

It was raining as the train pulled out, but he kept his sunglasses on.

I said, 'Do you think Mam's going to be all right?'

'Why wouldn't she be?' he said.

It was a Monday, as I recall. Monday we generally had cold meat and pickles, and a milk pudding to follow. Rice was my favourite, but I didn't object to sago or tapioca, provided there was jam to go with it.

I said, 'I don't know. Suddenly she's all on her own. I keep thinking of her, dishing up one plate instead of three.'

'It's the natural course of things,' he said. 'All these years she's groomed me for stardom and now I'm on my way. That's more important to her than having to eat her tea on her own. Anyway, Teilo'll probably turn up.'

I'd seen pictures of the *Queen Mary* in the newspapers but nothing prepared you for walking out of the shed and seeing the curve of her bow towering over you. Her name alone must have been fifty feet long, and the sun had broken through, bouncing off the shine off her new demob paint. Glossy black and white, and her raked funnels dark orange. She was beautiful.

Sel was eager to go aboard and sign on, but I persuaded him to wait with me a few minutes and watch all the comings and goings. A big fancy motor car was being lowered into the hold and two ratings were carrying vases of white chrysanthemums up the gangplank, floral arrangements taller than they were. There were crates stacked all over the dockside and a young Yank overheard us guessing what was in them. 'Eleven thousand pounds of sugar,' he said. 'Twenty thousand bottles of beer. I see you're new boys. What's your trade?'

He was Jim Ganey, Dining Room Waiter, First Class, and he had all the answers. 'That automobile is the property of Lord Freddy Orr,' he said. 'He likes to while away the crossing losing at poker. And the chrysanthemums are for the Duke and Dukess. The ones you Brits ran out of town. I've sailed with them before and I can tell you, they always travel with a quantity of flowers.' We were going to be sailing with the Windsors.

Sel said, 'How about that, Cled! I could be doing a Royal Command Performance sooner than I thought.'

But Ganey said, 'Don't fool yourselves. Once their stateroom is fixed up to their liking they stay put, save theirselves the bother of getting pestered by nobodies.'

I'd have liked to take a look around but there was a band call at six o'clock and we had three queues to join before we could go anywhere and the first one was to join the union.

Sel said, 'I'm not joining any bloody union.' But it was that or go home and the representative didn't appear to care which way he jumped as long as he made his mind up and stopped holding up the queue. It was a terrible shock to him, to be spoken to like that. There were all types signing on and Sel wasn't accustomed to the rougher element. He couldn't take his eyes off them.

And then we got our quarters. A four-berth cabin, aft on R deck. Sel said, 'There must be a mix-up. I should have my own cabin. I'm a vocalist.'

'Intermission singer,' the Ship's Writer said. 'R64. Next!'

Sel went very quiet. At home he was accustomed to a room of his own, with his costumes hung on padded hangers and a lace mat on his bedside table. He was very particular about his bits and pieces. Mam mopped his lino twice a week and dusted where she could, but she never moved anything because he liked everything just so. If ever we went to our Dilys's for tea he'd start tidying her spoon drawer.

I said, 'Cheer up, our kid. At least they've put us together.' We were sharing with a bass player called Feifer and a drummer called Wilkie. Bunk beds and tin lockers, and two strangers watching every move you made. Feifer was a bad-tempered type, used to lie in his cot eating slices of raw onion, and Wilkie was plain light-fingered. My shaving set from Greely's disappeared before we were out of sight of land. It was a good thing I was there, to show Sel the ropes and make sure nobody nicked his brilliantine.

He said, 'This is insulting. Where am I supposed to hang my suits?'

I said, 'We could be worse off. People like the greasers and the bellboys are ten to a billet.'

'Yeah,' he said. 'Could be worse. That's *your* way of looking at a situation, Cled. Could be better. Should be better. That's *my* way of looking at things.'

The night before a sailing was always organised chaos. Crew who turned up at the last minute, crew who didn't turn up at all, companion ways like Piccadilly Circus, trolleys of liquor and cigarettes and linens being pushed along the working alleys. 'Burma Road' they called it down there. And all the while cargo being winched aboard. Three tons of butter, according to Jim Ganey. Fifty thousand pounds of spuds.

We had a pep talk from Massie, the entertainments manager. 'Punctuality, ladies and gentlemen,' he said. 'Please remember to adjust your timepieces every night. And remember you're here to do a job of work. Don't venture into passenger areas. Don't presume to fraternise with the clientele. Any questions?'

I don't think he expected any.

'Yes,' Sel said. 'How about if the clientele try to fraternise with me?'

'Mr Boff,' he said, 'I believe you're engaged as a vocalist. This is no time to try being a comedian.'

We piled down to the mess room for Beef à la Mode with three veg, cheese and biscuits and a choice of ice cream, then somebody set up a card school and a dartboard in the post room. You couldn't have your usual recreational facilities the night before sailing or the night before docking. The social club was in the baggage area.

Sel was sitting down the table from me, chatting to an older man with epaulettes on his shirt.

I said, 'Are you coming for a game of arrows?'

'No,' he said. 'I've made other plans.'

I heard somebody say, 'Good lad. Keeping Mother happy. You'll go far.'

Sel's new pal was Mess Room Steward Noel Carey, but everyone called him Mother and he took a shine to Sel right from the start. You need company if you're below decks all the time. We musicians at least got to move about a bit, but Carey never went up for air. He led a lonely life, but Sel humoured him, and when Mother Carey had been humoured the door to the pantries would swing wide open. Once my guts had got accustomed to the way the ship rolled, I enjoyed a late supper, after showtime. Ham and eggs, or a flash-fried steak slapped between two slices of bread. All thanks to Sel's cheery personality. But a ship's crew is a close community. You need to go carefully. He said, 'I'll see you later. Noel's got something he wants to show me.'

I said to him later, 'We only just got here, so take things steady. When you're a newcomer you have to be careful not to tread on anybody's toes.'

'What?' he said. 'Whose toes?'

I said, 'That pantryman with the gappy teeth. After you went off to see Mr Carey's theatre programmes he said, "I wonder if he's going to show him his etchings as well?" sarcastic like. I think I detected a note of envy.'

'Don't worry about me,' he said. 'Envy's something I'm going to have to get accustomed to. Listen, I had a look in one of the First Class staterooms. You get a three-piece suite, Cled, not just a bed. And a coffee table and a drinks cabinet. That's the way to travel.'

I said, 'You'll be getting the sack before we've even sailed. You heard what the boss said. No snooping off limits.'

'I wasn't snooping,' he said. 'Noel took me up and showed me around. It's beautiful, Cled. Elegant. That's what I'm going to have some day. A stateroom, with a pink leather settee and a telephone and a fresh bowl of fruit every morning.'

'Shut yer yap, pretty boy,' Feifer said. 'Some of us is trying to sleep.'

SIX

There was no peace once the boilers were fired and the baggage lifts started up, but Sel lay on his bunk like the Queen of Sheba anyway, cucumber slices over his eyelids and curlers in his quiff. 'Preparing to meet my public,' he said. 'You don't get a second chance at first impressions.'

I said, 'Come upstairs with me. You're the one with the open sesame. See if we can get near a rail. Watch for big names arriving on the dockside.'

The word was Henry Ford was expected plus a Guinness millionaire, a mysterious star of the British stage and, of course, the Duke and Duchess.

Wilkie said, 'You won't see them. They'll come aboard from a launch once we're under way.'

But I went up anyway with a little Eyetie from the Tourist Class barber's shop who knew a window we could watch from, and we had company. A girl called Ginger from the beauty parlour, very jolly with lovely knees. She let me light two smokes for her before she mentioned she had a fiancé.

Her friend was quieter. Black wavy hair and skin so pale you could see the veins on her temples. Hazel. Not my usual type. 'Look,' she said, 'There's Lady Clackmannan.'

But it was only Lady Clackmannan's maid, down on the quayside supervising where the trunks were going.

'Princess Olga,' she said. 'Mr Vansittart.'

She was reeling off all these names, but they were just the servants down there. Hazel worked in the passenger laundry, so it was the maids and the valets she knew.

I said, 'Isn't it boring down there, dhobi-ing? Never seeing daylight?'

'It is not,' she said. 'Dhobi-ing! Cheeky beggar. What do you think I do? Bash shirts on rocks?'

Ginger said, 'Don't bite his head off. He's new.'

Hazel said, 'What's your name, new boy?'

'Cled Boff,' I said. 'Musician.'

'Well, Cled Boff,' she said. 'I hope you'll enjoy your work as much as I enjoy mine. I get to handle couture garments. They come to me when they need a delicate touch, see? Hopeless cases, that's my speciality.' She smiled at me. 'And every stain tells a story,' she said.

Ginger shouted, 'There's Rex Harrison!' And it was the actual man himself, climbing out of a taxi.

Sel was still stretched out on his bunk, reading *Tit Bits*.

I said, 'I think I just got lucky.'

'Oh yeah?' he said. 'I hope she won't be disappointed when she sees your love nest. I hope she likes the smell of second-hand onions. See any notables?'

I said, 'Rex Harrison. The Windsors' pug dogs. And there's a Princess Olga come aboard.'

He sat up. 'Really?' he said. 'What, tiara and everything?'

I said, 'No. Felt hat and an overcoat.'

'Glad I didn't stir myself, then,' he said. 'If I had a tiara I'd never leave home without it. I won the toss, by the way. I'm letting Tex do the big one tonight.' Tex Lane was the other support singer and the two of them had to cover six spots a night. If you did the First Class Dining Room, you finished with the ten o'clock spot in Cabin Class. If you did a turn in Tourist, you opened the late show in First Class, the Starlight Club in the Veranda Grill priming the pump for the star vocalist.

I said, 'I thought you were gagging to play the Starlight Club?'

'I am,' he said, 'but not the first night out. I want Tex Lane to go over the top first, let them see how mediocre he is. Suits me to warm up on the peasants. By tomorrow night I'll be ready for anything.'

He slipped in the back of the Grill after he'd finished his last spot for the night, although I didn't see him. He must have blended in well, in his new dinner suit and a crisp new shirt. Not like Tex Lane with his frayed cuffs. But Sel wasn't interested in Tex. Glorette Gilder was the one he was there to study, in her fishtail gown and her dangling earrings. 'She's nothing special.' That was his verdict. 'Wait till they see me in action.'

But a warm-up only got seventeen minutes: 'How High the Moon', 'Slow Boat to China'.

I said, 'I don't see that you've got a lot of scope. You're just there to air the room and Tex could hardly be heard tonight, for all the laughing and chattering. Nobody listens till the big name comes on. You're supposed to sing your numbers plain vanilla. No chatting to the audience. No holding a lady's hand.'

'Yeah?' he said. 'We'll see.' That was when he started developing his trade mark wink.

Of all the public rooms on board the *Queen Mary* the Veranda Grill was my favourite. It had a big curved window that looked out over the stern of the boat. Everything was cream and silver and mahogany, with soft pearly lighting and wide steps from the dining area to the dance floor, with thick black carpet and glass balustrades. I've played much bigger rooms since, and plenty of five star venues, but I've never seen anything to top it.

We were an eleven-piece band under the baton of Lionel Truman and everyone had better know their play list. 'Number twenty-four,' he'd say, quiet but clear, and we'd go straight into 'Tangerine'.

Even now, if somebody says 'Thirty-nine' I think 'Besame Mucho'.

Sel opened his first night with 'Blue Champagne' and 'Cruising Down the River', and then he unbuttoned his jacket for 'Moonlight Becomes You' I don't know if it was his silver cummerbund that got their attention but they piped down a lot more for him than they had for poor old Tex. He even got a little ripple of applause. 'Thank you so much,' he said.

He wasn't supposed to say anything. He was meant to finish his last song and clear off, but Sel never liked to be hurried. 'Tonight was my Starlight Club debut,' he said, 'and you couldn't have been a nicer audience.'

I heard Glorette whisper, 'Play me on.' But Lionel Truman hesitated and as long as he hesitated Sel stayed out there.

'Don't forget,' he said, 'Thursday night is Gala Night. I'll be here but it won't be Gala night unless you're here too.'

Glorette was getting irate. 'Play me on, you deaf old fucker,' she kept whispering and eventually Lionel lifted his baton.

But Sel still wasn't finished. 'Ladies and gentlemen,' he said, 'a warm welcome, please, for a lady who was playing the Veranda Grill while I was in short trousers. The one and only, the very fabulous, Miss Glorette Gilder.'

SEVEN

I didn't see Hazel again till our last night at sea. After showtime I always went to the Pig and Whistle with the rest of the boys. It was nice to wind down with a cold beer and a game of cards, or a sing-song round the piano, but Hazel didn't seem to socialise.

'I haven't had time to draw breath,' she said, when I did run into her. 'Pulled threads. Duck grease. You name it, I've had it this trip. Coty pancake on the neck of Mrs Vansittart's beaded silk.'

I said, 'You want to be careful, cooped up with cleaning products.' I told her about Sel's episode with DabAway.

She said, 'I wouldn't mind having a few visions myself. But I don't use a lot of chemicals. Guess what I use to lift pancake make-up? A heel of stale bread. Never fails. See, I have to be careful. I can't have my clients collapsing or going up in flames if somebody lights a stogie near them. Bread. That's the answer. And a slow gentle rub.' She brushed a bit of fluff off my shoulder.

'Hello, hello, hello,' I thought. 'Cledwyn, your luck is in.'

The question was where to take her. Last night out was clean-up night below decks so the place never went quiet. We went up on top to where you could have your dog walked by a bellboy. There wasn't anybody about. She had a smell of soapsuds when I kissed her. It was lovely, after days of Feifer's onion breath and Wilkie's socks. I only got as far as unbuttoning her cardie, though.

'That's enough,' she said. 'You'll be waking the dogs.'

'Funny you're Welsh,' I said. 'I'm hundred per cent Welsh myself.'

She said, 'Well, you don't sound it. You sound Birmingham to me.'

We got a two-day lay-over in New York.

I said, 'Got any plans, after we dock?'

'Sleeping,' she said.

I said, 'We could go dancing.'

'No,' she said. 'Perhaps another time. You go and enjoy yourself. There's nothing like New York, especially the first time. And don't bother going to bed tonight. The pilot comes aboard about four o'clock. You should bring Sel up here, watch the sun come up over the city.'

I couldn't persuade her to stay there with me.

'No,' she said. 'I'm going to tidy my work table, soak my feet and go to sleep.'

Playing hard to get.

So I had to make do with Sel for company. We stood on the starboard side, like Hazel had said, and watched New York appear. First everything glowed red and then it turned pale green, and by the time we were coming into the pier, everything was sparkling in the sunshine. The whole place looked like it was made of glass.

'I've arrived, Cled,' he said. He was looking radiant for a person who wasn't usually up before dinner time.

'No, Sel,' I said. '*We've* arrived.'

But the ship's whistle blew, so he could pretend he hadn't heard me.

We'd had a plan of campaign. Test the water with some booking agents, see a few sights, send postcards to Mam and Dilys. And we were going to watch what we spent.

I said, 'We should always have something put by for a rainy day.'

'Yes, Cled,' he said.

I said, 'And business before pleasure. We should do the agents first. You got your list?'

'Yes,' he said. 'But I'm not settling for any old ten percenter. It's got to be somebody who can bring in quality venues and a record contract. He's out there now, Cled, shaving, sipping his coffee. No idea that this is going to be his lucky day.'

He was only a few places ahead of me in the queue, but by the time I'd drawn my pay he'd disappeared.

Somebody said they thought he'd gone ashore with Mother Carey. Somebody else said he'd left with a bunch of boiler room boys. He was gone, that was all I knew, and he hadn't taken his good jacket with him.

Two of the clarinettists were going off to get one of those big American breakfasts. I said, 'I don't know what to do. I suppose I should go looking for him.'

'Save your shoe leather,' they said. 'You'll never find him. He'll be all right. You pal along with us.'

Which I did and I had quite a nice time, considering how worried I was about Sel, on the loose in a great big foreign city.

It isn't just the look of a new place that can muddle you. It's the smell of it and the noise. Steam leaking out of the ground and trains rumbling under your feet. Hot dogs and coffee and car horns tooting for the littlest thing. Even the girls were different: brighter and cheekier-looking, swinging along in their shiny nylons. The boys said they could point me in the direction of a bit of business if that was what I fancied, but I was contented just to look. Where the ladies are concerned I've never believed in paying for a thing when you might get offered it for free. I bought a little bottle of Evening in Paris scent in Macy's department store. If Hazel was willing to play ball it was hers. If not, there'd be others. Scent never goes to waste.

'The theatres,' I said. 'That's what I want to see.'

And I wasn't disappointed. Mary Martin was appearing in *South Pacific* at the Majestic, Carol Channing was in *Kiss Me Kate* at the Mansfield and *Brigadoon* was playing at the Ziegfeld. But the biggest thrill was Radio City Music Hall with pictures outside of all those high-kicking lovelies and Sold Out stickers across the Frank Sinatra posters. It made me realise what a fall Sel was heading for. It was one thing to be the toast of the Nechells Non-Political, but something else to come to a place like New York and think he could ever be a match for the big boys. We finished up in a club on 52nd Street called the Three Deuces listening to the great Art Tatum. I hadn't realised he was black till I saw him in person. When I look back on my first time in New York that's what I think of: seeing black people. And the meatball sandwiches, so big you needed both hands and dripping with gravy. And the adverts that lit up in Times Square. There was one that made smoke rings from a cigarette, and one that looked just like a waterfall, only it was all done with light bulbs.

I never did find out how Sel had passed his time. All I know is sign-on time was nearly up and he hadn't appeared.

I said to Massie, 'I won't be able to sail without my brother.'

'Entirely up to you, Mr Boff,' he said. 'But you'll be leaving without your papers.'

Then he rolled in, with two days' beard and a package under his arm.

I said, 'Dilys was right. You're not safe on your own.'

It struck me, seeing him unshaved, how much he looked like our dad.

'I'm here, aren't I?' he said. 'What's your grouse?'

I said, 'Try any agents?'

'Fuck agents,' he said.

Two days in the company of E deck types and that was how he was talking.

I said, 'Well, you'd better buck up. If you go on tonight looking like you do now, you'll be out of a job. You make Tex Lane look dew-fresh.'

'Yeah?' he said. 'And fuck you too.'

But Sel could always turn himself around for an audience. By seven o'clock he was shaved and shampooed, and ready to give them 'They All Laughed' in First Class cocktails. He was wearing his latest purchase: a white tuxedo with a black satin shawl collar.

I said, 'How much did that set you back?'

'It's an investment,' he said. 'Look like a star, you're halfway to being a star.'

He looked like a Latin American bandleader to me.

EIGHT

I wished Uncle Teilo could have been there to see us, 'chugging back and forth on some tub' as he'd put it. The *Queen Mary* was no tub. She was a floating palace. You could go to the pictures, in a proper cinema with flip-up seats, or play ping-pong, or keep fit in the gymnasium, riding on a bicycle that was nailed to the floor. You could get a shave and have your nails buffed, send a telegram, get your trousers mended. There were even churches: a normal one and a Jewish one. And there was plenty of entertainment: a band, a string trio and two feature pianists, four showcase ballroom dancers, and Sel and Tex and Glorette. It must have been a headache if you were a passenger, deciding how to fill the days. I'd have been worried there wasn't enough time to sample everything.

It was different for us, of course. I enjoyed the work. Lionel Truman led a good band and I liked the camaraderie of it, but when you weren't working you were very cooped up and five days at sea could seem longer than five days in Saltley. It was very gloomy below decks. The walls were painted dark-green up to the dado. You needed the lights on all the time and you could never get away from the vibration of the turbines and the smell of cooking and machine oil and men's socks. Tempers were liable to get frayed, as they did between Sel and Mess Room Steward Carey.

Carey was a man who got very attached to people and if he liked you he expected to monopolise you. So when Sel went down to G deck one afternoon, taking up the offer of being shown around by one of the firemen, Carey got overexcited and fetched a knife from the galley. 'Guided tours, is it!' he shouted. 'I know their game!'

Hazel was on her break. We were having a cup of tea.

'I'll kill him,' Carey was shouting. 'I'll kill them both!'

He'd been at the cooking brandy. You could smell it on him.

I said, 'God Almighty, Hazel, I'd better run and warn Sel.'

But there were three hundred yards of boiler rooms and he could have been anywhere. I didn't like it down there. I never liked the idea of all that steam being pent up.

Hazel had fetched two big kitchen porters in case assistance was required, but Carey had shut himself in his cabin in the meanwhile and was promising to do himself an injury, and as everybody seemed to be ignoring him I surmised it wasn't the first time this had occurred.

I said, 'I couldn't find Sel.'

'Shaft alley,' somebody said. 'That's where he'll be.'

I said, 'I don't know where that is.'

Everybody laughed.

Hazel said, 'Pay no attention, Cled. And don't worry about Mother. You couldn't cut hot butter with that knife he was brandishing.'

I said, 'I get the impression Carey isn't a family man. I suppose things can get out of proportion when you don't have a home life. It's a shame he's gone off the deep end, though. He's been very fatherly to Sel.'

Hazel said, 'I don't know about that. Ask me, half the crew belongs in the madhouse.'

She'd put a saucer over my teacup, to keep it warm while I was searching for Sel. It's funny the little things that make you fall for a girl.

I said, 'Are you going to let me take you dancing when we get to Southampton?'

'Maybe,' she said.

I knew one of the pastry chefs was keen on her. I'd seen her chuckling with him.

Sel didn't have a good trip sailing east that first time. There was

52

the upset with Carey. Then one of the pianists complained about him improvising in the Midships Bar so he got a stripping down from Massie about doing what he was paid to do and not a note more. They started trying to needle him in the mess room too, calling him Sally instead of Sel.

'Sally, Sally, don't ever wander,' they'd sing, hoping to aggravate Mother into grabbing a knife again.

On Channel night I went looking for Hazel before we started the show in the Veranda Grill. She was working on a silk blouse with a piece of tissue paper, trying to get a water mark off it.

I said, 'Well, have you made your mind up? What's it to be? Coming ashore with me or sleeping your life away?'

'I don't drink, mind,' she said.

I said, 'That's all right. You can have a port and lemonade.'

'Cled,' she said, 'invite Sel to come with us. He seems very down in the dumps.'

We had a nice crowd in for Gala Night. Tex got in a bit of a tangle with 'Fascinating Rhythm' but nobody appeared to notice and Tex couldn't have cared less. He knew Sel outshone him. I think he was just vamping until something else came along; a rich widow looking for companionship, or death from strong drink. It's only when you're on the up that you care how highly you're rated. The downward slide is the downward slide wherever you are on it.

I said to Sel, 'Me and Hazel are going to the Imperial for afternoon tea after we've docked, but I don't suppose you feel like coming with us?'

'Yeah, all right then,' he said. 'Keep an eye on you, you old goat.'

The ladies always liked him, laughing at his silly jokes, telling him all their business. Not that he ever had a lot to show for it. I was the one who got results.

'Hazel,' he said, 'I want to pick your brain. What's the best thing for my patent leather shoes?'

'Vaseline,' she said.

He said, 'And what about the black satin on my revers?'

'Potato water.'

'This woman', he said, 'is a treasure.'

He was holding her hand.

'Now what about old Chufty Auchtermuchty? I was watching him during the cocktail hour. He looks like a man who doesn't always know where his mouth is. You been removing stains for him?'

'His name's Lord Auchinloss,' she said, 'and I'm not telling.'

He said, 'All right, just tell me this, you know that furry thing he wears between his legs all the time?'

She was laughing. 'That's called a sporran, Sel,' she said.

'I'll take your word for it,' he said. 'But seriously, what would you do with that if he brought it to you and asked you to take care of it?'

'Throw it a steak,' she said.

They were in a silly mood, the pair of them.

I said, 'Don't let us keep you, Sel. I expect you're keen to go and meet your pals.'

It was seven o'clock before I got shot of him.

Hazel said, 'He's lovely. I have enjoyed myself.'

I said, 'I hope you're not using me to get to him because you'll be in for a disappointment. That business holding your hand? It's just acting. He's got no time for romance. All he's interested in is seeing his name in lights.'

'He's still lovely,' she said. 'He has a very happy attitude to life.'

Of course, she didn't know the half of it. She hadn't seen him moving furniture half an inch till it was just so. She hadn't seen him throw out a perfectly good egg cup because it had got a little chip on the rim.

Still, after Sel's patter and three port and lemons she did allow me to get more serious with her. One of the telephonists she shared with had stayed aboard and I daren't risk R64 in case Wilkie rolled in drunk, so we ended up in the Ripening Room.

Hazel had learned her trade at a high-class dry cleaner's in Belgravia, and then joined the *Queen Mary* after her refit at the end of the war.

I said, 'Don't you get tired of not having a place of your own?'

'It's economical,' she said. 'It means I can save up.'

I said, 'What for? Your own laundry?'

'No,' she said. 'I'd like a seaside guest house. Different people passing through, in a good mood because they're on holiday. Nice bed linen and towels and a brass dinner gong.'

We had Fred Astaire on our next passage to New York, a lovely, quietly spoken gent. I got him to autograph a First Class menu for Dilys. She was thrilled. Hazel came ashore with me that trip. I bought her a Pepsi at the Spanish Garden and took her to Radio City Music Hall to see Jerry Vale and the Rockettes. Where Sel got to I'll never know, but for a boy who liked scented soap he kept some very low company.

Every sailing day we'd go up to watch for celebrity arrivals. Douglas Fairbanks Junior, Constance Bennett, Gloria Vanderbildt, Vincent Price. Kings, princesses, millionaires, we entertained them all. But my greatest highlight was the time Gracie Fields was aboard. She was an old friend of our leader, Lionel Truman. 'Come down to the Pig and Whistle, Gracie,' he said. 'Give the crew a treat.' And she did. I played for her, 'Sing As We Go', 'Orphan of the Storm', 'I Took My Harp to a Party' and they were packed in like sardines, singing along with her. Her voice wasn't properly trained but she was a real card. Sel turned up when the party was in full swing, pushed his way to the piano.

I said, 'Fetch Hazel.'

'Fetch her yourself,' he said.

He wanted to get into the limelight with Gracie and the mess room crowd were egging him on. 'Go on, Sally!' they were shouting. 'Give us "Sally from Our Alley". You and Gracie together.'

She said, 'And who's this when he's at home?'

I said, 'This is my brother Sel. On his way to stardom.'

'Not with my audience, he's not,' she said. And although they did sing it together and she pretended to be amused, I could see she didn't like it. They were two of a kind, Gracie and my brother. Very 'hail fellow well met' provided you remembered who was the great star.

Still, it had been a big moment for me, playing for a singing legend, and Hazel missed the whole ruddy thing.

I said, 'Where were you?'

'Working, Cled,' she said. 'I sometimes think they sit in their state-rooms doing nothing but throw food and spill ink.'

I said, 'Well, I had a great triumph last night.'

'So did I,' she said. 'I got a big mayonnaise stain off an organdie skirt and four hours' sleep.'

She could be testy, even then.

Sel was riding pretty high by the time we reached Southampton too. He'd had a couple of billets-doux passed to him, and presents, at the Au Revoir Gala. A tiepin from a lady in First Class and an alligator photo frame from an old gentleman in Cabin Class.

'First stop the Imperial?' he said.

I said, 'I don't know. Hazel's tired.'

He said, 'Then you and me can go drinking.'

I said, 'How is it when we get to New York I don't see you for dust and yet you're hanging around me like a bad smell when we get to Southampton? What about all your pals?'

'Going home to see their mams,' he said.

I said, 'Do you want to?'

'Not worth it,' he said. 'We'd only be there five minutes. Let's go to the Yard Arm and plan worldwide fame.'

NINE

The thing about working on the *Queen Mary* was you didn't really get to see the world. You got to see galleys and corridors and Wilkie's scabby foot dangling down from the top bunk.

Sel said, 'I'm not sticking this much longer. There's no scope.'

I said, 'Then do something about getting an agent. Next leg, when we get to New York, don't run off like a dizzy kid.'

'Yeah,' he said. 'Definitely next time. I'm not getting due recognition with this lot.'

I said, 'We'll put our suits on. Decide on a couple of songs.'

'Yeah,' he said. '"Some Enchanted Evening". I see that becoming my signature tune.'

I said, 'And I think we should go back to being the Boff Brothers. Sel Boff, accompanied by Cled Boff, it sounds too complicated.'

He said, 'I don't know. I might start being just "Selwyn", you know? Like Hildegarde?'

I said, 'Then what would I be? I'm not being "Cledwyn".' I hated 'Cledwyn'.

'Quite right,' he said. 'It sounds like a boarding house. This Hazel? Are you two getting serious?'

I didn't have an answer to that. Sometimes, in the fruit store, I thought we were. Then I'd catch her chuckling with that pastry chef. 'I'm a single woman,' she'd say. 'I can chuckle with anybody I choose.'

I said, 'Why? You interested?'

'She's nice,' he said. 'And it strikes me, if you're serious about her you'll probably want to stay put. There doesn't seem much point in you trying out for agents if you're contented where you are. See what I mean?'

I said, 'And who's going to play for you if I don't?'

'I'll find somebody,' he said. 'Don't feel you have to throw up your chances with Hazel just to play for me. Accompanists are ten a penny, Cled.'

The ruddy nerve of it. But it did make me wonder how I stood vis-à-vis Hazel. I said, 'If I got a chance in America, would you come with me?'

She said, 'What kind of a chance?'

I said, 'With Sel. I'm a class instrumentalist, Hazel, as you'd know if you'd seen me in action with Gracie Fields. I don't have to play in a ship's band for ever more.'

She said, 'You only just started. And what would I do?'

I said, 'You'd find something. You could work in a dry cleaner's.'

She said, 'But I'm happy here. Where? What dry cleaner's?'

I said, 'We could get married.'

'Oh, I don't know, Cled,' she said. 'I'm in no hurry. I saw what my mam had to put up with all those years. Anyway, who's going to give you this big chance in America? I'll think about it if something happens and not before.'

But on that trip two things happened. Mr and Mrs Hubert F. Conroy came aboard, on their way home from London where they'd been celebrating thirty-five years of marriage. And Glorette Gilder was quarantined with a temperature of 105° and a nasty rash.

They asked Tex Lane to stand in first but as Tex himself admitted they were leaning on a weak reed. Being a front-liner is a high-pressure business. 'Give it to the boy,' he said. 'He's hungry for it.'

And that was how Sel got his chance as featured vocalist, with two hours' notice. He unpacked his gold suit and Hazel steamed the creases out of it and goffered the frills on his dress shirt; Mother Carey brought him a cheese omelette on a tray, and while Tex opened the batting in the Starlight Club, Sel lay on his bunk wearing nothing but his Y-fronts and a mud pack.

He must have been nervous. I know I was. But he didn't show it. He made his entrance cool as you like, strolled on, carrying a tea towel and two plates, deadpan face. 'OK,' he said. 'Who ordered the turbot?'

Glorette used to just stand there, like she was propped up and daren't move. A smoker's voice and low-cut backs, they were her stock-in-trade. But Sel was a natural. Put him in front of a microphone and there was no stopping him. 'Old Black Magic', 'If I Loved You', 'Beginning to See the Light'. 'The Anniversary Waltz', for Mr and Mrs Conroy. 'A Dream is a Wish Your Heart Makes', for 'anyone who ever wished upon a star' as he put it.

It was nearly daybreak before they let him go and he was buzzing. 'Eh, Cled, eh!' He kept hugging me and thumping me on the back. 'They loved me! And just wait till the next show. Tonight I'm really going to shake my feathers.'

I said, 'What if they let Glorette out of quarantine?'

'Get down to the infirmary,' he said. 'Put a pillow over her face.'

But there was no need. Glorette was out of action for the whole crossing and Sel saw this as his big chance. 'Come upstairs with me,' he said. 'I'm going to need extra shirts.' There was a branch of Austin Reed in First Class, but it was strictly off limits for us.

I said, 'Smile nicely at Hazel and she'll freshen your things up between shows.'

'I know she would,' he said, 'but that's not the point. What kind of star wears the same shirt three nights in a row? Anyway, come on up, see how the other half lives. How we'll be living.'

There were stewards you had to get past. Tourist Class weren't allowed into Cabin Class, Cabin weren't allowed into First Class and crew weren't allowed anywhere except in the line of duty. But Sel breezed us both through, greeted the gatekeepers like old friends, told them we were on urgent outfitting business for the Starlight Club.

'Ask for George,' one of them said. 'He gets stuff brought back, already worn. He'll fix you up with something.'

He did too. He had a dress shirt with a pin-tucked bib and a slightly imperfect cuff, and a silk waistcoat with a seam that had taken too much strain.

Sel said, 'How about shirt studs? Have you got anything glittery?'

But everything George had was from Garrards, top of the line, in beautiful silver-bronze display cases.

Sel said, 'How about on loan, like a library book?'

George said he didn't really see how he could, considering the value of the goods.

'Unless somebody stands surety for you,' he said. 'How about your uncle? Won't he treat you?'

I always had a more mature appearance than Sel.

Sel said, 'What, Uncle Cled? No, he's as tight as a duck's arse. Oh well, I'll just have to hope nobody notices I'm wearing the same old studs.'

That was when Hubert Conroy stepped forward. 'Why if it ain't Mr Starlight!' he said. 'Can I help? My money any good around here?'

So Hubert left a precautionary deposit with Austin Reed and Sel walked out with a set of lapis lazuli shirt studs and a new name. Hubert only called him 'Mr Starlight' because he couldn't remember his name. All he knew was he'd seen him in the Starlight Club. But anyway, it stuck. Ever after that Sel styled himself 'Mr Starlight'.

Hubert said, 'Come and meet Kaye. She's in the Garden Lounge ordering tea and pastries.'

Hubert was a retired refrigeration tycoon from Los Angeles, California. He was a big man, very friendly considering his wealth, and he knew what he liked. 'It's a pleasing thing', he said, 'to find a vocalist singing tuneful songs and not ignoring his audience. Eye contact, that's what I like. There are too many performers who act like they're singing to an empty room, never mind the poor Joe who's paid for his seat. And enthusiasm is another thing I like. Me and Kaye have seen big names and there are some come out on the podium and look like they're doing you a biggest favour just being there. You this boy's manager?'

'No . . .' I said.

He said, 'Well, you should be. I know a good thing when I see it and he'll go far. Have a pastry.'

Kaye wanted to know all our history and Sel was never afraid to embellish a story, or 'make it more entertaining' as he put it. How we'd grown up barefoot and starving. How we'd had to sing for our supper even when we were nibs, and then the Virgin Mary had visited him on his deathbed and told him to head for America.

I said, 'That story better not get back to Mam. You'll get a clip round the ear.' We'd always had shoes and three meals a day.

He laughed. He said, 'It won't get back to her and anyway, I was just giving value. Fans want a story. Rags to riches or riches to rags. Mam'd understand that.'

We were walking aft along the sheltered promenade when we ran smack into Milligan, the Ship's Writer. He never forgot a face. 'Well, what have we here?' he said. 'Two lost boys.'

You got a warning the first time you went out of bounds. After that they sacked you.

Sel said, 'I'm glad I've run into you. I've been thinking, now I've replaced Glorette I should be getting my own cabin.'

Milligan looked at him. He said, 'On this occasion I'm going to pretend I'm deaf as well as blind, Mr Boff, but it'll only be temporary, the same as your promotion, so don't depend on being so lucky a second time.'

Sel never batted an eye. 'Temporary!' he said. 'We'll see about that.'

His name was on the agenda they printed every day. The first time it said 'Tonight in the Starlight Club, Sel Boff replaces Glorette Gilder who is indisposed'. The next day it said 'Midnight in the Starlight Club, Selwyn, with the Lionel Truman Band'. The last day it said, 'Au Revoir Gala with Mr Starlight, Midnight in the Veranda Grill'.

I said, 'You must be driving them round the bend in the print room.'

'Not at all,' he said. 'I've brought a bit of interest and variety into their lives. And I've been talking to Lionel, too. I'm going to loosen things up. Take requests, talk to people. I'm not up there to see how fast I can race through the play list.'

I said, 'Well, while you're redesigning the show, you might think of singing one of my compositions. That'd give the evening a bit of added interest.'

'Such as?' he said.

I said, 'How about "You're the Vinegar on my Chips"?'

'I don't think so, Cled,' he said. 'I think it still needs work.'

See, he was all for himself.

He wore the blue lamé jacket for the Au Revoir, with the lapis studs in his shirt and he fetched Kaye Conroy up to the microphone, kidding her to do a daft old Max Miller song with him, 'La-di-dah-di-dah'. Now there's a song that needed further work. But he pulled it off, wisecracking between verses. He had them in stitches. And then he did a canny thing. He changed the mood. Number 22: 'Till Then'. He played it straight to settle them down, and then he went roving, like he'd started doing at the Birmingham Welsh, casually looking for a place to perch. But I knew him. He'd already weighed up the scene. He knew exactly who to aim for. Mrs Gertie Walters, widow of Walters the suet king and worth a mint, but Sel didn't pick her out because of that. He picked her because she was sitting on her own, looking wistful, and he took her hand and sang to her as if he was singing to our mam.

> Although there are oceans we must cross
> And mountains that we must climb
> I know every gain must have a loss
> So pray our loss is nothing but time
> Ooooh ooooh . . .

He closed with 'A Grand Night for Singing', then straight into number 49, 'We'll Meet Again' and there wasn't a dry eye in the room.

It was a grand night for singing, and for playing. I was proud to be there; proud to think he was family. I thought, 'Perhaps he has got what he takes. If he can light up an agent the way he's lit up this crowd . . .' This wasn't the Nechells Non-Political. This was Lord and Lady Delacourt, and Aly Kahn, plus a very big name in suet.

We didn't go to bed. We never did before a New York docking. Mother Carey made us smoked salmon and scrambled eggs, and then we went up to the dog deck to watch the pilot take us through the Narrows. There was the kind of mist you get before a hot day so they blasted the foghorn a few times, bottom A. I loved the sound of it.

I said, 'So today we go looking for an agent.'

'Correct,' he said. 'Hubert sees me in musical shows for family audiences. Hubert's got contacts in Los Angeles.'

Hubert Conroy giving him this inflated opinion of himself didn't help Sel strike the right attitude when we went to sign off. Glorette Gilder had got a clean bill of health for the next sailing.

Massie said, 'You can put your iridescent garments back in mothballs, Selwyn.'

Sel said, 'You're not having her back, after the way I performed?'

Massie said, 'Of course I am. Glorette is our featured vocalist.'

Sel said, 'You're out of your mind.'

But as Massie said, Sel had only ever been a stand-in. And he'd been paid extra.

Sel said, 'What about the paying public? Why don't you ask them who they'd rather see?'

Massie said, 'Do you mean the passengers who just disembarked, or the passengers who'll be arriving on Thursday, expecting to be entertained by Miss Gilder?'

I said, 'Leave it, Sel. You've got your bonus.'

'Mind your own!' he said. 'And you want to wise up, Massie. Call yourself an entertainments manager? You wouldn't recognise entertainment if it flew in wearing a leopard-skin jockstrap. I've had offers from California, you'll be interested to hear.'

Massie said, 'That's neither here nor there. Miss Gilder has a contract.'

'Well,' Sel said, 'now we all know which old lizard is sucking your dick.'

Massie sacked him on the spot. Ripped up his discharge book. 'I'll not delay you a moment longer, Mr Boff,' he said. 'I'm sure California is impatient to have you.'

Sel stormed off, left me with everybody staring at me. They'd all been earwigging, of course.

I found him in the cabin, sitting on his valise, trying to fasten it. 'Don't start,' he said.

I said, 'Nice work. You're out of a job, out of a bed for the night and you'll be out of money by tomorrow the way you spend it. You haven't got the sense you were born with.'

'No?' he said. 'Well, I've got no regrets neither. I'm ready to move on. Onward and upward.'

I said, 'Don't you move in any direction. You're to wait here while I see to a bit of business.'

'Just don't go crawling to Massie,' he shouted after me, 'because I wouldn't take his poxy job back if he came in here on his knees.'

But it was Hazel I had to see.

I thought, 'Well, this isn't quite how I planned it, but why not? She's a pretty little thing, hard worker, not averse to a roll in the Ripening Room.'

I intended asking her to come with me. We could have got engaged, set ourselves up in America. She'd have been handy to have around with Sel, too. He was more likely to listen to her. But there he was, when I got to her billet, leaning in her doorway chatting her up, still in his whites. That ruddy pastry chef.

I said, 'I see.'

'What?' she said.

I said, 'I thought we were a pair, Hazel. I thought we had a future.'

'Oh, for heaven's sake!' she said.

He sidled off, scared I was going to put one on him.

I said, 'Sel's given his notice. I was going to ask you to come with us, but now I see how the land lies . . .'

She said, 'The land doesn't lie anyhow. But anyway, I wouldn't walk away from a good job. I've got my security here.'

I said, 'Right then.'

'Look,' she said, 'I wish you well, Cled. But I never made any promises. I'm happy in my work. And I'm too young to get serious.'

She wasn't that young. Neither of us was.

I said, 'How about that pastry chef? You looked pretty engrossed with him.'

'Oh for crying out loud, Cled,' she said. 'He slips me a cream slice sometimes, that's all.'

After all the nylons I'd brought her.

I was in a very difficult situation. I'd have signed on for another stint, but I couldn't just go and leave him behind. He was full of big talk, but talk doesn't pay the rent and there was a careless side to him, too, after he'd had a drink. He'd follow the lead of any bunch of delinquents. If I wasn't around to keep an eye on him he was liable to wake up one morning, dead in a gutter. I'd never have heard the end of it from Mam and Dilys.

I caught him, ready to leave without me. I said, 'Now what are you going to do?'

'Brush this lint off my blazer,' he said. 'Alert New York to my arrival.'

'Well,' I said, 'never let it be said I shirked my responsibilities. I've decided I'm coming with you.'

'Yeah?' he said. 'Please yourself.'

TEN

Sel wanted to stay in a hotel. He believed if you wanted to be treated like a star you should live like one, but I soon put a stop to that. I could remember how Mam used to put her money in piles, this one for the electric, this one for coal, robbing Peter to pay Paul, and hiding it all over the place to keep temptation out of the way of Gypsy. And now it was my job to keep Sel on the straight and narrow. We took accommodation in a rooming house on West 43rd Street, rent paid a week in advance, and had our dinners at a cafeteria called Horn and Hardart. The food was in little compartments and you walked along with your tray and picked out what you could afford. Beans on toast. Lemon meringue pie. You could eat very well there for very little.

We started at the top of the list. The Aaronson Agency said they didn't see people who walked in off the street. The Colbert Agency said they were only seeing recommendations.

Thursday afternoon I watched the *Mary* slide past the end of the street. Sel was out, fetching our business cards. An agent called Milo Freeman had invited us to leave our card with him, only we didn't have one, as such. Sel had shot straight off to find a printer. 'An investment,' he called it. Any excuse to spend money.

I said, 'I waved goodbye to my future this afternoon.'

'No,' he said. 'You waved goodbye to your past.'

Then he showed me the business cards. 'Cunard front-liner, Mr Starlight' they said.

I said, 'Where's my name?'

He said, 'It looked too fussy with both names. Anyway, you'll be playing for me when I do try-outs, so they'll know you're on the payroll.'

I said, 'I'll tell you what makes them look fussy, you slippery bastard. Having that great big star instead of a normal dot over the i.'

'Trust me, Cled,' he said. The number of times I heard that. 'I know what I'm doing. I know what catches people's eye.'

We got to the Vs on the list. Marcia Vine, who also happened to represent Glorette Gilder. She said, 'Take my advice you'll hitch a ride home. This town's full of singers with more talent than you and most of them are working as soda jerks.'

We tried Patch Wolff.

Sel said, 'I've got a feeling about this one.'

'Boys,' Wolff said, 'in the unlikely event I start representing sugar-frosted shit, I'll confine myself to the home-grown product.'

Sel said, 'I think we should head west. Hubert said to look him up. He knows names.'

I was getting tired of hearing Hubert Conroy's name. I said, 'We've already gone west. Two more weeks' rent and we're flat.'

'Oh ye of little faith,' he said. I was ready to wring his ruddy neck.

There were a couple of dancers staying in our digs and I got talking to one of them, waiting on the landing to use the facilities.

She said, 'I know where they need a rehearsal pianist.'

And that was how we turned the corner.

It was a touring production of a show called *Daisy Days*, never did make it on to Broadway. The place smelled of sweaty shoes and the piano needed tuning, but it put a few dollars in my pocket and then way led on to way. That's how it is in show business. You can't go to the Labour Exchange. You have to keep your ears open and your craft honed. Just before *Daisy Days* opened I heard that an audition pianist was needed for *More Is Better!* and then the caretakers at the Polska Club, where the auditions took place, told me about a little piano bar that gave new faces a try.

Sel came along with me but they didn't want him. It was a very small room and the vocalist who's willing to sing quietly hasn't been born. All they needed was somebody like me, tinkling in the background. They gave me a Friday night, with no assurances, but I ended up with two nights a week till further notice. I was the one bringing in money, I was the one who could write and tell Mam I was appearing at the Sinbad Club on Madison Avenue, and that was a hard thing for Sel to swallow.

He got more and more morose. He wouldn't even stir himself to send Mam a postcard because she'd be expecting him to be the toast of the town, wherever he was, and he couldn't bring himself to fib to her. Not in those days, at any rate. He said, 'I should never have let you hold me back. I could have gone straight to California, linked up with Hubert Conroy if you hadn't taken my money.'

But I hadn't taken it. I was eking it out. And if it hadn't been for me he'd have had to find a way home before he starved. Intermission singer on a banana boat, that's how he'd have ended up. Anyway, I was on my way to another audition job one morning and my route happened to take me past the Milo Freeman Agency. He was the only one who hadn't given us a flat 'no', so I thought I'd look in on him. And that was what changed everything.

It was a scruffy little place. He shared a receptionist with the private detective on the floor above him.

I said, 'Had any more thoughts on Mr Starlight and accompanist?'

'God in heaven,' he said, 'I was about to pray for a miracle and you walk through the door.'

Milo represented a songstress called Ruby Farrell, who was meant to be appearing at the Judge House Hotel, Indianapolis, except she'd suffered a ruptured appendix. He said, 'You boys available?'

I said we were.

He said, 'Sure now? You gonna call the main attraction before you commit yourself?'

But we didn't have a telephone, for one thing, and for another, I'd left Greely's to become a world traveller, so I wasn't going to turn down Indianapolis, wherever it was. 'No,' I said. 'I'm the one who makes the decisions. We'll be here at four.'

I was so excited. I took those stairs two at a time when I got back and there he lay on the bed, curlers in his quiff, practising his signature. I said, 'Get the valises out. We're on our way.'

Milo was offering us two weeks at the Mark Twain in Peoria, Illinois after we'd done Indianapolis.

Sel said, 'Where? I'm not going to some dump in the sticks. I'm holding out for New York.'

I said, 'In that case you'll be holding out on your own. This is a great chance, Sel, and I'm taking it.'

He said, 'They won't take you without me.'

I wasn't sure if they would but I called his bluff. 'Oh, yes they will,' I said, 'it's already agreed.'

That got him to his feet.

Milo looked so happy to see us. 'Here they are!' he said. 'The Starlight Brothers! The answer to my prayers.'

Sel said, 'No, not the Starlight Brothers. Mr Starlight, with Cled Boff on backing.'

Milo said, 'Brothers sounds better. Family acts are very popular. I have the Betsie Sisters out in Nebraska singing up a storm, three big girls with faces that could turn milk, but I just had a request for them to extend their tour.'

Sel said, 'Nebraska! Who the hell cares about Nebraska! I'm Mr Starlight and I want New York.'

I could see him blowing both our chances. It was lucky for him Milo was the fatherly type. 'Listen,' he said. 'Forget New York. This town knows what it likes and saccharine is not the flavour of the month. The good news is there's a great big country out there eager to be entertained. Millions of regular folks who see nothing wrong with being a corn ball. Now, how about "The Boff Brothers"?'

Sel said, 'We've been that. It didn't work. He's Cled Boff now and I'm Mr Starlight, and that's how it's got to be.'

Milo said, 'OK, OK. Maybe family acts have peaked.'

Sel said, 'And I get to pick the songs.' He'd always picked the songs.

I said, 'I wouldn't mind if you'd pick one of mine once in a while.'

'Write one worth singing, then,' he said.

He was full of himself. 'About these venues?' he said. 'Are they any good?'

'High-class hotels,' Milo said. 'Businessmen. That's who you'll be playing to. Conventioneers.'

Sel said, 'Will they have their wives with them? The ladies are the ones that really go for me.'

Milo said, 'Is that a fact? Well, some of those guys are sure to have gotten lucky. They'll have company even if it ain't the married kind. But they won't want pyrotechnics after a heavy meal. Just easy listening and some of that crazy British talking you boys do. You can't go wrong.'

We had to get a train Monday night out of Penn Station and change at Washington DC.

'When you arrive,' Milo said, 'get a shave, get a shoeshine and take a cab. Don't act cheap.'

Sel never needed encouraging in that respect. He went straight out and bought a pair of snakeskin slip-on dress shoes to celebrate.

I said, 'Well, Mr Moneybags, there go your dinners for the rest of the week.'

'Good,' he said. 'If I starve, my suits'll hang better.'

So we were back in business, thanks to Ruby Farrell's bad luck. Dead men's shoes, Sel called it. And it wasn't the only time we did ourselves a bit of good by stepping into them.

We performed two hours a night, with Sundays off if we weren't travelling and as many steak dinners as we liked. I loved it, but Sel was frustrated. He wanted an audience that paid attention to him, not businessmen playing the big tycoon with their floozies, not love-birds chinking their glasses and nibbling each other's ears. 'I'm bored,' he kept saying. He'd sleep in till about twelve and I made it a point to have something lined up for us; a livestock show, a trolley car ride, an exhibition of quilts. But the afternoons still dragged and he started consorting with kitchen porters. He was gone for hours with one of them, reckoned they'd been in somebody's motor out to a farm where you could pick your own pumpkins. I never did work out why. They didn't appear to have picked any.

Indianapolis and Peoria may have been dead men's shoes, but Lansing, Michigan and Toledo, Ohio weren't. We got them on our own merits, a month at the deWitt, which was time enough for me to enjoy a little liaison with the deputy housekeeper, an older woman and very appreciative, and then a month at the Maumee Criterion, with a view of the bay from our billet, if you stood on a chair and leaned out a bit.

Then someone else's misfortune turned to our advantage. I was called to the telephone. It was Milo. 'The opportunity of a lifetime,' he said. 'Get yourselves to Chicago first thing Sunday. You've got two nights at the Palmer House.'

Our next engagement was supposed to be the Allegheny in Pittsburgh. I said, 'What about Pittsburgh?'

Milo said, 'I'm sending Lew Brown to Pittsburgh in your stead. I want you to have the Palmer House. The Empire Room supper club is the type of venue where Sel can really shine. It's his birthday and Christmas all rolled into one, Cled, and I'm depending on you to make sure he realises it.'

We were substituting for Jackie Brennan, who'd had a sudden death in the family.

Sel said, 'I don't know that these dining rooms are the kind of engagement I want. I need a proper audience to work with, not punters with their snouts in the trough. You shouldn't have taken it without asking me.'

I said, 'How could I? You'd disappeared as per. Driving around with some street arab, looking at vegetables, I suppose. And I took it because Milo says this is a premier venue. So what's it to be? Chicago or back to Saltley?'

'Saltley?' he said. 'I'm never going back there. I'd sweep the streets sooner.' That was a joke. Still, he thought better about the Palmer House and packed his bag. He said, 'But from now on I don't want you accepting any more engagements without asking me. And we're getting ourselves a map. I don't think Chicago is anything like on the way to Hollywood.'

That was his big new idea; if New York didn't fall into his lap he'd go into musical films. I seemed to be hearing Hubert Conroy's name more and more, and Sel wanted to keep heading in his direction. But according to Dolly, one of the hotplate waitresses at the Criterion, Milo was right. The Palmer House was a pretty fancy joint and not to be sniffed at. She even took the precaution of getting our autographs before we left. 'You may be nobodies right now,' she said, 'but you never know.' As a matter of fact I gave her more than my autograph.

Dolly was right. The Palmer House was a top-notch venue. Dining rooms, banqueting rooms, ballrooms. They could seat thousands and the lobby was like a cathedra: marble columns and a great big lofty ceiling covered with paintings and gold leaf. The first thing we were told was that in future we should use the service entrance and we were accommodated in an inside room where you had to keep the electric light on all day, but the piano was a Blüthner and the steaks were so tender you could eat them with a spoon.

We were getting ready for our first night there when the lapis shirt studs reappeared, supposed to have been on loan from the shop on the *Queen Mary*. I said, 'You stole them.'

'No,' he said. 'Just forgot to take them back.'

I said, 'Hubert Conroy left money to guarantee them.'

'So?' he said. 'I'll pay him back. All the more reason to go and see him.'

That supper club attracted a high-class crowd. Good-looking ladies in silky dresses and furs and lipstick. If we'd stayed a bit longer I'd have set my stall out. As it was, our two nights stretched to seven when Jackie Brennan's bereavement took longer than they'd expected and we got a very nice write-up in the *Chicago Tribune*.

> Now here's a thing! [it said]. A new act wowing them at the Palmer House niterie and it isn't even home-grown! British vocalist Mister Starlight accompanied by his brother Cled

Boff are currently replacing Supper Club regular Jackie Brennan. Mister Starlight delivers a nice line in Sammy Kaye songs, but more than that, he sprinkles them with glitter dust and serves them with those dimpled smiles no girl can resist. And not only the girls. Moms love him too. I predict a great future for this likeable songster. Mr S and his brother are appearing with the Dick Kennett Band and comic Jerry Jaspers, through Sunday. Don't miss 'em!

We bought three copies and clipped them out; one for Mam, one for Dilys and one for our scrapbook. We never did meet Jackie Brennan but I'd have liked her to know that her sad loss turned into a big gain for us.

Milo came out to see our last night. 'Now we can go places, boys,' he said.

Once you'd succeeded at the Palmer House, other doors opened. That winter we played the Detroit Statler and the Cleveland Grand, the Peabody Hotel in Memphis, Tennessee and the Belle Rive in Kansas City. All big, fancy hotels with an elegant clientele. Milo said, 'These are the places where you'll get a following. Folks who've made a buck without growing highfalutin and know how to enjoy their money. The kind of folks who'll take you into their hearts.'

But Sel was never content. He didn't like the way people walked in front of him to go to the toilet. And some places he didn't even have a little podium to stand on. He just had to perform from the dance floor. It was a good job he had the height. 'When I get my own show,' he'd say, 'I'll give them entrances. I'll have a drum roll and backlighting, and then there I'll be, poised at the top of a lovely staircase in a fabulous costume.'

His shiny jackets were gone, except for the glistenette one which he kept as a souvenir. We wore dinner suits for the supper clubs, but Sel made a feature of his ties and cummerbunds. He'd started making his own, stitching spangles on them. He was quite handy with a needle. He'd never darn the holes in my socks, though. 'Paint your toe black,' he'd say. 'Buy a new pair.'

Spend, spend, spend, that was him. Shoes, shirts, waistcoats. He'd started out with one bag and by the time we got to Kansas City he had three. And whichever town we were in he'd go scouting for shiny beads, to individualise his accessories. 'So I don't get mistaken for a singing waiter,' he'd say. And he'd end up leaving half of them behind. You could have followed our trail just looking for sequins on hotel carpets.

'They call me up', Milo said, 'and ask for the boy with the smile and the glitter, so don't hold back.'

Sel never held back in his life. Except in one respect.

The ladies were like bees round a honey pot with him, but he had no interest in romance. While we were appearing at the Peabody there was a lady sat in a ringside seat night after night and after every show there'd be a note waiting for him, reminding him which room she was in.

I said, 'Go on, why don't you? Get yourself a bit of experience.'

As far as I knew he still hadn't got off the mark. He reckoned he had but he'd never provide me with any details, so I didn't believe him.

I said, 'There's nothing to it, you know? It's as natural as breathing.'

'I need my beauty sleep,' he said. 'You go, if you're so keen for somebody to put her out of her misery.'

I said, 'No thank you. I've made my own arrangements.'

'Yeah,' he said. 'With a turn-down maid.'

She may have been a turn-down maid. She never turned me down, though.

He said, 'Cled, my mind's on my career. I don't want sidetracking. I don't want complications.'

I said, 'One of these days you'll meet somebody and lightning'll strike.'

'No,' he said, 'I don't think so.'

And it's true he never did have a lot of luck in love.

We were getting along right enough in those days. He was willing to put in some work in the afternoons, trying out new songs, then he'd go off for an hour or two with one of his new pals. A bellhop usually, or a porter. One thing about Sel, there was never any side to him. And they were nice enough boys. They had to be, to work in such high-class establishments.

The Peabody was my favourite. I played the baby grand in the lobby every evening while the dinner crowd were coming in. There were beautiful dusty-pink settees where you could sit and get a proper cup of tea. And then, of course, there were the ducks. They brought them down in the lift every morning. Sel liked to sleep late, but I always made a point of being down in the lobby at eleven o'clock, to hear the music start up and see those little ducks come marching out for their dip in the fountain.

It was the duckmaster who sold us our first car, an old Plymouth sedan, and it was a porter called Jefferson who taught me how to drive it, so all in all I have very happy memories of the Peabody. Memphis was a strange place, though. I went to the zoo one afternoon and they wouldn't let me in. 'No whites today,' the cashier said.

Funny town.

Milo got us the Baker Hotel in Mineral Wells, Texas for Christmas of 1951, in a very good line-up: the Desmond Trio, a Chinese illusionist and Patti Page top of the bill. But neither of us liked it there. It was too big for itself somehow, fourteen storeys high on the edge of a one-horse town. 'A carbuncle sitting on a pimple,' Sel called it.

Then, a lot of the guests were there for their health, taking the waters and sitting around in dressing gowns looking sorry for themselves. It didn't seem like Christmas.

I said to Sel, 'It doesn't seem right, walking around in shirtsleeves in December.'

'Yeah,' he said. 'I really miss waking up with ice on the inside of the window.'

He didn't seem to get homesick like I did sometimes.

I said, 'Don't you ever think of Ninevah Street?'

'Yes,' he said. 'I think of Mrs E peering round her curtains when they go there to film the story of my life.'

According to Mam, Mr and Mrs Edkins were great friends of hers all of a sudden. 'Mrs E went with her sister to see the Illuminations,' Mam wrote, 'so I told Mr E to come to me for his tea while she was gone. Men never eat properly if they're left. I didn't expect anything in return but he very kindly insisted on sweeping my chimney, so that was nice.'

I said, 'I don't know. It'd be nice not to be living out of suitcases all the time.'

'Don't live out of a suitcase, then,' he said. 'Be like me. Wherever I am, I can make it home.' And he would spread his stuff everywhere, photos and little knick-knacks people had given him, and he'd buy plants, even if we were only in a place for a few days. 'Know what I think we should do?' he said. 'Finish this booking and go to see Hubert and Kaye. We're practically almost there.' Of course, that was a non-driver speaking.

I said, 'I don't see how we can walk away from good money.' Milo had got us the Flame Room in Minneapolis for February.

Sel said, 'You've got to stop looking at things that way. You're not at Greely's now. Nose to the grindstone. Grateful to have a few quid in your pocket. You have to visualise the big picture. That's what I do. Nice cars, swimming pools, maids, drivers. I'm a big picture person.'

I said, 'And I'm the little things person who got us this far. Remembering what time we have to get to places. Putting oil in the motor. Getting your trousers pressed. I'm a ruddy sight more to this outfit than a piano player, Sel. And I'm tired.'

'Yeah,' he said, 'you look it. You should try the waters while we're here. Relax a bit. Just take a back seat for a while. Apart from the motor. I don't know where the oil goes and I don't want to know. But I'll take care of the trousers and stuff.'

I should have known he was up to something. I phoned Milo to see what he had for us after Minneapolis.

'Who can say?' he said. 'I'm surely not putting you boys up for anything else till I know you're serious. It seems early in a career for a vacation, Cledwyn, but what do I know?'

Sel had told him we didn't want the Flame Room.

I said, 'He's made a mistake.'

Milo said, 'I agree. But I can't make him do it. I'm sending them Gene Tully. There's a boy who deserves a lucky break.'

I said, 'Are you still representing us?'

'If there's anything to represent,' he said. 'Tell you what, Cled, give me a call when you're through vacationing. I'll see what I can do for you. If anybody remembers who you are.'

Sel was out, taking a steam bath.

I was ready for him. I said, 'Well, now you've done it. Halfway across America with a drawer full of bow ties and not a pot to piss in. California! Milo would have got us something in California if you'd given him time. But you have to go and ruin everything. You're loopy. You're not Vic Damone yet, you know. You're not Mario ruddy Lanza. Carry on like this and you'll be on queer street.'

He just laughed. 'Big picture, Cledwyn,' he said. 'What do I keep telling you about the big picture? By the time we're done in California, the Flame Room won't be able to afford us.' The thing with Sel was he wasn't corrected when he was a bab. He wasn't a naughty lad because he didn't really go in for things that lead to trouble: fighting, hitting cricket balls through windows. But Mam never told him his limits. If he said he wanted to make rock cakes, he wasn't told he couldn't. There'd be flour everywhere and sugar underfoot, and sometimes they were burned on the bottom, but with Mam it was always, 'Oh, they're lovely, Selwyn. They melt in the mouth. You are a clever lad.' In my opinion that's why he grew up so cocky. That's why it never occurred to him that things wouldn't always go his way.

Anyway, we played our last night at the Baker, packed our bags and started heading west.

I said, 'I hope you're not expecting a welcome committee?'

We were sitting in a diner in Amarillo.

'No,' he said. 'No, I'm expecting closed doors all over again, but I intend opening them. When I had my vision and she told me to come to America, she meant California. I can feel it pulling me.'

I said, 'I bet Mam misses you.'

We'd been gone nearly two years.

'She's all right,' he said. 'There's only one thing matters to Mam: that we're making a future for ourselves. She always knew I'd leave. I always knew I would. Anyway, Dilys keeps an eye on her.'

I said, 'Not very fair on Dilys, is it?'

He said, 'Look, I haven't come here to get out of looking after Mam. I'm here because it's meant to be. And by the time she really needs looking after I'll afford the best wheelchair money can buy. Fur-lined. With a big Gary Cooper lookalike to push her around. But right now I'm going to California, whether you're up for it or not. We can go our separate ways, it's up to you.'

I said, 'And how do you think you're going to get there without me? Who'll drive you if I don't?'

He looked around. 'He will,' he said. And he winked at some young truck driver sitting in the corner eating pancakes.

He would have done too. He'd have gone off with a stranger and ended up dumped on the roadside without a pair of cuff links to his name.

ELEVEN

Sometimes people only tell you to look them up if ever you're passing because they know you won't ever be passing, but that wasn't the case with Hubert F. Conroy. I never met a more genuine man and when we did pitch up, with our exhaust pipe hanging off and no fixed abode, he took us in and treated us like family.

Hubert and Kaye had a beautiful home up its own private driveway in Beverly Glen. We had to stop three times to ask directions and one gent we asked, clipping the edges of a lawn, took a long hard look at our old motor and suggested we'd made a mistake with the address, and when we found it, I understood what he was getting at. It was a palace, in the Spanish bungalow style, with archways and wrought-iron doors. Cigarette lighters on every occasional table. A lady called Willa who cooked and cleaned. And a swimming pool, of course.

Sel said, 'This is it, Cled. This is the kind of place we're going to have, after we get our big break. Can't you just see Mam, sitting on a patio in sunglasses and a pair of peep-toe sandals?'

I couldn't imagine any such thing. Apart from His Numps, nobody in Saltley owned a pair of sunglasses. There was no requirement for them.

I said, 'If you can point us in the direction of a boarding house . . .' but neither of them would hear of it.

Hubert said, 'Hotels are where you stay when you don't have folks in town. Don't matter how fancy they are they make a person feel lonesome and I've spent enough time on the road to know. Too many empty rooms in this place anyhow.'

Kaye said, 'Conroy's right. Stay as long as you like. It'll be like having Junior in the house again.'

Hubert and Kaye had had a son, Junior, dropped dead of natural causes when he was twenty-three. I think that's why they made such a fuss of us.

'Make yourselves at home,' Kate said.

And Sel took her at her word. He loved to splash around in the pool, although he never did bother learning to swim. He just stayed in the shallow end. Then he'd flop on a reclining chair and study Kaye's magazines, deciding what kind of bedheads he was going to have when he made the big time.

I said, 'Now we're here we should get back with Milo. Tell him to fix us up with some hotels.'

'Supper clubs!' I heard him say to Kaye. 'People chomping on their celery and clattering their soup spoons. A vocalist gets no respect.'

I said, 'I'll tell you who gets no respect, a person who sits in a paddling pool all day and doesn't pay his way.'

Hubert Conroy was a man who'd started from nothing so I thought he'd back me up. He said, 'Cled, let me tell you something. I worked hard, it's true. There were weeks when I hardly saw Kaye and Junior. But I didn't make any money till I started working smart. And that's something Sel seems to understand, not to wear himself out chasing after dumb things. You have to survey the scene and spot your chances, and you ain't likely to do that if you never lift your nose from the grindstone. So enjoy your vacation.'

'Anyhow,' Kaye said, 'supper clubs are a thing of the past. Television. That's the future.'

We were familiar with television, of course, having travelled. Hubert and Kaye had three tellies even back in those days, but our mam was the first person in Ninevah Street to get one, and that was years later. Dilys and Arthur bought one so they could watch the Coronation but they always did keep abreast of new gadgets. Dilys was the first in their road to get an all-electric washtub too.

I said, 'I don't see how a television show can be a patch on a class act, seen in the flesh. I can't see it catching on.'

Kaye said, 'I can tell you why it'll catch on. Human nature. Folks love to sit in an armchair. I do it myself. I sit down to watch Miltie Berle and before I know it I wasted a whole evening. Time was me and Conroy'd drive to the Ambassador, get dinner and a floor show.'

'Dragging a tired working man from his rest,' Hubert said.

Kaye said, 'See what I mean? Human nature. That's why we should be investing in television. And armchairs. And snack foods folks can eat without taking their eyes off the screen.'

That was how Kaycee Munchies got started. And that wasn't the only thing.

Kaye had heard about a new company that put television shows on to moving film, so you could show them any time, anywhere, and she persuaded Hubert to invest in it. 'Think about it,' she said. 'If you're starring in a Broadway show you have to turn up every night. If you get sick, they cancel or the stand-in goes on and either way the punters ain't happy. And you're only ever as good as your last performance. The greatest talents on earth have off days. But if you make television appearances and commit them to film the show can always go on. On and on. You can be the other side of the world, filming something else, or taking your wife on a cruise – are you listening to me, Conroy? – and your reruns'll still be out there, keeping your face where folks'll remember it and making you good money. You could be dead and you'll still be earning.'

'I like it,' Hubert said.

And one of the first things Kaycee Productions did was ask us to record something for a new show, *Variety Cavalcade*.

That got Sel off his deckchair. He said, 'I want to be backlit, so you can just see me in profile, leaning against the piano, as if I'm chatting to Cled. Black tuxedo, black tie, rhinestone cuff links. I'll do 'Embraceable You', 'Music, Music, Music!', 'Sugar-coated Lies'. Keep changing the mood. And I want the camera to stay on my best side.'

It was filmed in a lot on Van Ness Avenue, nothing much there except cables all over the floor, lights and a camera and a man on a trolley with a microphone boom. Russ Berdahl was the producer. That afternoon they were filming a vent act with a wooden horse, a guitar duo and Mr Starlight. Mr Starlight accompanied by Cled Boff, that is. Sel started straight in. Marking out where he was going to walk to during this song, what he was going to do during that song.

Russ said, 'Whoa there! I don't want you walking anywhere. See this camera? We can't just move this baby. So I'd like you just to choose your spot and stay there. Stand and deliver!'

Sel said, 'What's going to happen when you get a knife thrower on the show?' He always had to argue. It wasn't enough for him we were liable to be on American television, seen by thousands of people.

We did one run-through and one take. Berdahl said we were great, but we didn't feel great. When you're playing somewhere like the Empire Room, you rise to your audience and your surroundings. But the Kaycee studio was just a couple of big breeze block rooms and the only people who were there were too busy checking their dials to give you a smile or tap their feet.

Sel said, 'What about applause?'

Berdahl said they'd put that in later.

Sel said, 'I'll do it again. There were a few things I wasn't happy about.'

'No time,' Berdahl said. 'And everything was just perfect.'

It turned out it wasn't quite perfect. Sel had a shadow from the microphone across his chin and he looked like a dog on a choke chain, trying to remember to stand still. 'Lesson number one,' he said. 'Never leave anything that matters to other people. From now on it's going to be in the contract; staging, lighting, the lot. I'm taking control.'

I said, 'You can't start laying down the law. We're just starting out.'

He said, 'That's exactly when you do lay down the law, before they get into the habit of pleasing themselves. Start as you mean to go on, Cled. And I mean to have everything perfect.'

We went back to the Conroys and sat around the pool.

Sel said, 'Kaye, I don't know if this is going to work.'

She said, 'It was only a try-out. Think ahead. Think of all those folk who're going to see you at the flick of a switch.'

'I am doing,' he said. 'But it was Mr Starlight playing in a mortuary. There was no atmosphere.'

She said, 'We'll make atmosphere. We'll hang drapes behind you.'

I said, 'We used to have a potted palm, remember, Sel?'

Kaye said that could be arranged too.

Sel said, 'I didn't like having to stand still either. They must be able to move the camera, otherwise how do they film cowboy films?'

I said, 'I can tell you that. You have to have a camera on a dolly.' I'd read about it in *Moviegoer* magazine. I said, 'And I'll tell you what another problem was. No audience. I can play to an empty room. Often have done. But Sel needs an audience. Doesn't have to be a big one. But he's like a torch with no batteries otherwise.'

Hubert said, 'The boy's right. When we seen you in the Starlight Club you were a real live wire. The audience never knew what you'd do next. And you seemed like you were enjoying yourself. That was the main thing about you. You were real natural and friendly and happy.'

Kaye said, 'Well, there y'are then. We have to get you an audience. Conroy, we're gonna need a bigger studio.'

Hubert said, 'This woman won't rest till she's spent my last dime.'

'I'm gonna make you more than I ever spent,' she said. 'We'll film the whole show in front of an audience. Maybe everybody'll perform better that way.'

So Kaycee Productions launched *Variety Cavalcade*, filmed at the Topanga Ballroom. We did the first two in front of an invited audience, which actually meant the Conroys papered the place with their friends and relations, and we recorded two shows back to back. Then they gave it out on KC radio that if people wanted seats they could line up round the back of the Topanga, first come first served. By the third week they were turning people away.

Variety Cavalcade went out after a show called *Murder Mystery* so we got big audiences right from the start. As Kaye said, this was one of the beauties of television. If folks watched one programme there was a very good chance they'd stay where they were and watch whatever followed on. And it was a lot easier for them than getting dressed up and driving to a club. They could sit at home in their carpet slippers. They could watch it while they were eating their tea.

We did twelve shows and every one we did was better than the last. It was mainly ladies who queued to get tickets, housewives, and Sel had a knack with them. He'd go into the audience and start chatting to them, asking them about their frocks or their kiddies, acting like he had all the time in the world, even though everything had to be done to the split second.

Kaye said, 'You make it seem so natural.'

'What do you mean?' he said. 'It *is* natural. They're nice ladies. It's just like leaning over the garden wall.' Leaning over the garden wall in a hundred-dollar jacket.

He started developing an American way of speaking too. He'd pick somebody out of the audience and bring her up to the microphone to sing along with him, just like he'd done with Kaye on the *Queen Mary*. He'd put his arm round her and crack a joke, to stop her feeling nervous, and afterwards he'd say, 'Now you're a TV star! See how easy it is?'

We cut a promotional record: 'Younger than Springtime' with 'Harbour Lights' on the flip side, and then we were signed to do twelve more programmes, with a local firm putting up money, so the show got a new name. *The Bartine Variety Half Hour*. It was called sponsorship. Three times during the show Sel had to say, 'Don't forget, folks, spend five dollars at Bartine's Household Linens and get a free copy of my latest record.' '*My* latest record' was how he always put it, '*I'm* making a new record.' But it was always me who wrote home, me who sent newspaper clippings to Mam and then copies of *our* records to Dilys, so I made sure they knew. I didn't let them run away with the idea that he was the only recording star in the family.

That first disc did so well Bartine's ran out after two days and there was an incident in their towel department, caused by disappointed ladies. It was the lead story on KCR News that evening, even though there was trouble brewing in Indo-China, looked like it might turn into another war, and Clark Gable had just resigned from MGM.

Kaye said, 'We should follow through with another disc. Bring it out in time for the next series.'

I said, 'And we should record some of my songs. For added family interest.'

Sel said, 'Cled, I can't see Parlophone falling over themselves for "Renée on My Knuckles".' I'd never have suggested any such thing. That was a personal lyric composed after a disappointment of the heart. Writing that helped me pick myself up. At least I could comfort myself that I'd never followed Renée's wishes and gone in for a tattoo.

Kaye said, 'The hell with Parlophone. Everybody's knocking on their door. We'll start our own label.'

Hubert said, 'Darling, the idea of business is you're supposed to make more money than you spend.'

'And I will do,' she said, 'if you'll just cut me a little slack here. Mr Starlight is starting to roll. I can feel it in my bones.'

Hubert said, 'That's rheumatics.'

'Conroy,' she said, 'it's only money. You can't take it with you.'

So we cut our first commercial disc with Kaycee Records: 'Momma Knows Best' with 'Busy Being Lonely', which Sel always insisted was the B side. All I know is that record got into the hit parade and if I'd been given better advice I'd be a richer man today.

We were still living with Kaye and Hubert, and I felt the time had come for us to move out. For one thing, I'd started seeing Minnie Beck. Minnie played tenor sax in Ina Ray Hutton's All Girl Orchestra, five feet two and eyes of blue, and we'd met on the set of *Variety Half Hour*. But the nature of her work meant she travelled a lot. We had to make the most of our time together.

Sel said, 'Bring her back here. Kaye won't mind.'

He still didn't really understand the needs of a red-blooded man. His idea of recreation was water fights with the boy who came to clean the pool.

Kaye said, 'He's a late developer. Junior was the same. He never got around to dating, he was so wrapped up in his basketball. You find yourself a little love nest. Sel has a home here as long as he wants it.'

But then the fans started turning up. The nice ones just walked by, or stood outside for a bit, hoping to catch a glimpse of us. Some of them got cheekier, though: ringing the doorbell, peering through the windows. Willa answered the door one evening and there stood a girl wearing nothing but a cowhide duster coat.

Hubert said, 'How could you tell?'

Willa said, 'I'm saying no more. But she'll be back and others like her, and I'm not paid to answer the door to crazies.'

Hubert said, 'Sel, I'm sorry, but the help ain't happy and if the help ain't happy I get no peace. I'd say the time has come. You have security considerations.'

Sel said, 'Yeah, I should have seen this coming. I'm going to have to move to a secret location.'

Kaye said, 'You'll need an unlisted phone number.'

Willa said, 'And a pail of cold water. In case your help finds any undressed persons on your doorstep.'

It tickled me the way they all assumed it was Sel those girls were after. 'Busy Being Lonely' was a Cled Boff original and I had my following. I had my offers.

Set in a sea of laughing faces
I read the sadness in your eyes.
I know you from a thousand places
Your lips that smile, your heart that cries.
Are you busy being lonely?
If I should cross the room to touch you
Would you give this boy a glance?
If I told you I could love you
Would you take another chance?
Or are you busy, pretty lady,
Being lonely?

BOFF

TWELVE

Every month we sent money to Dilys with instructions to make sure Mam had everything she needed. She was still holding out against the upheaval of getting a bathroom, but she did agree to a gas fire and a new mattress.

I said, 'Get her a telephone. We'll pay.'

Dilys said, 'She doesn't want one.'

I wondered how we'd ever lived without one. Me and Minnie talked most days when the band was on the road.

Dilys said, 'She doesn't want one because everybody in Ninevah Street'd expect to use it. I'm not bringing it up again, Cled. I go over twice a week. I dry her sheets if the weather's bad. I do look after her. But she's so bloody cussed.'

I said, 'I know. That's why we want to do our bit.'

Dilys said, 'Don't worry. She's all right. And you'll have plenty of time for doing things. She's going to live to be a hundred. Unless I strangle her first.'

I said, 'There's talk of us getting our own show.'

'Yes,' she said, 'Mam told me. She's very proud, you know?'

I said, 'I know. It's all I hear: "My Selwyn, the star".'

Dilys said, 'No, I meant Mam's very proud of *you*. She might not say it, but she is. We all are. And that's another thing to consider, now you're both doing so well. If Dad ever thought Mam'd got money he'd be back like a shot, I guarantee it. Sel's already had a mention in the *Evening News*. All it needs is for Gypsy to read something. You don't want him getting any ideas.'

I said, 'I don't think Dad ever read the papers, did he?'

'No,' she said. 'He certainly never read the Situations Vacant.'

'We're looking into buying property. You'll all be able to come and visit.'

'Oh, I don't think so, Cled,' she said. 'I can't see that happening. I do miss you, though. Perhaps you'll be able to get back soon, have a little holiday?'

I said, 'We're very busy. Things are really on the up for us. And it's beautiful weather here. Every day feels like a holiday here.'

'Does it?' she said. 'That's nice.'

Houses were easy to find in Los Angeles. Clean new places with picture windows and lawns and fitted carpets throughout. They were building them as fast as they could pour concrete, all along the San Fernando Valley. And then there were the other places, for people who couldn't afford a house: caravans, but not just for holidays, like at Weston or Burnham-on-Sea. People were living in these, permanent. They were hooked up to the electric light and running water, but they were still only vans, taken off their wheels and resting on cinder blocks. Trailer parks. They fascinated Sel. 'Stop the car,' he'd say. 'I want to sit and look. 'Look at all those telly aerials,' he'd say. Every van had one.

'These people are my audience, Cled,' he said. 'Regular folks trying to get by. Nice ladies who'll never get taken to a supper club in their lives. Never have a gent hold their hand or buy them a gardenia. And I'm there, inside their houses. They know if they switch on at a certain time I'll be there, like family, only more reliable. That's what makes television special. People feel as though they know you, because you've been in their front room.'

I said, 'So?'

'So,' he said, 'you have to keep that in mind. You have to speak their language, put them at their ease, but you've got to look like a star. Friendliness combined with glamour. It's a balancing act. Get that right, Cled, and we've got a licence to print money.'

That was the first 'we' I'd heard in a long time.

We bought a two-storey house on Mission Avenue, with a garden and a row of Monterey pines behind it that sheltered it from the wind. I'd have bought a place of my own, only Minnie wasn't ready to settle down. 'Are you kidding?' she said. 'I'm a modern girl.'

I said, 'And I'm offering you a modern house. Fitted kitchen, car port, everything. Just say the word.'

'Honey,' she said, 'we'll have more fun if I just visit. Know what I mean?'

Sel turned out to be quite a homemaker. He went shopping with Kaye and picked out cushions and crystal ashtrays, and some lovely oil paintings: sunsets, horses galloping along a beach. Sometimes he'd buy a length of material and not bother getting it made up. He'd just throw it over the settee or drape it over a curtain rail. 'I'm experimenting,' he'd say.

We had a party to celebrate moving in: salted nuts, stuffed eggs, cheese and pineapple chunks on sticks. Sel spent all day rearranging the furniture, checking the glasses didn't have smears, making sure everything was just so.

Kaye said, 'That boy is going to make some girl very happy.'

Minnie said, 'You reckon? I dunno. He never showed no interest in me.'

We were only at Mission Avenue a year, but it was a good year. We were hardly off the television screen and Sel started to become known for his costumes again. He'd design them himself and then have them made by a lady called Celeste Strong. 'Not lamé,' he said. 'Lamé's for girls. Rhinestones are what I want to get into. Gorgeous detailing that catches the light.'

Kaycee Productions had a better set-up by then. They had a camera that ran on tracks, so Sel could move around and flash his rhinestones. And the two of us were getting on very well. If Minnie was in town, Sel'd make himself scarce so we could have the house to ourselves. And if he was having a pal over for beer and backgammon I'd go to the pictures or visit the Conroys. They were all nice enough lads, like the Mexican boy who did our garden, but they didn't have a lot to say for themselves. They'd just smile. I think a lot of them were overwhelmed, getting invited into the home of television stars. I think some of them were hoping to get into show business themselves.

Kaye used to say, 'He better be careful. One of these days he could bring home a murderer. Talk to him, Cled.'

But he switched off whenever I brought it up and I learned to do the same when he got on to the subject of my hair.

A man's hair does get thinner as the years pass. I just changed the way I combed it and there was nothing wrong with the way I looked. But Sel had a real thing about it. 'Cled,' he'd say, 'you've got to get a toupee. If you get one now people won't notice. Leave it till you've gone bald and everybody'll remark.'

I said, 'I'm not getting one. Baldness is a sign of manliness. Look at Yul Brynner. Women go crazy for him.'

Sel said, 'But we've got our image to consider.'

I said, 'I didn't know we had an image.'

'Of course we do,' he said. 'It's glamour. Glamour, glamour, glamour.'

I said, 'Hang about. You always reckon it's the "regular folks" we cater for. Well, "regular folks" don't care if a bloke's thinning on top.'

'Remember what I told you,' he said. 'Show business means added value. Why bother switching on to see the same thing you can see over the breakfast table? They expect to see something special, Cled. Classy suit, diamond cuff links. Perfect hair.'

'Perfect rug,' I said. 'I'm not doing it.'

And I never did.

We moved on from Mission Avenue for various reasons. The fans had started finding us for one thing, peering through the windows, leaving lipstick kisses on the glass. Also, Sel wanted his own swimming pool. And then I lost Minnie, just when I thought she was ready to get engaged. Well, she was. The band was playing in Atlantic City and she got enticed away by a fruit-canning magnate. He saw her in a show and liked the look of her so much he sent her a box of chocolates with a diamond ring hidden in one of the soft centres. A dangerous stunt, when you think of it. It could have turned out very tragic.

Fortunately for Mr Canned Fruit, it didn't. But for a while after that I didn't really care where I lived so when Sel moved to Strawberry Ridge, Encino, I went with him.

He said, 'You'll be renting from Starlight Realty.'

I said, 'Who's Starlight Realty?'

'I am, you plum duff,' he said.

It was to do with tax. That kind of thing interested Sel. I preferred a wage packet myself, but he always wanted a slice of the business. He had shares in Kaycee Productions. Shares in Kaycee Snack Foods. Years later I found out he'd bought the building where Celeste had her workrooms. He liked buying corner lots. And then, when they knocked all that area down to build a convention centre, of course he made a lot of money on it.

We started doing live performances between television series and we recorded three albums, *Starlight Serenades*, *Softly Starlight* and *Starlight Just for You*. And then there were the personal appearances. We'd get asked to cut the ribbon and open a new shop.

'You his minder?' they'd say sometimes, like that ignoramus at the petrol station we inaugurated in Irvine.

But the fans recognised me. They were always thrilled to meet the man who made the actual music. Some of the questions I used to get!

'Why do you talk so weird?'

'How much do they pay you for a show?'

'Will he sign my panties?'

Sel didn't encourage anything like that. Winking at them, putting his arm round them while he was chatting to them during a show, that was one thing, but when he met them anywhere else he could be quite old-fashioned. And he definitely wouldn't handle anybody's undies.

So then I'd get, 'Will you sign them?'

There were some things you'd get asked every time.

What was his favourite colour? Anything that sparkled.

What did he like for breakfast? French toast with maple syrup, although by the time he got up it was hardly breakfast.

Had he got a girlfriend? He had a routine for that one.

'Yes,' he'd say, 'I'll show you her picture.' And then he'd open the locket he had on a chain round his neck, with a picture of Crackers. 'Isn't she adorable?' he'd say.

Crackers was his first little dog. She was a West Highland terrier. He carried her around in his dressing-gown pocket when he first had her, and she'd sleep on his bed. He was never without a dog after that.

Strawberry Ridge was a better location from the point of view of privacy. The road wound up a hillside and you had to know it was there to find it. We didn't have a number either, nor even a name board, so if fans did come looking they couldn't be sure of picking the right house. We had four bedrooms and two bathrooms, and Sel kept on to Dilys about visiting. But Arthur never cared for travel.

Sel said, 'Let the girls come, if you won't. Uncle Sel's treat. They can come to the studio, see how we make a show.'

'They've got to settle down to work, Sel,' she said. 'I know you mean well, but you mustn't start turning their heads, giving them luxury holidays. Arthur'd have a fit.'

And Mam wouldn't come either.

> You keep your money in your pocket [she wrote]. Teilo wanted to take me on a charabanc to Brighton, sixty-five shillings all in, but I'm not a person who needs holidays. Anyway, I've got a promising boy going for his Grade Four so it's out of the question.
> Now, Selwyn, be careful with these houses. Don't spread yourself too thin. Give Cledwyn so much every week, to put by for you, then you'll have something for a rainy day.

He laughed. He said, 'I suppose it's too much for her to grasp. Well, she'll see. Film Star Row, here I come!' He'd got his eye on some land between Santa Monica and Malibu. 'No more second-hand houses,' he said. 'From now on I'm going to design everything. I'm going to build a place with its back nestling against the wall of the canyon and its front facing the ocean, all glass, with a veranda the length of it and a heated sea water pool. I'm going to have bathtubs in the shape of cockleshells.'

He bought the land. But then, before he'd done anything with it, we had a few of those rainy days Mam had worried about.

THIRTEEN

Television was changing. Instead of little companies like Kaycee, the big networks were taking over in Los Angeles. Sel said, 'It can only be a good thing. Think of the audiences! Soon the whole country'll be watching me.'

But the networks weren't interested in *Mr Starlight Sings*.

Kaye said, 'I don't understand it. They've taken *Variety Half Hour*.'

Hubert said, 'Never mind. You've given the boys their start. Now call it a day. Spend some time with your ever-loving husband.'

But Kaye wasn't ready to give up. She said, 'Maybe it's your costumes, Sel.'

Every show we recorded he wore a different jacket and every jacket Celeste made for him had more sparkle than the one before. So we made a new sampler with Sel back in a normal tuxedo, but they still wouldn't buy.

'Too unusual,' Kaye said, 'that's what I'm told. Too hokey. Too unusual. These New York executives don't seem to have the first idea what regular folks like to watch.'

Hubert said, 'Darling, in business you gotta know when to walk away. TV's getting bigger than you'll ever be and you know what? Regular folks'll settle for whatever they're given. They'll just tune in to something new and forget they ever watched *Mr Starlight Sings*.'

I said, 'We can always go back to the supper clubs.'

Sel said, 'Not me. I'm bigger than that now. And if NBC don't want me that's their hard cheese. I shall have the last laugh. There'll come a day when they'll be begging for me.'

I said, 'And in the meanwhile? You've got bugger all in the bank.'

'Maybe so,' he said, 'but I've got assets. And so I'm sticking with Kaycee. I'll stay local, stay where I'm appreciated. There's a way through this; I just haven't figured out what it is yet.'

And it was Bob Barney, the producer at Kaycee, who worked out what the answer was. Back in those days the networks didn't have enough shows of their own to keep going all hours. It was the little local stations, hundreds of them, that filled in the gaps. Barney said, 'They need shows and we've got them. We can sell them the tapes and they can find the sponsors in their own backyard. Think of all those towns, all with businesses like Bartine's.'

That was how Kaycee Syndication went into business, sending out samplers of *Mr Starlight Sings* to stations across the country. And back they came, every one of them a refusal. Waterloo Local said a man in bejewelled apparel was too risky for Iowa; Dodge TV said Sel smiled too much and LRTV said even in a normal suit he wasn't to their taste. They said his hair was too long and girlified for Arkansas.

Kaye said, 'What's wrong with these folks?'

Barney said, 'Well, he is different. And they're all buying *The Kooky Levine Show* like there's no tomorrow. Maybe Mr Starlight is just a California kinda thing.'

Kaye said, 'Maybe, but I'm not convinced. I'm going to give this my best shot. I'm going out there. I'm gonna find out what they've got against smiling and nice wavy hair.'

Hubert said, 'Don't do it, darling. It's a fool's errand.'

Kaye said, 'Conroy, you said this boy had something and you were right. You started all this.'

'Don't remind me,' he said. 'But I didn't expect him to break up my happy home. If this is worth abandoning a good husband for I'll eat my hat.'

Kaye said, 'I'm not abandoning you. If I was gonna do that I'd have done it years ago, while I still had my figure. I just want Sel to get the audience he deserves, plus I'm sowing a little seed corn for you, sweetness. And you won't starve. You've got Willa.'

'What about kisses?' he said. 'I ain't kissing the help.'

Willa said, 'And the help ain't kissing you.'

Kaye was gone a month, accompanied by a salesman, and they came home with ten contracts. Ten sounded all right to me.

Hubert said, 'Ten? Ten! You left me at the mercy of Willa Lightfoot four whole weeks for ten sales? Well, enough is enough. Know a mistake when you see one, darling.'

'I do,' Kaye said. 'But it's not me that's making a mistake. It's these dumb advertisers. This boy is bankable and I'm going to prove it.'

The next month Kaycee sold us to twelve more stations, and then another seven, including LRTV who had reconsidered about hair worn over the collar.

'See!' Kaye said. 'It's taking off.'

Hubert said, 'Twenty-nine deals in three months! I'll be six foot under. I'll be in Forest Lawn before you've even covered your costs.'

Willa said he was behind her in line for an early grave the way things had changed in the Conroy household. The lady of the house absent and those left behind doing nothing but get underfoot.

Then Cornhusker, one of the first stations to take *Mr Starlight Sings*, came back for more and so did FWTV.

'By popular demand,' Kaye said. 'Is that an apology I hear, Hubert Conroy?'

'No,' he said. 'I couldn't even if I wanted to. I'm too weak from neglect.'

But after that things really began to roll. By the time we'd recorded the next run of thirteen shows, we had nearly a hundred syndication deals. Kaye had Willa put Hubert's golf cap on a serving dish at dinner time.

'OK!' he said. 'You launched him. Now stay home. Please!'

Sel insisted on making changes for the second series that was being syndicated. He said, 'I'm changing the set. I go into the viewers' living rooms so I want them to feel like they're coming into mine. I want a sofa, and a little occasional table, and framed photos on top of the piano: Mam, Gaynor and Betsan.'

The trouble was we didn't have a photo of Mam.

'Never mind,' he said. 'We can get one from a picture library. Any nice head and shoulders'll do. They're not going to see it close up.'

I said, 'Mom might not like it.'

'She doesn't have to know,' he said. 'Anyway, it's only to give the idea of a family get-together. Fake living room, fake photo, what's the odds? Everything's fake on television.'

So we got the new set, as per his instructions. It wasn't till years later somebody wrote a piece reminiscing about the early days and remarked that the living room wall used to wobble if Sel went too close to it, and how everybody wondered why he had a photo of Gladys Cooper on top of the piano but nobody liked to ask. Crackers was in the second series too. He trained her to sit on the sofa nice and quiet and look into the camera when he told her to and cock her head to one side. By the time we did our third series Crackers was getting nearly as many letters as we were.

People think Sel was the big heart-throb, but I had a very big following myself. Sometimes they wanted a signed photo, sometimes they wanted my body. I had quite a few turn up at the Topanga Ballroom when we were recording, but we had security by then; a big boy called Ferd who knew ju-jitsu. Kaye had insisted. She said, 'You don't know who's out there. You could get disfigured by some crazy with a knife. I don't want you getting close to any fans without Ferd there to protect you.'

Of course, I was at liberty to make my own arrangements, after hours, if a pretty girl wanted to show me her appreciation. I had one or two who were just using me, asking about Sel while I was trying to romance them, but generally I could see that type coming. And I never took any fans back to Strawberry Ridge. Me and Sel had agreed. Home was strictly home. He had some nice things by then: musical boxes, little animals made out of crystal. Even fans can be light-fingered. They'd take plants out of the garden, light bulbs from over the front door.

Also, there was the point that Sel didn't want people seeing him. 'When I'm on, I'm on,' he said. 'I give them everything. But when I'm off, I want to please myself.'

And they'd have been very disappointed to see Mr Starlight pleasing himself. Slouching around in a pair of baggy old shorts, eating ice cream, picking tickle fights with Ferd or the pool boy.

We were becoming very popular with the older ladies, so another idea Sel had was to end every show on a holy note. He said, 'I serenade them, I make them laugh. But these are church-going ladies, Cled. I want to cater to that side of things too. It'll be a nice way to finish. "One Little Candle" or "I Heard the Voice of Jesus", or "Danny Boy". How you end a show matters just as much as how you begin it.'

I said, 'Not on a harmonium, I hope?'

Kaye said, 'I think it's a terrific idea, but I'm just wondering how you're gonna look, singing hymns in sequinned revers? How about a nice Pringle sweater?'

So that's what he tried, but it didn't work. Out of a suit Sel looked quite a porker and wearing a woolly accentuated it. He said, 'No. I'll stick with what suits me. Let's have just a head shot for the last number, and soft focus. That way the sequins won't intrude.'

One of those clever-dick commentators from New York called Sel 'The Holy Glitterball rolling across the Midwest and gathering momentum'. But those Jesical endings became quite a feature and the viewing figures said it all. Sponsors were lining up to get us: One Step floor polish, Huntly lawn mowers, Brite tooth powder for smokers, Malto night drink. Sel had to record those bits separately. 'After a show', he had to say, 'I find there's nothing helps me unwind like Malto. Just add hot water and sleep tight. And remember, Malto now comes in vanilla flavour too!'

We never needed to buy floor polish or anything like that any more. The garage at Strawberry Ridge was stacked so high with free gifts from our sponsors that the motor had to stand out front. It didn't matter. You get no weather to speak of in California and, according to Sel, it was only a matter of time until General Motors would be giving us a Cadillac.

FOURTEEN

'Your father', Mam wrote, 'is now drawing his old age pension, so he'll be able to sleep under his own roof instead of traipsing the country looking for work.'

Dilys said, 'What did I tell you? Don't send any more money to Mam. If you want her to have something, send it to me. Better still, hang on to it. If the life of luxury doesn't materialise he might clear off again.'

I said, 'I don't know. Mam's not getting any younger. It'd be nice for her to have company. Have a man around the house again.'

Dilys said, 'She's got men. Mr E's always available if her hinges need oiling. If she can't unscrew the top off a jar. And Uncle Teilo goes for his tea. Well, he did do, till Gypsy breezed in. Teilo's nose is really out of joint.'

I said, 'But does Mam seem happy to have Dad back?'

'How would you ever know?' she said. 'She's always talked a load of old cobblers about him so I don't bother listening. I'll tell you what I think. The minute he twigs there's no money he'll be gone. You heard it here.'

Three months, he lasted.

'Your father', Mam wrote, 'has gone back to Shrewsbury for a little holiday. There wasn't a lot for him to do here, especially with me so busy with *Maid of the Mountains*.' She'd been playing for the Aeolian Operatic Society at Digbeth Hall. 'Isn't it funny how we're all in the world of entertainment now, apart from Dilys and your father.'

Dilys said, 'That's not right. There's no bigger comedian than Gypsy. Know what he told her? He had to see a man about some racing pigeons. Well, he's gone.'

I said, 'Did he ask you for money?'

'Never came near,' she said. 'He wouldn't dare. And now, listen to this. Mam's decided she would like a telephone after all.'

'It will make it easier for your father to keep in contact,' Mam wrote, 'and I shan't allow neighbours to take advantage. I shall have a saucer beside it for them to leave their thruppences.'

'Halle-bloody-lujah,' Dilys said. 'Now I can check up on her without trailing over there. You should see her when she answers it. She picks it up as if it's going to bite her. Next thing is the bathroom. I think she's softening.'

I said, 'As long as she doesn't want gold-plated taps.'

'Well,' Dilys said, 'who can say what we've started? She'll be bathing in Channel Number 5 before she's done.'

So we started being able to talk to Mam again, or at least we talked to her and she shouted back. I suppose she thought her voice wouldn't carry. Uncle Teilo appeared to have slipped back into Dad's vacant chair. 'Teilo wants to take me to Blackpool for the Illuminations,' she said, 'but I'm not going.'

I said, 'Go! Enjoy yourself! You never go anywhere.'

'I do enjoy myself,' she said. 'I'm rehearsing *Bless the Bride* with the Aeolians. Did I tell you they've been on strike at Greely's? Thank goodness Selwyn took you away from all that. Bunch of communists.'

I said, 'Our new record's doing pretty well.'

'Of course it is,' she said. 'Oh, now what was it I had to tell you? Teilo?'

I could hear him in the background. I said, 'Has he moved in with you?'

'He has not!' she said. 'He's just popped in for liver and onions. It's not worth cooking for one. He says a girl you used to know on the clubs, Avril. She's appearing at the Hippodrome. Frankie Laine is top of the bill. Teilo says that could have been you if you'd stayed here. He didn't need to stay here, Teilo. He had Selwyn to take him to the heights of fame.'

As far as Sel was concerned we hadn't quite scaled the heights. 'Television gets your face known,' he said, 'but it's live appearances that get people excited. It's time to go back on the road, really meet my public.'

But Kaye Conroy said she'd taken us as far as she could. 'You need a promoter,' she said. 'You need a whole buncha people for a touring show. And I'm supposed to be a retired person. If I don't start following Hubert around in the golf cart once in a while, there's no telling. He might trade me in for an older woman. Talk to Kick. I think he's looking for a change.'

Kick Valentine was our musical director on *Mr Starlight Sings*. 'Yeah,' he said. 'I'm ready to travel. Where are we going?'

Sel's first idea was he was going to organise everything himself. He didn't trust people to do things right.

Kaye said, 'Sure. Next stop the morgue. You'll kill yourself! You gonna start stitching on your own sequins? You gonna fly your own plane? Why don't you just ease up a little, be a little more trusting? Why don't you talk to somebody you worked with before?'

And that was how we came to link up with Milo Freeman again, to take *Mr Starlight Live* out on the road. A full-length show, with an eighteen-piece band, a backing quartet called the Joytones and a support vocalist, who sang during Sel's costume changes. It took weeks to find the right girl. They were too glamorous or not glamorous enough. Too much personality. Too many ideas of their own.

He said, 'This is Mr Starlight's show not *Opportunity Knocks*.'

In the end the job went to Kitty O'Malley and as far as I was concerned she didn't have too much of anything. We had quite a thing, me and Kitty. I'd say, 'If you can't sleep, you know where to find me.'

'Oh, Cled,' she'd say. 'I don't know if I could trust myself!'

I've found fame to be a great aphrodisiac.

We opened the show at the Mount Storm Arena, Cincinnati with the worst band I ever had the misfortune to appear with. Kick had used a local contractor to put a band together and when rehearsal time came, the afternoon before the show, five of them didn't turn up, four ladies on saxophone and a cornet player, couldn't get away from their day jobs. And that was only the start. Even when we had them all assembled Kick couldn't get them to finish a number in unison.

Sel heard the racket. He said, 'OK, get rid of the monkeys. Where's my band?'

Kick said, 'Sorry, Sel. Just give me another half-hour with them. It's the guys. They're holding back, allowing the girls to finish first. Funny, really.'

Sel said, 'I'll tell you how funny it is, Kick. You just used up the one blooper you're allowed. So by the time I get to Omaha you'd better have a real band for me, rehearsed and ready to go.'

Kick said, 'They're called for two o'clock. Until I see them I don't see what else I can do.'

Sel said, 'That was before you forfeited your night's sleep. You can travel overnight. Rehearse them in the morning. Rehearse them till they're perfect. This is Mr Starlight you're working for, not Amateur Night.'

I felt sorry for Kick. Sel could be like that. Nice as pie one minute, then screaming and shouting because everything wasn't laid out exactly how he liked it in his dressing room: dusting powder at three o'clock; photo of Mam at eleven o'clock, cuff link case at twelve o'clock; costumes hung in reverse order on the rail; Crackers's water bowl placed on its special mat. It was like a parade ground back there some nights and Sel was the sergeant major, but as soon as it was showtime he was different again.

The house lights would go down and there'd be a drum roll. Then Kick Valentine would come on while we were playing 'Starlight Serenade'. 'Ladies and gentlemen,' he'd say, 'tonight Starlight Entertainment is proud to present, truly a star of stage, TV screen and hit parade, the one and only . . . Mr Starlight!'

And we'd play him on. He liked stairs to trot down, which wasn't easy to arrange at some venues so we started travelling with our own little set of steps covered with red carpet and he'd stand on them, waiting, behind a back curtain. 'Well, look at you all!' he'd say. 'Fancy you being here! Now I really feel like singing!'

We played the Gladstone Bowl, Kansas, Bluff Runs, Omaha and the Mile High, Denver, all sold out. He did three costume changes every show and in the second half he'd go down into the audience to let them admire Celeste's handiwork.

Some smaller places we played we didn't have a band. Just me on piano and Don Smith on bass. Those were the nights when he'd do a chat routine with me. 'Meet my big brother, Cled,' he'd say. 'Cled, are you awake?'

'I think so,' I had to say. 'If I'm not, there are an awful lot of people sitting around in this dream.'

'Cled,' he'd say. 'Do you know where you are?'

'Yes,' I had to say. 'Stage left, first half, second number.'

Milo said, 'They love you, Selwyn. There's only one thing I'd say. Keep them wanting more. No encores. Just say goodnight and go.'

That was how his beg-off came about. 'Thank you, thank you,' he'd say. 'You've all been so kind; now I'm going to let you go home. Night night! Sleep tight!' And it didn't matter how much they stamped and whistled, he'd never go back on. They'd put it out on the loud-speakers – 'Mr Starlight has left the building'. But there'd always be fans waiting outside, hoping to get lucky.

Milo said, 'We should think about your fan clubs, Selwyn. They're springing up everywhere. Maybe give a little reception before a show? Let some of them come and meet you in your dressing room?'

Sel said, 'I'll think about it.'

Milo said, 'What's to think about? These girls are your fans. Without them what are you?'

'A star,' he said, 'and a star keeps a certain amount of distance. I don't want any of them getting any big ideas.'

By the time we got to Las Vegas, *Star!* magazine was after him for his life story.

* * *

Me and my brother [he told them] are very close. He's a good deal older than me and he was still an amateur when I'd turned professional, but we're a good partnership, so when agents started asking me to come to the United States, I insisted that Cled had to be part of the deal. That's the kind of family we are. Sometimes folk can't believe we're brothers. But Cled provides a good dependable backing and I provide the glamour. He looked out for me when I was knee high to a grasshopper so the least I can do now I'm a star is keep him on my team.

I said, 'You've got some ginger, making me sound like a charity case.'

'They put words in my mouth, Cled,' he said. 'That's magazines for you. You say one thing and they twist it into something more interesting.'

I said, 'You could have mentioned who wrote "Busy Being Lonely". That would have been interesting.'

'It never came up,' he said.

I should have seen which way the wind was blowing.

Sel loved Las Vegas. It was too rough for my taste, like a place out of a cowboy picture. In those days it always seemed liable to get blown away or covered with sand but that never bothered him. He liked his bone china and his gardenia soap, but he liked cowboy towns too. 'You know what?' he said. 'I think I'll buy a parcel of land here. I'd like a place of my own.'

His house in Malibu was only half built. Ocean Star, it was going to be called.

I said, 'You're stretching yourself a bit, aren't you? How many houses can one man need?'

'I don't know,' he said. 'What kind of star has one home? Better to buy houses than pay hotel bills. I think I'll build a bungalow here. Vegas is a bungalow kind of town.'

We did two more runs of thirteen shows for Kaycee and cut a long-playing disc of our most requested songs, then we went east, back on the road.

106

I said to Kitty, 'We could share a room this time, get to know each other a bit better.'

I knew she was keen from the way she hung around Sel, using him to get closer to me.

She said, 'I think we have to be professional about this, Cled. We're part of a team and we can't afford to let our passions run riot.'

Playing it cool, as they say. She was a sexy little minx. If her legs hadn't been so shapeless she could have been a real pin-up.

Every show was sold out before we'd even left home and everywhere we went Sel was mobbed. Ladies wanting to touch him and a lot of them you'd have thought were too old to be interested in any such thing. He was two hours signing autographs in Pittsburgh and in Baltimore the police couldn't control the crowds.

Milo said, 'One of your fans lost her footing and got trampled. You should visit her in the hospital.'

Sel said, 'That's a great idea. I'll wear just a grey two-piece.'

Kitty said, 'A sweater'd be better. Friendlier.'

He was always being sent jumpers by his fans, but knitwear didn't really flatter him. In my opinion a sports jacket would have been the thing for visiting hospitals, but he didn't own a sports jacket.

He said, 'While I'm there we should do some other stuff. Visit some sick kiddies.'

Milo said, 'That's my boy!'

Sel said, 'Send out for teddies. Teddy bears and dollies and fluffy dogs. I'll go laden!'

There was a picture of him in the papers the next day, chatting to a little boy in an iron lung.

He said, 'I don't know why I didn't think of it before. It only takes an hour, it costs peanuts and the publicity's great.'

Milo said, 'We'll make it a regular feature from now on. This has gone down so well.'

Just as well because the show itself got a very nasty write-up. '*Now with Added Frosting*' it said.

* * *

> British phenomenon Mr Starlight has made glitter his trade-
> mark but he proves the old adage that glitter doesn't always
> signify gold. His songs are sentimental, his voice is unre-
> markable and he parades pictures of his dreary family in an
> attempt to convince us he's just like one of us. No need to
> try so hard, Mr S. We're convinced! Take away the rhine-
> stones and what do you have? A third-rate crooner with an
> ingratiating smile. Mr Starlight's current tour looks set to
> break box office records, which just goes to show you can
> fool an awful lot of the people an awful lot of the time.

Sel didn't care. He said, 'Give me that review. I'm nearly out of toilet paper.'

In Wilmington Milo arranged a 'surprise' hospital visit, so Sel could hand out fluffy toys and have his picture taken with a kiddie in a wheelchair.

Kitty said, 'You know what'd be neat? If everything had your name on it. Like the bears could wear Mr Starlight bow ties, and the dolls could have stars on their dresses.'

Sel said, 'Great idea. Look into that, would you, Milo?'

In New Jersey Sel agreed to give his first backstage reception for members of his fan club. 'As long as it's kept under control,' he said. 'We'll give them tea and biscuits, and signed photos.'

Milo said, 'They won't care about refreshments. They're coming to meet you in person, get their own personal photo taken with you, close up.'

Those fans brought him so many red roses apparently there wasn't one left to be bought anywhere in town. But the critics weren't throwing him any bouquets. The one from the *Pleasantville Post* wasn't pleasant at all:

> Further evidence, if evidence we need, that The Change
> makes women lose what little mind they have. Can there be
> a more unedifying sight than six thousand matrons slavering
> over this podgy, powdered, simpering boy? They squeal

when he opens his mouth. Heck, they squeal when he puts one foot in front of the other. Just when you thought you walked into a bonny baby contest by mistake, the Wunderkind toddles off into the audience and gives them his breathily insistent version of 'Tenderly'. Then, while you're still wondering about this boy in big girl's sequins, he turns the tables yet again and delivers a wide-eyed 'Lost Chord' back to back with 'Ave Maria'. What a choirboy! Didn't he do well, Mommy? Feet up, pat him on the po-po.

'Boo-hoo,' Sel said. He was laughing. 'Boo-bloody-hoo. I wonder how many handmade suits Mr Pleasantville Post has got hanging in his wardrobe? I wonder how many fan letters he gets through his letter box?'

It had become quite a topic in the newspapers, why men didn't like Sel and women couldn't get enough of him. They stopped people in the street and interviewed them. One man said he'd never heard of Mr Starlight, which was ridiculous. He must just have crawled out of the Burma jungle. Another one said he didn't care for Sel because he didn't seem like a normal man and then his lady wife said, 'Exactly. He's sweet and polite. And I'll bet he doesn't sit around in an undershirt, scratching himself.'

Of course, she was going by what she'd seen in the magazines. I suppose his fans thought he was like that all the time, sipping tea, wearing monogrammed slippers. One of the ladies' journals said the question on everybody's lips was who'd be the lucky girl to win his heart, and then a person on ACLR's *In the Air* radio show said Mr Starlight's heart appeared to belong to his mother, unless anyone had different information. Blow me if the very next day he didn't take Kitty shopping for a mink stole and who should they happen to run into but a pack of photographers. After all that hanging about, all those years of not showing an interest in girls, then he had to make a move on one of my prospects.

I said, 'You're just doing this to try and thwart me.'

He said, 'All I did was to buy her a wrap. I can't help it if the papers go off and write fairy stories.'

I said, 'Well, you know me and Kitty have something going.'

'That right?' he said. 'What kind of thing would that be? She come to you for fatherly advice?'

I said, 'I thought you were a third-rate crooner. I didn't realise you'd turned comedian.'

'Cled,' he said, 'there are a lot of things you don't appear to realise. There are pianists queuing up to play for Mr Starlight. You're only where you are because of me and I've only kept you on to stop Mam worrying. You don't fit in. Look at you. You're old before your time, old and dreary.'

I said, 'I don't think you are interested in Kitty really. You're just using her.'

'Bugger Kitty,' he said. 'I'm talking about you. I'm talking about a bad comb-over and a dingy old top plate. The chambermaid last night thought you were my dad, not my brother, and I can understand why.'

It was the toupee business all over again. And dentures. He wanted me to get some of those big shiny American teeth.

I said, 'You ought to be glad I keep a low profile. Do you want me to give you a run for your money? Show them who's the real musician in the family? Eh? I can play anything. And do you think you're the only one the ladies flock after? When it's a real man they want, it's me they come to.'

He said, 'You're small potatoes. If it wasn't for me you'd still be playing at the Non-Political. Probably not even there. You wouldn't have got as far as Southampton without me. Mr Starlight is what all this is about. The world's full of flyblown old club pianists, but there's only one Mr Starlight.'

I reminded him I was the one who passed Grade 8 piano.

'Yeah?' he said. 'And I got a merit badge for knowing how many beans make five. Stop kidding yourself. You're no bloody Hildegarde and you're no Cole Porter, so just be grateful I'm the kind of star who believes in family.'

I said, 'I'm warning you, you toy with Kitty's affections and you'll have me to answer to.'

He just laughed. 'What's it to be?' he said. 'Pistols at dawn? Grow up, Cled. Grow up and smarten up. Get some hair and get some teeth, or sling your hook. What's it to be?'

I said, 'It's been nice knowing you.'

He stormed off. He had a car waiting to take him to New York to be interviewed by Ed Sullivan. Kitty went with him. A little fur scarf and some girls are anybody's. We'd had quarrels in the past. I thought it would all have blown over by dinner time.

But when I got back to the hotel I had Milo on the phone. 'Cledwyn,' he said, 'what the hell is going on? I'm the one supposed to make the announcements around here. You boys had a tiff? You been upsetting Sel?'

I said, 'I'm the one who's upset.'

'Now, now,' he said. 'You have to help me here. We appear to have a situation on our hands and I need the facts. Is it true you're leaving to pursue your own interests?'

Sel had given it out on live wireless that I was leaving the Mr Starlight team to pursue my own interests.

I said, 'It's a joke.'

Milo said, 'It isn't a joke. He's given Kick orders to get another pianist for the rest of the tour.'

I said, 'Where does that leave me? Are you still my agent?'

'Come and see me,' he said. 'Drop by tomorrow.'

Sel wouldn't talk to me. He'd locked himself into his hotel suite with that Jezebel, O'Malley, and he wasn't taking phone calls.

I said, 'Milo, two can play at that game. I'm going solo. What have you got for me?'

He said, 'It's a tough one.' How he'd gone on about me being a class musician. He said, 'Solo pianist. No gimmicks. I don't know. I'll see what I can do. Unless you've reconsidered? There's no shame in improving on the hand Mother Nature deals us. A good-quality hair boost product can make the world of difference.'

His attitude was annoying me. I said, 'I haven't reconsidered.

111

And the other thing is I'm owed money. I was booked for a six-week tour.'

Milo said, 'But you were the one who walked out, Cledwyn. You could be sued for breach of contract. Not that that's Selwyn's style. Flesh and blood means a lot to him, I know. Show business and family, though, it's a tricky mix.'

I said, 'You've changed your tune. You were the one wanted us to be a family act. You were the one who went on about the Betsie Sisters.'

'The Betsie Sisters are like three legs on a stool,' he said. 'One's no good without the other two. You and Selwyn are a different case. He's big now, Cledwyn. He doesn't need anybody.'

I phoned the Conroys.

Kaye said, 'I don't know what to say, Cled.'

I said, 'I could do a show for Kaycee. I've got some ideas.'

She said, 'Well, we're kinda concentrating on quiz shows right now. But if anything comes up . . . At least you got Strawberry Ridge. Property prices there are shooting up.'

But I didn't any more. Sel had persuaded me to sell my half to Starlight Realty and be a tenant.

Kaye said, 'Well, he won't see you without a roof over your head. Know what? If you're set on going solo you may find it easier back in the old country. I guess you still got contacts there?'

Everybody shipped out to Dayton for the next leg of the tour: Kitty, the new bodyguard, Kick Valentine and they never even said goodbye. Bunch of Judases.

Milo said he had a cheque for me if I cared to drop by his office. 'Selwyn insists on you getting paid for the whole tour,' he said. 'I can't name another star who'd be as generous. So I hope you'll move on now, make a fresh start, no hard feelings.'

I said, 'I have very hard feelings. He's dumped me, like one of his old suits.'

'Take my advice,' he said. 'Don't be bitter. And know your limits. This kind of money will see you clear for a while, but not if you start talking to lawyers.'

I said, 'I've never talked to a lawyer in my life.'

'Smart boy,' he said. 'Keep it that way. Now, if you'll oblige with a signature I can give you your cheque. You decided yet where you're headed?'

'England,' I said. 'I've got various avenues I'll be looking into. Various opportunities I'll be following up.'

'Great,' he said. 'Sounds good. Be happy, Cledwyn.'

I intended to be. There was a certain little bus conductress who might be glad to hear from me, for one thing. The ladies are very susceptible to a gent once he's been on the television.

FIFTEEN

I called in to a place on 50th Street to get a shave and while I was waiting my turn I studied a face I was pretty sure I recognised. I said, 'Did you ever work on the Cunarders?'

He looked at me in the mirror.

I said, 'Were you on the *Queen Mary*, about five years ago?'

'Yeah,' he said.

I said, 'I did a few crossings myself, as a bandsman. Before I got into television.'

'Oh yeah?' he said.

After that I made it a point to carry a couple of my newspaper clippings in my wallet. People can be very sceptical.

He said he'd been two years in New York City. He said he'd had enough of being cooped up on a boat, never seeing daylight. 'Decided it was time to see the world,' he said.

But he hadn't exactly gone far. He was still only two blocks from the pier. He was still lathering chins.

I said, 'I played in twenty-nine states.'

'That right?' he said.

I had a suitcase sticker from every one of them as well.

'Where are you playing tonight?' he said. 'Carnegie Hall?'

That's the kind of jesting you get if you stay unassuming, if you don't allow stardom to spoil you.

I said, 'I've played venues bigger than that. I was with Mr Starlight.'

That got his attention. 'I've seen him,' he said. 'He's big. He in town?'

'No,' I said. 'He's in Ohio. We split up. I'm pursuing my own career now.'

He said, 'You telling all to the newspapers?'

I said, 'I am not.'

'Pity,' he said. 'I'll bet you got some weird stuff on him.'

I said, 'How do you mean?'

He sniggered. 'Oh, you know,' he said. 'He's not quite right, is he? Puts me in mind of my Uncle Phil.'

I said, 'Why? What did your Uncle Phil do?'

'Nothing,' he said. 'Never did a thing. He just wasn't quite right.'

I said, 'Do you see any of the old crowd when they're in town?'

'Dunno,' he said. 'I see a lot of faces. You looking for somebody?'

I said, 'No. Nobody in particular. I'm sailing home. Just wondered if I'd see any familiar faces.'

'You going on the *Mary*?' he said. 'I wouldn't. Not this time of year. I'd wait for the *Elizabeth*. She's been fitted with new stabilisers.'

And that was what I did. I stayed at the Edison Hotel but I had my dinners at the Automat, just like the old days. The shop windows were all trimmed up for Christmas and I bought a few bits and pieces from Filene's for the ladies back home. Woolly gloves in nice cheery colours for the twins, scarves for Dilys and Mam, and a marcasite brooch in case my luck was in with Renée.

I had a lovely time, strolling the streets, pleasing myself for a change instead of running after Sel. I even went back to the Sinbad Club and introduced myself to the new manager. He was very interested to hear how I'd gone on to greater things after I'd left there. He said if he'd had more notice he might have been able to find a slot for me. The only crimp in my week was not being able to buy copies of our hit single, 'Busy Being Lonely'. None of the sales clerks seemed to have heard of it.

I said, 'You should know your stock.'

But it was all Rosemary Clooney, Rosemary Clooney.

One girl said, 'What label is it on?'

I said, 'The *Bartine Variety Half Hour* label.'

'Hunh?' she said.

Ignoramus.

The *Queen Mary* was sailing that night. I went down to the pier, for old times' sake, ate a bag of roasted chestnuts, listened to the whirr of the cables and watched them loading provisions. Then I went to a diner on 48th Street which did a very acceptable all-day breakfast. The more I thought about what had happened between me and Sel the happier I was to be out of it. All those different towns where you didn't know anybody. Having to play the same old stuff all the time. And that barber had hit the nail on the head. There was something not quite right about Sel. Taking his own knife and fork with him everywhere he went. Getting in a paddy if the help moved one of his figurines half an inch when she was dusting. He was loopy. I was glad to be going home.

She'd been sitting at a corner table. I hadn't noticed her. 'Cled?' she said. 'Is it you?'

It was Hazel.

Well, the bloom had gone off her, no mistake, and I suppose it showed in my face. I didn't intend upsetting her. I hate to be the cause of waterworks in a lady.

'I know what you're thinking,' she said. 'What do you expect? Time's rolled on. I see a difference in you too. What happened to your hair?'

She sat down opposite me. 'I saw a picture of Sel,' she said. 'Mobbed by fans.'

Autograph hunters, that's all. I wouldn't have called it 'mobbed' exactly.

She said. 'You working for him?'

Too many ruddy questions.

I said, 'I didn't work *for* him. I worked *with* him. We were a partnership. But I don't work *with* him any more because I'm ready for a change. I'm going to be concentrating on my songwriting.'

'Did you fall out?' she said. 'You were always falling out.'

I said, 'We parted by mutual agreement. I had a hit single, you know?'

'No,' she said, 'I didn't know. That's nice.'

I said, 'How about yourself? Still in charge of delicates?'

'Yes,' she said. 'Though it's not the same. Ladies aren't dressing the way they used to. You don't see as much organdie or beading. There's not the challenge there used to be.'

I said, 'I'm surprised you're still working the liners. The way you were saving up, I thought you'd have had a chain of laundries by now.'

'Well,' she said, 'things didn't go according to plan.'

I bought her a slice of pie and a cup of coffee, and she sat and told me her story. How she'd found herself in the family way and been forced to give up her job and go away for a while.

I said, 'It wasn't me caused it, was it?' I knew really it couldn't have been. Me and Hazel had never gone quite to that extent. She'd always kept her girdle on.

'No,' she said. 'It wasn't you.'

I said, 'Was it that pastry cook?'

'It doesn't matter who it was,' she said. 'He's long gone.'

I said. 'What did you do?'

'Went home to St Asaph,' she said, 'looking for a bit of Christian charity, but my dad had got himself a new lady friend. They told me to clear off. My dad told me never to darken his door again, Cled. And I haven't.'

She'd finished up in a Methodist home for fallen women and had a little baby girl and put her up to be adopted. Then she'd had to wait to get her old job back. She said, 'So that's what happened to my savings, Cled. And now I'm not bothered. Now I just work to keep a roof over my head.'

I said, 'I often thought about you. Wondered how you were going on.'

'Did you?' she said. 'Well, now you know.'

I said, 'It's a pity I didn't see you before I bought my ticket. We could have travelled together. As it is, I'm going on the *Queen Elizabeth*.'

'That's all right,' she said. 'I wouldn't have seen anything of you.

Not unless you got sauce on your tie. You're sailing First Class, I suppose?'

I said, 'No. I've worked too hard for my money to throw it away. And I've seen too much of what goes on behind the scenes. You can still find an Elastoplast in your soup, doesn't matter how much you're paying. Anyway, I'd have come looking for you. Remember the Ripening Room? I always think of you when I smell melons.'

'Do you?' she said.

She looked so washed out. She had a little bit of silver coming in on her temples.

I asked after Lionel Truman and Massie. Both retired.

I said, 'How about Mother Carey?'

She said. 'I heard he shut himself in a meat locker, throwing a tantrum over some slight. Nearly froze to death. But it must have happened while I was gone. I don't know if it's true. Ginger married a black man from Jamaica. Jim Ganey moved to Union Castle.'

I said, 'What about you? Think you'll ever leave?'

'No,' she said. 'I'll be there till they have to sew me into a sack and tip me over the side.'

She still had a pretty smile.

'I shall have to be going,' she said. 'I'm due back.'

I walked with her to the pier. I said, 'It's funny, I've been to hundreds of places now, but nowhere else sounds like New York.'

'Yes,' she said. 'Funny that.'

'Hazel,' I said, 'wait for me in Southampton.'

'What?' she said.

We were having to shout over the traffic.

I said, 'Wait for me. So we can talk.'

'How can I?' she said. 'We'll have sailed again by the time you dock.'

I said, 'Give them notice.'

She said, 'What do you mean?'

I said, 'Give your notice and we can get married. We can buy that guest house you used to talk about. Get your little girl back.'

That started the waterworks again.

She said, 'I can't get her back. Once you've given them up that's that.'

I hadn't appreciated that.

I said, 'We can get married anyway, if you like?'

She said, 'Why would you do that?'

I said, 'Why not? We got on all right before, didn't we? And now we're both at a loose end.'

She said, 'I've got to go, Cled. I'm late.'

I said, 'Will you wait for me?'

'I don't know,' she said. 'What if you change your mind?'

She was halfway up the crew gangway.

I said, 'I'm not going to change my mind. Are you going to wait for me?'

'I'll think about it,' she shouted. 'But I don't know. People let you down.'

And she was gone.

I didn't sleep much that night, going over everything. It was Renée I'd been thinking about, sitting there in the diner, wondering if I'd be able to rekindle something with her, wondering if she was still available, or married with kiddies, gone to seed. And then Hazel had claimed me. Not as well stacked as Renée, but nice, in her own way, and as Mam always said, better bread today than jam tomorrow because tomorrow never comes.

I took the marcasite brooch back, to see if I could exchange it for a ring. The girl said they didn't do exchanges.

I said, 'Only I'm probably getting engaged.'

She said, 'So, she gets a ring *and* a brooch.'

I said, 'Look, it's not that I haven't got the money. I've had a song in the hit parade. But I've already got a scarf I can give her, or gloves, so she won't expect a brooch as well.'

'Lucky lady,' she said. 'Caught herself the last of the big spenders. Mister, why don't you go to Woolworths? You can get the wedding band too, while you're there.' And I would have done, except the big question was would Hazel be waiting for me when I got to Southampton?

SIXTEEN

The ladies and gents at my dinner table were quite fascinated to hear from someone who'd experienced life below decks. It gave them a better appreciation of the luxuries they were enjoying, being able to visualise all those busy bees, out of sight, starching shirts, peeling spuds, rolling pats of butter. There was just one couple I didn't take to, and as it turned out they were a bit peculiar, going off in a huff, asking to be moved to another table. All I'd said was, on a liner like the *Queen Elizabeth* the beautiful public rooms represent the tip of an iceberg. I don't see how I was supposed to know she was a nervous traveller. But the husband cut up quite ugly. 'Thanks, big mouth,' he said. 'It's only taken me five years to get her aboard a liner.'

Of course the crew were surprised to learn I'd been a Cunard man myself. I made a point of introducing myself to them, especially the band members. I thought they'd be interested to hear about my experiences under Lionel Truman. But even in five years things had changed. The play list was shorter. Standards were lower. They were a jaded bunch. No *esprit de corps*. And none of them had even heard of Glorette Gilder so she'd evidently faded from the scene.

I didn't bring up Sel's name. I wasn't in the mood to answer a load of silly questions about him. I'd decided to travel incognito and it was no disadvantage. I still had women running after me. There was one sad creature, all on her own, kept turning up wherever I went. Sun deck, smoking room, you name it, there she'd be, looking like a pipe cleaner with specs. I'm sure she'd have been grateful, but I just couldn't bring myself to oblige.

Then there was the married one. She started giving me the eye after I'd let slip about having starred on American television. Running her tongue over her teeth, sitting up on a bar stool criss-crossing her legs. I wouldn't have minded. She had a nice pair of pins on her. It was her husband I was worried about. He had a thick bull neck on him and a boxer's nose. It was probably just as well we ran into a gale the second day out and seasickness saved me from myself. No matter how still I lay it felt as though something was sliding around inside my head, banging on the inside of my skull. The first night I thought I was going to die and by the next morning I was hoping I would, and when I finally lifted my head from the pillow, as we were coming into the Solent, I found I'd dropped so much weight I could pull my trouser belt in a full notch.

I thought, 'Renée won't know me.'

Then I remembered Hazel. I'd made her an offer she'd be a fool to turn down, but you never know with women. They decide things for the daftest reasons. I stood by the rail while we were being warped in, collar up against the wind, hat brim pulled down, and it crossed my mind I didn't have to go through with it either. She might not recognise me, looking so lean and hungry. I could probably slip by her and be on my way. So I thought, 'Well, the way I'll play it is I just won't search for her face in the crowd. I'll just look straight ahead and see what happens. Destiny. Kismet as it's called in the musical. Or was it Carousel? Anyway, Hazel was right at the front when I got into the passenger terminal, nose powdered, mouth lipsticked, so I knew what her answer was.

'Cled,' she said. 'Did I dream it?'

I remember thinking, 'Well, that's that, then.'

Sometimes it's better to have these things taken out of your hands. I said, 'What do you reckon, then? Shall we give it a try?'

'Yes,' she said. 'Let's give it a try.'

We went straight to the Majestic for tea and toast and sexual intercourse. She still had that lovely smell of soapsuds about her.

She said, 'Where were you thinking of for the guest house?'

'I don't know,' I said. 'I haven't decided. Somewhere classy. Torquay, or Bournemouth. Somewhere with sea views.'

'Lovely,' she said. 'We can have different colours for the bedrooms. The Rose Room and the Azure Room and so on. And just half-board. We don't want people coming back in the middle of the day, getting underfoot. Just bed, breakfast and an evening meal.'

I said, 'And we'll have a piano in the lounge so I can tinkle the ivories after dinner, to entertain the guests.'

'Oh, Cled,' she said. 'I'm so happy.'

So I gave her the brooch and one of the pairs of woolly gloves, and that was that. Well, Betsan never kept anything for more than five minutes and it had crossed my mind she'd be just as happy with a box of Milk Tray.

'My fiancé,' she kept saying. 'Mr Starlight's brother.'

I bought a little second-hand Wolseley the next morning and then I telephoned Dilys. 'I'm on my way home,' I said, 'so warn Mam. I'm engaged to be married.'

Dilys screamed. 'You got Sel with you?' she said.

Hazel was nervous, of course.

I said, 'Nothing to worry about. She'll like it that you're Welsh.'

She said, 'You're going to see some changes, Cled. Five years.'

Mona's Hosiery had become a ladies' hair emporium. The Empress of India had a new front door. That was about all. Spooner's were still putting an apostrophe in 'Roasting Chicken's' and Jewkes's still had that empty hairnet card in their window. I said, 'It's gloomier than I remembered. We had our own orange trees in Encino.'

It started raining as we pulled into Ninevah Street, same as the day me and Sel left. I said, 'I'm glad I've come back with you on my arm. Things to look forward to.'

She squeezed my hand.

Dilys had been watching for us from Mam's front window. She came running out, smiling and hugging and kissing and carrying on. 'You little tyke!' she said. 'Springing this on us. What ever happened to your hair? Hello, pet. I'm the sister.'

Mam hadn't come to the door.

I said, 'Is she all right? I expect I'll see a change in her?'

'Wishful thinking,' Dilys said. 'She's indoors with a face on her like a trod chip.'

I noticed the Edkinses' curtains twitching.

Dilys took Hazel under her wing right from the beginning. 'Don't mind me,' she said. 'I'm barmy. And don't mind our mam. The first forty years are the worst.'

Mam looked exactly the same as the day we'd left. I believe she was even wearing the same cardigan. She was never known to perspire, so her clothes lasted for ever. But the house was different. There was a gas fire instead of the old coal grate, and a new three-piece suite, cottage style, and pictures of Sel everywhere, cut out of magazines. She said, 'You'll have to have shop-bought biscuits. Springing this on me. If you'd given me notice I'd have baked a cake.'

Dilys said, 'Oh, Cled, it is grand to see you. We haven't half pined for you.'

Mam had gone into the kitchen to put the kettle on. 'No we haven't,' she shouted. 'We've been all right.'

Dilys said, 'Now, how about Sel? He never said a dickybird about this when I spoke to him. When's he coming?'

'When he's good and ready,' Mam said. 'He's got better things to do than waste time sailing across oceans. And when are you going back?'

Hazel said, 'We're not. Cled doesn't play for Sel any more. We're going to open a boarding house.'

If it had been up to me I'd have broken the news piecemeal.

Mam came out of the kitchen. 'Now what have you gone and done?' she said. 'You're meant to be looking after him. He's only a bab.'

I said, 'I did look after him. And he's not a bab. He's a ruddy great lummox and getting a bit too full of himself. I could tell you some stories.'

Mam said, 'I don't want to hear stories. You'll get gumboils, telling lies. Turning up here with a woman, springing weddings on us. Is she expecting?'

'No,' Hazel said. 'I'm not. And it wasn't Cled's fault Sel sacked him. I'm very fond of Sel, Mrs Boff, but from what I hear he acted very hastily.'

Dilys said, 'What happened, Cled? He didn't sack you?'

I hadn't wanted to go into all that business just then. I'd been hoping for a nice welcome for Hazel and a bit of appreciation for everything I'd done, but Mam hadn't even shook her by the hand. I saw red. I said, 'We had a falling out. But I was ready for a change anyway. He's too much of the big shot these days, wheeling and dealing and riding around like King ruddy Farouk. He was on at me all the time to get a wig, since I've gone thin on top. Reckoned I was spoiling the look of things. Not glamorous enough, that's what it amounted to. The trouble with Sel is he's all sequins and no technique.'

Dilys said, 'Don't be bitter, Cled. I hate to think of you quarrelling.'

I said, 'I'm not bitter. Things have turned out very well for me. I bumped into Hazel again and I'm a very happy man. We'll open our boarding house, with different coloured bedrooms and a supper club ambience, and you'll be able to come for your holidays.'

Mam said, 'We don't need holidays. We need people to do as they're told and not leave their brother in the lurch. And you haven't gone thin on top, Cledwyn. You've gone as bald as a coot.'

Dilys and Hazel went through to wash the tea things.

Mam said, 'Where's she staying?'

I said, 'We thought Dilys and Arthur might put her up. And I could have my old room. Seeing as Sel's not here.'

Mam said, 'You can't. It's not aired.'

Dilys shouted, 'Then air it, Mam. Use that electric blanket we bought you that's never been out of its wrapping.'

Mam was very begrudging. 'Well, don't touch any of his stuff,' she said. 'When he comes back I want him to find everything as he left it.'

Hazel said, 'Guess what, Cled? All this time you've been gone and your mam's still got your razor by the sink.' She must have imagined it, though. There was no razor there when I looked for it later on.

I was all for naming the day, but there were a couple of flies in the ointment. Everybody said I should make up with Sel and wait till he was free to attend, but I wasn't going to phone him. I'd sent a message through Milo and that was as far as I was prepared to go. I looked in on the Birmingham Welsh and the Non-Political, willing to sign autographs, but it was the same everywhere I went.

'Where's that famous brother of yours?'

'What's it like having a star in the family?'

Same silly questions, over and over.

I said, 'I'm going to get a board made and walk up and down Colmore Row. Yes, he's In America. No, he has no plans to return. And yes, isn't it marvellous that a boy from Saltley, who can hardly read music and never had a girlfriend nor any breath control to speak of, has turned out to be the big singing heart-throb. Ask me it's a ruddy miracle.'

Arthur laughed. He said, 'And I'll walk behind you with one that says "Judge not your brother".'

Christmas came and went without any word from him. Just a hamper each for Mam and Dilys from Harrods of London, with tinned ham and pickled walnuts and fruit cake.

Then there was the mix-up over my money. I had to wait till Mam was in bed before I could phone Milo. I didn't want her listening in. I said, 'This can't be right. I'm owed royalties.'

'Tax,' he said. 'I guess you didn't allow for tax.'

I said, 'Have they hit Sel too? He must owe more than I did.'

'Can't discuss that with you,' he said. 'But Sel did take expert advice. You could have done the same.'

I said, 'Is that it, then?

He said, 'You want someone to check the figures? I can arrange that, if you're willing to pay.'

I said, 'It's just not as much as I was expecting.'

'Cledwyn,' he said, 'in my experience it never is.'

I had to break the news to Hazel. I said, 'I think I've made a mistake.'

She said, 'You've changed your mind about getting married?'

'No,' I said, 'but you might not want me after all. I don't think we've got enough for a place in Torquay.'

'Never mind,' she said. 'There's other places. Llandudno's very nice.'

I said, 'I'm sorry. I've let you down.'

'Cled,' she said, 'you haven't let anybody down. I'd be on the scrap heap if you hadn't come along. Let's get married at Easter.'

Then the question was what to do about Gypsy.

Dilys said, 'If he comes, I won't.'

Me and Mam had quite a chat about whether efforts should be made to find our dad. I said, 'I feel he should be invited, even if he won't come.'

Mam said, 'Well, he does move about a lot. I'm not sure where we'd find him just now.'

I said, 'Why is that, Mam? I never knew a man spend so little time in his own home.'

'He had to be willing to travel,' she said. 'It was very hard to find work.'

I said, 'But now he's got the old age pension?'

'Well,' she said, 'what is there for him here? He's been accustomed to travel. And I'm so busy. I'll never retire.'

I said, 'It must have been lonely for you, all these years.'

'I've been all right,' she said. 'I've had my joys. But you're right, we should drop a line to his last known address, tell him there's a wedding coming off. It's the correct thing to do. Always do the correct thing, Cledwyn.'

We didn't hear back, needless to say.

We were married on Easter Saturday, us and about five hundred others. It was like the old production line at Greely's. Arthur put ribbons on his motor and drove Hazel to the Register Office, so she'd feel like a proper bride, and Dilys and Uncle Teilo stood as witnesses for us.

I think Betsan was disappointed we didn't have any celebrity guests. 'It'd be great if Elvis came,' she kept saying. The whole world was going Elvis Presley crazy.

After the ceremony we went out to Great Barr and Dilys put on a wonderful spread: baked gammon and sherry trifle and a cake iced by Gaynor with silver balls and a little bride and groom. They toasted us in hock wine, with a ruby port for Mam because hock was made by the Germans and they'd killed her brother Amos, and anyway, she didn't really drink.

When we were saying our goodbyes, Mam said, 'Keep your head screwed on, Cledwyn. Don't go throwing your money about.'

Anybody would have thought it was me that had just had my picture in *Tit Bits*, sitting in a new Cadillac in a three-piece mohair suit. Apparently his telegram arrived just after we left. 'Lucky beggar,' it said. 'All the best. Starlight.'

SEVENTEEN

We bought a house in Llandudno on Happy Valley Road, just below the Great Orme, and we worked flat out, bringing it up to scratch. We had ten bedrooms and none of them had seen a paintbrush for years. That first season we were too late to feature in the brochures, but we still had quite a few guests. If people rang our doorbell on spec, they only had to step inside to see it was a nice place. There was no smell of old cabbage at Hazelwyn. We had air fresheners throughout.

Hazel took care of the rooms and the laundry and the catering, with a girl to help during August when we had a full house. Getting twenty cooked breakfasts on the tables before the bacon fat goes cold takes more than one pair of hands. I looked after the bookings and the finances, and made sure the clients were happy, remembering their little likes and dislikes, regaling them with stories about my years in show business. We had quite a photo gallery in the dining room, pictures of me playing at the Peabody and the Palmer House, and one of Sel that Hazel had insisted on. It all helped to break the ice and keep conversation trickling along.

Every evening we served soup, meat and three veg, and a choice of hot pudding, ice cream or cheese and biscuits, and we provided extras, on request, like packed lunches for people going up to Caernarvon for the day, or Snowdon. Milky drinks were available at bedtime, and a draughts board and a pack of cards in the guests' lounge, in case of inclement weather.

The only thing that saddened me was we didn't have space for a piano nor the time for me to do any composing. I missed bringing pleasure to an audience and as soon as our guests heard about my hit single they wanted to hear me play, but there it was. As Hazel said, when you run your own business, sacrifices have to be made. Hazel wasn't musical, of course.

We hadn't planned on going in for a family till we'd had a few seasons with Hazelwyn running to our satisfaction, but these things happen and anyway, Hazel wasn't getting any younger. Our Jennifer Jane was born on 4 December 1957. My thirty-sixth birthday, and I couldn't have asked for a nicer present.

Dilys said, 'What did Sel say?'

I said, 'Nothing. I haven't phoned him. And I'm not going to neither.'

She said, 'Will you stop this? You're like a mardy kid.'

I didn't care. He'd started it.

'I'll phone him, then,' she said. 'He'll be thrilled to mint balls.'

And when we took Jennifer Jane to Ninevah Street when she was five weeks old, to introduce her to the family, there was a beautiful rocking crib waiting for her, white rattan with flowered sheets and a quilted bumper and two pink waffle blankets, shipped from a very high-class shop in Los Angeles. 'To Jennifer Jane from Uncle Sel,' the card said. 'Hope you're better looking than your Dad. Come to think of it, you're bound to be.'

Dilys said, 'Cheeky beggar! Don't worry, I'll tell him. She's beautiful. Like a delicate little flower.'

Mam said, 'Selwyn was only making a humorous quip. It's his way of showing he's forgiven Cledwyn for running out on him.'

Hazel said, 'Not that old chestnut. We must have told you a hundred times it was Sel's doing, not Cled's.'

Mam said, 'I'm not going into that. Selwyn's not here to speak up for himself. He's gone to expense and sent a beautiful cradle, for a child he'll probably never see. Selwyn always does the right thing, that I do know.'

And he did turn out to be a good uncle. He sent quite a sum to Dilys for her girls' eighteenths, to be put in the bank for them for later, and he never missed a birthday or Christmas with Jennifer, although she was three years old before he met her. Of course, he loved shopping, and not just for himself. He could shop all day and by the time he got home he'd have forgotten half of what he'd bought. He'd phone sometimes, after he'd broken the ice with the cradle. 'Put her on,' he'd say. 'Tell her it's her Uncle Sel.' He just liked to hear the funny little noises they make. 'I envy you, Cled,' he said.

I said, 'No sign of activity on the romance front?'

He just laughed.

I said, 'How's Kitty?'

'Kitty who?' he said.

And then when I got off the phone, I had Hazel quizzing me. 'Who's Kitty?'

Jennifer was a sunny baby, and the Hazelwyn Guest House was doing very well. We were pretty contented, really, although Hazel did have a few black moments, dwelling on the little baby she'd given up.

I said, 'Cheer up! You've replaced her now. You've got Jennifer Jane.'

'You don't *replace* a child, Cled,' she said.

Some days whatever I said was wrong. In the end I left Dilys to deal with all that side of things. Hazel had told her all about the business of the baby, so whenever Dilys and Arthur came to stay, in the off season, she'd send me out with Arthur for a game of crazy golf so she could spend on hour with Dilys and enjoy a nice cry. Funny creatures, women.

Sel had got his own show at the New Frontier in Las Vegas. People'd say things sometimes. We had one clever dick staying with us. He said, 'You must feel like Cinderella, stuck here frying eggs.'

But I had no regrets. I said, 'I've played in Las Vegas, thank you very much. I had my fill of luxury hotels and standing ovations. I like being able to walk down to the seafront, get a breath of soft Welsh air before I start on the breakfasts.'

'Still,' he said, 'golden discs.'

But those records weren't anything special: *Starlight Songs* and *Love by Starlight*, the same old stuff rehashed. He could have done with something novel. Something by Cled Boff.

Then a book was brought out, about the house he'd had built on Rancho Drive: Desert Star. He sent copies to everybody. We got two, so Hazel insisted on putting one on the hall table, next to the guest register. 'It's a conversation piece,' she said.

Desert Star was a pink stucco bungalow, designed by himself, with a front room big enough to hold the Treorchy Male Voice Choir and a swimming pool with a big mosaic star in the bottom. 'All the light fittings were specially imported from Venice, Italy,' Hazel would read aloud in bed. 'Mr Starlight relaxing in a favourite zebra-skin chair in his book-lined den.'

He was in all the pictures, of course. You could never keep him away from a camera. Sel on a big white settee with Crackers and two more Westies he'd acquired, Brandy and Soda. Sel in the kitchen, with Pearl who looked after him, pretending to supervise her chopping an onion. Sel in his bedroom, with pink satin sheets and a fur rug, and a painting of the Virgin Mary looking down at him. And Mam's favourite: Sel in his swimming pool being served a beverage by a boy in a Tarzan suit. Once he hit the big time Sel always kept a boy. He never learned to drive, for one thing. I don't think he even learned how to turn the wipers on.

Then Nerys, who helped in the kitchen, borrowed the bloody book. Started quoting from it while I was trying to concentrate on my frying pans. 'Mr Starlight has no fewer than three pianos in his Las Vegas home,' she said, 'including one reputed to have been played by world-famous composer Franz Liszt.'

I said, 'Nerys, that's ridiculous. Three pianos and he can't play a note.'

Hazel said, 'Ignore him. He had a bad night with cramp and now he's in a mood.'

Nerys said, 'I wonder you don't have a piano, Mr B.'

Hazel said, 'Here we go.'

I said, 'I don't have a piano because my wife needs a whole room for her towels and bedding. Other people manage with an airing cupboard, but not my wife. She thinks she's still on the *Queen Mary*.'

Nerys said, 'My Uncle Penri has a piano, Mr B. He never plays it since Aunty died.'

Hazel said, 'We don't have room, Cled. I don't care how cheap it's going for.'

But that was all right. Penri said I could play it in his house, whenever I liked. He let me have a key so if I wanted to play on a Thursday afternoon, which was when he played for the Lorina School of Dance, I could just let myself in.

Hazel said, 'You haven't got time, Cled.'

I said, 'Yes I have. If you've got time to keep leafing through that book, keeping me awake with light fittings from Venice, Italy, I've got time to play piano in the afternoons.'

'I see,' she said, 'Sel gets three pianos, so you have to fritter your time away round at Penri Clocker's. What next? You going to start swimming at the corporation baths? Tell them to bring you a drink on a tray to the shallow end? You going to find yourself a film starlet?'

Sel was a regular in *Celebrity Secrets* and *Out and About*, and once in a while there'd be a picture of him squiring a pretty girl to a nightclub. Dilys would say, 'Perhaps this is the one. Perhaps he's going to settle down.'

And Mam would always say, 'There's no hurry.'

Sometimes he'd walk out with older ladies too, like Thelma Arden who lived across the street from him on Rancho Drive. She'd been quite big in films before the war. It was Thelma he took with him when he was invited to the White House to sing for President and Mrs Eisenhower. It was a very great honour, of course, and it was soon after that he converted. He became a fully paid-up American.

Mam said, 'Quite right too. This country never appreciated him. It had its chance.' He had a bit of a following in Britain, but he was up against artists like Dickie Valentine and Ronnie Hilton, boys who just wore a nice collar and tie and didn't run around in the audience. Boys who had more tuneful voices. Americans are more excitable and over there Sel had all the following he could wish for. But it niggled him to be overlooked by the old country.

Dilys used to say, 'When are you coming back?'

'When I need a police escort,' he'd say.

Then Milo pulled it off.

Sel telephoned Mam to tell her. 'Book yourself a permanent wave,' he said. 'I'm coming to the London Palladium in the spring and you're going to be in the front row of a box.'

Then the arguments started. Mam expected us all to go to every show he was doing: the Palladium, the Leeds Empire, Cardiff Stadium, Birmingham Hippodrome.

I said, 'I can't trail around the country like that. I've got a living to earn.'

'Not in March, you haven't,' Mam said. 'Nobody goes to Llandudno in March.'

That's what you get when you're in the hotel business. People think you only work half the year. I said, 'And Arthur can't just drop everything neither. Nor Betsan and Gaynor. And we've got a bab, don't forget. Jennifer can't stay up, sitting in smoky theatres.'

Mam said, 'You've just got a monkey mood on you. You're just jealous.' And there was a bit of a stand-off until we had something else to argue about.

Dilys's girls were both courting and there had been talk of them getting engaged at Christmas, a double celebration. Then, when we heard Sel would be paying a visit Dilys thought they should have a double wedding too. She said, 'We've waited long enough for him to come so you'd better get on with it while he's here.'

Mam said, 'And get your pictures in the paper with your famous uncle.'

Gaynor said she didn't want her picture in the papers and Betsan said Elvis was what she'd call famous.

Betsan was seeing Terry Eyles, who worked in a clock spring factory in Loveday Street, and Gaynor was seeing Clifford Millichip, who had his dispensing certificate and was on his way up at Boots the Chemist. Everything was agreed and the church was booked, and a nice private hotel out near Sutton Coldfield for the reception. There were frocks being made left, right and centre: wedding dresses, bridesmaids' dresses, evening dresses for Mam to wear to Sel's shows. And big silly hats were bought, that you could only ever wear the once.

Then, just before Sel was due to arrive, Betsan broke the news that she was expecting and after that it wasn't wedding bonnets we needed. It was steel helmets.

EIGHTEEN

The big question was whether Terry Eyles would stand by Betsan. Arthur was sent to talk to him man to man, but Arthur wasn't up to the job and Terry still appeared to be wavering, so our mam went down to Loveday Street herself and had him fetched out of work and gave him such a telling off he clocked out, jumped on a bus and wasn't seen again for quite some time.

Dilys said, 'She's stuck her oar in one time too many.'

Mam said, 'Somebody in this family had to show some leadership. I've written to your Aunty Gwenny. She'll have to have Betsan there, till it's all blown over. And Gaynor and Clifford can have a quiet wedding, befitting the change in circumstances.'

Betsan said she wasn't going anywhere and Gaynor said she'd only ever wanted a quiet wedding, but expense had been gone to and bridesmaids' dresses had been made.

Dilys said, 'There was no need for all this upset. Brides expecting, it happens all the time. All that matters is that Betsan doesn't get herself in a state and bring things on too early.'

Mam said, 'Betsan already brought things on too early.'

Ruddy families. Sel was well off out of it.

Dilys said, 'All that matters is that that little bab has a good home and it will do, whether Terry Eyles ever shows his face again or not. I'll mind it myself if I have to and Betsan can go back to work.'

Mam said, 'That'll be a nice thing for the neighbours, an unmarried mother walking around in broad daylight. Well, I've done my best, God knows. But bad blood will out.'

Hazel said, 'Your mam's got a nasty mouth on her, Cled. Why don't you ever stand up to her?'

I said, 'I don't even know what she means by "bad blood". There's nothing untoward on Arthur's side. Perhaps she means our dad. He was definitely irregular. Perhaps she's seen the light at long last.'

'Oh, Cled!' she said and she threw a dish mop at me. It was that time of the month, I expect. She said, 'It's not badness that makes babies! It's feelings and the heat of a moment. Well, Dilys and Arthur are doing the right thing by Betsan and we should be behind them a hundred per cent.'

So by the time Sel docked at Southampton, Hazel wasn't speaking to Mam, Gaynor wasn't speaking to Betsan and the whereabouts of Terry Eyles were still unknown.

We watched Sel's arrival at Victoria railway station on the television news. 'Crowds of excited fans', they said, 'greeting the Birmingham boy who came home a star. Extra police sent for.' He was wearing a fur coat, right down to the ground, waving and grinning and calling out, 'Hi, there! Y'all here waitin' on somebody special?'

Hazel said, 'Oh, love him, he's turned American!'

He'd put on weight as well.

I drove to Birmingham the next morning. Sel was having a car sent to take us to Claridge's Hotel in London, Mam and Dilys, with me to keep the peace. It was a black Bentley with leather seats and a driver in a hat. Mrs Grimley was pretending to do a bit of weeding by her front door.

Mam said, 'You go and get in the car, Dilys. I'll just check everywhere's locked up. I'll just pay a penny.'

Ten minutes Dilys was sitting out there. Mam was farting around putting stuff in a carrier bag: custard creams, pear drops, socks from Aunty Gwenny, white heather bath salts. 'Things he'll have missed,' she said. 'How are things looking outside?'

I said, 'Same as they were five minutes ago. Will you get a move on!'

She said, 'I'm surprised the Edkinses don't just happen to be passing by.'

I said, 'They're watching from their front window. It's cold out there.'

That satisfied her. She didn't want to leave the house till she was sure Ninevah Street was watching her go.

I was glad to sit up front with the driver and chat. Leave the pair of them to sit in the back, staring out of the windows and having the hump with one another. He had some stories about the people he'd driven: Lady Docker, Mr Pastry, Albert Dell the hangman. And of course, I had my own anecdotes: Patti Page, Rosemary Clooney. I'd known them all.

He thought he remembered my hit single. He said, 'There's nothing to beat a live show, though.'

A man after my own heart. I said, 'I've made dozens of television programmes but playing for Gracie Fields was one of my greatest thrills.'

'Tommy Steele,' he said. 'I had him in the car the other week.'

I said to Mam, 'Now when we arrive, leave everything to me. I'm used to these grand hotels.'

But she had to take matters into her own hands. 'I'm visiting my son,' she said to the doorman. 'Selwyn "Mr Starlight" Boff. He's appearing at the London Palladium. Dilys, your skirt's all creased. If you smoothed it down . . . Cled, here's sixpence for the driver. You bring our gowns in and I'll tell this girl to announce us.' Then the carrier bag split so we had pear drops all over the floor of the lobby.

Dilys clung on to my arm all the way up in the lift.

I said, 'It's only our kid we're visiting.'

'I know,' she said. 'Doesn't feel like it, though.'

Sel was in a corner suite with a view of Hyde Park and a fireplace and a grand piano. He was on the telephone when we walked in, leaning against the mantelpiece warming his backside on the fire. He said, 'Let's talk later. I gotta run now. Something important just came up.' And then he did a funny thing. Even though Mam and Dilys were there, that he hadn't seen in a very long time, it was me he came to first. He made out to wrestle with me and gave me a hug, then he stood back and inspected me and I do believe he had a small tear in his eye. He was looking very well: suntanned and shiny and everything immaculate, hair, nails, trouser creases.

He took Mam in his arms. Neither of them said a word. He just picked her up and swung her round, with her feet off the ground.

She said, 'I think you've grown.'

Then he brought Dilys over, so he had them sitting either side of him on a big settee, and he rang for tea and cucumber sandwiches to be brought in. 'I'll be mother,' he said. 'How do you take it, Dilys? I can't remember.'

She was quite shy with him. We all were, in a funny way. There can be a lot of silences after ten years.

He'd booked the suite next door for the three of us.

I said, 'You didn't have to pay for me. I could have found digs.'

'Cled,' he said, 'don't be an idiot. I want you here, with Mam and Dilys. I want you to make sure they're all right. Know what I mean? Make sure they're not backward about asking for anything they need. Anything at all. And I want you to ride with them to the theatre. Ladies should always have an escort.'

Mam said, 'I suppose you've heard? Betsan's defying me. I arranged for her to go to Aunty Gwenny's but will she!'

I said, 'Mam! This isn't the time.'

'Of course it's the time,' she said. 'He has to be put in the picture. We need a man in this family. Someone to back me up. See, Selwyn, your brother allows his wife to wear the trousers and Arthur Persons wouldn't say boo to a goose. And all the while Betsan is going to the bad. But I know you won't let me down.'

'Well,' he said, 'how about we talk this over in a day or two? When I'm in Birmingham? Time's getting on now.'

'Whatever you think,' she said. 'I know I can depend on you.'

'Good,' he said. 'Because I have to think about getting to the theatre and you'd better go and unpack. And prepare to be titivated. There's a beautician coming for you at six, manicure, facial, the works. And when she's finished with you, Cled, with any luck she might have time to look at you girls as well.'

I said, 'As long as there's no rugs involved.'

He laughed. 'Mam,' he said, 'I've got something I want you to wear.' He went into the bathroom and came out with a beautiful corsage, roses and stephanotis. 'There you are,' he said. 'Now everybody's going to know you're the most important lady in the house.'

And Mam came over quite girlish, trying it out on her shoulder, admiring herself in the mirror. 'Once upon a time,' she said, 'a lady always got flowers. In the days when gentlemen were gentlemen.' If she ever had flowers from our dad she'd have paid for them herself. Or they'd have been off the back of a lorry. 'And that's what you are, Selwyn,' she said. 'A true gentleman. Because of being raised correctly.' And she gave Dilys such a cheeky look.

I noticed Dilys had hardly touched her cake and she was usually very partial to a chocolate dainty, but she didn't say anything till we were inside our own quarters with the door shut.

'Doesn't he look well?' Mam said. 'Every inch the star.'

Dilys said, 'You just had to go and do it, didn't you, Mam? You just had to go and spoil my day.'

I left them to it. I was hoping to catch the football results.

Then the phone rang. 'Cled,' he said, 'I think I dropped a clanger not getting flowers for Dilys as well. I thought she looked a bit wistful, didn't you? Can you rustle something up? Just phone downstairs, tell them to put it on my bill. Something nice, but not as big as Mam's. You know the drill.'

I said, 'Break a leg.'

'Gotcher,' he said. 'And Cled? It's great to see you. Really.'

His name was up in lights. I could see it as we turned into Argyll Street and it caused me quite a pang. I could have been up there with him. Should have been, by rights. The Boff Brothers. He was appearing with Tommy Trinder, Shani Wallis, a skiffle band, some tumblers called the Five Corsairs and an escape artiste called Zeno. And the Tiller Girls, of course. It was a top-notch show.

Don Arrol was the compère. 'Tonight,' he said, 'a warm welcome, please, for someone making their first appearance at the Palladium.

A shy, retiring Birmingham boy who took on America and won. Mr Starlight!'

And on he came, riding on the back of a motorbike, with a cloak billowing out behind him, purple with silver stars and a black satin dinner suit underneath. The bike stopped and he just sat there on it till the audience calmed down. 'Go round again,' he said to the boy who was driving him. 'I'm not sure they've noticed me.' He always liked to start off with a laugh. And then he made a big feature of the cloak, messing around, showing it off when he should have been singing his opening number. 'Isn't it fabulous?' he kept saying. 'If the sequin industry goes into a decline, don't come crying to me. I've done my bit.'

He sang 'All in the Game' and 'A Certain Smile', and then he said, 'This is a very special night for me, folks. My first time in this wonderful theatre. My first appearance back in good old England after far too long. And the first show where I've had a very, very special person in the audience. Can we have some lights, please?' And they brought a spotlight up on our box. I could feel Dilys cowering down behind me in her seat.

'My mam,' he said. 'Give us a wave, Mam.'

And bugger me if she didn't do it. I reckon she'd been studying on the Queen Mother.

He sang 'You're My Girl' and 'Many Loves, Penny Loves', and then the boy came back on with the motorbike and he jumped on. 'Wait there!' he shouted. 'I'm just going to slip into something more comfortable.'

And in the time it took the band to play 'Sentimental Me' he was back on, in white tie and tails, every inch of it covered in sparkle. 'Y'all wearing your sunshades?' he said.

There were women screaming and some of them were trying to get down to the front of the stage.

He said, 'I see three girls here who'd like to inspect the goods. Is there a steward down there can give them a hand?'

And while he sang 'The Roving King' the three ladies were brought on stage, to see his costume close up and guess how many sequins were on it. 'So what do you think?' he said. 'Do you like it?'

'Beautiful,' they said.

He said, 'Well, that's good, because you helped pay for it!'

He sang them off with 'Because of You' and he closed with his usual: 'May the Good Lord Bless and Keep You'.

'Thank you, thank you,' he said, just like Milo had told him. 'You've all been so kind; now I'm going to let you go home. Night night! Sleep tight!'

Mam and Dilys were both crying.

And I must say, for all the differences we'd had, I was very proud of him myself, to see him where he'd always sworn he'd get to some day, and the audience in the palm of his hand. It would just have been nice if he'd mentioned our hit single.

Anyway, we went backstage so I got to see some of those Tiller girls close up, check if what they had was absolutely real, and it was. Mam and Dilys met Tommy Trinder and had their pictures taken, which was a thrill for them, and then we got whisked away to Claridge's in the Bentley.

Dilys said, 'I shan't sleep a wink.'

Mam said, 'It's been a wonderful day.'

Dilys said, 'It has.'

One thing about Sel playing the Palladium, it had got Mam and Dilys to agree on something. And they still had his Birmingham appearance to look forward to.

NINETEEN

He flew in to Elmdon Airport and went straight to the television studios to be on a programme called *Lunch Box*. 'I'm still the same lad who left Brum ten years ago,' he said. 'I may be recognised everywhere I go, but I still like the simple things in life: walking my dogs, eating ice cream and watching a movie in my Vegas home, relaxing on my deck in Malibu, just watching the ocean.'

After *Lunch Box* he was booked to open a new mini-market, that used to be an ironmongers on Hayward Street, and pay a visit to the Milk Maid factory, to see some of his old pals and inaugurate a new choc ice called the Starlight Bar.

Then his driver brought him home, nudging the limousine through the crowds while we were all freezing our nuts off.

Mrs Grimley said, 'I expect you wish you'd persevered now, Cled. I bet you wish it was you coming home in a Rolls-Royce.'

And Mrs Edkins said, 'I knew from when he was a bab he was meant for big things. I read his palm.' Which just goes to show what silly twaddle women say when they're overexcited.

The newspapers were there too, of course. They asked him what his plans were, after the tour. 'I'm going to a family wedding,' he said. This was strictly against orders. Mam didn't want the press turning up if Betsan was likely to be there, flaunting herself in a smock.

Somebody said, 'How about you, Sel? Any sign of wedding bells for yourself?'

'Wait and see,' he shouted.

And Mam said, 'There's no hurry.'

He signed a load of autographs and then he finally came indoors. It was a comical sight. He was wearing a wolfskin coat and it was so big there was hardly room for anybody else in Mam's living room. Jennifer was fascinated by that coat. She went straight to Sel and sat on his lap.

He said, 'Look at you in your pretty dress. We shall have to get you up on stage, so you can sing a little song with your Uncle Sel.'

Hazel said, 'No, Sel. It'll be past her bedtime.'

Betsan was babysitting for us, so Hazel could come to the show. 'Time she got some practice in,' Dilys said.

Sel said, 'But I thought you'd all be there.'

Dilys said, 'You'll see Betsan at the wedding.'

'Can't miss her,' Mam said. 'There's enough of her to see.'

He went up to look at his old room, knocked one of his little pottery puppy dogs off the dressing table swinging round in his big coat.

'Don't worry,' Mam said. 'I'll sweep it up.'

He said, 'I don't know why you don't clear the whole lot out. Give yourself more room.'

'I don't need more room, Selwyn,' she said. 'I'm here all on my own.'

Hazel winked at me.

The limousine was too long to turn round so they had to reverse all the way down the street. It was very overcast but he kept the light on inside the car, making sure everybody got a good view of him. That was the last time he ever set foot in Ninevah Street.

Hazel was smiling and chatting to the neighbours, holding Jennifer Jane up so she could wave him off.

I said, 'You're in a good mood.'

'I am,' she said. 'I'd forgotten how lovely he is.'

I said, 'He has beauty treatments, you know? Sunlamps. It's not all natural.'

'I don't care,' she said. 'He's still lovely. But so are you. You're not bad for an old-timer.'

143

I thought, 'Hello, hello, hello. Somebody's frisky.' I said, 'And what were you winking about, upstairs?'

'Your mam,' she said. 'I don't need more room, Selwyn. All on my own here.'

I said, 'What? Don't tell me there's another razor in the kitchen?'

'No,' she said, 'but somebody's got their feet under the table.'

I said, 'How do you know?'

She said, 'Because there's a can of lighter fuel in the pantry and two packs of Senior Service, unopened. So somebody's on the scene. Unless your mam's become a secret tobacco fiend.'

I said, 'Do you think it's Uncle Teilo?'

'Could be,' she said. 'What does it matter? Everybody needs a bit of company.'

There must have been five hundred waiting for him outside the arena, all ladies, all squealing and pushing. Vera Muddimer was there, in charge of his fan club contingent. They had flowers and cards for him, and presents. Thirty jumpers at least, and all the wrong size because he would fib when he talked to people like *Celebrity Questionnaire*. He always reckoned he was a steady ten and a half stone, but it was a long time since he'd been any such thing. Six foot one in his stocking feet, he reckoned. Five foot eleven standing on tiptoe more like.

He had a full supporting line-up: Jewel and Warriss, the comics, a rockabilly band from Dudley, supposed to be the coming thing, a Scottish vent act called the McDummies and a support vocaliste called Cherry Buxton who sang things from *The Merry Widow*.

Sel was top of the bill.

A girl was waiting for us as we went in, VIP hostess. 'Mr Boff?' she said. 'Mr Starlight would like a word before the second half. If you make yourself known at the stage door somebody'll take you round.'

Dilys said, 'I wonder what he wants?'

Hazel said, 'I think I know.'

I thought I did too.

Doug, the new bodyguard, was straddled across the doorway, arms folded over his chest.

I said, 'I'm family.'

He said, 'That's what they all say.' Then he gave me the nod. Jumped-up gorilla.

Sel was sitting in his Y-fronts and his socks, drinking vodka and sucking on a cigarette.

I said, 'Why don't you have an orange squash? No wonder you sweat. You'd do better without strong drink and cigarettes.'

'No I wouldn't,' he said. 'The liquor relaxes me and the smokes keep me from eating. See? A balanced diet. Cled, I'm going to spring a bit of a surprise this show. I want to bring the family element back into it.'

I said, 'I thought you might. What do you want me to play?'

'Not you, you berk,' he said. 'Mam. I want to fetch her on stage. Do you think she's up to it?'

To see him sitting there, fat rolling over the top of his shorts, it was amazing to think how trim he'd looked leaping around at the Palladium.

I said, 'What are you going to do with her?'

'Piano lesson,' he said. 'Don't say anything to her. I want everything to look natural. But do you think she'd like it?'

I heard a bell go.

He said, 'You all right, our kid?'

I was all right. I wasn't the one that was sweating.

He said, 'You didn't really expect to play, did you?'

I said, 'Don't be ruddy daft. My playing days are through.'

'That's right,' he said.

His dresser came in, with a corset and a tin of dusting powder. 'First bell's gone,' he said. 'You've got more company outside, trying to get past the guard dog, but it's time we started getting you into this.'

I said, 'Right! Now I see how it's done. You're all trussed up under your sequins.'

'It's murder, Cled,' he said, 'but I have to do it. Doesn't matter what I do the weight goes on. I've got slow glands.'

Doug put his head round the door. He said, 'I've got more family out here.'

And in walked our dad. 'Hello, son,' he said. 'Nice to see you doing so well for yourself.'

Me and Sel hadn't seen him since just after I was demobbed. He'd shrunk a bit but that was the only difference I saw in him. His eyes still roved around while he was talking. He was always on the lookout for anything he could pocket.

Sel said, 'Where did you spring from?'

'Out of town,' he said. 'I've had quite a trek to come and see you.'

The dresser was trying to push Sel into his corset.

Sel said, 'Big of you to put yourself out.'

Dad said, 'I'm retired now, son. It'll be easier to keep in touch.'

Sel said, 'Yeah, I bet it will. Does our mam know you're here?'

Dad said, 'You shouldn't force yourself into a thing like that, son. You'll harm your insides.'

Sel said, 'I'll harm your insides, you work-shy bastard. Retired! As far as I recall you were never anything else. Made the effort to see the show, have you?'

Dad said, 'Tickets are a price, aren't they?'

Sel said, 'Well, there you are. I could have comp'd you, if I'd known you were alive.'

He only dressed as far as his shirt and trousers, everything in gold that night. He called it his Sun King outfit. But the cape didn't go on till he was in the wings, just before his entrance.

The dresser said, 'Shall we make arrangements for the onward journey?' gesturing to Gypsy with his eyes.

Sel took another nip of vodka. 'Yes,' he said. 'Ask Doug. He'll take care of everything.'

Dad said, 'I'm not a well man, Sel. The state of my chest, I could go any time. Be nice if we had time to talk.'

Sel said, 'Yeah, wouldn't it have been? Thirty-two years and we just never got round to it. How time flies!'

Dad said, 'Don't be like that. Times were tough. We had the Depression. Then the war. Your lot don't know how easy you've had it. Putting food in the babs' mouths, that was our priority. We did

146

whatever we had to. As long as you didn't go without, we didn't mind the hardship and separation.'

Sel said, 'You're breaking my heart. I don't remember any food parcels, do you, Cled? I don't recall any postal orders arriving.'

I said, 'How come you never wrote?'

Gypsy didn't even look at me.

Sel said, 'Yeah. How come we never got birthday cards?'

'Claudication of the arteries,' he said. 'It's agony to hold a pen. Growing old is no fun, Sel. Every day's a struggle.'

Sel said, 'How much?'

Gypsy sat down.

Sel said, 'Don't get comfortable. It's time you were on your way. I've got an audience waiting for me. How much do you want?'

He said, 'I haven't come looking for a handout, son . . .'

Sel said, 'Good.'

Dad said, 'I'd just like us to get to know one another better, before it's too late. I'll give you my address. I'm in Stoke-on-Trent. Nothing fancy, of course, just the one room. But it's all right, apart from the damp. I expect Annie's in clover now, though. You always were a good boy to your mam.'

Sel jumped on him. 'Mam's none of your business,' he said. 'She looked after us and now I'm looking after her, and as far as I recall you were never in the reckoning. Now, my man Doug is going to give you a glass of orange squash and ten pounds for your train fare, and then you can bugger off back to Stoke-on-Trent. I don't want to see you hanging around when I come back after the show.'

Gypsy looked at me and then at the tray of drinks. I think perhaps he thought I was Sel's man, Doug.

I followed Sel outside. I said, 'Can you believe it? Shall I tell Mam?'

'No,' he said, 'not a word. I don't want her upset. And don't worry. Doug'll get rid of him.'

I said, 'Do you realise he never even spoke to me? I don't think he even knew me.'

'Yeah,' he said. 'Ain't you the lucky one?'

The lights were going down by the time I got to my seat.

Hazel said, 'Well?'

'Nothing,' I said.

'It doesn't look like nothing,' she said, 'if your face is anything to go by.'

Then Mam shushed her because Sel had had his drum roll.

He came on pulled along on a little platform with wheels, only they were hidden under a big cloak with the sunray collar. He had two boys at the front and two at the back acting as brakes, all dressed as footmen. The ladies were all ooh-ing and aah-ing. 'What?' he said. 'This old thing?'

You'd never have known, watching him, what a wreck he'd looked sitting in the dressing room in his shorts. He opened with 'The Night Is Young' and 'Only Forever', and then some youngsters were brought on in wheelchairs, to sing 'Inchworm' with him.

He sat on the edge of the stage, dangling his legs, mopping his face. That's drink for you. He said, 'People keep asking me about the girls in my life, so tonight I thought I'd introduce you to someone very special. Come on down, Mam!' He did 'Sentimental Me' and 'Forever' while Mam was fetched down.

Hazel kept whispering, 'I knew it! I knew he was going to do something!'

Then there was a trumpet fanfare.

'Ladies and Gentlemen,' he said, 'making her stage debut tonight, my Queen of Hearts, my mam!'

And the four footmen carried her on in a sedan chair.

Dilys said, 'Oh, my good God! She's nothing to do with me.'

He sang 'In a Golden Coach', then he had the pianist move over so he could sit with Mam and pretend to have a lesson from her, like he was a kid again, which raised quite a laugh.

He said, 'Do you know you're pushing me off this stool?'

'No,' she said, 'but you hum it and I'll pick it up as we go along.'

So, of course, she got a round of applause.

I said, 'She'll be expecting her own show at this rate.'

Dilys said, 'I hope she gets it. I hope it involves a lot of travel.'

He serenaded Mam with 'Little Old Lady'. 'As taught me by my good friend Gracie Fields,' he said. Gracie would have been very surprised. I doubt she even remembered him.

He finished with 'All the Things You Are' and then the old usual, and he got a very warm ovation.

'Marvellous,' Arthur kept saying. 'Absolutely marvellous. Good tunes, good jokes.'

Gaynor said, 'He didn't tell any jokes.'

Dilys said, 'Did Mam know he'd be calling her on?'

Hazel said, 'Cled did, didn't you? They were down in the dressing room, hatching a surprise.'

I said, 'More than you know. Gypsy turned up while I was down there.'

Dilys's face fell. She said, 'It's never over, is it? Just when you think you're shot of him, back he comes. Just when you're enjoying yourself.'

I said, 'Don't worry. The heavy had instructions to send him on his way. You're not likely to see him.'

Gaynor said, 'Who's Gypsy?'

Hazel said, 'Never mind. Let's go down, see those lovely costumes close up.'

Dilys said, 'I'm not going. Not if he's around. I'll get back. Make sure Jennifer Jane's all right.'

I said, 'He won't be around. Sel sent him away with a flea in his ear.'

Dilys said, 'I don't care. I'm not risking it. The rest of you go.'

I said, 'Sel'll be disappointed.'

Hazel said, 'Never mind. He'll understand. Don't make a fuss, Cled.'

The dresser was just coming out as we got to the dressing-room door. 'He's decent,' he said. 'Ready to receive.'

I said, 'No complications?'

'No,' he said. 'Everything tidied away.'

He had the gold suit over his arm, drenched with sweat.

Hazel said, 'Do you know what I'd do with that?'

'Put it in a darkened room?' he said. 'Send for bomb disposal?'

'Cat litter,' she said. 'That's the best thing for smelly delicates.'

I said, 'My wife was First Class laundress on the Cunarders.'

'Really?' he said. 'That must be useful. Perhaps you can recommend something for getting a blot off an escutcheon.'

Using language like that in front of my wife.

Sel was showered and shampooed and sitting in a nice robe sipping French champagne with Mam.

She was high as a kite. 'Come along in,' she said, as if it was her dressing room. 'Do you know who we just had in here?'

I looked at Sel, but he shook his head.

'Only the Lord Mayor of Birmingham,' she said. 'And McDonald Hobley, off the television. Local dignitaries and well-wishers. Come and sit over here, Gaynor. You never know who might turn up.'

And how right she was. We hadn't been there long before Uncle Teilo walked in. 'Sel,' he said. 'I think it's time you knew the truth. I'm your father.'

Mam flushed scarlet. 'Teilo Morris!' she said. 'What a lie!'

'Now, Annie!' he said. 'Where's the harm in telling him? He's entitled to know. And it's not as though Gypsy's ever coming back. You don't need to worry about him.'

Sel gave me the eye.

Mam said, 'I'm not worried. And there's nothing to tell. Have you been drinking?'

Gaynor said, 'But Gypsy did come back. Uncle Cled said.'

Mam said, 'Be quiet, Gaynor. You don't know anything about this.'

And Arthur said, 'It's getting a bit crowded in here. Why don't me and Clifford go and fetch the cars?'

Sel said, 'No, Arthur, you stay where you are. Top your glass up. You're family. Teilo's the one who's leaving.'

Teilo said, 'I know it must have come as a shock to you, Sel. But I wanted to clear the air. I only wanted you to know the truth.'

Sel said, 'You're a bloody liar, Teilo. You've had the hump with me ever since I signed on with Ted Sibley, and now you're just trying to get back in with me. Well, you don't bother me. You're laughable. But I won't have you upsetting Mam.'

Mam said, 'I'm not upset. I know what I know.'

Teilo said, 'I'm not after money, if that's what you mean. I just wanted you to know. And it'll take a while to sink in. But you know where you can find me. My door's always open, Sel. Blood's blood, after all.'

I felt sorry for him, really. Teilo did a lot for us when we were starting out.

'I'm thirty bloody two,' Sel shouted after him. 'What do you want to do? Buy me a train set?'

Mam said, 'Teilo's not been himself. The clubs have fallen off since everybody got television. He's not been himself at all.'

Gaynor said, 'I still don't know who Gypsy is.'

Sel said, 'Arthur, if you could take Mam and Hazel, I'd like Cled to ride back with me for five minutes. We've got a bit of business to see to.'

Hazel gave me an old-fashioned look. She said, 'I hope you won't be long, Cled.' She didn't want to be stuck with Mam.

Sel was staying at the Plough and Harrow Hotel but he got Doug to drop us in Monument Road so we could walk the last bit and slip in the back way. There'd always be a lady or two who'd find out where he was staying and they'd turn up, hoping to get to know him better. It had happened to me, but I could take it in my stride. One of the perks of the trade, I always thought. But Sel never liked situations. He liked his ladies but not individually. Not if they got too close.

I said, 'What a night!'

'Yeah,' he said. 'All those years without a dad and suddenly I've got two.'

I said, 'Gypsy took the hint, then? Mam didn't see him?'

'No,' he said. 'He took half a bottle of vodka and he cleaned me out of smokes, but Doug got rid of him. Tell me about this business with Betsan.'

I said, 'I think Mam's making matters worse. I mean, it's very sad.

She's a cracking girl and now she's soiled goods, but sending her away's not going to achieve anything. Betsan's decided she's going to be one of these unmarried mothers and Dilys is encouraging her.'

He said, 'What do you think?'

I said, 'I don't know. Hazel had a kiddle, you know? Gave it up.'

'No,' he said. 'I didn't know that.'

I said, 'She gets very low sometimes, thinking about it, but of course, that could just be Hazel. Women are complicated creatures.'

He said, 'Well, I don't like Mam upset, Cled. She's head of the family. We'd none of us be here if it wasn't for her and I think Dilys could show her more respect. I think I'll have a word with Arthur about it, after Gaynor's wedding.'

Waste of breath, that. Arthur might do a lot of cogitating at his desk at Aldridge's but at home he did whatever Dilys told him.

I said, 'What do you reckon about Teilo?'

He said, 'It doesn't bear thinking about. I don't look like him, do I?'

He didn't look anything like him.

I said, 'When you think, though, he did used to come round a lot.'

'He did,' he said. 'And there we were thinking he was just partial to Mam's sausage and mash.'

We laughed.

He said, 'I'm glad we're pals again.'

It was never of my doing, falling out.

He said. 'Straight up now, Cled, didn't I do you a favour? If you hadn't gone when you did you wouldn't have met Hazel again. Settled down. Had young Jennifer. You weren't cut out for the life I lead.'

I don't know about that. I could have handled it. And I might have settled down with somebody else. Like Kitty O'Malley. I said, 'Hazel wasn't my only prospect, you know. I just happened to bump into her when she was down on her luck. I just felt sorry for her.'

He said, 'You're such a romantic. Anybody ever tell you?'

As a matter of fact many of the ladies have said the very same thing.

It was nearly midnight but he would have drinks served in the lounge. We talked about old times.

I said, 'The Belle Rive was a great hotel. That and the Peabody. Very swish.'

He said, 'I hate them all. Sleeping in my own bed, that's what I like. That's the great thing about Vegas. I stay put and the audience keeps changing. The Baker. I hated the Baker.'

I said, 'Me too. I never slept well there.'

He said, 'They reckon it's haunted, you know? They reckon this place is haunted. The Grey Lady.'

I said, 'Have you had any more visitations? Any smiling nuns?'

'Oh yes,' he said. 'I get visitations all the time.'

I never knew if he was pulling my leg.

'As a matter of fact,' he said, 'I think I'm having one just now. Is that Old Man Edkins standing over there gazing at me, or am I losing my mind?'

And indeed, it was Mr E from next door, weaving across the lounge, looking a bit the worse for wear. 'Hello, Selwyn,' he said. 'I've come to tell you something. I think it's time you knew. I'm your dad.'

TWENTY

Gaynor and Clifford were married as planned, with our Jennifer as flower girl and Sel as guest of honour, with a Tiller Girl called Nola as his date. It was a nice wedding although Betsan couldn't be there due to swollen ankles, and the Millichip relations gave Sel and Nola a wide berth. Apparently strings had been pulled to keep them off the top table. That's the beauty of a buffet, of course.

I said to Arthur, 'What's their problem? Anybody'd think Sel's not house-trained.'

'Well,' he said, 'Clifford's people don't like a lot of ostentation.'

But there wasn't going to be any ostentation. Sel wore a nice charcoal-grey suit and a red tie, and Nola was in acqua, with a little matching hat.

Gaynor said, 'It's a question of conversation. What would they find to say to each other? Clifford's people are college educated.'

Dilys said, 'All they have to do is sit and eat a chicken salad. It's not the *Brains Trust*.'

Mam said, 'Selwyn has his School Certificate. He can mingle with anyone. Of course, I can't speak for the person he's brought with him.'

I said, 'And how about me? I've been in show business and they don't seem worried about conversing with me.'

Sel said he hadn't even realised he was being snubbed by the Millichips. 'The Mouseshits' he called them, after that. 'Don't worry,' he said. 'Put me and Nola with the riff-raff. We don't care where we sit.'

Dilys said, 'Well, I don't like doing it, but you'll probably have a better time. I'll put you with some of Gaynor's pals from work. They'll be thrilled.'

Sel said, 'You know what's wrong with this country? Too many folks like the Mouseshits. They think small and yet they're so bloody self-satisfied. If you think big, they can't wait for you to fall on your arse. And if you don't, if you make a success of yourself and enjoy the fruits, they call you "vulgar". Well, fuck the Mouseshits and the horse they rode in on. Give me America any day.'

Arthur said, 'You're not tempted to come back, then? You'd be able to afford a nice place in Shirley.'

Sel said, 'Shirley! I like a place where it's not an offence to be a protruding nail. Las Vegas is my kind of town. Everybody wants to be a major player in Vegas. And the higher you climb, the more stuff you get, the more you flash it about, the more they love you. Flash Harry, that's me.'

'Will Saltley songster wed leggy lovely?' it said in the *Evening Mail*. There was a picture of him arriving at the church.

The gossip column in the *Sunday Express* wasn't so friendly.

> This may be a foolish question [it said] but why are the women of this country so exercised by the continued bachelor state of Selwyn 'Mr Starlight' Boff? He's only thirty-two years old – no great age; he suffers no shortage of female companionship – witness his recent assignations with Palladium hoofer Nola Nugent; and it must be obvious to a blind man in a London fog that Mr Boff's heart is already spoken for. He loves himself. He loves his mother. Beyond that he likes to keep his public guessing.
>
> Well, Mr S, we know the answer. There'll be no wedding bells for Miss Nugent, nor any other eligible misses. Selwyn Starlight isn't the marrying kind. You read it here.

Sel was livid.

I said, 'Don't buy newspapers, then. What you don't read can't worry you.'

But he couldn't resist. He lapped it up when they said nice things about him, so he sometimes had to take a drubbing. To me it didn't seem worth getting upset about.

I don't think Nola had had any expectations. She was just a nice well-built girl. 'A sweet guy.' That was how she described Sel.

I said to Hazel, 'I don't know what all the fuss is about. I was still single when I was his age. Nobody pestered me about it.'

'You weren't a sex symbol,' she said. 'Nobody was interested in you.'

That's all she knew.

Mam said, 'And there's nothing to say a boy has to get married. Ivor Novello never did.'

Still Sel reckoned he could have sued the *Express* to ruination. He said, 'They're suggesting I'm not a real man. They're intruding into my private life.' Of course, some people would say if you let *Star!* magazine take pictures of you sitting in a bubble bath sipping a glass of Babycham you don't have a private life any more, but Sel never agreed with that argument. He said, 'I'm going to let it pass this time but only because I don't want the inconvenience of a court case. I've got a diary full of commitments. I haven't got time to keep flying over here, chasing scandal rags.'

Mam said, 'Quite right. Don't give people the satisfaction. Now we've got something to tell you. I'm going to America.' She looked like the cat who'd got the cream.

Arthur said, 'I'll be jiggered. That'll be the first holiday I ever remember you taking.'

Mam said, 'It won't be a holiday. I'm going to take care of Selwyn and his luxury homes.'

Hazel said, 'I thought Pearl looked after you, Sel?'

'Yeah,' he said. 'Well, I take a lot of looking after.'

Dilys said, 'Mam, you're not to start making trouble. Pearl's been with Sel years. You're not to upset her.'

Mam said, '*I'm* not a troublemaker, Dilys. I just do my best to help.'

I said, 'How long are you going for?'

'For as long as I'm needed,' she said. 'And don't any of you try to stop me.'

Dilys was trying not to smile too much.

Sel said, 'She can stay as long as she likes. I might give her a regular spot on the show.'

Mam said, 'So you see, Dilys, I'm going where I'm needed. Going where my advice gets listened to. And you won't miss me. You'll be too busy pandering to Betsan; minding that illegitimate child.'

Sel delayed sailing so Mam could travel with him.

'We'll have a stateroom, of course,' she was telling everybody. 'You get a settee and a bell to ring if you want anything.'

Mrs Edkins said, 'You'll be wrecked, Annie, sleeping on a settee. I'm surprised Selwyn's not getting you a bed.'

'She can't help it,' Mam said. 'She's never travelled and she never will.'

Hazel said, 'Teilo's going to miss you.'

Mam didn't bite.

Hazel said, 'If I were you, Mam, I'd get rid of that lighter fuel that's in the pantry. It could stink the place out with the house closed up.'

Mam said, 'That wife of yours, Cledwyn. She's mental.'

I said to Dilys, 'She could be gone months. What do you think we should do about the house?'

'Don't know,' she said. 'Think we could get some gelignite?'

But then the day after Mam and Sel sailed Terry Eyles turned up and offered to do the decent thing by Betsan. I don't know whether she accepted him because she wanted him or because she didn't want to be a burden on Dilys and Arthur, but in the long run it made no difference. Terry never really settled to married life and Betsan ended up as one of those single-parent families anyway. Still, Ninevah Street came in handy. Betsan and Terry moved in there and they had a baby boy, named Ricky after Ricky Valence, who'd just had a song in the hit parade.

I wrote Mam a letter once a fortnight without fail, and enclosed snaps of Jennifer Jane or newspaper cuttings we thought would interest her: the 1962 Golden Daffodil Awards, with Hazelwyn getting a special mention for comfort and cleanliness. A piece about a Chinese restaurant opening in Pentrefoelas. But not the story that appeared in the *News of the World*:

SNUBBED! The father music star Mr Starlight left behind. The damp walls of disabled pensioner James Boff's bedsit are covered with photos of his famous son. 'I'm very happy for his success. Only sad he didn't find the time to visit me when he was in the country.' Chronic asthma sufferer Mr Boff says his doctors have told him the climate in California and Nevada, where his son has luxury homes, would help his condition, but it looks unlikely that he'll ever afford to make the trip. 'It would be nice to see him one last time, though.'

I said to Dilys, 'What shall we do about it?'

'Burn it,' she said. 'No, don't even waste a match on it. Put it on your compost heap. And don't ever mention it to Mam. I want her to forget all about England, forget about Gypsy. I want her left where she's happy.'

Mam was happy at Rancho Drive and yet she wasn't, Pearl being the fly in the ointment. From the minute Mam arrived there she wanted to get rid of her. 'Now I'm here it's money thrown away,' she said. 'And she's been allowed too much rope. Laying down the law. Telling me about my own boy.'

I said, 'Well, Mam, Pearl's been with him a few years. They're bound to have got into their little ways. And if Pearl goes and then you come home, what will he do?'

'I'm not coming home,' she said. 'I'm staying where I'm needed. Nobody knows Selwyn like I do. He gives his all, as you know, and when the show's over he still isn't finished. Sometimes he has to go out afterwards to attend to business and he doesn't need her waiting up, checking up on him, interrogating his protégés.'

That was a new one on me.

Penri was very good on long words. 'Oh, yes,' he said, 'a protégé. From the French. It could be somebody learning their craft from him. Or just somebody he's trying to encourage.'

I said, 'It can't be the first thing. He doesn't have any craft to teach. It must be for backgammon.'

I said to Sel, 'Mam tells me you've got boys you're encouraging.'

He laughed. 'Yeah?' he said. 'Yeah, I think she likes it. She says it keeps her young.'

Mam said, 'You know Selwyn. Generosity itself. Bringing young-sters home, offering them a square meal. I see no harm in it, as long as they wipe their feet and say thank you. And that woman may as well do some cooking. God knows we pay her enough.'

I said, 'Is Mam causing trouble with Pearl?' Dilys was worried there'd be a bust-up and Mam'd be back in Birmingham to torment her.

'No,' he said. 'They're never happier than when they're arguing. You could make two Mams out of Pearl but that don't mean Pearl always wins. Anyhow, I'll be taking Mam on the road with me soon, so Pearl'll get some peace.' He was taking ten weeks off from the New Frontier, touring Wisconsin, Illinois, Ohio and Michigan with Mam and two of his dogs. 'Gotta keep those ladies sweet,' he said. 'Can't let these youngsters have it all their own way.' Troy Shondell, Roy Orbison. Open-neck shirts and tight trousers, that was the direc-tion music was heading.

So Mam went on the road with Sel, making an appearance in every show. Sometimes they'd do the piano lesson routine or she'd come on in the middle of a song, bring him a clean hanky or tell him off about something, to raise a laugh. Sometimes, if it had been a long day, she'd just sit on a couch with his dogs and he'd sing to her.

I said, 'I hope she never sees any of those old Kaycee telly shows, with Gladys Cooper's photo on top of the piano.'

'She won't,' he said. 'There's a thing called editing. Anyway, I'm keeping her too busy for her to worry about ancient history. She cuts the ribbon now, when I open a shopping centre. She's started getting fan letters.'

I said, 'Who from?'

'Older ladies mainly,' he said. 'Thanking her for being an inspiration. Asking her advice about things.'

I said to Mam, 'What kind of things?'

'Family matters,' she said. 'Wayward children and lack of standards. You wouldn't believe some of the stories they send me. They feel they can turn to me, you see. They look at Selwyn and they wonder why their own children haven't turned out so well.'

I said to Hazel, 'It's always Sel, Sel, Sel. Always the golden boy. You'd never think there were three of us in the family. You know why? Because he never answers her back.'

Hazel said, 'Neither do you, so that's not the reason.'

I just don't like upset, that's all.

Mam got a spot in a magazine called *Coffee Break*, giving advice on subjects of interest to the ladies. It was called 'Ask Mrs Boff'. She didn't have to read the letters that came in or write the actual advice. They had somebody in the office to do that. But she had her picture at the top of the page and she got paid. And then one of Sel's old sponsors, Creamola, signed them to do an advertisement together, for their new tinned custard, in regular and banana flavour.

'Mom,' he had to say, 'no one makes custard like you do. What's your secret?'

'No secret,' she had to say, holding a tin of Creamola behind her back. And then she had to wink at the camera.

Sel said, 'She's a natural. One-Take Annie they call her.'

Pearl was annoyed. 'He don't even care for custard,' she said to me. 'He likes ice cream.'

Looking through the knot hole
in Grandpa's wooden leg,
I slipped and sprained my eyebrow on the pavement.
Go fetch the Listerine,
Sister's caught a cold,
And a boy's best friend is his mother.

TRADITIONAL

TWENTY-ONE

We might have spared Mam Gypsy's trouble-making, but it wasn't long before there was a story that couldn't be kept from her. Sel was appearing in Grand Rapids, Michigan but he hadn't taken Mam with him. She'd been asked to open a new facility for the elderly in Orange County.

According to the newspapers, a boy who was on the lighting crew claimed Sel had lured him into a dressing room and kept him there against his will. He said certain demands had been made of him. He'd reported it to the police, only not till two days after.

I said to Hazel, 'I never heard anything like it. If it had been one of his fans . . . some of the suggestions I used to get . . . I wouldn't dare tell you. They'd make your hair curl.'

'You have told me, Cled,' she said. 'A thousand times.'

I said, 'But a gaffer's runner? Why would he go to the dressing room? If Sel had any demands about lighting it'd be the lighting director he'd send for. He's very particular about lighting. But *demands*? I don't see what demands he could have made.'

Hazel said, 'Perhaps he wanted him to play backgammon.' Sometimes Hazel would say the first silly thing that came into her head.

Mam said the whole business was about money. 'Selwyn's known for his kindness to youngsters,' she said. 'And this is the kind of risk you run when you're in the limelight. There's always somebody waiting to take advantage of a person's good nature and innocence.'

Then Kaye Conroy telephoned me all the way from Los Angeles.

162

Usually we only heard from the Conroys at Christmas. 'This is an ugly story,' she said. 'Have you talked to him?'

When he was touring we didn't hear from him for weeks.

She said, 'Well, I left messages in Toledo and Cincinnati but he didn't call me back. I hope Milo Freeman is taking care of things. Sel thinks he can always smile his way out of trouble but in a situation like this smiling ain't gonna be enough. That boy claims he was assaulted.'

I said, 'Never! Sel wouldn't harm a fly. When we were lads he wouldn't even play cowboys and Indians. Dollies' tea parties with Joan Wagstaff, that was him.'

'Yeah,' she said. 'I know what you mean. But still, he has a powerful build. If ever there was any kinda . . . misunderstanding . . . he'd be a hard man to fight off.'

It made me think of those high jinks he used to like with Ferd when we lived at Strawberry Ridge.

I didn't get to talk to him till the tour was over and the story had gone quiet by then. I said, 'What was that all about, then? One of them tickle fights?'

'Yeah,' he said. 'Something like that.' He seemed to find it all very amusing. 'Don't worry,' he said. 'He settled. They always settle.'

I said, 'What do you mean, "always"?'

'Oh, you know,' he said. 'Pity this one turned out so greedy. He was cute.'

I said, 'So there was truth in the story? Was it backgammon?'

He just laughed. He said, 'How's Jennifer Jane doing at school? Tell her to work hard. I want her to be a lawyer when she grows up. Every family needs a lawyer.'

Of course, Jennifer was only seven.

I said to Hazel, 'Well, you were right. It was backgammon. And then I suppose things got out of hand. It can happen. There was a girl came home with me one time, when we were recording shows at the Topanga . . .'

'I know,' she said, 'I've heard that one before as well.'

I don't think she had.

She said, 'Cled, has it ever occurred to you, about Sel? What type of man he is?'

I said, 'Jammy, that's what type he is. Whatever scrape he gets into he'll always laugh his way out of it.'

'Yes,' she said, 'jammy maybe. But you must realise he's got tendencies?'

I was shocked. I said, 'How long have you been harbouring that idea?'

'Oh, for goodness sake, Cled!' she said.

I said to Penri, 'Hazel's got it into her head that Sel might be pansified, but how could he be? He was voted Most Romantic Man of the Year two years running by readers of *True Romance* magazine.'

Penri's advice was to put it out of my mind and I did. Sel brought out two new albums: *Rocking by Starlight*, trying to follow the latest trend and not to my taste, and *Starlight Moments*, with more slow-beat, tear-jerking type of tunes. They both sold well.

If you listened to Mam everything was wonderful. 'He can name his own fee these days,' she said. 'I was invited to Lola Wynn's house, to a star-studded pool-side party. Dirk Diamond was there. And Abby Laverne. We've got shows booked nearly two years ahead and we're doing another custard advertisement, new creamier Creamola.'

Pearl told a different story: 'I'm reconsidering my position.'

I said, 'Is it Mam again?'

'No,' she said. 'She don't bother me. But Mr Sel's out till all hours. If he wants company I don't know why he doesn't bring it home. We got a big enough house. Ask me, folks out at that time of night are looking for trouble. And Malibu is nothing but Sodom and Gomorrah. I've told him he'll have to find somebody else to take care of him at Ocean Star. Somebody who doesn't need their sleep.' People who haven't been in show business find it hard to understand the hours you keep. She said, 'You should hear some of the carrying on down the street. Car doors slamming. Dancing and squealing till all hours.'

I could have done with a bit of all-night dancing and squealing myself.

We always closed from November till Easter, but we weren't idle. There's a great deal of wear and tear in a guest house, so every room had to be redecorated. And then, you always had to be working out new features to keep you ahead of the competition. We went en suite with three of the bigger rooms, which put us streets ahead of the Tal-y-Bont next door. En suite was quite a novelty in Llandudno in 1965.

Dilys and Arthur generally came in the off season, so Dilys could help with the paper hanging. And after Terry left her Betsan would come too, with little Ricky. It was nice for them to get out of Ninevah Street and breathe some good Welsh air. Dilys used to say, 'Why don't you take Hazel away for a week, have a change of scene? We'll mind Jennifer Jane.'

But to be honest, the shine had gone off things between the two of us. She had no interest in hearing my stories. It was a kind of envy, I suppose, for the life I'd led before we were married. And there wasn't much activity on the bedroom front. She always seemed to have her head stuck in a magazine.

I said to Penri, 'I think to a certain extent Hazel has withdrawn into a fantasy world.'

'It can happen,' he said.

And Hazel wasn't the only one. All of a sudden Sel was rethinking his career. According to the *Sunday Pictorial* he'd got the sack from Network Nationwide. 'Lights Out for Starlight', it said. 'American television company NNTV have not renewed their contract with British-born songster, Mr Starlight. The network's decision to axe his long-running show follows a series of disclosures about his personal life.'

'A pack of lies,' Mam said. 'He'd already told them he didn't want another series. He's decided to be a film star instead.'

Dilys said, 'What disclosures? This better not be Gypsy making trouble again.'

There'd been the story about the boy in Grand Rapids and then as far as I knew the only other thing had been a row with the tax people over various houses he owned.

But as he said, he didn't actually own them. Starlight Realty did. 'I'm incorporated, Cled,' he said. 'Mr Starlight leases those properties. A certain lifestyle is one of the tools of my trade, so I should be allowed to write it off.'

Arthur said, 'Why wouldn't the television people make changes? People can't be expected to watch the same thing year after year.'

I said, 'That's just where you're wrong. If you'd worked in television, as I have, you'd know to give the viewers what they already like, not chop and change and confuse them. In show business you're never afraid to serve up old favourites.'

Hazel said, 'Well, you all know what I think.' But we weren't going to go into that again, with Jennifer Jane flapping her ears.

Dilys said, 'I'll tell you what it is. They're getting rid of him to make room for the Mersey Sound. That's what everybody wants now.'

It wasn't what I wanted.

'Anyway,' she said, 'I could never imagine him looking right on the telly. The screen's too small. I don't see how you'd get a proper feel for his costumes. He belongs on a stage. He's the kind of star you have to see in the flesh.'

And that was Sel's version of things too. 'I'm going back on the road,' he said. 'That's what I do best. Getting out there, talking to my audience. I'm looking at movie scripts as well. We're getting some very interesting offers. And did I tell you, I'm going to be the new face of Stay Slim?' Milo had got him another advertising contract.

I said, 'Will Mam be in it too?'

'No, not this one,' he said. 'But it's lots of lovely money. And a free lifetime's supply of diet products. I'll have some sent to you.'

I said, 'Don't bother. Nobody in this house has time to get fat. You might send some to Dilys, though. She's tried carrot sticks but she never looks any different.'

The first film he made was called *Wheel of Fortune*, with Brock

Murphy and Nadine Gray. Sel played a singer in a nightclub. Played himself, really. Then, as soon as he'd finished filming he went back on the road, to Colorado, Oklahoma and Texas, with guest appearances by Mam and the dogs. But ticket sales were so poor for Houston they cancelled his second show and when the write-up of the film came out he had another disappointment:

> This tired offering has one of the strangest pieces of casting since Bette Davies played a cockney waitress. Mr Starlight, famously prone to getting locked in cupboards with Best Boys, plays Miss Gray's lover with all the passion and conviction of a porky, lukewarm cousin. Don't give up the day job, Mr S.

The Stay Slim didn't appear to be working.

I said to Penri, 'I think young Selwyn's got problems. I think he's peaked.'

And Penri said, 'It's easily done.'

I lost count of how many times Hazel saw that picture, though I didn't care for it myself. Give me a good shoot-out or a car chase any day. Nadine Gray was a bit of all right, though.

I said, 'He's risen too high too fast. He's not had time to learn his craft.'

He'd already started on another film, *The Run-Around*, but the doctor signed him off for a week, with a relaxed throat, and somehow he never went back. They replaced him with Mitch Moran and dubbed the songs. Then he lost his regular spot at the New Frontier because they were closing for demolition.

I said, 'Well, he's had a good innings, for somebody with no proper training.'

Hazel said, 'What training? There's no training for lighting up a theatre, Cled. Either you've got it or you haven't. And he's got it.' Of course, Hazel had no experience of the cruelty of show business.

I called him up. I said, 'Whatever happens, you know you've always got a home here.'

'What the hell for?' he said. 'I'm all right. I'm just resting up, enjoying my new hot tub, courtesy of Star Spa Inc., doing a little strategising. Watch this space, Cled. You're gonna be seeing some exciting changes.'

TWENTY-TWO

'Milo's putting out a press release later today,' he said, 'but I wanted to tell you myself. I'm getting married.' Her name was Bliss Bellaire and he'd met her on the set of *The Run-Around*.

I said to Hazel, 'See? Now admit it. You were wrong about him having tendencies.'

She said, 'I'm admitting nothing. Anybody can get engaged.'

I was happy for him, though. Sometimes it just takes a long time to find the right person.

Dilys was over the moon. Pearl said if he was happy she was happy. Mam said, 'She's a bottle blonde, but I'm bearing up as best I can.'

The wedding was going to be in Malibu, on the sun deck at Ocean Star, and Sel was acting like a girl, dizzy as a humming top, planning everything: jasmine and tuberoses, and a priest in pastel vestments.

I said, 'What's wrong with a Register Office?'

'No,' he said, 'I want God at my wedding. I want this writ in the Book of Life. Looking at the divorce rate around here, it strikes me folks need all the help they can get. And I want all of you here, too. I want Jennifer Jane to be a flower girl and Ricky to carry the ring cushion. I want it to be a real family occasion. And *Celebrity Secrets* are acquiring exclusive picture rights: the wedding, the honeymoon cruise, everything.'

Hazel said, 'I give it six months.'

The engagement was in all the magazines, with pictures of them picking out the ring.

Bliss was a beautiful-looking girl, ash-blonde and a lovely embouchure. She'd appeared in a lot of films, only nothing we'd ever heard of. When they asked her what had made her fall in love with Sel she said he was the most perfect guy she'd ever met, romantic, considerate, cultivated.

I said, 'Wait till she leaves one of his towels crumpled.'

They asked Sel if he hoped to have kiddies and he said, 'I'd like a houseful. I think I'll make a pretty good father. I've been an uncle since I was nine, you know. And I'm a great-uncle. So why not a Great Dad!'

At first Sel said it wouldn't be a long engagement. He said, 'We'd have loved a June wedding but we both have so many professional commitments.'

Bliss was due to start filming *The Curse of the Reptile* and Sel had a big tour of Canada.

Mam said, 'There's no need for him to rush into anything. He's young still.' But he was going on thirty-nine.

I said, 'What about you? After the wedding?'

She said, 'How do you mean?'

I said, 'Well you can hardly stay there, living with newlyweds.'

'I don't see why not,' she said. 'Nobody's said anything to me about being thrown out on the street.'

I said, 'Perhaps he'll buy you a place back here. A nice little bungalow.'

'I'm not coming back,' she said. 'My blood's thinner than it was. And anyway, this marrying hasn't happened yet and perhaps it never will. When he wakes up and realises he's being had.'

I said, 'You've got to give her a chance.'

'I am doing,' she said, 'I know how to behave. Even if she is a gold-digger.'

I said, 'Well, Sel's talking about all the kiddies they're going to have. You'll have to learn to get along with her if she gives you grandchildren.'

Hazel came up right next to the telephone and went 'Ha!'. There was no call for that. Mam never interfered with the raising of

Jennifer Jane. As a matter of fact she hardly ever saw her.

Mam said, 'I've already got grandchildren. I don't need any more. I'm a television personality now.'

The Canadian tour went off all right, though he wasn't playing to such big houses any more. Then he toured Minnesota, and the Dakotas and Wyoming, and sang at two big benefit shows in New York and Washington DC, raising money for backward kiddies. But by the time he was back in Las Vegas with time to spare, Bliss had had to go to Red Rock Canyon to play a saloon floozie in a cowboy film. They'd been engaged twelve months and there was no sign of progress.

It's my opinion they'd have carried on like that for years if *Whisper* magazine hadn't brought out a piece asking questions:

> What's Lover Boy up to this time? Ask any lady of a certain age and she'll say Mr Starlight is the son every mother wishes for. Ask the girls, they'll say he's their dream date. Ask us, he's just teasing. He has no more intention of going to the altar with Bliss Bellaire than he does of flying to the moon.

'I could sue the bastards,' he said. 'But I'm not going to. Love's turned me soft. Me and Bliss have named the day, Cled. We're getting married on my birthday. So get your bags packed. And send me Jennifer Jane's measurements. Celeste's designed a dress for her, like the petals of a flower, each one a different shade of pink, and little fairy wings that strap on the back. She's going to love it.'

Of course, June was out of the question for us. Jennifer Jane had school and we had our guests. Some of our regulars booked with us straight after Christmas to be sure of getting their usual room. You can get somebody in to fry the breakfasts and you can get somebody in to make the beds, but there's no substitute for resident proprietors. You get to know your clients and they look forward to catching up with you once a year. It was the difference between winning a Golden Daffodil or just an Also Commended.

Hazel said, 'You go. I'll manage. I'll ask Nerys if her sister can give me a hand.'

I said, 'I think I should be there, don't you?'

I said to Penri, 'I feel damned if I do, damned if I don't. Hazel says I should go, but you know what women are like. Half the time they don't mean what they say. And if I go and enjoy myself, that won't go down very well. You know? Sel's probably invited people like Kitty O'Malley. I've got a lot of history over there.'

Penri said, 'It's a dilemma.'

I said, 'I think the only thing to do is this: go, but pretend I've had a rotten time.'

'And bring her back a little something,' he said. 'To show you were thinking of her. A stick of rock. Or a souvenir teaspoon.'

It was my first time in an aeroplane and my guts were churned up. You hear of terrible things. For two pins I'd have cancelled. But when it came to it we were treated like royalty. We had First Class seats and proper meals, and Ricky was given colouring books and a trip up to the cockpit to see the pilot. And those air hostesses were a treat for the eyes: natty little suits and high-heeled shoes. One of them was making quite a play for me, bending over, making sure I was strapped in.

I said, 'Good job for you I am!'

She laughed. I got de-luxe treatment from her; extra peanuts, tea topped up as often as I liked. Especially after I'd told her about my career in show business.

Ocean Star was like an anthill when we got there: decorators hanging silver bells and white ribbons everywhere, florists arranging big vases of baby's breath, three lads erecting a nuptial gazebo on the veranda.

Mam and Pearl weren't speaking, and a glazier had had to be sent for because a photographer had fallen through a window-pane, trying to get an exclusive.

But Sel was letting it all wash over him. 'It's going to be a perfect day,' he said. 'Come and see the suit.' Celeste had made him a two-piece Italian-style in silk.

I said, 'I thought it was the bride who was supposed to wear white?'

'It's ivory, Cled,' he said. 'Ivory photographs better than white.'

I said, 'I've brought a light-grey wool from Hepworth's. I assume you'll want me as best man?'

'No,' he said, 'I'm not having a best man. I'm having a best woman. I thought it'd make a talking point.'

Dilys said, 'Not Mam?'

'No,' he said. 'I did ask her, but she wasn't sure she could stand for long enough, with her bunions. It's going to be Pearl. A black lady best man. I'll be starting a trend.'

It was going to be a night-time wedding with hanging vines and fairy lights, so it would look like a starlit occasion even if it turned out misty. Milo was flying in from New York. Thelma Arden was driving from Las Vegas. And the bride was on her way from Butler, Pennsylvania with her mother and father. She was spending her last night as a single woman at the Malibu Beach House Hotel.

I said, 'Is Kitty coming?'

'Kitty?' he said. Pretended he didn't know who I meant for a minute or two. 'What, *Kitty*?' he said. 'No. I lost touch with her long ago. Why?'

I said, 'Just wondering who I'm going to dance with at your wedding.'

'Pearl,' he said. 'And Mam. And your sister. You've got a lovely little wife at home, Boff, so keep your sneaky eyes on the road ahead.'

I said, 'Yeah, well, you'll find out. You and Bliss have had a test run, I hope?'

'None of your business,' he said. 'But I will tell you one thing. Since I met her I haven't looked at another woman.'

I spent an hour at the Conroys' the morning before the wedding and that was a sad occasion. Kaye was hoping to attend the ceremony but Hubert wasn't a well man: heart trouble, brain trouble.

Kaye said, 'It's like he's not here any more, only he is. And sometimes he won't even be left with Willa.'

Hubert smiled at me but I don't think he knew me.

Kaye said, 'How's the bridegroom?'

173

I said, 'Running around, tying bells and love hearts on everything. I've never seen him so happy.'

'Wonderful,' she said. 'I was beginning to have my doubts, you know, Cled? The way he was conducting himself. Well, anyway . . . He's such a darling boy. Maybe he just made friends too easy. But we know he'll make a sweet husband. I just hope this girl treats him right too. You met her yet?'

I hadn't, of course, and I never did. Just after I got back to Ocean Star, the bride's father arrived. 'The wedding is off,' he said. 'Verna has changed her mind.'

Bliss's real name was Verna Schlitt.

Sel ran to the phone. But Mr Schlitt said she wasn't at the hotel, nor even in town and that he wasn't at liberty to divulge her whereabouts.

Sel looked terrible. All the colour had run out of his face. He said, 'I talked to her yesterday. She was happy enough yesterday.'

Dilys said, 'Perhaps it's nerves.'

'Yeah,' Sel said. 'It'll be nerves. She'll be all right if I talk to her.'

Mr Schlitt said, 'It ain't nerves. The marrying is oft, O-F-T. Verna has had her eyes opened to certain facts.'

Dilys said, 'What certain facts?'

Mam said, 'Shut up, Dilys.'

Schlitt said, 'I ain't going into all that in front of mixed company. He knows what I mean.'

Sel said, 'This is devastating. This can't be right.'

Schlitt said, 'Verna's the one entitled to devastation. She's suffering disappointment and loss of expectations.'

Mam said, 'Don't listen to him, Selwyn. He's just after money.'

But Mr Schlitt said Verna was a rising star. He said, 'My girl don't need money from no washed-up faggot lounge singer.'

Well, that did it.

Mam said, 'Throw him out, Cledwyn. Duff him up and throw him out! Don't worry, Selwyn. It's all for the best. There are plenty more fish in the sea.'

Dilys said, 'Perhaps it's all the razzmatazz, Sel.'

Betsan said, 'Yes, like Terry. It was the thought of all the fuss and photos gave him cold feet.' Of course, with Terry Eyles it wasn't just his feet. He never did warm up to married life.

Sel said, 'But she likes razzmatazz. She usually does. But I don't want her upset. Whatever it takes. I'll marry her at a drive-up wedding window if that's what she wants.'

Mr Schlitt said, 'She don't want. Here's your ring. Now stay away from her.' It was some ring.

Sel said, 'The ring's hers. She can keep it.'

But Mam snatched it up off the table and put it in her pocket.

Sel said, 'Look, please, just ask her to call me. I just want to talk to her.'

Schlitt said, 'Are you dumb as well as unnatural? She won't be coming within a country mile of you, you shirt-lifting son of a bitch. Using my kid, creating smokescreens. Well, I'll tell you something. Schlitt women marry *real* men.'

Mam was bobbing about, very excited. 'Hit him, Cledwyn,' she said. 'Hit him fair and square.'

I never hit a man in my life and I wasn't going to start with Mr Schlitt. He was built like a prop forward.

Pearl was shouting, 'Don't worry, Mr Selwyn. Clarence been sent for. He'll see this person off the premises. They'll be no hitting in my house.'

Clarence was a handyman, on call to every house in Coldwater Canyon and related to Pearl in same way. But Mr Schlitt was gone before Clarence could be found, and Dilys and Mam and Betsan started arguing, about who had been to blame for Terry Eyles's poor showing as a bridegroom and a husband, and little Ricky fell asleep on a leather couch, first time he'd given in and closed his eyes since we'd set off from Ninevah Street.

Sel went to his room. He said, 'I'm not at home to anybody except Bliss.'

Mam said, 'You go and lie down, sweetheart. I'll get on the telephone to Milo. He'll take care of everything.'

She couldn't wait.

'All cancelled!' she said to Milo. 'Tell the priest not to come and the photo people. Irreconcilable differences, that's what you should say, although between you and me, he's had a lucky escape. He's sleeping now. On no account to be disturbed.'

But Pearl made her own rules. She went in to him with a dish of ice cream. 'You go in to him, Mr Cled,' she said. 'I put Rocky Road and Cheesecake Flavor, to revive his spirits, but that boy needs his brother.'

I said, 'Pearl, did you think there'd be a wedding?'

'I'm not here to think, sir,' she said. 'I'm here to pick up.'

His bedroom colour scheme at Ocean Star was baby-blue and oyster, and the ceiling was painted midnight-blue with silver-leaf stars. There were two couches, piled with cushions, and a king-size bed with light bulbs in the headboard, and satin sheets and pillows embroidered with his name.

I said, 'That headboard doesn't look very comfortable.'

'Cled,' he said, 'why's she done this?'

His dogs were fussing around him. They seemed to know he'd had a setback. He still had two Westies in those days, and a mongrel called Lucky and a skinny, nervy little thing called Martoonie that he reckoned was an Italian Greyhound although she looked like a whippet to me.

I said, 'I'm sorry you've had a disappointment, our kid.'

He said, 'If I could only talk to her. Perhaps it's not her. Perhaps her dad's holding her prisoner.'

I said, 'Mam and Milo are taking care of everything.'

'What?' he said.

I said, 'Telling the magazine. Cancelling the harpist.'

'God!' he said. 'The photos. Fuck! That's another thing. She was thrilled about *Celebrity Secrets* giving us a big spread. It's Schlitt. Has to be. He's brainwashed her.'

I said, 'A dad wants the best for his daughter.'

He looked at me. He said, 'I was the best. In a million years she'll never find a man who'd treat her better.'

I said, 'I know that. Sel, these "certain facts" he brought up?'

176

He just sat there, scratching Lucky behind his ears.

I said, 'Hazel wondered . . .'

'I wanted to get married, Cled,' he said. 'I really wanted to.' And he started crying, which was a very hard thing to watch. He was always such a smiler as a rule. He said, 'I can't help it. I am what I am. But I'd have been good to her.'

I didn't like facing him with it. We'd never had anything like that in the family. But it had to be done. I said, 'Is it . . . men?'

He said, 'We might have had kiddies. I'd have tried. I'd love to have kiddies. What am I supposed to do? All the rest of you have got families. Why can't I have one?' He was a sight, with his nose red from crying. He wasn't so much the Lover Boy, with ice cream dripped on his shirt and his slacks all rumpled. His hair was skew-whiff too, though I couldn't have said why at the time.

I said, 'These men? How does that work, exactly?'

He just rolled over, turned his back on me. 'I want to be alone,' he said. 'I want to go to sleep.'

I phoned Hazel. I said, 'Looks like you were right. Sel's a pansy.'

'Cled,' she said, 'it's three in the morning.'

That was hardly my fault. I said, 'The wedding's off.'

'Naturally,' she said. 'Why are you whispering?'

I said, 'I don't want Mam to hear. How do you think I should break the news to her?'

'It's not your news to break,' she said. 'Poor Sel.'

I said, 'What about Dilys?'

She said, 'I don't think you'd be telling Dilys anything she hasn't worked out for herself. Are you coming straight home, then?'

But we weren't. We were going to Vegas with Sel, keeping him company till he felt up to facing the world. Milo put out a statement to the effect that Mr Starlight and Bliss Bellaire had called off their marriage by mutual agreement and Bliss Bellaire's publicist put out a statement that she was in exciting discussions with Paramount about a new movie. Actually, she ended up on afternoon television, bringing the contestants on for *Name that Tune*.

Milo said, 'As long as you're all in town I'd like to see a photo opportunity. Mr Starlight enjoying a well-earned vacation with his British family. You know the kind of thing.'

We made a number of photo opportunities that week. We all went to the Lucky Horseshoe for a steak dinner, to show that Mr Starlight hadn't lost his appetite, which is where Betsan caught the eye of Larry Chase. He was at a nearby table and sent a note across to her, said she was the sweetest-looking girl in the room and could he take her to a show?

Mam said, 'No, he cannot. She's made her bed.'

Dilys said, 'Ignore her. You go if you want to. Enjoy yourself.'

Then Thelma gave a nice party, to lift Sel out of the doldrums. Bob Mitchum came. Debbie Reynolds. Just a hundred close friends and of course a lot of them remembered me.

I said, 'We should give them a little show, our kid, like the old days.'

He said he didn't feel like it but even Mam backed me up. 'Whatever happens,' she said, 'the show goes on. That's the mark of a true star.'

So we moved the baby grand into the room that opened on to the swimming pool and gave them all a treat.

I said, 'We should think of re-forming.'

He said, 'I don't think so, Cled. I can't see Hazel moving to Vegas.' I said, 'Hazel'll do as she's told.'

I don't know what they all found so amusing about that.

The day before we were due to fly home Larry asked Betsan to stay on, to be his wife and help him run his chain of mini-golf courses, which she did. I wasn't there for the nuptials myself, but Dilys and Arthur flew out, and young Ricky got to be a ring bearer after all. Sel loaned them one of his Cadillacs to take them to the Little Church of the West and paid for the wedding breakfast and had Ricky to stay with him and Mam while Betsan and Larry honeymooned at Ocean Star. He was very generous as an uncle, even if he was unnatural in other respects.

I brought that up with Dilys during that long journey back from the wedding that never was. I said, 'I suppose you realise about Sel?'

'Yes,' she said. 'I suppose I do.'

I said, 'How could such a thing have come about do you think?'

'Well,' she said, 'He was always different. Artistic.'

I said, 'What I don't understand is when he was a nipper he never played with boys. So how come that's what he's keen on now? Is it something he's picked up?'

'I don't know,' she said. 'Wouldn't make any difference if I did. There won't be any wedding and he won't be having any babs. All he'll get is called names. It makes me sad, Cled. It makes me very sad indeed.'

TWENTY-THREE

The first season we noticed things were changing was 1968. We had vacancies most weeks and some of our regulars didn't come. People who'd stayed with us for years didn't get in touch. Business went downhill pretty fast and it wasn't only us. The Tal-y-Bont had vacancies too. Everybody said it was because of Spain. They said why would anybody come to Llandudno and get rained on when they could go to Spain and fry for nearly the same money. Personally, I couldn't understand why folk would pay to get sunstroke and bad guts when we had beautiful scenery to offer and good clean water, but a new trend had set in and there wasn't much we could do about it.

Hazel said, 'There's not enough work for two of us. You'll have to get a job.' She kept circling adverts with her biro: warehouseman, school caretaker, transistor radio assembler. But as I said to Penri, my business was show business.

'It is,' he said.

I said, 'It's in the blood, but somebody like Hazel, who's only ever seen the mundane side of life, can't understand that.'

'Cledwyn,' he said, 'I'm going to share a thought with you. Turkey and Tinsel mini-breaks.'

This was a new concept. A Christmas holiday with all the trimmings, but not at Christmas time and not at holiday season prices.

Penri said, 'They're becoming very popular with pensioners. People who'd be at home on their own on Christmas Day or dragged round to their relatives. See, on a mini-break they have nice company and all the extras too. Things they wouldn't bother with at home, paper hats and cranberry sauce. And entertainment. Party games and music from real artistes. Not the same old telly programmes year after year.'

I said, 'I see what you're getting at. But we don't have a lot of room for party games at Hazelwyn. And we usually do our redecorating in the winter.'

'No,' he said, 'bear with me. I didn't mean Hazelwyn. I meant *I'm* starting to do them, at the Saltdene in Abergele. Christmas carols and seasonal singalong numbers. I'm getting an electric keyboard. It's got built-in Bossa Nova rhythm and it fits into a case you can carry on the bus. Now, this is where you come in . . .'

I said, 'I don't think I could ever play a plastic keyboard, Penri. I've been accustomed to quality instruments. I suppose I could offer myself to places that had a decent piano.'

'I didn't mean that,' he said. 'There's not that many openings in Tinsel and Turkey. I can't have you muscling in on my territory.'

I said, 'I thought you said they were getting very popular?'

'They are,' he said. 'But not that popular. What I meant was, you could take over from me at the Lorina School of Dance. I'll gladly put in a word for you.'

Hazel wasn't very happy. She said, 'You could have got that job at Gamble's Shoes if you'd put your mind to it. Playing in a tinpot dance school! That's not a proper job.'

I said, 'I'm using my professional skills. And if Jennifer Jane would care to learn ballet I can get her the classes half price.'

Jennifer Jane said, 'No thank you.'

The Lorina wasn't much but I did enjoy it. Ballet, tap, modern dance, whatever they needed I was the man. Madame Lorina found me to be a much more versatile musician than Penri Clocker. 'You'll go far,' she said.

'I've already been,' I used to say.

She meant well. She just had a tendency to forget what she'd been told. And it was through her I got the chance to play for the new summer show rehearsals at the Pavilion Theatre in Rhyl.

Hazel said, 'What time will you be back?'

I said, 'When you see me. It's not a nine till five job.'

'I know that,' she said.

Who can say? Perhaps if she hadn't been so sarcastic, perhaps if she'd shown more interest in my work, I might not have strayed. Then again, we'd started putting up travelling salesmen and some of them treated the place like home. For all I know she may have slipped one of them an extra rasher.

Anyway, there I was at the Rhyl Pavilion, trying to rehearse a strangulated tenor, when love walked right in and drove the shadows away. It was little Avril, who'd debuted at the Birmingham Welsh the same night Sel collapsed with suit poisoning. I said, 'It may be twenty years but you don't look a day older.'

'Strike a light!' she said, 'I'd never have remembered you. How did you recognise me?'

I said, 'I never forget a cleavage.'

'Sel Boff's brother!' she said. 'I've told that story a few times! How I cradled him in my arms till the ambulance came. Remember the colour of him? We thought he'd had it. But look at him now. Hasn't he done well?'

You get used to it. People being so dazzled with your brother they overlook your achievements. Later on, after she'd heard my success story, Avril was putty in my hands.

I said, 'What are you doing here?'

'Looking for Bryn,' she said. 'It's time we were making a move.'

There I was, rehearsing the new Bryn Reynolds Summer Spectacular and there she was, Mrs Bryn Reynolds herself.

I said, 'I heard you played the Birmingham Hippodrome.'

'I did,' she said. 'Then I married Face Ache. Moved to Knutsford and called it a day.'

Reynolds was an impresario. He put shows on all over the north-west; variety shows for families who still came on proper holidays.

I said, 'It would have been nice to go for a lemonade. Catch up on the lost years.'

'Can't do it,' she said. 'We're due in Manchester at seven. Next time you talk to Sel tell him I've never forgotten that night. I always say, if only he'd opened his eyes and looked up, seen what I had to offer, he might have turned out normal. Know what I mean?'

I said, 'Well, I'm told Sel was probably a lost cause from day one. But you certainly improved my circulation. Still are doing, as a matter of fact.'

She said, 'I could always drive over next week.'

I said, 'That's a long drive for a lemonade.'

'Well,' she said, 'I'm sure you'll think of something else, to make it worth my while.'

Little scorcher.

We started seeing each other, once a week in the beginning. I lived for those Mondays. Avril gave me a welcome in the hillsides and no mistake.

'Extra rehearsals,' I used to tell Hazel.

She'd say, 'Anybody would think it was Covent Garden.'

No disrespect to Hazel, but she never had Avril's allure. Hazel was the kind of girl you marry. And the only trouble was the back of a motor isn't very satisfactory, especially not at our time of life. There was Penri's house. I could have come to some kind of arrangement with him. But I didn't dare. It was too close to home.

I said, 'Of course, if you left Bryn and I left Hazel . . .'

'Now, Cled,' she said, 'let's not have any silly talk. If only you could get a summer season somewhere, then we could have ourselves a little love nest.'

And blow me down if Bryn Reynolds didn't ask to see me the following week, greeted me like an old friend. 'Cled,' he said, 'you were a pro at one time, I know. I might have something for you. Aberystwyth. Bobby Bly's got gallstones. I'd need you for ten weeks.'

I said, 'I'll take it.'

Bryn said, 'Think about it. Let me know tomorrow.'

I said, 'I don't need to. I'll take it.'

Hazel said, 'You might have asked me first.'

I said, 'It's the chance of a lifetime.'

She said, 'It's Aberystwyth, Cled. Where does that leave me?'

183

'Running Hazelwyn as per,' I said. 'I can drive back on Saturday nights, if you like. There's no show on Sundays. And I can go back on Monday mornings.'

'Well,' she said, 'you've obviously got it all worked out.'

Jennifer said, 'What is it you're going to be doing?'

I said, 'Playing the piano.'

'Who for?' she said. 'Is Uncle Sel coming?'

My own child and yet she had no concept of me as a solo artiste.

I was in a very presentable line-up at Aberystwyth. Barry Maguire was top of the bill, doing impersonations. Then there was a black tap dancer, a vent act called Titch and Lofty, a troupe of yodelling dachshunds and a couple who sang light operetta. I closed the first half with a piano medley called 'Through the Decades', everything from Scott Joplin to Gilbert O'Sullivan. And when the show ended I wasn't finished. Two or three nights a week I had Avril waiting for me at our digs. We told the landlady we were Mr and Mrs Boff but she must have had her suspicions, the amount of wear we gave that bed. Saturday nights after the show I'd drive home to see the family and get my laundry done. It was very hard to act natural when I was feeling so happy.

Hazel used to say, 'You're in a good mood. You'd better go to Aberystwyth every summer.'

But it was Rhyl and Prestatyn Bryn offered me for the following season.

Hazel said, 'I suppose that means you'll be home every night?'

I could see my arrangements with Avril about to go down the toilet.

Hazel said, 'The thing is, Cled, I can't have you rolling home late, banging doors and waking my gentlemen. They have to get up in the morning and do a day's work.'

I said, 'Perhaps it'd be better if I stayed in digs. Just came home on the weekend like last year?'

'Yes,' she said. 'Perhaps it would.'

It wasn't a brilliant line-up. Stan Butterworth, the balloon magician, a mime act from Poland, a comedy duo called Howie & Frank, and a vocalist called Dudley Ellis. Ticket sales were very slow to start with. I think it was because the weather was pleasant. Rain is what you pray for when you're doing a summer spectacular. What made the difference was a little idea I'd had with my friend Penri Clocker. A promotional disc. I got Avril to float the idea with Bryn.

'Cled,' he said, 'I've had a brainwave. We should cut a disc promoting the show. Dudley on vocals, you on backing.'

I said, 'That's a very good idea, and funny you should bring it up because I've got the very song for you.'

'"Summer Holiday",' he said. 'It's obvious.'

As I explained to Penri, Bryn Reynolds was a man who was used to getting his own way, but every cloud has a silver lining and every record has a flip side. And the main thing was Radio Conwy played it all day, every day. '*Summer Holiday*' on the A side and, on the B side, a Boff and Clocker original: 'Rhyl!'.

By the end of that summer everybody was singing it. Why we weren't able to get it properly reissued I shall never understand.

I said to Jennifer Jane, 'Now what do you think of your old dad, eh? Now I'm in the hit parade? I'll bet they're all talking about it at school.'

She said, 'I'm afraid they are.'

She cracked me up.

I said, 'Great elms from little acorns grow. This year Rhyl. Next year, who knows. Blackpool, maybe.'

Hazel said, 'I wonder if fame is going to change you?'

Her sneering didn't bother me. I was on the up. I was back where I belonged, tinkling the ivories, name on every bus shelter in town. There was only one worry on my mind: Bryn. If he'd ever found out about me and Avril it would have been the end of my career revival.

But Avril never appeared to worry about anything. 'Relax!' she'd say. 'He thinks I'm at the hydro getting beautified.'

'Relax!' she'd say. 'He's in Lytham looking at a new venue.'

And then he turned up, just before the matinée one Wednesday. It was towards the end of the season. 'Cled,' he said, 'a word.'

I could hardly hear what he was saying for the blood pounding in my ears. Avril was supposed to be in Wilmslow, at a ladies golf lunch, but she was actually two streets away, luxuriating after a morning of love.

'That brother of yours,' he said. 'Mr Moonshine?'

'Starlight,' I said.

Bryn said, 'Yeah! Whatever became of him?'

That's the cruelty of show business. One minute you're a top-liner, next thing you're just a custard advert. Sel was getting by. He compèred a daytime talent show on the telly, talking to the turns and singing a couple of songs, and he still did celebrity appearances with Mam, cutting the tape to open new shopping centres. He performed live sometimes too. They still liked him in Vegas and he was part owner of a club called the Double Down, so he wasn't hurting for money. When that terrible business happened in Aberfan he'd sent them a very handsome cheque. But times had changed. He'd tried going more rockified, but that didn't suit him, and there wasn't the same romantic interest in him, because of the stories about boys. Women had come to their senses. Some women. So, sadly, he hadn't managed to stay at the top and to a lot of people that's the only place that counts. They soon start asking, 'Whatever became of him?'

I said, 'He's still out there. Why?'

He said, 'I'd like to get him over here next summer. A name from the past always pulls them in.'

I said, 'Where?'

'Morecambe,' he said. 'The Winter Gardens.'

I said, 'You offered me Morecambe.'

'That's right,' he said. 'The pair of you. The Boff Brothers reunited.'

I said, 'Not the Boff Brothers. That's history. We'd have to have separate billing. I've got my own following now, since "Rhyl!".'

'Yes,' he said. 'Whatever. Tell him to call me.'

I said to Sel, 'I know you won't be interested but I'm just delivering a message.'

'Don't be so sure I'm not interested,' he said. 'I've never turned work down on account of a modest venue. There are folks who go to Morecambe who'll never get the chance to come to Vegas and who am I to deprive them? They all buy records.'

Hazel said, 'Oh, how lovely! And tell him he's to come back here with you on the weekends. I don't want him staying in a hotel when he can be with family. Tell him I can see to his costumes.'

Avril said, 'Great news about Sel. I can't wait to see him again. Has he still got those lovely dimples?'

I said, 'He's no kid any more.'

She said, 'Do you know who he always reminded me of? Audie Murphy in *Red Badge of Courage*. Anybody else ever remark on that?'

As I pointed out to her, Audie Murphy was a hero. Audie Murphy got the Medal of Honor. Whereas Sel didn't even get through basic training.

'Never mind,' she said. 'He had a sweet face and he taught me a thing or two. It was him told me I should pile my hair up on top and catch it with a rhinestone pin.'

I said to Penri, 'I'm beginning to think this is a mistake. I can't have him taking over.'

He said, 'You'll have to be very firm.'

I said, 'He's got to realise I'm in the driving seat now.'

'You are,' he said.

Then Bryn undermined me.

Sel's costumes arrived at the end of April. Two big trunks with everything rolled in tissue paper.

Hazel was like a kid on Christmas morning. 'Look at the work that's gone into these,' she kept saying. 'And beautiful colours. One thing about Sel, he's not afraid to wear colours. Try one on, Cled. I'd love to see you in lilac.'

That was a joke. Sel must have been nudging thirteen stone by then.

She said, 'You look like a clown in it.'

Not the only one, neither.

I said, 'You're always going on about not inconveniencing your gentlemen and now look at the place. Sequinned jackets hanging everywhere. It's like living in Santa's grotto.'

'They're not inconveniencing anybody,' she said. 'They're a talking point.'

I said to him, 'You've sent far too much gear. A few of those glittery bow ties would have done. If that. Audiences don't care about that kind of thing any more.'

'I care,' he said.

He arrived the first week of May. Mam didn't come with him.

I said, 'I suppose she's getting frail?'

She was eighty-one.

'No,' he said. 'She's fitter than you are. She's too busy to come. She's shooting a new advert. It's an electric armchair that does everything: reclines, rocks, vibrates, mixes you a Martini. And anyway, she wouldn't leave Ricky. She thinks if she leaves him with Pearl for five minutes he'll start turning black.'

Young Ricky wasn't getting on with Larry, his stepdad, so he'd moved to Desert Star to live with Sel and Mam. 'Just till things calm down,' he said. 'Mam understands boys.'

He stayed at Hazelwyn for a couple of nights, to humour Hazel. He said, 'So, Jennifer Jane, it turns out you've inherited your mummy's brains as well as her good looks.'

She had her head in a book all the time, studying hard. She was hoping to become a doctor.

'Good job,' he said. 'If you'd taken after your daddy you'd have turned out daft, with no hair.'

She said, 'I'm not Jennifer Jane any more. I'm Jennifer.'

'Right,' he said. 'I stand corrected. And are you going to come to Morecambe, see your Uncle Sel in action?'

'Don't think so,' she said.

I said, 'This is what television's done to entertainment. Nobody can be bothered going to a live show these days, not unless you offer them Herman's Hermits or the Gee Bees.'

He said, 'I can't complain about TV. It's been good to me.

Anyway, I'm here to enjoy myself. And I've had people recognising me already, this afternoon when I was out.'

I said, 'That was because you were the only man going up the Great Orme in a white leather suit.'

Hazel said, 'Well, *I'll* be coming to Morecambe to see you, Sel.' She'd never bothered to come and see my shows. Just as well, though. It might have led to complications with Avril.

Me and Penri had been working on another song, in the hopes of building on the previous summer's success, but then Bryn got it into his head to turn the spotlight on Sel. He had him record 'Summertime', with 'Yesterday' on the B side, and he arranged for the *Sunday Express* to mention him in an article called 'Whatever Happened To . . .' about has-beens.

Hazel said, 'That's cheeky.'

Sel said, 'No, I don't mind. I know I'm not exactly at my peak. And I'd rather be called a has-been than a never-was.'

We opened the week after Whitsun. Me and Sel had top billing, with Micky Michaels, the comic, a Country and Western group from Widnes called the Rattlers, a memory man – I forget his name – and Zuleima, the Human Rubber Band. It was a very slow start. It was all very well him running on, twirling round, showing off his jacket as if we had a sell-out at the Topanga Ballroom, but when a theatre's half empty you can feel it. It gets into your guts.

We did a mix of nostalgia numbers and novelty songs: 'As Time Goes By', 'When Somebody Thinks You're Wonderful', 'A Windmill in Old Amsterdam'. There was one matinée we played, Sel giving his all in a pink sequinned jacket. 'All together, now!' he said, for a reprise of 'I Do Like To Be Beside the Seaside' and I'll swear there was nobody out there, only the usherettes.

Then we had a cold snap so things picked up, punters glad to get in out of the wind and enjoy a first-rate show. Sel started getting ladies up out of the audience, just like the old days, to admire his costume or sing along with him.

'It's such a thrill seeing you in the flesh,' one of them said.

'Cled,' he said, 'you might have told me my fly was unbuttoned.'

189

That got a laugh.

'How about a request?' he said. 'Anything you like. Cled here can play anything. Rachmaninov. Chopsticks.'

'"The Boy I Love",' somebody shouted. That raised a laugh too.

Hazel was disappointed that he didn't come back to Llandudno with me every opportunity but he had other things on his agenda. Weekdays he'd hang around with me, especially if Avril was in town, laughing and larking about with her instead of taking a hint and making himself scarce, but Saturday nights he'd have a car collect him straight after the show and he'd be gone till Monday afternoon – in Liverpool or Manchester, I suppose, looking for others of his tendency.

I said, 'You be careful. You're on my patch now. Any scandals and my career'll be affected as well.'

He said, 'You're something! *You* are telling *me* to be careful? Tell you what, Cled. I just hope Bryn Reynolds isn't the jealous type. I hope he isn't in possession of a shotgun.'

Me and Avril were always very discreet. I said, 'We're only friends.'

'Oh yeah?' he said. 'That's some kinda friend, drives all the way from Knutsford for a Bacardi and a packet of crisps. And I didn't realise Hazel had such a modern outlook, allowing you to have that kind of friend. The kind that stays the night.'

I said, 'I don't see how you can comment, never having settled down yourself. You don't know what it's like. The same old routine year after year.'

'No,' he said, 'it's true, I don't. Even though I wouldn't have minded trying it.'

I said, 'And from what I hear it must be like Crewe Junction at your place. A different face on the pillow every morning.'

'Face on the pillow!' he said. 'That's a lie! Nobody puts their face on my pillow.'

I said, 'Well, whatever it is they do, only don't tell me because I don't want to know. But me, I've put in nearly twenty years with Hazel.'

He said, 'You make her sound like the night shift at Greely's. Poor little Hazel. But I tell you what, Cled, I'm not going to say another word. I'm not that interested. I always believe what goes on in a person's bedroom is their own fucking business. What do you say?'

Oh Rhyl!
The inspiration of a tune
You stand beneath a Conway moon
And murmur softly, some day soon
Return you will
To lovely Rhyl.
Prestatyn's nice in its own way
There's nothing wrong with Colwyn Bay
But please believe us when we say
Return you will
To lovely Rhyl.

CLOCKER AND BOFF

TWENTY-FOUR

We were playing to full houses by the end of the season. Linking up with me had given Sel a new lease of life and it was quite on the cards that we'd be offered something even better for the following summer. But then September came and it turned out to be a black month for us all round. First we heard Hubert Conroy had passed away in his sleep and then Arthur dropped dead at his desk. He was only two weeks off retirement. Two people came from the Personnel Department at Aldridge's, turned up on the doorstep and broke the news to Dilys, just like that.

It was Gaynor who phoned us. She said, 'You'll have to come. Mother has to be supervised and I can't leave Clifford on his own all day.' Gaynor and Clifford had their own chemist's shop at Alum Rock by then. They'd never gone in for a family.

Hazel said, 'You and Sel go. I'll come for the funeral.'

I said, 'Why can't you come now? This is a job for a woman.'

'Because I can't swan off and leave my gentlemen,' she said. 'This is a business I'm running.'

Jennifer Jane said, 'Why do we have to have all these men in the house anyway?'

There was one gent Jennifer Jane particularly disliked. She said she didn't like the way he came down to breakfast in his slippers.

Hazel said, 'Well, that's a hanging offence.'

Jennifer said, 'I'd have thought we could have our house to ourselves now Daddy's top of the bill.'

Hazel said, 'Being top of the bill, Jennifer, will very likely be a flash in the pan and if you're going to college for five years we need steady money coming in.'

Sel said, 'I've told you, I'll pay for her to go to college. I want her to discover the secret of eternal youth. But you do what you have to do. Me and Cled'll go and rally round Dilys. You follow when you can.'

I took care of things at the undertaker's and Sel sat with Dilys. I never know what to say to people at a time like that. I said, 'Would you like Mam to come home?'

'No,' she said. 'Funnily enough, I wouldn't.'

We could have had a slot on the Friday but we had to wait for Betsan to fly in. That meant Tuesday was the soonest we could get the deed done. Sitting around, drinking tea, listening to Dilys crying. I couldn't even phone Avril for a bit of light relief.

When Hazel finally arrived I said, 'On Tuesday, I think I'll give the cremation a miss. I'll stay here, in case anything crops up.'

'Nothing will crop up,' she said, 'because I'll be here, cutting the sandwiches and you'll be where you should be, at your sister's side.'

Sel said, 'We should have it catered.'

'No,' she said. 'I've already told Dilys, I'm doing ham sandwiches and fruit cake. And they can have tea or sherry. Sel, you go and buy the sherry.'

On the Tuesday they closed Aldridge's for the afternoon as a mark of respect. It all went off according to plan. Sel sang 'The Old Rugged Cross' and the crematorium laid on a vicar to say a few words. I'd never realised Arthur's middle name was Hampton, after Harry Hampton, centre forward for Aston Villa when they won the League Cup in 1910. It's funny the things you don't know about a person till they're dead.

Gaynor and Betsan and Clifford rode with Dilys in the front car, and me and Sel followed behind with Arthur's brother and sister-in-law.

I said, 'Who was the little old chap talking to you at the back of the chapel?'

He said, 'You didn't recognise him either? It was Teilo. He's gone all skin and bone. I didn't know him till he spoke.'

I said, 'What did he say?'

'Oh, you know,' he said. 'Hello, son. How's Annie? Be nice if we could be friends. Be nice if we could have a drink, for old times' sake.'

I said, 'Will you?'

'Not bloody likely,' he said. 'Start socialising with one dad, the other two are liable to turn up.'

Mr and Mrs Persons' faces were a picture.

'Anyway,' he said, 'I'll be gone.'

I said to Sel, 'I thought you might stay on a bit? Keep Dilys company?'

'Can't be done,' he said. 'I've got commitments. She can come back with me and Betsan, have a change of scenery. Perhaps she'd like that. Funny, isn't it, you make plans. There he was, sharpening his pencils, dreaming about that big fat pension from Aldridge's, and the next minute, gone. "When I retire," he used to say. What a mug. Learn from this, Cled. Tomorrow doesn't always come. Whatever it is you want, get on and do it.'

I said, 'I do.'

As we walked through the door Hazel said, 'Roll your sleeves up, you two. Cled, you hand the sandwiches. Sel, you help me with beverages. Listen, more tragedy. Bryn Reynolds's wife. It's true what they say. Bad news always comes in threes.'

Everything inside me stopped still.

The first edition of the *Evening News* lay on the dresser in the hall. 'Motorway carnage', it said. 'Avril Reynolds, well-known on the Birmingham club circuit, was one of three killed in a pile-up in fog on the M6.'

Hazel said, 'Only forty-five. What a waste. You seen her recently, Cled?'

I looked at her.

She said, 'The paper's full of car accidents. Thick fog all over that side of the country and yet it's beautiful here. I think we could put a few chairs in the garden. It might lift the mood a bit if people can circulate and look at the flower beds.'

I didn't say a word.

Sel grabbed hold of Clifford. He said, 'Clifford, take these sandwiches round. I need Cled for something.'

'Sel!' she said. 'Where are you taking him? I need you to pour the sherry.'

'Five minutes,' he said. 'We'll be back directly. But I've got to get some smokes.'

He walked me outside to my motor.

I said, 'You've got smokes. You opened a new pack just before the hearse came.'

'Get in,' he said. 'Just sit quiet, till you've pulled yourself together.'

I don't know how long we sat.

I said, 'I can't go back in there, sipping tea, talking to strangers. I can't do it.'

He said, 'I'll do the talking, you do the sipping. It'll be worse if Hazel sees you going to pieces. Then you'll have some talking to do.'

I just wanted to be on my own, so I could think about what had happened. I said, 'This is judgement on me, Sel.'

'Judgement!' he said. 'It's a car pile-up. It's people driving too fast in fog. Now get a grip on yourself. If you can't do it for Hazel, do it for Dilys.'

I said, 'That's going to be my punishment, never being able to talk about her. After you've gone home, there won't be anybody who knew, anybody I can talk to.'

'Ever hear of a thing called a telephone?' he said and he got me in one of his bear hugs. I could smell that orange stuff he'd started putting on his face.

Two men from Aldridge's had stepped outside for a cigarette. 'Look at that pair,' I heard one of them say. 'Must be the widow's side of the family.'

It was even worse after the well-wishers had all gone and the washing up was done. Everybody sat around, talking about the best way to get over a bereavement. Get a little part-time job. Do voluntary work. Join a bowls club.

Sel said, 'You should come and stay with me. Perfect weather. Beautiful house. Lovely garden. Swimming pool.'

'And your mam,' Hazel said. 'Just what you need, eh, Dilys? Back under the same roof as your mam.'

Sel said, 'She wouldn't be under the same roof. Not exactly. She'd be in one of my guest bungalows. Anyway, Mam's all right. She's mellowed. And Ricky's there. And Betsan and Larry aren't far away. I reckon I should buy more land. We could have ourselves a whole compound. We could be like the Kennedys.'

Gaynor said, 'What about your pipes? If you go to America you'll have to drain them. I can't keep running over from Alum Rock all the time, keeping an eye on things.'

Hazel said, 'Betsan, how come you're allowing your gran to raise Ricky? He should be at home with you.'

Betsan said, 'He can come home any time he likes, but he has to learn to get along with Larry.'

Hazel said, 'It doesn't seem natural to me, a boy his age being raised by a woman in her eighties.'

Betsan said Larry had done his best. She said she had to put him first.

Hazel said, 'Well, I think you're making a big mistake. Your child is always your child. Whereas husbands come and go,' which started Dilys weeping again.

'They do come and go, Hazel,' she said. 'And you might keep that in mind. You and Cled should cherish each other a bit more. You look at one another like you lost a shilling and found sixpence. Sel's the only ray of sunshine in this family, bless him. But you don't need to worry about my pipes, Gaynor, because I'm not going home with him. I'm staying here with my memories.'

Dilys had insisted we have her bed. She said, 'I don't want to wake up in it without Arthur.'

So Hazel lay next to me, prattling on. 'You look terrible, Cled. What's the matter? I'm sorry if I've not cherished you lately. I've

197

been busy. You've been away. Have you got a pain? Tell me if you've got a pain. Have an aspirin. Have a Rennie. I don't want you collapsing on me like Arthur.'

That was how I started serving my time, listening to her when I wanted to be alone with my thoughts. Avril wasn't the greatest beauty but she had musicality and a vivacious personality and a double D bra cup. She could go to bed in the middle of the afternoon and not worry about a thing. She never asked me to leave Hazel. She never really complained about Bryn. 'He's not a bad old stick,' she'd say. 'But all he thinks about is business. Counting his money, that's what lights Bryn's fire!'

She'd turned Aberystwyth into paradise for me, and Rhyl and Prestatyn, and then she was gone. It felt like winter, without any prospect of spring.

TWENTY-FIVE

I t was just as well Dilys didn't go home with Sel, because there was a nasty surprise waiting for him when he got off the plane. He was on the cover of a magazine called *Uncensored*. 'The Secret Life of Mr Starlight,' it said. They'd found three men willing to come forward and say things about him. One of them said Sel had struck up a conversation with him in Pershing Park, Los Angeles and offered him a beer. 'I'm not that way myself,' he said, 'but I was young and he was a strong man and he wouldn't take no for an answer. It was just the once, but I knew who he was. My mom had all his records.'

They'd raked up the Conroys' pool boy too, from all those years back, and one of Sel's drivers. I suppose they paid them money. It was just a scandal rag on sale in supermarkets and it wasn't as though it was the first time there'd been stories. But this time he said he was going to sue.

I said, 'Well, you were a big pal of that pool boy. What about the other two?'

'I don't know,' he said. 'The world's full of boys.'

I said, 'Then you shouldn't go to court. You'll just get tied in knots by lawyers. And they'll put Kaye Conroy on the stand. You don't want to put an old lady through that. And what about Mam? Why don't you just let it lie.'

'That's the thing, Cled,' he said. 'Time after time I have done. I've never talked about my private life. I never wanted to and I still don't, but now my fans are going to read this stuff and it's going to cost me. These scumbags are the ones who started it, not me, and now I'm going after them.'

He was right about it costing him. A daytime telly series got cancelled and he fell out with three different lawyers, and in the end it was open season on Mr Starlight. He'd always had a big following in Baltimore, but a paper there ran an article about him calling him Mrs Boff's Fruit Pie, and Bliss Bellaire was in the *Enquirer*, recycling her old line about him being the perfect gentleman, except she'd altered her tune a bit. 'He was a little too perfect for a red-blooded girl like me,' she said. 'There comes a time when all that restraint ain't so flattering to a girl.' Of course, Bliss Bellaire wasn't exactly a girl any more, nor a film starlet as they described her, but that's magazines for you.

Sel put out a statement saying he intended fighting a pack of filthy lies that were making his elderly mother ill. 'I believe in family,' he said. 'Ask anybody. I adore women and women adore me. Ask my fans. I may not have been lucky enough to find the right girl and settle down, but that's no reason to tar me with disgusting names and cause distress to my loved ones. Don't these people have mothers?'

Our Jennifer said, 'I don't see what all the fuss is about. He can't help the way he is. It's only like being left-handed, or having red hair.'

I was shocked she even knew of such a thing, but she had just started her medical studies at Liverpool University and I suppose doctors have to know about all kinds of things. I said, 'It doesn't run in families, though?'

'No,' she said, 'I don't think so. I expect it's hormones. He probably got the wrong hormones before he was born.'

I told Sel. I said, 'Jennifer Jane says this problem of yours is caused by hormones. A lot of things are, apparently.'

He said, 'Is that right?'

I said, 'Yes. She reckons there'll probably be a cure for it some day.'

'Well,' he said, 'there you go! I didn't even know I had hormones. Thank God somebody in this family's getting an education. How about you, our kid? How are you?'

I said, 'Nothing wrong with my hormones.'

'No,' he said. 'I meant how *are* you? Have you seen Bryn?'

'Next week,' I said. 'I'll call him next week.'

Hazel had been nagging me as well. 'At least send him your condolences,' she kept saying. 'If you're going to earn a living you're going to need Bryn Reynolds.'

I said, 'It's not easy, Sel, keeping it to myself.'

'No,' he said, 'I can imagine. Well, tell Jennifer Jane to get to work on that cure. Tell her to burn the midnight oil. I'll pay for the test tubes. And remember, if there's anything I can do, I'm here if you need me.'

I said to Penri, 'I think Sel's hoping we can get back together again, do another season. He won't come right out and say it, but he's been dropping hints.'

He said, 'A big name like Mr Starlight, you could likely get Blackpool. I'd speak up if I were you. Cled. I'd strike while the iron is hot.'

So I picked up the telephone and called Bryn. I said, 'I was very sorry to hear of your sad loss.' I'd practised saying it.

'To tell you the truth, Chegwin,' he said, 'things weren't the way they seemed between me and Avril. She went her own way and I went mine, had done for years. As a matter of fact she was going her own way the night she . . .'

I said, 'On the M6. I read about it. In fog.'

'Correct,' he said. 'On the M6. In fog. With Stan Butterworth. You're probably shocked.'

I didn't know what to say.

He said, 'I was shocked, Chet. I mean, we're all grown-ups. We are all free to make our own arrangements. But it's always been a rule of mine not to mix pleasure with business, and I thought Avril did the same. Well, I was wrong. Stan Butterworth. After all I'd done for that man. Well, you reap as you sow. He's blown his last balloon.'

I'd been picking myself up, starting to feel a bit better, and then he had to go and tell me a thing like that.

He said, 'Now, I was wondering about you for Pwllheli. I've got

Rita Delmonte top of the bill, a band called the Nite Riders, and Titch and Lofty. Remember them from Aberystwyth?'

I remembered them very well. I was wondering whether Avril had shared her charms with Lofty as well as me and Stan Butterworth. Or was Lofty the doll? Anyway, that decided me. I couldn't work for Bryn Reynolds any more. Too many bitter memories. I said, 'No thanks, Bryn. As a matter of fact me and Sel may be joining forces again. There's talk of a United States tour.'

Then I had to tell Hazel. I said, 'I might go back on the road with Sel.'

'Where?' she said. 'Back on the road where?' She laughed when I said I was going to talk to Sel about a tour of the Midwest. 'That'll be a long way to bring your laundry home,' she said. 'You're dreaming. Well, you'd better wake up and talk to Bryn Reynolds.'

I said, 'I already did. All he had to offer was Pwllheli so I told him no thank you.'

She said, 'Then you can just phone him back and tell him yes please. You've got to do something, Cled. I can't have you mooching around here, burning electric and being sarcastic to my gentlemen.'

That was because I'd laughed one time when some novelties salesman suggested we were both in the same line of business. 'Sales is a solo act,' he said. 'Every time you walk in to see a buyer and slap your order book on the counter, it's like standing in the spotlight at the Swansea Grand. You're out there on your own.' Anyhow, I don't believe he heard me laugh. He was too busy fascinating my wife with his Welsh dragon pencil tops.

I said, 'Bryn Reynolds isn't the only one putting shows on. I've got contacts. I might get a season in Spain. Benidorm. There's plenty of work there. I'd be gone for months. Would that suit you?'

'Spain!' she said. 'More silly talk. And meanwhile somebody else is snapping up Pwllheli. You know your trouble, Cled? You've got a highly inflated idea of yourself. To hear you talk you're some big star. Well, you're not. You're run of the mill. You think you're God's gift to women. Well, you're not that either.'

Jennifer Jane slammed her bedroom door. It was already closed, so she must have opened it so she could slam it.

I stayed very calm. I went upstairs, packed a bag and slipped out the back way. I said, 'I've had enough, Penri. Enough of not getting due recognition.'

He said, 'Pwllheli wouldn't have been bad. You might have built on it, for next year.'

I said, 'It's not just that. I've had enough of men in shiny-arsed suits winking at my wife, giving her promotional biros. Enough of the bloody buggering rain.'

He said, 'I can see you're out of sorts.'

I did phone Hazel.

She said, 'If you look lively and get down to Moira Street, Probert's are looking for a piano salesman.'

I said, 'I'm not going to be a piano salesman, Hazel.'

She said, 'Are you in a railway station?'

I said, 'No. I'm at London airport.'

She said, 'Does that mean you've left me?'

And then my money ran out.

TWENTY-SIX

'I'll send Blue,' he said. 'He'll meet you off the plane.'
There had been a lot of changes at Desert Star and Blue was
one of them. He was Sel's driver, bodyguard and personal assistant, and he lived in one of the guest bungalows. Sel had bought the
house next door and knocked it down, so he could enlarge the garden
and have more rooms built. From the street all you could see were
yuccas and prickly pears, and a high wall painted pale peach.
Everybody knew who lived there, but nobody made a fuss about it.
That was a nice feature of Las Vegas. You didn't get people cruising by, rubbernecking, not in those days.

He'd had a glass arcade built between the pool and the breakfast
terrace, filled with banana palms, and a pair of panthers guarding
each end. They were life-size, covered in flock and wired up to roar,
except to me they looked more like they were yawning than roaring
and the noise they made sounded like a toilet chain being pulled. But
Sel was very proud of his jungle atrium, as he called it. His pride
and joy, though, were his raised flower beds filled with Mr Starlight
roses. 'Fortunes may change,' he said. 'Sometimes you're in, sometimes you're out. But once you've had a floribunda named after you
they can't take that away.'

Mam was very happy about me visiting. It was the warmest
welcome I ever remember getting from her. 'This is how we should
be,' she said. 'Proper family together. We don't need outsiders.'

Sel said, 'Hazel's not an outsider. Cled should have brought her
with him. I'd love to have her here.'

A trial separation, that's how I saw it. Time for both of us to review the situation.

Mam said, 'Wives hardly ever fit in. You do your best to guide your boys but in the end you have to let them realise their own errors. Well, now Cledwyn has realised his.'

I said, 'It's not a question of errors. I'm here to talk business with Sel.'

'A bit late for that,' she said. 'You should have stuck with him when you had the chance. Made something of yourself instead of vegetating in Llandudno. Boffs don't run boarding houses. Boffs perform.'

I said, 'I perform.'

'Aberystwyth!' Mam said. 'Morecambe! They're for no-hopers.'

Sel said, 'Now, Mam! You didn't say that when I was there.'

She said, 'That's because you were only there out of the kindness of your heart. You went to give your brother a helping hand, instead of taking your mother on a star-studded cruise, which you could have done. What kind of business are you here for, Cledwyn? If you need work you can be my driver. Selwyn will pay you. Then I won't have to be driven around by a black man.'

I said. 'I'm here to talk Boff Brothers business. We had a great success in Morecambe, didn't we, Sel? Something we could build on.'

'Yeah,' he said. 'Yeah. I'm mulling it over. Why don't you take young Ricky to Malibu for a few days, while I'm mulling? Take one of the cars.'

Ricky hardly left his room, except for mealtimes. As Pearl said, he should have been in school but he'd never really settled down after Betsan uprooted him from Birmingham. He hadn't found it easy to make new pals. And not being gifted at sports hadn't helped him get along with his new dad. I think Larry might have taken better to a lad who could hit a ball.

Sel said, 'He'll be all right. He'll find something he's good at, give him time.' So he was allowed to stay at home, plucking at a guitar and trying out different hairstyles.

Mam said, 'He's been to school. He was too advanced for the class they put him in.' She made him sound like a chip off his great-grandad.

I said, 'Do you want to go to Malibu, Ricky?'

'Don't mind,' he said.

That was teenagers for you. No enthusiasm for anything. I'd read in the papers that they were becoming the most influential age group in the world.

I said, 'Want a trumpet lesson? When I was your age I practised for hours, didn't I, Mam? Trumpet, piano. I could show you the basics.'

'No,' he said, 'it's all right.'

Suited me. I didn't want to be a babysitter. I wanted to get my new career under way and it was proving very hard to get Sel to sit down and talk. There was never any sign of him till the afternoon. I'd have my breakfast outside, under the awning, and then play one of the pianos.

Pearl loved tunes by Jerome Kern. 'You better had stop, Mr Cled,' she'd say. 'I already polished this room twice over.'

I'd take the runabout sometimes, drive down to the Strip late morning and make myself known to the showroom managers, but it was Sel I was waiting on and sometimes it'd be three o'clock before he put in an appearance. And Mam was like a guard dog. She wouldn't let anyone give his door a gentle tap. 'He needs his sleep,' she'd say.

And Pearl'd say, 'Only because he stays up all night watching fool movies. What he needs is regularity and fresh air. He should play golf.'

A lot of Sel's neighbours whiled away their days at the Sahara Country Club, hitting a few balls and sinking a quantity of drink, but of course they weren't appearing in cabaret. I knew from my own days in show business that if you're in the spotlight till three in the morning you do need time out of the public eye. When you've been out there, practising your craft, you can't just come home, put the cat out and go to bed. You have to wind down.

His fans would have been surprised to see him when he did crawl out. In the magazine pictures he was always wearing silk pyjamas or a nice, cheerful leisure shirt. They'd show him arranging a vase of Nile lilies, or getting ready for a fancy dinner, checking the table settings were perfect. But that was done for the photographs. I never saw him in any silk pyjamas. He wore the same old dressing gown he'd had at Mission Avenue and he'd slop around like that till it was time for Blue to drive him into town. And there were never any fancy dinners either, although the table with the elephant tusk legs was always kept laid, with crystal and linen, and a little silver pepper and salt for every seat. You could walk in any hour of the day or night and think the Aga Khan was expected. But we ate in the kitchen as a rule.

Sel lived on ice cream and cigarettes but Ricky ate everything Pearl put in front of him: fried chicken, macaroni cheese. When Mam had first moved in there had been ructions in the kitchen. Pearl didn't understand about the kind of gravy we'd had in Birmingham and Mam was scandalised to see her putting strawberries in a lettuce salad. It had gone as far as bags being packed and they weren't Mam's bags. But Pearl loved Sel like he was her own, so she'd unpacked her bags and tried to work alongside Mam, and her patience had paid dividends because once Mam discovered the slot machines she lost interest in how the gravy was made.

She'd have Randolph drive her to the Tumbleweed with a bag full of nickels and dimes, and then he had to stay with her, so that if she needed to answer a call of nature she wouldn't have to leave her machine unattended and risk somebody else winning her jackpot. Four or five days a week she did that, if she wasn't booked to make a celebrity appearance. And Randolph had his instructions. Escorting Mam to the Tumbleweed took precedence over the gardening and the odd jobs, and when all her money was gone he had to top her up with more. I couldn't see any satisfaction in it myself, sitting in the gloaming when the sun was shining outside, but Mam never tired of it. She dressed up and kept to a timetable, as if she was going to a job of work. They had slot machines at the Flamingo, where Sel was showcasing. She could have gone there and had VIP treatment, but she said the slots at the Tumbleweed were better value and anyway, she didn't like distractions. People recognised her sometimes, from her custard adverts, and thronged her for her autograph.

She had me escort her to *Showtime with Mr Starlight* a couple of times too, although it had no appeal for me, sitting out there with the mugs when I should have been performing. I preferred a nice rib dinner followed by *Nudes on Ice*. You could hang your hat on some of those girls' nipples.

I'd say to Sel, 'Well? Have you mulled?' And I'd play one of his old favourites, 'An Angel Passed', 'Time on my Hands', to get him in the mood.

'I save that stuff for the ladies in Wisconsin,' he said. 'Here you're singing over the chinking of glasses, for one thing. And you have to keep things light and cheerful. People don't come to Vegas to have their heart strings pulled. They want "Zip-ah-dee-doo-dah".'

So I played 'Zip-ah-dee-doo-dah'. I said, 'I'm adaptable.'

'It's not that easy, Cled,' he said. 'I've got a regular set-up here. Dusty plays for me here, Tubby plays for me when I'm on the road. I can't start changing everything just because you've blown into town.'

I said, 'As I recall, from events in Atlantic City, you can do anything you like.'

'Cled,' he said. 'Don't get me wrong. It's nice having you here, but don't you think it's time to sober up? Work things out with Hazel?'

I'd had Dilys on at me too, and Jennifer Jane.

Dilys said, 'It makes me very sad, Cled, very sad indeed. And I don't want to hear any tales. Hazel's always been a good friend to me.'

Jennifer said, 'I don't want to hear anybody's side of it, Daddy. I've got exams.'

I said, 'I'm not going back, Sel. I'm like a lodger in that house. Waiting in line behind her gentlemen for the All-Bran every morning. Having to go to Penri Clocker's house every time I want to play. So if you don't want me here, just say the word. I'll make my own way. I've still got contacts.'

'Don't talk so daft,' he said. 'Of course I want you here. Look, I have got something in mind, if you were to be here permanent.'

I said, 'Now you're talking!'

He said, 'I'm not getting rid of Dusty and I'm not getting rid of Tubby, so you can forget that. But there's that lot I bought on Tropicana standing idle. I've had in mind to put a club on it, only I never seem to get round to it. That'd be something you could do.'

I said, 'You mean play?'

He said, 'First you have to build it, open the doors, do the hiring. After that you can play. Play, count the takings, do a striptease if you like. It'd be yours. But think it over, Cled. It's a big step. You should talk to Hazel.'

But Hazel didn't want to talk to me. The minute she heard my voice she'd put the phone down. And anyway, I'd already made up my mind, assisted by a certain little lady called Lupe Leon.

I met Lupe at one of Thelma Arden's parties, across the street from Desert Star. Thelma always had a house full of company. The Nulties, the Pecks, the Winegartners, the whole Vegas crowd, plus whoever happened to be in town: Harry Belafonte, Joey Bishop, Mitzi Lamour. People would gather around the pool or in the pool, because there was a fibreglass waterfall and a swim-up bar that served every drink you could name.

They'd wheel a piano out on to the sun deck and I'd be asked to play. Sel would never sing, though. Sometimes he didn't even show up, but if he did he'd just sit in the shade, drinking vodka and Coke. He got his suntan out of a bottle and the only pool he'd ever go in was his own. 'All those people!' he'd say. 'All those little bits of skin floating off! It's disgusting. Anyway, Thelma's pool is over-chlorinated. It'd ruin my hair.'

Thelma had a high-backed peacock chair she reserved specially for Mam, and there she'd sit, holding court and eating everything she was served. One of Pearl's cousins cooked for Thelma. There'd be sausages roasted on sticks and fresh-popped buttered popcorn, just to keep you going till the roast was ready. Loin of pork cooked on a spit, and baked potatoes and home-made ice cream. It was a very nice way of life and you could never do it in Llandudno. They don't have the weather for it.

When Lupe found out I couldn't swim she wouldn't leave me alone till I learned. She had starred in a number of films that called for a girl who could dive and turn somersaults and look good underwater, and when the demand for that fell off she'd gone into business, training her own squad of Aquarettes. They travelled all over the world performing in water spectaculars. Lupe could do anything underwater and she did. She definitely helped me to get over Avril. It was thanks to her I learned to do the doggy paddle. It was thanks to her I decided to stay on in Vegas and open the Old Bull and Bush: a traditional British pub, with horse brasses and a beam-effect ceiling and an upright piano played by Mine Host. I was star of my own show every night of the week, with good cold beer on tap and some toothsome wenches working the pumps.

TWENTY-SEVEN

Sel lost his libel case against *Uncensored*, but then he went back for more, a glutton for punishment, suing them for damages caused by invasion of his private life.

I said, 'How can you be entitled to a private life when you bring books out with pictures of you sitting in your bathtub?'

He said, 'Bringing out books is a way of allowing my fans to share my fabulous lifestyle. All my ladies, sitting in their little houses, dreaming. It cheers them up to see me with my nice things. It makes them feel like they really know me. And they're respectful, Cled. They enjoy what I give them and they don't ask for more. They never cross that line.'

I said, 'I don't see how you can pick and choose. Once you're known for being known, people are bound to start going through your dustbins.'

He said, 'Well, it's plain bad manners. If you invited me round for tea, you wouldn't expect me to start peering under your beds, rooting round in your cupboards. What's wrong with these jerk-offs? I work hard. I take care of my own. Why won't they leave me in peace?'

Milo said, 'Selwyn's trouble is he's old-fashioned. He needs to move with the times and quit beggaring himself with lawsuits.'

Milo was right. For one thing, homosexuality had come in. People had gone on marches demanding the right to it. There had even been a march in Cardiff. I remember Penri saying to me, 'I hope it doesn't become compulsory!'

I remember saying to Hazel, 'I didn't realise there were such things in Wales,' which got me into trouble with Jennifer.

'They're not things, Daddy,' she said. 'They're gays. And you didn't know about them because they were hiding in the closet. Well, now they're out and quite right too. It's healthier.'

I said to Sel, 'The way you are, you know? It's not the terrible thing it was. According to Jennifer Jane everybody's coming out of the closet.'

'Good,' he said, 'all the more room in there for me.'

Milo said, 'You could be the height of fashion.'

'No, thank you,' he said. 'Retro, that's me.'

I'd never heard it called that before.

The tide had turned against him, but he seemed to relish the idea of fighting it. 'I've done very well in life ignoring trends,' he said, 'so I see no reason to change.'

But then one man started taking a special interest in him and one man can drag you down, if he sets his mind to it. His name was Craig Vertue and I don't know what he'd done before, but by 1978 he was a full-time professional homosexual. He was everywhere: in the newspapers, on the telly. He was one of Sel's own kind and yet he turned on him. 'Men like Sel Starlight', he said, 'should be helping gay kids feel good about themselves. He should be saying "it's OK, love yourself". Starlight's fans are the very moms these kids are scared to come out to. He could make a difference. It offends me to see a man who could be a role model hiding behind his mother's skirts.'

Milo Freeman believed there was a whole new future for Sel, appearing on TV shows talking about how happy he was to be 'that way'. 'Gay Pride,' he said. 'It's kinda catchy. You could cash in big time. Look at Vertue. He's on the box more than you are. Think of all those fags who'll start buying your records.'

Sel said, 'You know, Cled, I always thought I was one of Mother Nature's slip-ups. Like having an extra finger? It's not the easiest thing in the world but it's not the worst. I never expected any sympathy. But I never saw it as something to brag about either. As far as I'm concerned it's just one of those things, but now, to listen to people like Vertue, it's better than coming up on the Treble Chance. According to him, the old marrieds are the ones to be pitied, sitting there in their fireside chairs, photo of the kiddies on the mantelpiece. A fate worse than death, according Craig Vertue. Well, he loses me there.'

Sel went to see Kaye Conroy. He said, 'Kaye always had the right instincts. I'd dump Milo tomorrow if she'd take me on.' He wanted to redesign himself, to get Vertue off his back and still keep his lady fans loyal.

'Get outta here!' she said. 'I don't want your ten per cent. I'm too old and tired. But I'll give you my opinion for free. Don't go baring your soul. Those shows, they're just a way of making cheap television and once you've given away your mystery you can never get it back. Don't go on marches. Don't start wearing badges, nor workmen's jeans. Have you seen the way folk are dressing these days? Have you seen that Barbra Streisand? You don't need to redesign anything. Stay as sweet as you are. Go back on the road and give them more of the same. Whatever happens, there'll always be a market for sequins and a nice demeanour.'

And he followed her advice.

Milo said, 'You can forget Fenway Park. You can forget the Megadome. They want Elton John.'

Sel said, 'Fair enough. Didn't you always tell me this is a big country? I'll go where I'm needed.'

He played towns so small they didn't even have a set of traffic lights and he blinded them with his costumes. 'Capes,' he said. 'I'm experimenting with capes again. Celeste's wiring me up with little electric light bulbs, and she's making some with surprise linings too, so just when they think they've seen it all I can swish it open and voila! Rhinestones as far as the eye can see! Some of them are so heavy Blue's going to have to walk behind me with it draped over a special trolley.'

Milo said, 'Crazy. He's spending more to earn less. Ruining himself.'

Sel said, 'Prairie Home, I opened in a gold Spandex all-in-one and matching boots, gave them "Sweet and Lovely" and "There'll Be Some Changes", then I said, "Well, now you've seen me in my gardening clothes I'll go and smarten up a little." That's when I hit them with the cape, duck egg velvet lined with premium marabou over matching trousers and a white lace shirt, They went crazy. Somebody shouted, "Are they real feathers?" so I had her brought up on stage to test them for herself. I said, "Don't be shy. Have a good feel. There's nothing fake in this show." They loved it. I'm climbing back, Cled. I'm so out of fashion I'm going to be the next latest thing.'

And in a funny way he was right. The more he stayed out in Nebraska and Iowa, pleasing the ladies, the more bad write-ups he got; and the more bad write-ups he got the more the ladies flocked to his shows.

Craig Vertue wrote, 'That self-loathing piece of work Mr Starlight is at it again, twinkling his way across redneck territory trimmed up like a Christmas tree. Does he think he passes for Mr Straight? Hello, Selwyn! Don't you know "straight" is so "yesterday"?'

He got nasty post too. Pearl showed me a parcel that was delivered one morning. You could smell what was in it. She said, 'He used to get nice things, Mr Cled. Scarves and candy and toys for the dogs, but now you never know what you'll find. I don't understand it. That boy never harmed a fly.'

I said, 'There are certain people who're annoyed with him. They think he should stand up and be counted, if you get my meaning.'

She said, 'I'm not paid to get meanings. I'm paid to pick up this house and take care of Mr Sel. Well, one of these days he'll be getting a bomb, then we'll all go up in smoke and that'll be that.'

Mam said, 'It's time he got himself a proper bodyguard, with a gun. That Blue does too much smiling and admiring himself in the mirror. He doesn't even have a proper name.'

I said, 'You realise what's behind all this, Mam?'

'I do,' she said. 'It's sheer envy.'

I said, 'No. It's about his private life. Everybody knows what he is, but Sel won't admit it. And he won't get any peace till he does.

He might just as well go on the *Johnny Carson Show* now and get it over and done with. Admit that he's a cream puff.'

She said, 'He is not! It wasn't his fault things didn't work out with that bottle blonde.'

I said, 'Mam, face facts. He wears Elizabeth Arden on his face.'

'Of course he does,' she said. 'So do I. We have to be photogenic at all times.'

I said, 'He played dollies' tea parties till he was nine.'

'And you wet the bed,' she said. 'But we don't talk about that any more.'

I said, 'All right. Why has he never married?'

'Because we're happy the way we are,' she said.

There was no talking to her.

I said, 'There's no shame in it any more, Mam. Everybody's equal now.'

'No they are not,' she said. 'Selwyn is one in a million and you're just making up stories. You're plain jealous because he's a star and you couldn't even get Pwllheli.'

But I hadn't wanted Pwllheli. And I'd put all that behind me. I was very happy, running the Old Bull and Bush, playing my cockney singalong medley every night, regaling the punters with my show business reminiscences. Jennifer Jane was talking to me again. I had Pearl to look after the inner man and Lupe taking care of all the other bits.

The only loose end was Hazel and Dilys never let me forget it. She said, 'She's not eating. She's wasting away.'

Of course, Dilys's idea of wasting away wasn't everybody's.

Jennifer said, 'Mummy's all right. She's going to keep fit. She's started having muesli instead of a fry-up.'

Dilys said, 'She hardly takes any gentlemen in now. She says she can't be bothered. It could be she's going through the You Know What.'

But Hazel had gone through the You Know What when I was still on the scene.

Dilys said, 'She's got that little baby on her mind. Wondering where she is in the world, wondering what's become of her. Sometimes they come looking for their real mam, you know, once they're grown? I think she's hoping her own little bab'll turn up.'

I said to Jennifer, 'Your Aunty Dilys thinks your mother's depressed. There's something you should know about. It happened years ago. Before you came along.'

She said, 'Not the little mishap? Mummy already told me.'

I said, 'What do you think?'

'What is there to think?' she said. 'She told me about Stanley as well.'

I said, 'Who's Stanley?'

She said, 'You know! Stanley. The biscuit salesman. I kind of knew. Still, it's pretty gross to be told.'

I said, 'What, is he on the scene? Is he living at Hazelwyn?'

'Not any more,' she said. 'You remember him! The one with the slippers.'

I said, 'So you think she's all right?'

She said, 'I'm sure she is, Why? You hoping to come back?'

That was out of the question, of course. I had a business in Vegas that couldn't be left. Cled Boff *was* the Old Bull. I said, 'No. I just wondered. I never wanted her to suffer.'

'Right,' she said. 'I'll tell her you asked.'

TWENTY-EIGHT

Over the years Sel and Milo had fallen out more times than I could count, but when he heard Milo had collapsed, eating a filet mignon at the Merimee restaurant, he rushed to New York to be at his side. 'Too late, Cled,' he said when he called. 'He never regained consciousness. That man was like a father to me.' Then he realised what he'd said. Sometimes, even when it's a sad occasion, you can't help but laugh. But Sel was a sentimental soul. He was very good at funerals. He was asked to be a pall bearer, but with his being six inches taller than the other gents, it would have given the casket an unsightly tilt, so he withdrew. But he did sing 'Oh My Papa' by special request of Milo's daughter. All the years I knew him I hadn't even realised he had a daughter.

I said, 'This could affect Sel's prospects. One thing about Milo, however bad things got he always pulled something out of the bag.'

Mam said, 'They'll be falling over themselves to represent him. He'll be able to pick the crème de la crème.'

Sel usually had a good nose for smelling a rat, especially the type of rat who talks business at another man's graveside, but it failed him for once. Maybe it was the upset over Milo that left him off his guard. Whatever the reason, by the time he came home from New York he was already under new management. The kind you might live to regret.

Hallerton Liquorish was a youngster, not much more than thirty, and full of big ideas. He represented a rock band called Scum that seemed to be famous mainly for the trail of stains they left wherever they stayed. If you offered me a thousand dollars I couldn't whistle you one of their tunes. He also had on his books a cabaret comic who was very popular due to the colour of his language and a certain Sheree, whose claim to fame was that he'd started life as a boy called Ed and somewhere along the way he'd got rid of his surname plus one or two other bits and pieces.

I said, 'Are you sure you're doing the right thing? What kind of company are you going to be keeping?'

'Never mind the company,' he said. 'I like this boy's attitude. He doesn't start telling you why you *can't* do things. Milo could be too cautious. But Hallerton, he's full of ideas and energy. I love that.'

Sel could have afforded to ease up if he'd wanted. He had all those properties bringing in rent and parcels of land he was sitting on. He owned the Double Down Club in Vegas and the Backdoor Club in San Francisco. He'd done very well out of his investments, made a killing when all the Kaycee companies were bought by Premier, and he'd made another smart move going into fitness and leisure centres with Betsan's husband, Larry. He could just have played the Show Room when it suited him and spent the rest of his time by the swimming pool, counting his money, but he wouldn't settle for that. The fact was when Sel wasn't performing he didn't really know what to do with himself.

I like a good murder mystery myself but the only books I ever saw Sel open were the ones about Mr Starlight. I'd sometimes play a game of pool with Blue, but Sel never would. He had a full-size table but I don't think he even knew how to hold a cue. Buying things was his only pastime. And then making more money to buy more things.

He said, 'Hallerton's lining up some great TV opportunities.'

The thing was, though, television had changed. Solo spots on family music shows were a thing of the past and Sel was into extra time for being a heart-throb. Those dimples of his looked all right on nicely lit photos, but on the screen he looked quite portly.

'Game shows,' he said. 'Hallerton's right. I've got exactly what it takes. I'm a household name. The ladies love me. And I'm quick with an audience. It'll be money for old rope.'

I said, 'Do you need the money?'

'I can always find a worthy home for it,' he said.

Silly things, he bought: a silver tea set, supposed to have belonged to some king of Portugal, yet nobody ever had tea at Desert Star; a chandelier he didn't have a place for; a fancy four-wheel drive for Blue.

Blue wasn't a boy I ever really took to. He was clean and polite, but there was a crafty side to him. He was paid, he got a beautiful place to live and all kinds of extras, anything he liked the look of Sel bought it for him and he was supposed to be on call to Sel around the clock, but the minute he thought he was off the leash, any time he was sure Sel wouldn't come looking for him, he'd be off downtown, drinking with boys of his own age. He was only twenty-four. It must have been boring, waiting around to drive the boss home from the Strip. Watching TV with him till he was ready to fall asleep. Once or twice I heard them having words. Blue was in the bungalow next to mine and Sel always came there last thing, not wanting to disturb Mam with the noise of them playing backgammon.

Sel recorded a pilot for a show called *Anybody Can Play*, which never came to fruition, and then one for VTV, reviving a programme that had been very popular in the Fifties. And that one flew.

'I got it!' he said. He was dancing around in his swimming trunks. 'You're looking at the new presenter of *Queen for a Day*!'

Pearl was thrilled. She said, 'I never missed a show. Artie Deane used to present it and I didn't care for him, but I still never missed a show. I cried buckets.'

I said, 'Will you do any singing, Sel?'

'Sure,' he said. 'I'll be singing *Queen for a Day*.'

Mam said, 'Whatever it is, I'm sure it'll be lovely.'

Betsan said it sounded like a freak show to her.

Three ladies were brought on, one by one, and Sel had to chat to them, find out the story of their lives and it would always be a hard-luck story. Then the audience had to decide which was the most tragic case, which was the most deserving of winning the prize, and according to how loud they clapped, so it registered on a dial and the lady who got the highest score was crowned Queen for a Day. The prize was a washer-dryer, a new frock, a manicure and various other kinds of beautification.

I agreed with Betsan. I said, 'What kind of person goes on the television to plead poverty? You used to turn the telly on to get taken out of yourself, see people with some talent, not people bragging about their tragedies.'

But Sel didn't see it that way. He said, 'These aren't the kind of ladies to feel sorry for themselves. They're just telling their story and having a bit of fun. Anybody can hit hard times. And nobody goes home from my show empty-handed. The runners-up get a bouquet and a jar of face cream. And they're all so sweet, Cled. I'd have three Queens every show if it was up to me.'

Queen for a Day went out twice a week, in the afternoons. While a series was running, Tuesdays and Thursdays from three to half past, you got no sense out of any member of the fairer sex. Pearl and Mam watched it, although on different sets. Thelma cancelled her golf for it. Lupe wouldn't answer her phone when it was on. Even Betsan tuned in. 'Just while I'm on the exercise bike,' she said. 'It helps pass the time.'

Sel had a big hit on his hands. After the first series Premier re-issued his old *Simply Starlight* album and it went straight into the charts. His face was everywhere again. The *Daily News* called him 'Her Majesty, Mr Starlight'. *Queen for a Day?* they said, or Queen for a thirteen-week series? The *New York Times* said the show had all the hallmarks of quality broadcasting: laughter, tears, a man in a shiny suit and a clapometer.

But Sel said smart-ass critics didn't bother him. 'They're a smug bunch,' he said, 'hanging around waiting to bury another tryer. Well, any damned fool can criticise.'

He was riding high and then he received the cherry to top it all: an invitation to attend a soirée at the White House. This wasn't a first. He'd sung for Ike and Mamie Eisenhower back in 1956 and that had been a great honour because it was before he'd become an American. But this time it was for President and Mrs Reagan and that meant everything to him. 'The pinnacle of my achievements,' he said. He was one of the Reagans' biggest fans. 'They believe in God, country and low taxes,' he said, 'same as I do. They're cheerful and friendly, and Nancy's so beautiful. I may just pick her up and bring her home, keep her on a shelf with my figurines.'

It was his White House engagement that prevented him flying to England for Jennifer Jane's graduation. And Lupe was very put out about the timing as well.

She said, 'You can't go. Sammy'll be in town. I'm giving a party.' I'd waited a long time to meet Sammy Davis Junior, but the day your little girl passes out as a doctor isn't a day you'll even consider missing.

Lupe didn't understand that. She'd never had children. 'Why bother?' she said. 'Hell, you haven't seen the kid in years.' Things became quite cool between me and Lupe after that.

Sel said, 'Tell them to put it back a week. I can't say no to the President of the United States.' But the University of Liverpool couldn't make allowances for Mr Starlight's social arrangements.

Jennifer said, 'Just as well. What if he'd turned up covered in flashing light bulbs? Anyway, I'm only allowed two tickets. I did tell you.'

It was a pity because he had been a big encouragement to her, sending her humorous little cards, and money, so she could study hard and not knock herself out working for pin money like a lot of them had to. It would have been fitting for him to be there.

But it wasn't to be. He had to go to Washington DC to sing 'Bless This House' and I had to go to England on my own. I had to face Hazel for the first time in five years.

TWENTY-NINE

I went to Dilys's for the night before I drove to Liverpool. She said, 'You're going to see a difference in Hazel.'

I said, 'I suppose you knew about Stanley?'

'Yes,' she said. 'No. It wasn't Stanley. You mean Trevor. Travelled in office stationery.'

I could have sworn his name was Stanley. I said, 'I'm sure Jennifer Jane said he sold biscuits?'

'No,' she said. 'Sticky labels. Window envelopes. All that sunshine must be addling your memory.'

I said, 'She involved with anybody at the moment?'

Dilys said, 'Are you?'

I said, 'When are you going to come and visit?'

'When it's time to bury Mam,' she said.

I said, 'Don't wait for that. She's going to see us all out.'

The graduation ceremony was at eleven o'clock. There were hundreds of people milling about outside the hall. It caused me a pang of sadness, seeing all those couples, arm in arm, sharing a proud moment.

I was waiting on line with my ticket when Hazel claimed me. 'Hello, Cled,' she said. 'You've got a suntan.'

She was wearing her hair shorter than I'd ever seen it, very sporty-looking, and a nice cherry-red trouser suit. She wasn't wearing her wedding ring. She noticed me noticing. 'Lost it,' she said. 'Down the drain, probably. It didn't fit me any more.'

I said, 'Well, we've got a nice day for it. I've brought my cine camera.'

'That's nice,' she said. 'Journey all right?'

I said, 'How are things?'

'Fine,' she said. 'Things are fine. The Cadwalladers have given up the Tal-y-Bont. Bought a retirement flat in Rhos. Sel all right? And your mam?'

It was a strange thing to be shuffling along in a queue having a conversation with your wife.

The three of us went to the Adelphi Hotel afterwards for an à la carte lunch. I ordered a bottle of their best champagne, but Jennifer said she'd sooner have a beer.

I said, 'We shall have to get used to calling you Dr Boff now. So what's next on the agenda?'

'MRCP,' she said.

More exams.

I said, 'At this rate you'll be running Glan Clwyd.'

'Yeah,' she said. 'That'd really be something to aim for.'

Hazel said, 'Conwy needs doctors, Jennifer. There's nothing wrong with going back to your roots.'

'Well, since you ask,' she said, 'I'm thinking of Australia. Somewhere where there are opportunities.'

Hazel put her knife and fork down. She didn't say anything, but she hid her meat under her veg and didn't eat another bite.

I said, 'Who's for pud?' I had my eye on the Steamed Syrup Sponge with Custard. I said, 'Pearl doesn't make custard. We've got a garage full of Creamola, but it's not the same.'

Jennifer said she didn't do puddings. 'Actually,' she said, 'I should be making a move. I've got stuff to do.'

Hazel said, 'Jennifer! Your daddy's come all the way from America to see you.'

'So?' she said. 'Nobody made him go to America. Did they?'

I said, 'Back to work, eh?'

She had to stay another year in Liverpool. Junior houseman, her job was called.

I said, 'Your Uncle Sel'd love to hear from you. He's very proud of you, you know?'

'Yes,' she said, 'I know. I wrote to him. We can get a beer later, if you like. I should be free about eight.'

Me and Hazel finished the champagne.

I said, 'It's understandable. I can't expect her life to come to a halt just because I'm in town. How about a crème brûlée?'

'Yes,' she said, 'I think I will. And I'll have a glass of Sauternes wine to go with it.'

I said, 'Got many clients in at the moment?'

'Two,' she said. 'That's all I do now. They look after themselves, really. They know where everything is.'

'Yes,' I thought, 'I'll bet they do.' I said, 'Dilys tells me you've started doing yogi.'

'Yoga,' she said.

I said, 'Get your legs round the back of your neck, can you?'

'No,' she said, 'I do it for inner tranquillity.'

I said, 'Betsan and Larry have a whole gymnasium in their house. Of course, it's his line of business. We've got one as well, but nobody uses it, really, apart from Blue.'

She said, 'He the boyfriend?'

I said, 'I don't know. He's on the payroll. He could be. Sel pads across the garden and watches telly with him. I mean, with those types how would you know? You're not going to see them canoodling on the settee, are you? I mean, what exactly do they do?'

'Cled,' she said, 'where have you been all your life?'

I said, 'So . . . Australia . . . I thought she might go to London, didn't you? Still, it might never come to it.'

'Oh, I think it will,' she said.

I said, 'Well, don't lose sleep over it. Twelve months from now she'll probably have some different scheme. She could be courting by then.'

'Yes,' she said. 'Courting. I haven't heard that expression in a long time.'

I said, 'And if she does go, you'll be able to visit her. Australia's not the other side of the world.'

I was hoping to cheer her up but I hadn't expected to make her laugh that much. People were turning round, looking at us, wondering what was so comical.

I said, 'Another glass of that Sauternes?'

'Yes,' she said, 'why not? And after that, I've got a double room upstairs, if you're in the mood for sexual intercourse.'

I hadn't lain in bed, dozing, in the middle of the afternoon since Avril. The curtains made everything look orange. I said, 'Did you plan this?'

'No,' she said, 'I don't plan anything any more. I expect you've got a girlfriend?'

As it happened I wasn't sure how things stood between me and Lupe. I said, 'Not really. The pub keeps me very busy. You seeing anybody?'

'Penri Clocker's a poor old wreck these days,' she said. 'Arthritis. Nerys takes him a dinner in every day, in an aluminium tray.'

I said, 'Remember the Ripening Room?'

She laughed. Her skin was still nice, for fifty-six. Very pale, but smooth. Lupe was the colour of mahogany.

I said, 'I've been trying to talk Dilys into coming to Vegas. Perhaps you could come with her?'

'The Lorina Dance School closed down,' she said. 'Did I already tell you that? And the Aphrodite chipper.'

I said, 'I've got my own bungalow, you know? Air-conditioning. Jacuzzi. Palm trees outside the window.'

She said, 'Dilys'll never come. She should do. See your mam one last time. But she won't leave her garden. She only comes to see me when the ground's too frozen for her to do anything else.'

I said, 'Hazel, I know we've had our ups and downs.'

'Mrs Cadwallader had a breast off,' she said. 'But she seems all right now. Yes, we have had our ups and downs, Cled. There have been times when I didn't like you very much.'

I said, 'Twenty-five years is a long time.'

'When you were doing those summer shows,' she said. 'Bragging about your hit single. Coming home smelling of women.'

I said, 'I never did.' I'd always been very careful about that.

'Now, Cled,' she said. 'It doesn't matter any more. You had your disappointments and you needed your little consolations.'

I said, 'I wouldn't say I've had disappointments. I've been successful in business. I've rubbed shoulders with the stars. Got a daughter who'll be able to take care of me in my old age.'

'It just seems to me', she said, 'you've always been in Sel's shadow. That must be hard.'

'Not at all,' I said. 'I'm a perfectly satisfied man.'

She said, 'Well, that's all right, then. Because what's Sel got, when all's said and done? Fifty years old and still living with your mam. Always having to get dressed up, always having to smile. Never knowing who his real friends are.'

I said, 'Are you going back in the morning?'

'Yes,' she said, 'in the morning. How about you?'

I said, 'Tonight. Take Jennifer for a beer and then head back to Dilys's.'

'Unless you stayed,' she said.

'Could do,' I said.

She said, 'It seems a pity to waste a double room seeing as Jennifer booked it.'

I said, 'It does.'

She said, 'You dripped custard on your nice shirt, Cled. I'll put it to soak in the sink. And then in the morning you could come back with me to Llan.'

I said, 'Well, there's my pub, that's the thing.'

'Just while I see to my gentlemen and pack a bag,' she said. 'If you really meant it. About visiting?'

THIRTY

I'd only been away two weeks but by the time I got back Blue was gone and I had a new neighbour: Brett. Another big blue-eyed boy. 'Husky' was how Hazel described him.

He was certainly nicer to get along with. He'd been a centurion in his previous position, at Caesar's Palace.

Hazel said, 'Why is your boyfriend living down the garden, Sel? Haven't you got room for him indoors?' She said it right in front of Mam.

Mam said, 'He's security. Twenty-four-hour security, protecting us from intruders. What's she doing here?'

I said, 'We don't get intruders.'

Sel said, 'It's only a matter of time. Either they'll be after my silver or they'll be after me. Thelma was broken into while you were in England. They took all her stereos and she slept through it all, didn't hear a thing.'

Mam said, 'And they left their visiting cards on her white carpet. She's had to have it all ripped up and replaced. Nobody has any manners any more, not even the burglars. I thought your wife was running a lodging house in Llandudno?'

I said, 'She's here on holiday.'

Sel said, 'Here on her second honeymoon, eh, Cled?' He was so thrilled I'd brought Hazel back with me.

I said, 'It's called a trial reconciliation.'

'Sure it is,' he said. 'Take her to Malibu. Take her to Van Cleef, buy her a new wedding band. Put it on my account.'

Hazel wasn't interested in going to California. She liked it at Desert Star. She swam in the pool every morning and used the treadmill that had been gathering dust. 'Why are we all eating on trays?' she wanted to know.

It was just a habit we'd got into: Mam in her room; Sel in his; Brett in the kitchen.

Hazel said, 'All these beautiful rooms. All that lovely food Pearl makes.'

'None of your business,' Mam said. 'We're happy the way things are.'

Hazel said, 'Well, at the very least I'm going to eat at a table, and Cled with me. Even if it's only the kitchen table.'

But Pearl insisted we should use the elephant tusk dining room. 'Now you're here, Mrs Cled,' she said, 'we're gonna do things properly.'

'When's she leaving?' Mam kept asking.

But Hazel was getting her sleeves rolled up at the Old Bull and Bush. 'Why don't you get some tankards, Cled,' she said. 'And a darts league? And who's this Loopy Lion everybody's worried I'm not going to like?'

'Don't leave us,' Sel kept saying to her. 'I know Cled's a boring old bugger, but we need your smiling face around here. This place was turning into an old age home.'

Mam was nearly eighty-nine. Pearl was seventy-five, Randolph must have been about the same. And young Ricky had moved out to live in sin with a pretty little blackjack dealer called Kim. Ricky was working part-time as a leprechaun at O'Lucky's Casino, but he was also starting to make a name for himself in the world of competitive eating. He'd got through the Nevada hot dog qualifiers, scoring thirty-eight in ten minutes, including the bread roll and tomato ketchup, so he was on his way to Coney Island for the 1981 championships.

Hazel said, 'I'd like to stay. But it's up to Cled.'

'Cled,' he said, 'beg this woman to stay.'

I said, 'I never thought you'd like it here.'

'Neither did I,' she said, 'but I do. I like the way people are so cheerful. I like being a thorn in your mam's side.'

Sel was still having trouble with Craig Vertue and others of his type. 'The Glads,' Sel called them. Glad to be Gay. They said he should be sending a message to young queers. 'Message!' he said. 'I already sent mine, Western Union. Mind your own business, stop. Stay out of mine, stop. Get a bloody life, stop.'

I said, 'What does Hallerton Liquorish think?'

He said, 'Hallerton thinks I should carry on doing what I do best, entertaining people. He wants to get me my own chat show.'

I said, 'I suppose your singing days are over.'

'Not at all,' he said. 'Once I get my own show, I shall be able to do whatever I want, in between chatting to my guests. A bit of the old soft-shoe shuffle with Liza. A little duet with Engelbert. And I'll tell you another thing. I'll only have true entertainers on my show, people *I* want. It'll be in the contract. I'm not having any boring old windbags on my show, flogging their latest book. You're going to have to sparkle to sit next to Mr Starlight. And I'll be a natural. I can sit on a couch and talk to anybody.'

It seemed a funny thing to get paid for, but as Kaye Conroy had rightly predicted, there was getting to be no place in television for skill and musicianship. 'Some day', she said, 'they'll have programmes about people doing absolutely nothing. Some day they'll have telly programmes about people watching telly programmes.'

But Sel loved television, especially if he was on it, and when he was invited to appear on *Levine Late*, hosted by Kooky Levine, he jumped at it.

Hazel said, 'Do be careful, Sel. What if you get asked something tricky?'

'I won't be,' he said. 'These things are all agreed beforehand.'

I said, 'Once those cameras are rolling anything could happen.'

'Cled,' he said, 'this is Mr Starlight you're talking to. You know me. Prepare, prepare, prepare some more. And I've got so much to talk about nobody else'll get a word in edgeways. My lovely homes, that's what people want to hear about. My work with sick kiddies. My fabulous lifestyle.'

We'd known Kooky Levine back in our early days at Kaycee, when he was trying to be a comedian. A hopeless case, in my opinion. He knew a lot of jokes but then, so does your average travelling salesman. There's more to it than that. You've got to have presence. You've got to have timing and a feel for your audience. But Kooky had managed to land himself a chat show, and Sel was invited to be on it with Chrissie France, another old friend from our supper club days, and Telly Savalas, who played Kojak. Only, as things turned out, Kojak cancelled at the last minute and they brought on a substitute. Sel came home from the studios looking very thoughtful.

Mam said, 'Did they love you, Selwyn?'

'Yes,' he said. 'They did.'

But then he went straight to his room and stayed there under a bed full of dogs till next day.

I said, 'What happened?'

'Vertue,' he said. 'He was the surprise guest. Don't worry. I fettled him.'

I said, 'Why didn't you pull out, as soon as you realised?'

'And disappoint my fans?' he said. 'Never. Anyway, I handled myself all right. It takes more than that dreary little runt to get the better of Mr Starlight. I came out on top.'

I said to Hazel, 'Talk about bad luck! Kojak cancelled and Sel's arch enemy was on instead.'

'You muggins!' she said. 'Kojak didn't cancel. It was all a put-up job.'

Then we saw the show.

Sel was in a jonquil flamenco shirt and burnt-orange pants embroidered with bugle beads.

Vertue was in his usual jeans and plaid shirt. He said his mission in life was to persuade gays to make themselves visible.

That got a laugh.

He said, 'Gays in the public eye should be just that, don't you think, Kooky? There are still queers hiding away in Straightsville afraid to come out and enjoy the daylight. Scared they'll lose their families, scared they'll lose their jobs. And that's no way for any human being to live, wouldn't you agree, Sel? As a completely impartial straight guy, Sel, wouldn't you say it's a tragedy to live a lie?'

Sel said, 'I've always believed in self-help. I've always agreed with the old saying, every cripple finds his own way of walking.'

Vertue said, 'Are you calling gays cripples?'

Sel said, 'You know damn well that's not what I said. But Craig, this is so boring. Why don't I tell you all about a plan I have to auction some of my spectacular costumes, to raise money for backward children.'

Vertue was wriggling around in his seat. 'Cripples! Backward children!' he said. 'What kind of language is that?'

Kooky said, 'How about you, Chrissie? Would you be glad to be gay?'

Chrissie France just sat there giggling.

Sel said, 'It's OK, Chrissie. Nobody's saying you have to be. Not yet, anyhow.'

Kooky said, 'Craig, our audience is maybe wondering, you're glad to be what you are and yet you're discriminated against? Is that right? Are you still a victim of discrimination?'

'Sure I am,' he said. 'My partner dies, do I have any rights concerning his cremation? No. His folks could spirit him away to Montana. Can we adopt? No. Can we take out a family subscription to the opera? No. But I'll tell you why I'm glad nonetheless. This is a battle to the death of the old order. Since Stonewall we've been throwing off our chains. Storming the citadels of repression and hypocrisy and I feel so proud to be a part of the struggle.'

He got a ripple of applause. He wiped a tear from his eye. 'In years to come', he said, 'there are going to be more than a few old closet queens who'll wish they'd been there too.'

Sel said, 'You make it sound like ruddy Agincourt.'

'Yes, well,' Vertue said, 'I guess this is something you can't comprehend, Sel, being such a down-the-line hundred-per-cent straight.'

He got a big laugh.

Hazel said, 'Turn it off, Cled. I don't want to watch any more.'

You could see the sweat breaking through on Sel's top lip. His shirt was straining at the buttons too.

Kooky said, 'Sel? A final word?'

Sel said, 'Yes. I'd just like to say to all those nice folk out there, don't lose sleep over this. Rise early, work hard, honour your father and mother. Keep your bedroom door closed.'

'OK,' Kooky said. 'We'll be back after the break with a song from Chrissie France.'

Hazel said, 'Whoever talked him into doing that show should be shot.'

I said, 'Nobody had to talk him into it.'

But he had looked terrible sitting on that couch. 'Like an over-weight old has-been,' Hazel said.

I said, 'But why did Liquorish get him to do it?'

'Because everybody'll be talking about it tomorrow,' she said. 'Because it made Sel look ridiculous and people love that. They'll show it over and over. You'll see.'

We didn't see Mam till the following morning.

I said, 'Did you watch it? What did you think?'

'I didn't need to watch it,' she said. 'Sel always looks lovely, whatever he does. It was on far too late for me.'

Sel said he hadn't bothered to watch either, but he'd been down in Brett's bungalow watching something. I'd seen him walking back to the house when I got up to pee.

'Vertue's a loser,' he said. 'I reckon I'm the most interesting thing that ever happened to him. Nobody would ever have heard of him if he hadn't picked on me. He should pay me a commission. Anyway, didn't I give him a trouncing?'

It was written up in all the papers. 'The old guard fighting off the new,' one of them said. 'Mr Starlight is Yesterday's Man.'

He said, 'Hallerton's been fielding calls all week. There's not going to be a studio couch in the country that doesn't have the impression of my backside on it.'

Hazel said, 'Be careful, Sel. Think of your fans. Think of how things look.'

'I am doing,' he said. 'That's why I'm going to Caliente Springs. Mudbaths. Gourmet salads. By the time I'm on *Johnny Carson* I'm going to look like a million dollars.'

THIRTY-ONE

Jennifer Jane didn't emigrate to Australia. She went to New Zealand to specialise in diseases of the heart.

Hazel: 'Well, that's that, then. I think it's time to get rid of Hazelwyn. What do you think?'

I said, 'You don't want to go back?'

'Not particularly,' she said. 'Why? Don't you want me here?'

It wasn't that. It was just taking some getting used to, after being a single man for a number of years. It wasn't only Lupe who had had her hopes raised. But I didn't have the heart to send Hazel away. She was so happy, puttering around with Sel's costumes, doing little repairs on them, chattering to Pearl in the kitchen.

I said, 'Yes. I'd like you to stay.'

Sel was very happy about it. 'Come to your senses at last,' he said. 'Hazel's a gem. Now we've got to work on Dilys. I'd love to get her out here.'

Hazel said, 'Leave Dilys to me. She'll come for your mam's ninetieth and she'll enjoy herself so much she won't want to leave.'

We were planning quite a gathering of the clan. Gaynor was going to come, first time she'd ever been abroad, although sadly Clifford didn't feel he could leave his shop. Betsan and Larry. Ricky and Kim. Even Jennifer Jane was trying to wangle some time off.

Sel was having Mam's portrait painted, top secret. There was a lady in Vegas who did it from a photograph and it was going to be unveiled the day of her birthday, when we were all assembled. He said, 'I've had a preview. It's beautiful. I think I'll get her to do me next, now I'm looking so rejuvenated.'

Sel had become a regular at the Caliente Springs health resort. He paid them good money and they fed him on celery juice. Pearl wanted to send Brett with a thermos of ice cream but Brett said it was more than his life was worth.

'Ten pounds,' Sel said. 'That's what the camera adds to you. So I've decided to lose twenty.'

I said, 'And how come your face is so shiny?'

He said, 'I think you mean dew-fresh. I've had a skin peel. You should get one.'

So the new slimline Mr Starlight kept popping up on chat shows, chatting with stars like Debbie Reynolds or Shelley Winters. Sometimes he'd take one of his little pooches along with him, as a conversational point. Sometimes he'd wear one of his beaded shirts and talk about the lack of glamour in the modern world.

I said, 'When's your next bout with Mr Vertue?'

'All in good time,' he said. 'It's some other poor bastard's turn.'

Craig Vertue was putting the arm on Rock Hudson.

'Buzzing round him like a blowfly,' Sel called it.

I said to Hazel, 'How can that be? Rock Hudson can't be a homosexual. He was married to a girl called Phyllis.'

'Who cares?' she said. 'All those beautiful films he made. And what's this Vertue person ever done? What pleasure has he ever brought to people?'

They finally met again on the *Merv Griffin Show*. Vertue, the same as always, blue jeans, thin as a garden cane, and Sel in embroidered trousers and a spotted shirt with big frilly sleeves.

Hazel said, 'He's turning himself into a fairground attraction.'

Sel was first on, talking about his early days. 'We had nothing, Merv,' he said. 'No toys. Hand-me-down clothes. I had to make my first costume out of one of my dear mother's tablecloths.' Ruddy whoppers, the lot of it. He had a farmyard and a bus conductor's outfit and roller skates.

Vertue was on after the commercial break. Sel always got to his feet when a new guest came on, even if it was a gent. But this time he didn't just stand there. He strode across to Vertue.

Hazel said, 'He's going to hit him!'

And that was what the audience seemed to think. Instead of applauding Vertue, it had gone quiet.

Sel towered over him. 'Craig,' he said, 'before you start, there's something I want to say. I know you'd like to make my life a misery, but it's not going to happen. You're just a humourless little creep, so I've decided to forgive you.' And he got him in a clinch and bent him over backwards and kissed him, a great big smacker, right on the mouth.

I said, 'Now that's something they'll show over and over.'

And they did. It became a very famous photograph.

Vertue just shook his head. And although he kept needling Sel as per, Sel was enjoying himself, winking at the camera, pretending to nod off when Vertue started his usual sob story.

Then he challenged him to an arm wrestle. 'Merv,' he said, 'I think you need more action on the show. So me and young Craig are going to provide it. We're going to settle our differences. Best of three.'

Sel won, of course. He always was strong, considering.

I said, 'You know something that mystifies me? His hair. It never changes.'

Hazel looked at me.

I said, 'Don't you think it's funny? His face gets older but his hair never looks any different.'

'It's a wig, Cled,' she said. 'Obviously.'

I said, 'Do you know that for a fact?'

'Yes,' she said.

I said, 'Did he tell you?'

'Yes,' she said. 'But he didn't need to. It's as plain as the nose on your face.'

I said, 'You've made my day. All those times he nagged me. All that grief he gave me.'

She said, 'You're not to bring it up. You're not to tell him I told you.'

I said, 'What does it matter, if you reckon it's so obvious?'

'His feelings matter,' she said. 'He doesn't like people knowing things about him.'

I said, 'I'm not people. What's he like underneath it? Is he as bald as me?'

'I don't know, Cled,' she said. 'I've never seen him. And if you say anything to him, I'll never forgive you.'

I didn't say anything to him. But the next time he was sitting cogitating on the edge of the pool I gave his hair a friendly tug and his hand flew up to save it. I jumped in, swam around for five minutes, then I hauled myself out and sat alongside him. I said, 'One thing about not having any hair. According to Lupe, you move through the water faster.'

He just sat there, dabbling his toes.

'All right,' he said eventually. 'So you've twigged. But you'd better keep your mouth shut. My fans love me the way I am and they don't want to hear any different.'

I said, 'I'm not going to tell. How come you've got that touch of silver on the temples?'

'Realism,' he said. 'Top of the range realism. Want to see?'

He had a Sheik of Araby theme for his bedroom at Desert Star. Orange silk swagged down from the ceiling and tacked to the walls, like a tent, and a black carved bedhead. Candle lanterns and cushions everywhere like an advert for Turkish delight. He'd had a pair of camel skin drums for bedside tables until they'd started to smell.

He took me into his dressing room, first time I'd ever set foot in there. There were dozens of suits and shirts lined up on rails, one for formal wear, one for casual, with a docket on each coat-hanger saying where he'd worn it and when. All his shoes were kept on trees. All his jumpers were folded on shelves, as if they'd never been worn.

He slid a mirror to one side and there was a cupboard behind it. Five plastic ladies' heads on a shelf, one bald, and the others wearing wigs. They all looked identical to me.

'No, they're not,' he said. 'That one's my newly trimmed look.

237

That one's my "due for a trim" look. This one's my "lightly bleached from the sun" look.'

I said, 'So what's that one?'

'Nightwear,' he said. 'It breathes better than the others.'

I said, 'And underneath, I suppose you're about the same as me?'

He said, 'We should start making a list for Mam's party. Get the invitations printed.'

I said, 'It's funny. I can't remember what it feels like to have hair. Why do you wear it in bed?'

'Because you never know your luck, our kid,' he said. 'You never know. I think we should have a dinner on the day of her birthday, just family. And then a bigger affair round the pool, for friends and neighbours.'

He'd sat down in front of the mirror. 'I thought we'd put on a little show for her,' he said. 'All her favourite songs?' He pushed his thumbs up under his hairline and worked them around as far as his ears, easing the wig away from his skin and, when he lifted it off, all he had under there were a few little whispy bits just above his neck. He said, 'Candy looks after them for me.' Candy was the girl who came once a week to do his nails. 'As you can see,' he said, 'this wouldn't be the right image for Mr Starlight. My fans have given me so much, Cled, so I make it a rule to keep on giving them what they expect: glamour, perfection. Understand? And that's why, if you ever breathe a word to anybody, I'll have Brett break your legs.'

I looked at him in the mirror. He winked at me. I was looking at an old man.

THIRTY-TWO

Dilys and Gaynor flew to Los Angeles to have a couple of days with Betsan before Mam's party. Betsan and Larry had a luxury home in Palm Desert. Larry's spa-gym leisure centres were doing very well. Then they all flew to Vegas. Sel had a costume fitting, getting ready for a new show at the Flamingo, so me and Hazel went with Brett to the airport. He was wearing a new livery Sel had designed for him, epaulettes and a peaked cap, but he didn't look very happy in it.

I said, 'What's up? Don't you like the colour?'

'Makes me look like hired help,' he said.

It was funny to see Betsan and Gaynor side by side after so long. You could argue Betsan had had a harder life, with Terry Eyles running off and leaving her with a bab to raise, but she looked ten years younger than Gaynor. That's a suntan for you. And having your own in-house fitness equipment.

Dilys said, 'I can't wait to see Sel. I hear he's been dieting.'

Hazel said, 'He goes to Caliente Springs and eats nothing but grapes.'

'Pineapple,' Brett said. 'He's on the pineapple diet. You can eat as much pineapple as you want.'

Pearl was out front in a clean apron and Mam came to the door when she heard the car. She was having one of her days of walking with a stick. 'I wouldn't need it,' she said, 'if there weren't dogs waiting to trip you up everywhere you turn in this house. You look washed out, Gaynor. You should take iron.'

Dilys said, 'Hello, Mam. You're looking spry.'

Mam said, 'I *am* spry. Roberts women don't deteriorate.'

Which wasn't true because Aunty Gwenny had to have water tablets and elastic stockings by the time she was sixty.

She said, 'You should get some weight off, Dilys. You'll never get to be my age, carrying all that weight. Selwyn's on the banana diet and he looks a picture. Bananas and ginseng.'

'And ice cream,' Pearl said. 'He still loves his Rocky Road.'

I wanted to take Dilys and Gaynor to the Old Bull and Bush, show them round my little empire, but Dilys wouldn't move till she'd seen Sel. She unpacked a photo album she'd put together. 'Here you are, Mam,' she said. 'The story of your life in pictures.'

Mam said, 'I don't need old photos. I'm on the television. Ninety years old and still working.' She'd just made a new advertisement for a safety buzzer that hung round your neck. It was for the elderly, in case they fell and need to buzz for someone to come and help them up.

Hazel started looking through the album. 'Who's this young soldier, Dilly?' she said. 'Is it your dad?'

Dilys said, 'No. I'm not sure who it is.'

Hazel said, 'What a shame. I suppose your mam's the only one who'd be able to tell us and she's not interested in looking.'

Dilys had even gone back to Ninevah Street and taken pictures, so Mam could see what had become of the old neighbourhood.

Mam said, 'I don't care about Ninevah Street. You have to look ahead, not back.'

But curiosity got the better of her. Hazel put the album down where she could reach it and she did pick it up. '1913,' she said. 'Priory Road. I was governess to three children, Gaynor, and I was only sixteen. See me? I wore my hair pinned up in those days. I always had pretty hair. It was a doctor's family. Three boys. I'll think of their names in a minute. And that's my brother Amos. Before he went to Flanders.'

There were pictures of all of us as kiddies and the outside of number 17, as it looked now, with double-glazed window frames and ruched blinds, and a sign that said 'Tara'.

I said, 'I thought they'd have knocked that down by know. Flattened the whole street.'

Dilys said, 'Oh, no. They call them starter homes now.'

Gaynor said, 'You haven't got a picture of Grandad.'

Dilys said she hadn't been able to find one.

Gaynor said, 'What happened to Grandad? I don't remember going to his funeral.'

Mam said, 'We lost touch. He always had to travel, to find work. We had the Depression and then the war. He was never the same, after the war.'

'Yes he was,' Dilys whispered to me. 'He was exactly the same.'

I couldn't help smiling.

Mam said, 'It was no laughing matter, Cledwyn. Those were hard times. Your grandad was a very gifted man, Gaynor. He had to travel to find the appreciation he was due. Same as Selwyn had to.'

Hazel said, 'What kind of business was your dad in, Cled? I don't remember.'

'Various,' Mam said.

Then Sel arrived and saved her from having to go into any details. We had an afternoon of jollification around the pool. Betsan painted Mam's nails. Hazel took Gaynor out to buy a swimsuit. Brett and Sel and Larry messed around with a giant water pistol. And Dilys lay alongside me on a lounger and roasted. 'I could get used to this,' she said. 'Sel looks terrible, Cled. Why didn't you warn me?'

I said, 'He's getting older. We all are.'

'Is that what it is?' she said. 'I suppose. You just don't expect it with Sel. You expect him always to look boyish.'

I said, 'I'll tell you something, if you promise not to let on.'

'What?' she said.

I said, 'That's not his real hair. It's a wig he's wearing.'

'Well, I know that,' she said. 'Everybody knows that.'

Jennifer Jane arrived late that night with a person we'd never even heard of: Fraser. She said he was a cardiologist, same as her, although he didn't look like one. He looked like a PE teacher.

241

Hazel said, 'You should have asked your Uncle Sel. You can't just turn up with extras.'

Sel said, 'It's all right, Hazel. There's plenty of room. I'll get Pearl to make up another bed.'

Hazel said, 'You will not. I'll do it. Pearl's got enough to do.'

Jennifer said, 'We don't need another bed. We'll bunk down together.'

Sel said, 'Not in my house, you won't. Whatever would your grandma say?'

'Jeeze,' she said, 'what's the big problem? I am twenty-seven years old.'

Fraser said, 'Calm down, Jen. No sense upsetting the olds. We'll get a hotel, no worries.'

Betsan said, 'I don't see what the fuss is about. Everybody sleeps together these days. It's been the trend for a long time.'

Sel said, 'Well, I don't follow trends, as you well know. And as far as I'm concerned Jennifer Jane doesn't get a double bed till I've sung at her wedding.'

So off they went, looking for a hotel, and it was after midnight.

'Bloody hypocrisy,' Jennifer said to me, 'considering the way everybody else in the family carries on.' And she slammed the door of the taxi so hard it made my ears ring. Nice start to a birthday party.

Hazel couldn't sleep and if she couldn't, I wasn't allowed. 'I'm embarrassed,' she said. 'Who is this Fraser anyway? And after everything Sel's done for her.'

I said, 'Times have changed, though. Betsan's right. Now they've got the Pill, everybody does it.'

Lucky buggers.

'I'm not talking about sex before marriage, Cled,' she said. 'I'm talking about manners. I don't care how old she is. As soon as she steps through the door tomorrow you're to make her apologise to Sel.'

But I didn't need to. Jennifer Jane ran straight to him and gave him a hug. 'Sorry,' she said. 'Jet-lagged. You know how it is?'

We all dressed up, even Ricky, black tie, best frocks. Except for the cardiologist. Jennifer Jane said it was called 'smart-casual', but it was what I would call a sports shirt and slacks.

The first thing was the unveiling of Mam's portrait. It stood six feet high and it was hung facing the front door, so it would be the first thing you saw as you came in. She was posed on a high-backed Lucite chair, wearing a red evening gown and a corsage of gardenias. Exactly as she was wearing for her birthday dinner. Everybody agreed it was a very good likeness.

Pearl brought in Mumm champagne and home-made cheese straws, and Sel proposed a toast. 'Mother, grandmother, great-grandmother, star of stage and screen,' he started.

Then Brett appeared, with a face like thunder. 'Well?' he said. 'Am I included or what?' They'd been arguing earlier because Brett thought he should have been invited to the dinner. He said, 'I thought I was family now?'

'You are, baby,' Sel said. 'But if you come we'll be thirteen round the table and I can't have that.'

Brett said, 'What about the slopehead? She ain't family.' Ricky's girlfriend was some kind of oriental. Very nice, though. Flat-chested, but always smiling.

There we all stood, champagne at the ready.

Sel said, 'Brett, don't make me mad now. Pearl's not complaining and she's not coming.'

I heard Pearl say, 'Pearl don't want to.'

Brett went off, scowling, and Sel picked up where he'd left off.

'We've all been privileged to know an amazing woman,' he said. 'A little girl from the valleys who went up to the big city to better herself. A wife and mother who always put her family first. And a natural talent, even if she waited till an age when most ladies are in their rocking chair before she became a star. They broke the mould after they made Anne Roberts.'

Hazel whispered to me, 'We can only hope.'

Sel said, 'So, Mam, here's to your next ten years!' And we all raised our glasses.

As soon as we went in Mam started rearranging the table. 'You move further down, Cledwyn,' she said. 'Then Ricky can sit by me. I don't see enough of him. And send Jennifer up to sit next to Ricky. That person she brought with her can sit with the Jap.'

We had melon with ham, veal cutlets with a selection of veg, and a strawberry soufflé.

Betsan said, 'Tell us about the olden days, Grandma. Tell us about Grandad.'

'Jennifer,' Mam said, 'have you got a ring?'

Jennifer said, 'Hunh?'

Mam said, 'Well, be sure you get one. You don't want to end up the way Betsan did.'

Sel said, 'What about when you were a girl? We'd all like to hear about that.'

'Best thing I ever did, leaving Pentrefoelas,' she said. 'It was all right for convalescents, but it didn't have enough scope for me. I was a trained pianist, you see. That's where you get your talent, Selwyn.'

Sel said, 'Well, Cled's the pianist around here.'

'But you could have been,' she said. 'You could have been any number of things.'

Betsan said, 'And where did you meet Grandad?'

'Can't remember,' she said. 'I had boys flocking around me. I could afford to take my pick and I chose the one with brains, like Gaynor did.'

Larry said, 'What about the next ten years? Any unfulfilled ambitions?'

'No,' she said. 'Except to meet Omar Sharif again. I met him at Thelma's, you know. Beautiful eyes. Beautiful manners. That's someone to model yourself on, Ricky. Omar Sharif or your Uncle Selwyn. Perfect gentlemen, both of them.'

Jennifer said, 'So what's your secret for a long life, Grandma? Ninety years old and your ticker's still going strong.'

'Hard work,' Mam said. 'Hard work, a sober life and a clear conscience.'

Dilys said, 'It didn't do Arthur much good.'

Sel said, 'What do you think of Las Vegas, Fraser?'

Fraser said he didn't understand how anybody could live there. He said it had to be the most dispiriting place in the world.

Betsan said, 'You've obviously never been to Saltley.'

Fraser said New Zealand had everything: rainforests, volcanic lakes, dolphins, snow-capped mountains.

Hazel said, 'We've got mountains here. We had mountains in Wales.'

'Sure,' he said, 'but we've got greenery and space. Opportunities. Law and order. Best place on earth, isn't it, Jen?'

We'd never called her 'Jen'.

Sel said, 'Well, it's a lucky man who finds the place he was meant to be. You like dolphins, and law and order. I look out across Vegas after the sun's gone down, see the Strip starting to sparkle, see my name in lights, that's what I love. And we're not short of space here, Fraser. There's nothing but bloody desert from here to Salt Lake City.'

Ricky and Kim couldn't stay for the evening party. He was going to Memphis, Tennessee for an eating contest, hoping to improve his personal best for glazed doughnuts; forty-one in nine minutes. 'Happy birthday, Gran-gran,' he said.

'Ricky,' she said. 'Why can't you find a nice white girl?'

We had celebrities wall to wall for the poolside party. Dino Martin, Prince Farakasi, the Kirk Douglases. I played the Chickering grand And we did a medley from Sel's hit album *A Boy's Best Friend*. He sang 'Through the Years', 'Mamma', 'The Girl Who Married Dear Old Dad' and the one that always got her blowing her nose, 'If You Were the Only Girl in the World'.

Mam danced with Sel and Milty Berle and Joey Bishop, and Hazel and Dilys got a bit silly with Burt Reynolds dancing a threesome. We had two beverage fountains, one for sparkling wine, one for non-alcoholic fruit punch, an eighty-pound spit-roasted pig and a chocolate mint layer cake.

And we finished off with a little firework display set up on top of the garden wall. 'Ninety Glorious Years' it spelled out at the end.

Hazel said, 'How does it come about that a nasty piece of work like your mam gets so doted on and we're lucky if we get a phone call from Jennifer?'

Dilys said, 'It's a different generation. They don't bother with things that don't interest them. No sense of duty. It's more honest, I suppose. Jennifer's busy with her own life now and what's she got in common with you? I'm the same with my pair. I look at Gaynor sometimes and wonder what to say to her. But I'll tell you why Sel panders to Mam so much, singing these silly old songs. He's scared of her. In a lot of ways he's still a kid. He daren't do different.'

But I'm not sure Sel was ever afraid of anything. I think he believed he'd been touched by angels' wings.

People were still dancing and Mam was still going strong, but Sel said he thought he might turn in.

Jennifer said, 'You all right, Uncle Sel?'

'All the better for seeing you,' he said. 'It's been a big day, though. Who'd have thought it, eh? All for little Annie Boff from Ninevah Street.'

Jennifer said, 'What's wrong with him, Daddy?'

I said, 'He's just not used to being up before midday.'

Pearl said, 'His tail light's out, Miss Jennifer. You're the only one around here appears to have noticed. He's still motoring, but his tail light's out.'

I said to Hazel, 'What do you think she meant?'

'I'd have thought that was obvious,' she said. 'I don't care how much they torture him at Caliente Springs. A man who eats a quart of ice cream every night shouldn't be dropping weight the way he's doing.'

Women! They're always reading between the lines.

If I were hanged on the highest hill
Mother, o'mine, Mother o'mine,
I know whose love would follow me still
O Mother, O Mother o'mine.

KIPLING

THIRTY-THREE

Dilys didn't fly home with Gaynor. She said, 'I'll go home when Sel stops looking like a death's head.'

Hazel and Dilys had both got it into their heads that he was ill, but he filmed a new series of *Queen for a Day* and then he opened a new show at the Flamingo, five nights a week, three costume changes per show.

Hazel said, 'I wish he'd cut down on the cigarettes.'

I said, 'He's got shows booked solid for the next twelve months. He's getting the swimming pool re-tiled. You don't bother with things like that if you've got cancer.'

Dilys said, 'All he seems to want to do is sleep.'

I said, 'He's always been like that. You haven't toured with him the way I have. He always slept in after a show.'

'I know that,' she said. 'But now he sleeps in when he hasn't done a show. Pearl says he used to like pottering around in the afternoon, rearranging his figurines, or going shopping. We haven't been shopping once since I've been here.'

I said, 'Sel, everybody's worried about you. Pearl says your figurines need dusting. Hazel and Dilys are moithering because you never go shopping. Thelma keeps telling me the name of her doctor. Now, what's up?'

'Nothing,' he said. 'Bring the girls to watch the new show tonight. They'll see for themselves. Mr Starlight is all revved up and ready to go.'

He'd always kept things light for the Vegas showrooms. 'It's not like a show for my ladies,' he used to say. 'These punters don't want their heart strings pulled. When you've spent all day at the crap tables, you need cheering up.' And his new repertoire was certainly very lively: 'Yes Sir, I Can Boogie', 'I Love the Nightlife', 'Singing in the Rain'. 'Glamour with a good beat,' he said, 'that's what I give them. "Be-bop-a-lula" in diamonds.'

He did the first set in a Capri-blue lycra all-in-one covered in teardrop sequins and matching high-heeled boots. 'Come Fly with Me,' he sang, 'The Lady Is a Tramp', 'Fever', cracking jokes, borrowing a Kleenex from three girls sitting at a ringside table.

'This air-conditioning too cool for you?' he said. 'I'm freezing. I'll just go put on a few more rhinestones. Back in two shakes.'

Those Flamingoettes were something, but I couldn't enjoy them with the lady wife sitting one side of me and my sister on the other, so I went round to see Sel during the break. Then I saw the change in him. He was slumped in an armchair breathing something through a mask. He waved me to sit down.

'Oxygen,' Brett said. 'He gets out of breath.'

I said, 'He always did. Who told him to take oxygen?'

Brett didn't appear to know. I sat and watched him, dabbing at the sweat, sucking on the gas.

'There!' he said. 'That's better. See? Good as new. The girls enjoying the show?'

I said, 'Is this what the doctor ordered?'

'Doctors!' he said. 'I don't bother with doctors. Hallerton gets it for me. That boy can get anything. Know what I mean? Anything at all.'

I said, 'You're sick.'

He said, 'I am fifty-five, Cled.'

I said, 'And I'm sixty-one, but I don't need breathing apparatus. Tell them you can't do the second show. I'll tell them.'

'Mr Starlight never cancels,' he said. 'The only show Mr Starlight ever missed was at Industrial Brush and that was due to the hand of God.'

Hazel gave him such a telling off when she heard about it. She said, 'Apart from anything else, it's dangerous. All those people smoking. You could cause an explosion.'

He winked at her. He said, 'Wherever I am, whatever I do, I cause an explosion.'

So he carried on, goofing around, like a spring chicken. His jacket had big pink roses on it, like a cover for a three-piece suite, except it was all sequins. He only slowed down for his final number. 'One for the road,' he said, 'and for my baby too' – 'September Song'.

Every night he played to a full room, every night he finished in a jacket that weighed a ton, but the last couple of weeks there were signs he was slowing up. Brett would be sitting outside in the motor, waiting to take him to the Strip, and Sel was still in his bathrobe, not even shaved. And it didn't go unnoticed in the press that he wasn't quite A1. Bambi Allen wrote about him in *Celebrity!*:

> Mr Starlight's new high-octane, diamond-studded show at
> the Flamingo, Las Vegas has done little to allay concerns
> about the super-trouper's health. The trim rejuvenated figure
> he unveiled six months ago is beginning to look plain
> haggard and word on the Strip is that Mr S is running on an
> empty tank. The big question is, what's wrong?

Hallerton Liquorish allowed it to be known that Sel had developed an allergy.

Mam said, 'I'm not surprised. He takes stray dogs in and he doesn't know where they've been.'

Dilys said, 'I think it's anaemia. You can't work as hard as Sel does living on pineapple and ice cream. You don't get the nutriments you need. That's the reason I don't diet any more.'

Mam said, 'The reason you don't diet any more, Dilys, is that you don't have any self-control. You never did have and that's why you've given in to obesity.'

I said, 'I wonder if it's drugs. He told me Hallerton Liquorish can get him anything.'

Hazel said, 'Meanwhile, he's getting worse. Why doesn't one of you just call in this doctor of Thelma's? Sitting around here theorising. Just do something.'

Mam said, 'It's none of your business. This is Selwyn's home. Mine and Selwyn's.'

Hazel said, 'Cled? Are you going to do something? You seem to be the man around here.'

Mam said, 'No he's not. I am. And if Selwyn doesn't want a doctor he doesn't have to have one. He doesn't like people going into his bedroom.'

Hazel said, 'Then he can see him in the front hall. He can see him in the jungle ruddy atrium. As long as he sees him. Cled?'

I said, 'It's a very tricky situation. Obviously, to a certain extent you have to respect a person's wishes. Then again . . .'

Hazel said, 'Right! That's enough. I'm getting that number from Thelma.'

Mam said, 'I think your wife's going mental, Cledwyn. I think she's the one who needs the doctor.'

Dilys said, 'I think Hazel's right.'

Mam said, 'You would do. You never did have a mind of your own.'

So Hazel set things in motion and Mam went and shut herself in her room, to mark her disapproval.

Hazel said, 'He'll come this afternoon. His name's Dr Rosen. Now you'd better go and tell Sel.'

I said, 'You go. You started all this.'

She said, 'I can't. Sel doesn't like women in his room.'

I said, 'Pearl goes in.'

'Pearl's Pearl,' she said. 'Go and do it, Cled, please, before I prove your Mam right and turn violent.'

His breakfast was on the side, not even touched. He was still in his pyjamas but he'd put his hair on.

I said, 'Is there something else you fancy? Slice of toast?'

He always loved marmalade. 'It's not that I don't want it, Cled,' he said. 'But I've got trouble with my dentures. I can't chew.'

He took his top plate out and showed me. His gums and his tongue and down into his throat as far as I could see, everything was covered with horrible white spots.

I said, 'Leave your teeth out. Let the air get at it.'

'I couldn't do that,' he said. 'What if somebody saw me?'

He looked so pathetic.

I said, 'I don't know how you're going to feel about this, but Hazel's asked Thelma's medico to come and see you. I told her she should have asked you first, but you know what they're like when they get a bee in their bonnet. Hazel can be very strong-willed and Dilys encouraged her. But if you want it called off just say the word and I'll tell her, straight.'

He didn't say anything. He just sat there and let the tears roll down his cheeks.

I said, 'Is that a yes or a no?'

He nodded.

I said, 'Is that a yes, you want the doctor or a yes you want the doctor cancelled?'

'Stay with me,' he said. 'When he comes, stay with me.'

I said, 'What about Mam?' Mam always expected to be in on anything involving His Numps.

'No,' he said. 'Just you.'

And as a matter of fact, Mam had Randolph drive her to the Tumbleweed for an hour. It wasn't her usual time for playing the slots, but she wouldn't stay around to see Hazel win the day.

Dr Rosen said Sel had a fungal infection. 'Easy to fix,' he said. 'But you're run down. I recommend you come in for a complete physical. A guy your age should do it anyway.'

Sel said he'd think about it.

I said, 'I think the doctor's right, our kid. You should look into things. Like why you're needing oxygen between sets.'

The doc said, 'What oxygen?'

Sel said, 'Thanks, Cled.'

Dr Rosen said good health was the best investment a person could make.

Sel said, 'Yeah? I've done pretty well with real estate myself.'

They laughed.

The doc said, 'These marks on your legs? Had them long?' They were like patches of corned beef. Sel said he hadn't noticed them.

Dr Rosen said, 'I hear the new show's great. I didn't catch it yet but everyone's talking about it.'

'Hottest ticket in town,' Sel said.

The doc said, 'Well, we can't allow Mr Starlight to lose his shine so we should set up this physical as soon as possible. When is good for you?'

Sel said, 'After Gladys Knight takes over. Next month.'

Dr Rosen said, 'Later today would work for me.'

There was nothing said for a few minutes.

Sel was just ruminating, gazing down at the blotches on his legs, his mouth all sunken without his dentures. 'Cled,' he said eventually. 'I'll need you to take care of a few things.'

Are we to part like this, dear?
Are we to part this way?
Who's it to be, 'er or me?
Don't be afraid to say.

CASTLING & COLLINS

THIRTY-FOUR

Brett drove Sel to the Lakeshore Clinic in the runabout and a youngster called Evie Paul stepped in at the Flamingo Show Room. 'Tell her not to make herself too comfortable,' he said. 'Tell her it's only for two nights.'

I said to Hazel, 'As long as there's a show most of the punters couldn't care less who they see. Ask them the next morning and half of them won't even remember.'

'I don't think anybody forgets seeing Sel,' she said.

He was very worried about publicity.

'We'll tell the truth,' Mam said. 'You're suffering from exhaustion. The truth is always the easiest.'

He said, 'No, not exhaustion. That makes me sound clapped out. It'd be better to say I caught something. Something you get over fast. Chickenpox. That's what I'll have.'

He was booked into Lakeshore as Amos Roberts, to ensure privacy. It was very nice: private rooms, choice of menu. Mam referred to it as 'Sel's little holiday'. Evie Paul described it as her lucky break. And Liquorish put out a statement that Mr Starlight had been forced to pull out of his show, the first time he'd done so in thirty-five years, due to influenza.

Pearl took the opportunity to springclean his rooms. 'He'll be home any minute,' she kept saying. 'Everything better be perfect.'

But Sel developed an infection on his chest, so he was kept where he was until he responded to the medication.

I visited him every afternoon before I went to the Old Bull, took him a few Agatha Christies and a pack of cards in case he wanted to play Patience.

'I'm all right,' he said. 'I can get eighty channels on this TV. I've found a few old Starlight shows. Remember that one we did with Doris Day?' They'd cleared up his fungus. He looked a lot better with his teeth in. He said, 'As long as I'm here, I think I might have my eyelids done. You interested in anything? Get those jowls lifted?'

I said, 'No, thank you. Women love me just the way I am.'

He said, 'What about the girls? Do you think Dilys'd like a facelift? I'll pay.'

Hazel said, 'Ask him if they can do anything for your mam. Personality transplant.'

I hadn't actually met Hallerton Liquorish, but I guessed who he was, sitting on the edge of Sel's bed, talking on the telephone. Hazel was with me that afternoon.

Sel said, 'Hallerton's getting me a second opinion.'

Liquorish didn't give us a glance. 'OK, done deal,' he said to Sel. 'I'm flying Alpert in from LA first thing tomorrow.'

I said, 'Who's Alpert?'

'The best,' Liquorish said. 'The very best.'

Hazel said, 'Is that what you want, Sel?'

He just shrugged his shoulders.

Hazel said, 'Does Dr Rosen know?'

Liquorish ignored her. He said, 'See, Sel, this is where California is ahead of the game. Lakeshore may be fine for aesthetic procedures but they're not up to speed when it comes to medical conditions. Folk are so goddamned healthy in Vegas. They just drop dead on the golf course. But LA doctors are the tops. They've seen everything.'

Dr Rosen said he never objected to patients calling in another opinion. 'I know Sel's anxious to get back to work,' he said. 'We're giving him pentamine. Normally I'd expect his chest to be clear by now. I don't know what to say.'

I called Jennifer Jane. I said, 'What do you think?'

'I don't know,' she said. 'I can't know everything. Tell him I love him.'

Mam said, 'He always had a weak chest, ever since he had the whooping cough.'

'Measles,' Dilys said. 'It was measles.'

'Whooping cough,' Mam said. 'Your memory's going.'

Dr Alpert said he knew of quite a number of cases like Sel's. He said, 'This kind of chest infection is on the increase and it doesn't respond. The purple lesions, they were something you only saw in old guys. Now we're finding them in young men. Sel's not young, of course, but he's the first case where I've seen both these things together. Plus he's losing weight. I believe he has something we're calling the Gay Syndrome.'

I said, 'Gay as in . . . ?'

'Correct,' he said.

I said, 'He's not going to like that. He doesn't like that word.'

'Yeah?' he said. 'Well, I guess we can call it something else. We can call it Compromised Immunity, but that doesn't change the facts. Sel is a sick man. Does he have a partner?'

I said, 'Dusty Hayes plays for him in Vegas. Is it catching?'

Hazel said, 'Not that kind of partner, Cled. *Partner*. Like I'm your *partner*.'

That was a new one on me.

She said, 'There's Brett. I suppose he's what you'd call a partner.'

Dr Alpert said Brett should drop by, get a check-up.

I said, 'It's not cancer, then?'

'No,' he said. 'But it's carrying off guys younger and fitter than your brother.' He said it wasn't so much a disease as a phenomenon and he couldn't be one hundred per cent sure Sel had got it, but it looked very much that way.

I said, 'How will we know?'

'If he doesn't start getting better,' he said.

I said, 'And who's going to tell him?'

'I already did,' Liquorish said.

Hazel said, 'I don't think you should have done that. I think that was a job for the doctor, or family.'

Liquorish laughed. He said, 'He was fine. Full of fighting talk.

You know Sel. We sketched out a press release. I'd like to get Bambi Allen on side with this. Offer her an exclusive. I'd like her to have a fabulous quote from Sel. Something humorous yet dignified. He's thinking about it.'

Hazel said, 'I expect you want to go in to him now, don't you, Cled? You wouldn't want him lying there on his own, would you, Cled? And before Bimbo Allen gets her exclusive, whatever that is, I think we feel Sel's family and friends should be told, don't we, Cled?'

Liquorish said, 'You're the sister, right?'

'Sister-in-law,' she said.

'Well,' he said, 'Sel's a professional, like me. He knows the importance of information management. He leaves me to do what I do best, so he's free to do what he does best. And I suggest you do the same. Go comfort his mother, buy him some grapes, plump up his pillows. Leave me to take care of the Mr Starlight story.'

She said, 'You'd better do the right thing by him. I'll be watching you. We all will.'

He snapped his fingers at me. He said, 'What about Action Man? He likely to be at home? Get him here. I'll tell Rosen to keep him under observation. We don't want him talking. Any talking to be done, I do it. I'll be back. Tomorrow. Friday. Shit, I have to fly.'

I said, 'You shouldn't have said that to him, Hazel. That side of things is none of our business. Now you've put his back up.'

'Good,' she said. 'Now go in to Sel. Go and talk to him.'

I said, 'You go in.' I didn't know what to say to him. I said, 'Women are better at this kind of thing.'

'Then fetch Dilys,' she said. 'Only don't just sit there, Cled. If keeping tabs on Mr Liquorish is going to be my job you're going to have to make yourself useful in other ways. Your mother. Go and talk to your mother.'

I said, 'Brett. I'll go and find him.' One thing at a time, I always say.

Brett had been going out a good deal while Sel was in the clinic and not needing a driver. He liked to go fishing for bass on

Lake Mead or drinking beer with his young pals from Caesar's Palace.

I tried the Four Queens and O'Lucky's and the Magnet. I tracked him down in Big Jim's eating a steak breakfast. I said, 'The boss needs to see you.'

'Yeah?' he said. 'He ready to come home?'

He seemed so happy, chattering away, I didn't like to tell him the outlook wasn't good. Poor bugger. It was like taking a dog to be put down and it keeps wagging its tail at you.

He said, 'He'll likely want to go to Malibu for a while. Rest up some more. Malibu's great.'

I said, 'I don't think he's well enough.'

'Sea air,' he said. 'That's all he needs.'

Brett was from a town called Enid, Oklahoma. 'Ran away when I was fourteen,' he said. 'Had enough of getting the strap from my old man. Sel's my family now.'

He was waiting in his room in a wheelchair. Everybody left Lakeshore in a wheelchair, even if all they'd had was their moles burned off.

Brett said, 'Are we going to Malibu?'

'Baby,' Sel said, 'I want you to do something for me. I want you to let Dr Rosen check you over. This thing I've got, you never know.'

Brett said, 'Is it clap?'

'No,' he said, 'it isn't. But I don't want you getting any kind of sick. I need you fit and well while I'm recuperating.'

Brett said, 'I ain't sick.'

Sel said, 'But do it for me anyway, baby. We did share an ice cream spoon.'

THIRTY-FIVE

Mam declined to believe Sel had a disease or even a phenomenon, which is what Sel preferred to call it. 'The phenomenon is suffering from a phenomenon,' he said.

'Vitamins,' Mam said. 'That's what he needs. Cod liver oil and malt.'

He said, 'She could be right. Get on the phone to Jennifer Jane. Tell her we want to know the minute she discovers vitamin F. And G and H. Tell her I'll take the lot.'

Dilys wanted a good British doctor to see him. 'Harley Street,' she said. 'He can afford it. We don't have to believe everything this Alpert doctor says.'

But Sel wasn't well enough to go to London. It was as much as he could do to walk outside and smell his roses. 'Tomorrow,' he kept saying. 'Tomorrow I'll probably feel like running through a few songs. Gotta start thinking about my cornbelt ladies.'

There had been a Midwest tour planned for the autumn, but Liquorish had cancelled it. 'Rescheduled,' he said.

Hazel said, 'When for?'

'To be decided,' he said.

Sel would just sit out by the pool for hours, gazing into space. He liked to have company but that was hard for Brett. A youngster like that, full of beans. He had been given a clean bill of health. 'Come back in a year,' they said.

So Brett kept busy, walking the dogs, going to the supermarket, lifting Sel into bed at night and the rest of us took turns to sit with

Sel. Pearl would bring her vegetables out. She'd sit peeling potatoes and talking to herself.

And Mam always came for a word before she went off to play her slots. 'You're looking much better today, Selwyn,' she'd say. 'I see a marked improvement.'

I was sitting with him one morning. Dilys and Hazel were doing aquarobics with Lupe Leon. Keep fit in water, supposed to be ideal for the older lady. I think Lupe only did it to try and get my attention. Prancing around in her bikini. Squealing and laughing and sticking her backside up in the air.

'Our kid,' he said, 'I think I'm finished.'

I said, 'Come on! That's no way to talk.'

'No,' he said. 'I've got this feeling. Funny, really. I'm the bab of the family. I should see the lot of you out.'

I said, 'Cures get invented every day. That's what Jennifer says. There's investigations going on we don't even know about. Chemicals bubbling over a bunsen burner. Atoms getting split. It's just a matter of time.'

'Everything is, Cled,' he said. 'Everything is. I just want to make sure everything's done right. I can't just sit here. Leave my fans wondering. I should announce my retirement and do a farewell show.'

I said, 'How can you? You can't even stand.'

He said, 'I could do it sitting down. Soft focus. Slow songs.'

I said, 'Forget it. You're looking too gaunt.'

'Yeah,' he said. 'I thought about that. I'll get Celeste to make me some jewelled kaftans. Put a bit of padding underneath. You look any size you want in a kaftan. I could look like Demis Roussos.'

'What do you think?' Brett'd say every day. 'Is he gonna make it?'

Hazel said, 'What we have to do, Brett, is hope for the best but prepare for the worst.'

I said, 'And if it should come to it . . . well, we'll see you all right. A good driver can always find work, same as a pianist.'

'Oh, I ain't worried about that,' he said. 'Anything happens to Sel, this place is made over to me. But I'd kinda miss him.'

I said to Hazel, 'Where does that leave us? I'll have to have it out with Sel.'

'I'd rather you didn't,' she said.

I said, 'What about the Old Bull? What if he's left him everything? That's my livelihood. And what about Mam? Where's she going to live? In Great Barr with Dilys?'

That made her stop and think. But I didn't bring it up with Sel. He was going through a bad patch.

Hallerton Liquorish telephoned every day. 'I'll be flying down,' he'd say. 'Maybe Monday. I have stuff Sel needs to sign. Next week,' he'd say. 'Things have been crazy, but next week for sure.'

I said, 'Did you know Sel left Desert Star to Brett?'

'Say what?' he said.

I said, 'He reckons Sel sort of adopted him.'

'Not sort of,' a voice said. 'Did it. It's in the will. I get everything.' It was Brett. He'd been listening in.

Liquorish said, 'Holy fucking shit. I'll be there tomorrow.' And he was, on the first flight.

Brett said, 'Sel, from now on, when folk want to talk to you, I should be there. You're in no state. I'm your son now, remember?'

Sel said, 'Hey, we're all on the same team. You, me, Hallerton. Cled too. Keeping Mr Starlight shining bright.'

Liquorish said, 'And I don't usually talk business in front of the kids.'

Brett said, 'I just don't want folks bamboozling you.'

Sel said, 'OK, OK. Just sit nice and quiet. That all right with you, Hallerton?'

Liquorish said, 'Whatever Mr Starlight wants, Mr Starlight gets. You're looking terrific, Sel! This is great. I see a difference in you.'

Sel said, 'You know me. The Come-Back Kid. I'm taking my vitamins and I'm saying my prayers.'

Liquorish said, 'And you are so in demand, I can't tell you. Kennett Shaffner wants to interview you on *Face to Face*. Bambi is preparing an in-depth. And Mimi Warren at *Hot!* has a great idea for a photo feature. Then there's a fabulous new thing called "Celebrity Hugs".

Some of Hollywood's biggest names are getting involved: Shirley Maclaine, Elizabeth Taylor.'

Sel said, 'You want me to hug Liz Taylor?'

'Always the comedian,' Liquorish said. 'No, but she'd sure like to hug you. It's to help allay public fears. People hear about this "Gay Plague" and they start worrying about contagion. But if they see their screen idols getting close up and personal, it'll make them realise there's nothing to fear.'

Sel said, 'Who saying that's what I've got?'

Liquorish said, 'Well, obviously some people *are* saying that.'

Brett said, 'Then you better put them straight. You better get out there and tell them. Sel has low blood. Ain't that right?'

Sel said, 'Hush, baby, hush.'

Liquorish said, 'Call it what you like. We have to be realistic here. I mean, obviously, people are speculating. And obviously, given the diagnosis, it's only a matter of time till it's out of the bag. I think we should take the initiative here. A pre-emptive strike. A nice piece on how Mr Starlight and his partner are coming to terms with . . . whatever you want to call it.'

'Son!' Brett said. 'I'm his adopted son, ain't I, Sel?'

Liquorish said, 'Oh yes, the adoption. You never mentioned that happy event to me, Sel. When did that happen?'

Sel sighed. 'It is something I've been thinking about,' he said.

'But not formalised?' Liquorish said.

'Not exactly,' he said.

Brett jumped up. 'See, Sel,' he said, 'just like I said. He's trying to bamboozle you with his ten-dollar words.'

Sel said, 'Please, baby. Take Peaches, get her coat trimmed. That's what would make me happy.' Peaches was the poodle.

I said, 'Only we were all wondering, after Brett said you'd left him everything, you know? There's Mam to think of. There's Pearl. There's your half-share of the Old Bull.'

'Cled,' he said, 'I haven't left everything to Brett. You got the wrong idea. I haven't left anything to anybody yet.'

Liquorish started laughing.

Brett said, 'Sel?'

Sel said, 'Leave it, baby. We'll talk later. Take Peaches.'

Liquorish said, 'Oh Brett, baby! You should check your facts before you start bragging. I don't think Daddy signed the papers.'

Brett jumped up and caught him with a fast upper cut, right across the mouth.

Liquorish went crazy. 'My teeth,' he was shouting. 'Did he get my teeth? Jesus! Five hundred bucks a tooth! I only just finished at the dentist.'

Brett ran out of the room, Liquorish ran after him, I ran after Liquorish.

Brett was yelling, 'I'll kill you, you sonofabitch.'

Pearl was outside mopping. She said, 'There'll be no killing in my house. Now quiet down. Mr Sel all right?'

Liquorish said, 'I'm the one just been assaulted.'

But he'd only broken the skin on his lip.

Brett said, 'He did sign. He told me. I'll get what's mine.'

Liquorish said, 'There's only one thing Daddy'll be leaving you and he already gave you that, I'll bet.'

I said, 'No. They told Brett he was all right.'

'All right now, maybe,' he said. He was dabbing at his mouth. 'But he'll get it. They all do. Hear that, shithead? You're toast.'

Brett was backing away. 'I'll get you,' he said. 'I'll come after you. All this'll be mine.' And he ran off.

We went back in to Sel.

Liquorish said, 'You should be careful. That boy is a wild animal. Now, I have contracts requiring your signature, VTV, Sony, Premier. That one is Paradigm Promotions, for their insurance. This one's the syndication deal we discussed, I put a mark where you need to sign. And there's our agreement with *Celebrity!*. There too. All straightforward. I have to see a doctor about this injury. I have to get a tetanus shot. I question the sanity of that boy, Sel, I really do. I'll swing by tomorrow, before I fly back. Firm things up for Mimi Warren. I don't want to overtire you. But I can't tell you how happy

I am to find you in such good shape. You carry on like this, Liz Taylor could have a wasted trip.'

'She will anyway,' Sel whispered. 'I'm not doing it.'

Elizabeth Taylor. The most beautiful woman in the world.

I said, 'If I put my pyjamas on do you think she'd hug me?'

That made him smile. He said, 'I've always thought Hazel has a look of Liz Taylor about her.'

Only in her colouring. She never had the build.

I said, 'It seems a pity not to let her come, if she wants to. It's all in a good cause.'

'See, Cled,' he said. 'If it turns out I can't beat this thing, I don't want to be remembered for how I died. I want to be remembered for my sell-out shows and my fabulous costumes. I want to be remembered for my beautiful homes. My work with sick kiddies. Do you understand? Is Brett back yet? I have to talk to Brett.'

All evening he kept asking, 'Where's Brett? Why isn't he back yet?'

But Brett was gone. Drinking with a bunch of centurions, I expect. And Peaches never did get her coat trimmed.

THIRTY-SIX

'I'll wear my Indian pink,' he said, 'and my Turkish slippers.'

Mimi Warren was coming with a photographer.

'A tasteful photo feature,' Liquorish said. 'And a few words from Sel.'

Celeste had made him a rail of those kaftans he liked to wear since he'd gone so scraggy. It was quite a production, getting him ready. Dilys put the orange beauty cream on his skin. Candy came in to do his nails and make sure his wig looked right. And Pearl had to judge when to put his dentures in. He couldn't wear them for long and they were a bit vague about what time they'd be arriving.

Six of them, it took. Mimi had an assistant, the photographer had one. Then there was a make-up girl and a boy to make sure the cushions looked right.

Sel said, 'They can go. Let them play in the pool. Mr Starlight does his own make-up.'

Hazel was the only one he'd allow to rearrange his clothes. 'Make sure my ankles aren't showing,' he said. 'My ladies prefer to use their imagination. Let me see those Polaroids. Maybe I should wear a shawl, for added interest. And let's have Rocky in a few shots. He's got more wrinkles than I have.' Rocky was an ugly little boxer dog he'd taken in. It had been found wandering with a gammy leg by one of Pearl's relations.

Sel kept up the smiles and the poses till they had no film left, but we had to use the wheelchair to get him to bed afterwards. You'd never think, looking at those pictures, what a sick man he was. He always had a knack with cameras.

It was a nice piece.

> When you've reached the very top, as I have [he said]
> you have the good fortune to be able to stop and take a
> breather and enjoy the view. That's what I've been doing
> since my recent illness. Relishing my achievements and
> rethinking the future. And you know what? I decided there
> was something crazy about the way I've been living,
> working so hard I never had time to walk my doggies or just
> plain relax, here in my lovely home. All work and no play
> can make even Mr Starlight a dull boy and I owe my fans
> one hundred per cent sparkle, nothing less. So from now on
> the world may be seeing a little less of me, but what they do
> see won't disappoint. I'll be taking time to do more charita-
> ble work – I've always loved working with children, as you
> know – and I've been asked to collaborate on a range of
> costume jewellery, replicas of some of the fabulous pieces
> I've been privileged to own. I also think it might be fun to
> create my own signature fragrance and, of course, write the
> amazing story of my life, an enormous task unto itself. I
> predict it'll run to several volumes, so you see, Mr Starlight
> isn't so much retiring as changing direction. This year my
> dear mother celebrated her ninetieth birthday, which I'd say
> is a very good omen for me.

Young Ricky brought him a book called *Defeating the Enemy Within*. He said it had helped him have the right attitude when he went into a contest against really stiff competition. The book said if you had a disease and the disease seemed like it was winning, you had to talk to it, man to man, tell it to pack up and leave. Sel had Dilys read to him from it every day. His eyes weren't so good any more.

I said, 'Do you think it works?'

Dilys said, 'No. But Sel does and I'd read Bradshaw's train time-tables backwards if it made him feel better.'

He liked me to sit with him and watch his old shows, the same stuff over and over. Then he'd nod off, but if I tried to tiptoe out he'd wake up. 'Is Brett here?' he'd say. 'Where's Brett?'

Nobody knew. His bungalow was just as he'd left it. He'd left two good leather jackets behind.

'Rewind the tape, our kid,' he'd say. 'I always liked that bit.'

It was a funny time. People wanted to know the latest news, only officially there wasn't any latest news. Officially Mr Starlight was taking a well-earned break. Even the national president of his fan club wasn't allowed to know. The gifts kept piling in: pyjamas and candied fruits and bottles of tonic wine. The letters came by the hundred. And Liquorish kept phoning with little ideas he'd had. Information management, as he called it. 'How about a talking record? Bedtime stories, narrated by Mr Starlight. How about a two-minute piece, fund-raising for *Kids in Need*? Just a head shot. Just a few words?'

Hazel was like a guard dog. She didn't even want Sel asked, but Mam always bypassed her. 'You'll feel better if you do something,' she'd say. 'You're like me. You're not suited to idleness.'

'I'll think about it, Mam,' he'd say.

'That's right, Selwyn,' she'd say. 'Because the more you do, the more you feel you can do.'

I'd been down at the Old Bull interviewing a new barmaid the morning Liquorish had called with his latest scheme. He wanted Craig Vertue to pay Sel a visit, to make his peace.

Hazel said, 'I told him, Vertue didn't need to come all the way to Las Vegas to do that. He can write it in one of his articles. A public apology.'

Mam said, 'You had no business answering telephone calls. Call him back, Cledwyn. It'll be a nice surprise for Selwyn. I think he'd enjoy a visitor.'

Hazel said, 'Ignore her. She has no idea.'

I said, 'We could ask Sel.'

Hazel said, 'No, Cled, it's not right. He's not well enough to know what he's agreeing to and anyway, it's nothing but a racket. It's only because of what he's got. Nobody'd be interested in him if he'd got emphysema. Well, I'm not going to allow it. There'll be no more strangers visiting and no more photos, not while I'm here.'

Mam said, 'He enjoys having his picture taken. It keeps his spirits up.'

I said, 'What do you think, Dilys?'

'I agree with Hazel,' she said.

'You would do,' Mam said. 'You never held an opinion of your own in your whole life. Being swayed by people who aren't even family. You'd listen to the milkman's horse.'

Hazel looked at me. Her eyes were blazing. She was looking for a fight.

Dilys said, 'Hazel is family, Mam.'

'Not by blood, she isn't,' Mam said. 'Not by my invitation. Cledwyn could have done a thousand times better if he wasn't such a fool.'

Hazel's voice was quiet at the start. She said, 'I'll give you proper family, you old besom. I've put up with you for thirty years. If we weren't family I'd have throttled you long ago. Done time for it and enjoyed it. They'd have let me out by now.' She'd been cooped up for days.

I said, 'Why don't you go over to Thelma's, pet, take a break? She's got company. Nancy Sinatra's over there.'

'Bugger Nancy Sinatra,' she said. That was when she started shouting. 'If I leave your mam unsupervised she'll let the whole ruddy circus in. She'll have him propped up for photos after he's dead and I can't trust you to stop her. You're such a mouse, Cled. You never stand up to her. None of you do.'

Mam was smiling. 'You wife's going mental,' she said. 'I knew she would, sooner or later. I can always tell the type.'

Hazel said, 'I'll wipe that smile off your face.'

'Can't hear you,' Mam said. 'We don't listen to mental cases in this family.'

'We'll see,' Hazel said. 'You'll be all ears in a minute because I'm going to bring something up that should have been said a long time ago. Shouldn't it, Dilys?'

And all the colour drained out of Dilys's face. 'Oh no, Hazel,' she said. 'Not that, please. Not now.'

I didn't know what was going on.

Mam got up to leave. 'I haven't got time to sit listening to loonies,' she said. 'I'm going to have five minutes with my boy. Make sure all this shouting hasn't set him back.'

Hazel said, 'Why don't you go with her, Cled? Settle her in a comfy chair and tell Sel we're all coming in. Because your mam's got something she wants to tell him.'

Mam was out of the room already, wheezing and leaning on her stick. Hazel's face and throat were flushed, and she was pacing up and down. It crossed my mind Mam might be right. You do hear of people snapping suddenly. Something pushes them over the edge and the next thing you know they've shot the whole family.

I said, 'Go and have a lie-down. I'll get you a cold flannel.'

'Pipe down, Cled,' she said. 'Come on, Dilys. It's now or never.'

Dilys said, 'I can't. Not yet.'

Hazel was tugging on her. 'Not yet?' she said. 'It should have been done years ago. And if you leave it any longer it's going to be too late. Then how will you feel?'

Dilys said, 'Stop her, Cled.'

But how could I? Nobody ever tells me what's going on.

Hazel said, 'How many times have we talked about this, Dilly? How many years have I heard you say you were just waiting for a chance? Well, sometimes you have to make chances. So here it is.' She was rubbing Dilys's hands. 'Come on,' she said, 'buck up and get in there before your mam starts spoiling everything. It's going to be all right, you'll see. You're going to feel wonderful afterwards. You'll feel like a different woman. Come on, Cled. Don't stand there catching flies. This is important.'

Sel was on the couch in his bedroom with Rocky and two of the mongrels. Mam was fussing over him. 'He's not to have upset,' she said to Dilys as we came in. 'Look at him. He's not so good today.'

'I'm all right,' he said. 'Leave the cushions where they are.'

'Mam,' Dilys said, 'I think Hazel's right.'

Mam never looked up. She was smoothing the coverlet on the bed. 'Look at these dog hairs,' she said. 'No wonder you can't shake that cough, Selwyn.'

Dilys said, 'Please, Mam. It could be now or never.'

Mam said, 'No need for it to be ever. Causing upset. We've always been happy. We'd be a happy little family if Cledwyn hadn't married that loony.'

Hazel didn't say a thing, but she never let go of Dilys's hand.

Dilys said, 'But I would like him to know. I always wanted him to.' She sat down next to Sel on the couch. 'Sel,' she said, 'I'm not your sister. I'm your mother.'

Sel looked a bit vague. He had been dozing.

Dilys said, 'I'm sorry for any upset, Sel, but I always wanted you to know. In those days . . . when it happened . . . I was too young, you see? And in those days . . . it wasn't like now. So I went away till I'd had you. And that was that. . . . So I'm your real mam.'

'Mam's my mam,' he said.

'That's right,' Mam said. 'I'm the one who raised you.'

Hazel said, 'Only because Dilys wasn't allowed. It was Dilys who *had* you.'

'Was it?' he said. 'How do you know?'

Dilys said, 'Because I told her. Hazel knows what it is to have given up a little baby. She knows the heartbreak of it. She's been a good friend to me. And she's right about getting things out in the open. Every day of your life I've wanted to tell you, Sel. I didn't want you thinking I was only your sister.'

He said, 'You've been a lovely sister.'

Dilys said, 'And if ever it had come out some other way, I didn't want you thinking you were unwanted.'

Mam said, 'It wouldn't have come out.'

Sel said, 'I wouldn't have thought that. I never felt unwanted in my life.'

271

Dilys was crying. She said to Hazel, 'He doesn't seem very pleased.'

Sel said, 'I don't know. I was just sitting here. And then this. Who needs two mams? And now I've lost a sister.'

Mam was fidgeting on the edge of a chair, excited. She could see things were going her way.

Dilys said to Hazel, 'Now what do I do?'

Sel said, 'Cled? Were you in on this? Did you know?'

I said, 'Not a thing. I've been down at the pub all morning.'

There were quite a few things I was still trying to work out. I said, 'Are you my mam too, Dilys?'

Hazel glared at me. 'Idiot!' she said. 'How could she be? Eight years old? Can't you count?' Shouting at me. I wasn't the one who'd upset the pigeon barrel.

Sel put his poor thin arm round Dilys, pulled her closer to him. 'Don't cry,' he said. 'I don't want you to cry.' Of course, if there's one thing guaranteed to make them cry all the more . . . He knew nothing about women, really. 'Strewth,' he said, 'this is a turn-up. I shall still have to call you Dilys, though. I don't think I could call you . . . anything else.'

'That's all right,' she said. 'It's the trend anyway, first names.' She sat there beside him, but she wouldn't look at him, bashful all of a sudden.

'Mam,' he said, 'come and sit here with me. I'll have a mam either side of me.'

Mam didn't move. She said, 'I'm having a dizzy spell.' But I helped her to her feet and she did go and sit next to him.

Sel smiled. He said, 'It's a good job I've got two arms.'

But nobody else was smiling.

He said, 'No more shocks, I hope? You haven't got anybody else waiting in the wings, have you?'

And that was exactly what I was wondering. I said, 'So if Dilys is his mother, who was his father?'

'Unknown,' Mam said. And then the whole room went quiet, except for Rocky scratching himself.

It was Hazel who spoke up. 'Go on, girl,' she whispered. 'You've done the hardest part. Finish what you've started.'

'Mam?' Dilys said. 'Where's the harm?'

'Lies and slander,' Mam said, 'that's the harm. Speaking ill of the dead, who can't defend themselves. You always were trouble, Dilys, right from a bab. It's always the girls that make trouble. Well, you've both got what you deserve, you and the loony. Daughters! My boys have never given me a minute's bother. Apart from marrying a troublemaker.'

Sel said, 'Well, you'll have to tell me now. I hope it wasn't Teilo Morris.'

Or old man Edkins, I was thinking, recalling the night of the three dads.

'No,' Dilys said. 'Our dad was your dad, Sel. It was Gypsy. So you are a Boff, through and through. We kept it in the family, see? But I swear it wasn't my fault. I swear I never encouraged him.'

'All lies,' Mam said. 'And now you've gone and given me angina.'

THIRTY-SEVEN

How could such a thing be? That was what I wanted to know. Married life isn't always satisfying, as I'd be the first to admit, but the world's full of understanding women and Gypsy was a good-looking type. He could have had Mrs Edkins next door, for one. I reckon she'd have had anybody. But for him to have had a young girl. His own youngster.

I said to Hazel, 'I don't know that I believe Dilys. She could have got into trouble with some lad and then blamed it on Dad. Just said the first thing that came into her head.'

'No,' she said. 'You're wrong.'

I said, 'Then why did she sit there hanging her head?'

'Because she's ashamed,' she said. 'All these years and she still blames herself.'

I said, 'So she did encourage him?'

She said, 'She was fourteen, Cled. He was her father. She wasn't out on a date with the boy next door.'

There wasn't a boy next door. The Edkinses didn't have children and Mrs Grimley had one girl and she had a hump on her back.

I said, 'I don't know. It still takes some believing.'

'Well, I believe her,' she said. 'I've heard the story enough times, how your mam threatened her if she ever opened her mouth. And she loves Sel. She wouldn't tell him half the truth.'

I said, 'Why did she tell you?'

'Women tell each other things,' she said.

I said, 'Do you think we should move out? I can't see you and Mam patching things up now.'

'I'm not going anywhere,' she said. 'I'm staying till it's over. I'm not leaving Dilys at a time like this, and I'm not leaving Sel and neither are you. And you talk about patching things up. I'll tell you something. If your mam had just raised him, if she'd taken on the job out of the goodness of her heart and then let him know the truth when he was old enough, I'd have been the first to give her credit, because at least Dilys got to see him growing up. At least she didn't really lose him, not the way I lost my little girl. But she took it too far. Threatening Dilys. Hiding it from Sel when he could have been told. And she's covered up for your dad when he should have been prosecuted. To hear her he was God's gift. Well, he wasn't. He was a criminal. So I can't feel a lot of sympathy for her, Cled, and I don't care if she's a hundred and ninety.'

Sel was going through Mam's birthday album when I went to help him into bed, looking at the photos. 'Did I dream it?' he said.

I said, 'I don't know what to make of it. Do you believe Dilys?'

'Course I do,' he said. 'Why wouldn't I? It's taking it in that's the hard part. So Betsan and Gaynor, they're my half-sisters, you could say. And then you. I'm your half-brother or your nephew, depending on how you look at it.'

I said, 'But about Gypsy? Do you believe that?'

'Yes,' he said. 'Everybody always said I was his double. Now we know why. I should be more than his double. Two doses of Gypsy in my blood.'

I said, 'And you know what they say? The acorn doesn't fall from the apple tree.'

'Thanks,' he said. 'See this?' There was a photo of Dilys, in the backyard at Ninevah Street, rocking Sel in his pram. You could just make out Mrs Edkins peering over the wall. He said, 'It looks different now, doesn't it? Now we know?'

I said, 'It was Hazel put her up to it, you know. She thought it'd be better if everybody knew the facts.'

'Yeah,' he said. 'So I gathered. I don't know, Cled. Sometimes I think people have too many facts these days.'

I said, 'I think Dilys is wondering whether she's done the right thing. I think it fell flatter than she'd hoped.'

He said, 'I love our Dilys, makes no difference if she's my sister or my mother or both. And I don't care who my dad was. I never did. Apparently he's who we thought he was and it makes no bloody odds anyway. We always knew he was a skiving piece of lowlife.'

I said, 'What about Mam?'

He looked beat. 'Look,' he said, 'she's the one who raised us, right? Leaving everything else aside, she's the one who did the work, put the grub on the table. Gypsy didn't cover himself with glory, did he? I don't even remember him being there. I can't remember a single teatime he sat down with us, can you? And Dilys couldn't have done any different. Fourteen years old. Poor bugger. Poor little bugger.'

We looked at the old snaps of Aunty Gwenny and Uncle Rhys standing outside their cottage at Nantglyn where we always went to recuperate from pleurisy or tonsillitis. Or to have a little baby on the QT.

I said, 'It does make you wonder, though. I mean, if nobody in Ninevah Street realised you were Dilys's . . . if Mam stuck a cushion under her pinny and nobody was any the wiser, and if Teilo Morris thought he could claim you as his own, and old Edkins too . . . what does that say about Mam?'

'It doesn't bear thinking about,' he said. 'It's too horrible to contemplate.'

We had a chuckle over that. Just about the last one we did have. It wasn't long after that we had to put him in nappies and get two nurses in, one for the day and one for the night. It was as though his body was shutting down, like Greely's factory the first two weeks in August, turning the machines off room by room, putting out the lights.

The worse he got the more we saw of Liquorish and the more we saw of Liquorish the oftener Craig Vertue's name cropped up. 'Cled,' he said one afternoon, 'I think I'll do it. Why not? Why carry a quarrel to the grave? Tell Candy I'll want the tousled look. And I think I'll wear the apricot terry.'

'You won't regret this,' Liquorish said. 'It's going to be a very wonderful moment.'

We had a sod's opera that morning getting him ready. It had been weeks since he'd had his dentures in and they didn't really fit any more. We propped him up with nice big pillows and put his fluffy robe on over a nightshirt, to bulk him out a bit. Then Dilys had to put his Pan Stik on.

'Blend it more,' he kept saying. 'I don't want Vertue seeing me with a tidemark. And then give me some blusher around the eyes. Just fluff it on and a little bit on the chin too. Tricks of the trade, see, Cled? Never meet your public without full battledress.'

Vertue was older than he looked on the television. Forty, I suppose, but one of those who never loses the boyish look. 'Believe it or not,' he said, 'there's always been a great affection between me and Sel. As his brother, you'll know what I mean. The toughest fights are with the ones you love.'

Liquorish said, 'And Sel loved a fight.'

'He did,' Vertue said. 'He was a worthy opponent.'

Hazel said, 'He's not dead yet.'

Vertue said men were dropping like flies. 'It's a holocaust,' he said.

But for a man who reckoned he was going to funerals every week, he seemed very shaken by the sight of Sel. And there was the smell, of course. He had fresh flowers in his room and scented candles, and the nurses sponged him down properly every time he was changed, but nothing really got rid of the smell.

'Sel, Sel, Sel!' Vertue said. 'My old sparring partner! It's been way too long.'

Sel smiled.

Vertue tried to move one of the dogs off the bed so he could perch there, but she wouldn't be moved. He pulled a chair up as close as he could without her baring her teeth at him. 'I want you to know', he said, 'I'm here out of love for you, old buddy. Unconditional love.'

Sel said, 'Watch your language, Craigie. My mother's in the house. Both of them are, actually.'

Vertue said, 'Still got that great sense of humour, Sel. That's good. That's so good. I can't tell you . . . These are terrible times. So many good men down. And ignorance everywhere you turn. AIDS is the new leprosy, Sel. Everybody's talking about it, everybody's scared of it.'

'That's right,' Liquorish said. 'It's very big.'

Vertue said, 'And you know what people think? They think, "Oh it's just something a bunch of fags have caught. They'll soon be gone and good riddance. As long as none of them leaves anything on *my* toilet seat. Uh-oh, better round them up, keep them behind barbed wire. Don't want them drinking out of *my* coffee cup." Well, now it's started. They're building camps.'

Sel said, 'Who is?'

'The US government,' he said, 'out by China Lake and Fort Irwin. It's the final solution all over again.'

'Get away,' Sel said. 'This is America.'

Vertue said, 'Yeah. Scared, straight America. I'm telling you, Sel. They're planning to round us up. I sleep with my passport under my pillow. If it comes to it, I'll make a run for Canada. Regroup. But it's not too late to stop it. Somebody like you can make a difference. Mr Starlight can put a face to AIDS. You're not just some poor anonymous queer. All those old ladies out there panicking, writing to their Congressmen, they love you. They won't want you rounded up.'

Sel said, 'Seems to me you're the one who's panicking, Craigie.'

Liquorish said, 'Can we do the pics now, before Sel gets too tired?'

They were terrible photos. Sel tried to wink for the camera, but it just looked as though his face had drooped and Vertue never did take a good picture.

Sel said, 'What's the caption going to say? One old shitter meets another?'

'Sel,' he said, 'let's not part like this. Nothing I did was meant personally. You're a nice guy. But there was a fight to be fought and we needed names like yours. Still do. It'll be a memorial to you.'

'I like that,' Liquorish said. 'A memorial.'

'On the other hand,' Vertue said, 'if you go straight from the closet to the grave, imagine what they're going to say. I hear "hypocrite". I hear "coward". I see a reputation in ruins.'

'Craigie,' Sel said, 'Mr Starlight's going to have to ask you to leave.'

Vertue looked at me. 'What can you do?' he said. 'I tried. What a stupid waste.'

I said, 'Well, we have got an elderly mother.'

'Yeah?' he said. 'And what does she think he's got? Food poisoning?'

THIRTY-EIGHT

Vertue was his last visitor, except for family. Ricky came most days, except when he had to go to Reno for a Buffalo Wing Eat-Off, and Betsan came twice a week to give Hazel and Pearl a break. Dilys said she didn't need one.

Sel suddenly decided he wanted the Christmas decorations put up, even though it was September. He loved Christmas. Normally he had a Black Forest pine in every room and a neon shooting star that moved along a gantry above the garden, a bit nearer the main house every night, until Christmas Eve. But we just did his room. He wasn't going anywhere any more. Randolph put up a nine-foot tree and ran the snow machine to make a tableau for the frosted deer, and Hazel and Pearl hung the decorations: ice garlands made out of plexiglass and little resin cherubs in red lamé robes.

I said, 'How's that?'

'Beautiful,' he said. 'And now there's one last thing.'

He wanted a priest.

Hazel said, 'What kind does he want?

I said, 'The kind that has holy water.'

Mam took straight to her bed. She said her sciatica was paining her.

Hazel said, 'Just go to any Catholic church.'

I said, 'Where? I don't know what to say.' I'd never talked to a priest in my life.

Dilys said, 'Go on, Cled, there's a good lad. Do it for me. Just tell them it's for somebody who's very ill. And I think you're supposed to curtsy. And kiss his ring.'

I said, 'If you know so much about it, why don't you go?'

Hazel said, '*I'll* go.'

And she was back within the hour with Father Victor from the Guardian Angel Cathedral. 'See?' she said. 'That's how easy it is. And I didn't have to kiss any rings.'

He was very young, for a priest. Very modern. Jeans and a crewcut and a little black handbag. He was with Sel for an hour, just the two of them, and I couldn't hear a word of what was said, even with my ear up against the door. Then he came out.

I said, 'All finished?'

'Just beginning,' he said. 'Any chance of a soda? Do you know if your brother was baptised?'

Dilys said not.

I said, 'He did go to Sunday school for a while.'

'No,' she said. 'That was Band of Hope. And he only went until they had their summer outing to Weston.'

He said, 'Could you ask his mother?'

Dilys said, 'He wasn't christened, Cled.'

I said, 'I'll ask her anyway. You know what she's like.'

Mam was hiding in her room, playing on her one-armed bandit and avoiding contact with Rome.

I said, 'Can I come in?'

'Has he gone yet?' she shouted.

I said, 'No. I need to ask you something.'

'Ask me from out there,' she said. 'I'm not decent.'

So I had to stand, shouting through a closed door. 'Was Sel ever christened?'

'No. There was a slump on.'

'Would you like to see him christened?'

'Can't hear you,' she said. 'Tell me later. I'm asleep.'

Father Victor said Sel had to be baptised first, and then everything else would follow on: Holy Communion, Extreme Unction, Eternal Peace. He said, 'Normally he'd have a sponsor. Is there someone you can think of? A member of the Catholic Church? A close friend?'

We couldn't think of anybody. Pearl and Randolph were Baptists, Brett was a Lutheran atheist and anyway he was gone, and the agency nurse said she worshipped Mother Earth. I tried Thelma.

'Well, I'm Jewish,' she said, 'but let me think for five minutes. Do I have five minutes? Is he dying?'

You wouldn't have thought so. He was sitting up in bed giving his orders. He wanted ivory candles and white flowers and his purple kaftan. He wanted all the dogs to be present.

Dilys said, 'If we can't find anybody, does that mean he can't be done?'

But Father Victor said in an emergency he'd go ahead anyway. He said Sel was as ready as any man he'd ever seen.

Then Thelma called back. 'I knew I'd think of somebody,' she said. 'Lupe. She's on her way.'

Mam wouldn't be coaxed out of her room, but the rest of us were all there. Pearl held a candle and Dilys held the bowl of water, and Lupe Leon drove straight over in her tracksuit, hair still wet, and stood as his godmother. He was baptised Gregory. Father Victor had suggested it. He said Saint Gregory was very popular among singers, plus he'd suffered from tummy troubles during his life on earth, so it was doubly suitable. Also, of course, Sel always loved Gregory Peck.

He seemed very happy and serene afterwards, holding on to the crucifix the padre had given him. It did make you wonder. Dilys asked for a blessing and she got a brochure too, about going the whole hog and becoming a Catholic, although she hasn't followed it up so far.

Pearl put on cold meat loaf and hearts of palm salad afterwards, 'I don't have a thing in,' she said. 'If a person was given a day's notice she wouldn't have to send company away starving.'

But she put some of her brown sugar shortbread in the oven. Father Victor didn't go hungry. It was getting dark by the time he made a move.

'What a wonderful occasion,' he said. 'Such grace. I hope you felt it too.'

I walked him through the garden to the back gate and as we came out on to Rancho Drive there was a bright white flash, then two more. 'Ah!' he said. 'The gentlemen of the press.'

The death watch had started.

Hallerton Liquorish moved into the Continental Hotel and issued a bulletin every day: 'Gravely ill with pneumonia. Mr Starlight's condition continues to worsen.' Craig Vertue wrote in the *LA Times* that he had visited the bedside of Sel Starlight, but had failed to persuade him to go public with what everyone knew to be the cause of his illness. Bambi Allen's office asked us to keep her apprised, and more than fifty Mr Starlight regional fan club presidents took turns keeping the vigil, including Vera Muddimer-as-was, who came all the way from Kingstanding. 'The pleasure he's given all of us over the years,' she said, 'it's the very least I can do.' She sat with him for five minutes, but Sel didn't really know who she was. He wasn't all there, towards the end, but he gave her a wink and a smile. We had to keep his curtains closed all that last week in case anybody slipped over the wall and tried to get a photo. The cars were bumper to bumper in the street, some with well-wishers, some with the vultures.

I said, 'I feel sorry for the neighbours.'

Thelma said, 'Don't think about it. It's the neighbours who should feel sorry for Sel, not even allowed to die with a bit of sunshine on his face.'

But it was silence he couldn't stand. If the telly was turned off he'd grow very agitated. His favourite was an old *Mr Starlight Christmas Special* so we just kept playing it, over and over. Young Sel, with his curls and his dimples, in a green velvet Beau Brummell coat and a white shirt with a ruff at the neck, singing 'Home for the Holidays' to Jack Benny and Zsa Zsa Gabor. Sometimes his lips would move, as if he was trying to sing along.

Hazel said, 'You'll have to talk to your mam, Cled. Her head has to come out of the sand before he goes.'

Mam had stopped going to the Tumbleweed. That was the only way you'd have guessed anything was wrong.

I said, 'She won't listen.'

Hazel said, 'Well, say something anyway. Poor Annie. I feel sorry for her, now it's come to it.'

I persuaded Mam to take a turn round the garden with me. She was pretty sturdy, for ninety. She only relied on her stick if she saw a dog in her path and the dogs were all indoors with Sel. They wouldn't leave his side, except for calls of nature. I said, 'There doesn't seem to be anything else they can do for Sel. His chest's worse this morning.'

'Yes,' she said.

I said, 'Dr Rosen says he's slipping away.'

'Yes,' she said. 'I know. I'm ready.' She was very calm.

I said, 'At least he's peaceful.'

'Yes,' she said.

I said, 'It'd be nice if we could all get along with each other now. For Sel. No more quarrelling.'

She didn't say anything.

I said, 'I don't think it did any harm, Dilys telling him where he came from, do you? I think it was the right thing.'

She said, 'I've always done the right thing by my children, Cledwyn. I can't answer for anybody else.'

I said, 'Father Victor's going to come back. You know? For the end. He's very nice, really.'

Silence again.

I said, 'Mam, you do realise what kind of funeral it's going to be? Sel's decided and we can't go against his wishes.'

'No,' she said. 'Well, it doesn't matter. I shan't be there.'

And she wasn't. Pearl went to clear her dinner tray and found her having some kind of seizure. It was the second one that finished her off. The ambulance was chased all the way to the Sunrise Emergency Center, reporters thinking it was Sel, thinking they were in with the chance of a photo, but Mam never knew anything about that. They said she hadn't suffered.

'No,' Dilys said. She was dry-eyed. 'Mam never suffered.'

And when we got back to Desert Star we had other things to think about. The press were back, annoyed about the goose chase they'd been on and Hallerton Liquorish had paid a call. He'd wangled his way past the night nurse and got himself a dog bite on his ankle and Sel's signature on a new will. It must have been a very shaky signature.

I said to Hazel, 'Where were you?'

'Running up and down with a stepladder and a mop handle,' she said. 'Stopping photographers poking their cameras over the garden wall.'

I said, 'Where was Pearl?'

'Training a hosepipe on the ones I missed,' she said. 'Never mind. That signature won't be worth a light. You all right, Dilys? You look all in.'

Dilys said, 'I'm all right. I just wish she'd gone sooner. Given me more time with him.'

Hazel said, 'You had your way in the end, that's the main thing. You stood up to her and had the final word.'

I said, 'It was as if she knew. That last walk I took with her round the garden? It was as if she knew her time had come.'

Hazel said, 'She was ninety. She hardly needed a crystal ball.'

I said, 'Well, she was a remarkable woman, you must admit.'

'Here we go,' she said. 'Rewriting history. She was horrible, Cled. She was a poisonous old meddler. Look how she treated Dilys. Think of the names she called me and I never did anything to cross her, not till the end.'

I said, 'She was just an old lady.'

Hazel said, 'She wasn't "just" anything. She was very, very nasty. All that sentimentality over Sel and over that child molester she called a husband, and yet she treated you like dirt. So don't get misty-eyed around me, Cled. I'm glad she's gone. And I'll be even happier when they've put a good heavy stone on top of her.'

Pearl stripped the bed in Mam's room. She brought a waste-paper basket to show us, full of ashes and photos half burned. She said,

'She been burning her effects. She musta heard death's chariot coming for her.'

Dilys said, 'Leave everything, Pearl. Rooms can be cleared any time. Sel's the one who matters now.'

His eyes were open, but he was very pale. 'Brett?' he kept asking. 'Turn the sound up on the telly, baby,' he said. But it was turned up.

He lasted two more days and the agency said they'd have to send a new nurse. The one we'd got used to had already booked her holidays. 'I hate to leave him,' she said. 'He's been so sweet. But I'm going to my sister's wedding.'

We could have done without that upheaval. The old one did as she was told regarding his wig, but the new girl argued about it every inch of the way. She said, 'I'm here to make him comfortable and he isn't comfortable sweating under a thing like that.'

Hazel said to her, 'If you knew him, you'd know he's never comfortable without it.'

'Well,' she said. 'It's not normal procedure. What's the big deal anyway? Was he somebody?'

If she'd followed instructions that last picture of him would never have been taken.

Hazel was convinced money had changed hands.

Father Victor came about an hour before he died. 'May the Lord who frees you from sin, save you and raise you,' he said.

Sel was trying to sit up. His chest was bad. Dr Rosen had come but we hadn't alerted Liquorish. He was in the habit of just turning up anyway.

Sel was still calling for Brett, right up to the last. Then he asked for Mam. We hadn't told him. There didn't seem any point.

Dilys said, 'I'm here, our kid.'

It seemed to pacify him. 'Lovely,' he said. 'It's all been so lovely.' And then it was all over.

Dr Rosen said, 'The death certificate. You know what I have to put on it? I'm obliged, by law.'

Hazel said, 'It hardly matters, really, does it? He's dead. His mam's dead. They can all come crawling out of the woodwork now.'

286

And when I went out with Randolph to let the hearse pull inside the gates, there was a helicopter circling overhead, and Liquorish was in the pool with a pair of total strangers, photographers from *Zoom!*.

THIRTY-NINE

'What a tragedy,' Craig Vertue said on *Late Night Live*. 'Sel Starlight could have become an icon of gay pride, but he clung to hypocrisy. Well, dead men have no secrets. What must all those fans of his be thinking now?'

The national president of the Official Mr Starlight Fan Club soon told him. 'He was every mother's ideal son,' she said. 'Every sister's favourite brother, every girl's perfect date. We don't need an autopsy to know he had a kind heart. We don't need any doctor's report to know he infected the world with joy. Now we pray that he's allowed to rest in peace.'

'One of the twentieth century's unsolved mysteries,' the *Daily News* wrote. 'How did Mr Starlight conquer America? How did a British boy, a closet queen with a mediocre voice and a gruesome family entourage, come to be worth an estimated ten million dollars?'

'Mega-weird,' celebrity party-goer Bliss Bellaire was quoted as saying. 'And not quite the perfect guy everyone thought. No one knew Sel the way I did and I'll be revealing all in my forthcoming memoirs.'

'BATTLING BRETT', the *Nevada News* headline said. 'Former Caesar's Palace centurion Brett Maples has announced he intends to contest the will of his long-time companion, Sel "Mr Starlight" Boff. A document signed by the controversial showman just before his AIDS-related death allegedly gave control of the five-million-dollar estate to Starlight's agent Hallerton Liquorish.'

The embalming company said they guaranteed complete security but after the photo of him without his hair started doing the rounds we hired Pinkerton guards, just to be sure. It took five vans to carry all the flowers and traffic was nearly at a standstill along the Strip. He was late for his own funeral.

The Flamingo had put his name up one last time and as his car drove past, they dimmed the lights. Dilys was holding up pretty well, till that happened. We buried him alongside Mam at the Oasis Memorial Park, in his sun-kissed wig and a replica of his favourite suit; a white three-piece covered in gold rocaille beads and Swarovski crystals.

'Sad day,' Liquorish said.

Hazel said, 'It'll be a sadder day for you when you try to get that forgery proved.'

'He signed it, fair and square,' he said. 'Sel's wishes. I'm only carrying out Sel's dying wishes. People often change their mind at the last minute. I believe he realised it'd be an unfair burden on his bereaved family. Better to hand everything over to someone who knew his affairs inside out.'

I said, 'I'd just like to know about the Old Bull and Bush. Half of that's mine.'

'I'll be in touch,' he said. 'Great ceremony, by the way. Beautifully staged.'

Hazel said, 'You're not to talk to him, Cled. You're not to tell him any of your business.'

I said, 'I just thought I should bring it up. We'll have to stay on the right side of him, in case this will stands up. We could be up the Swanee.'

'Liquorish is the one who's up the Swanee,' she said. 'There's nothing left.'

I said, 'What do you mean, nothing?'

'All given away,' she said. 'Ocean Star to Dilys. The Double Down to Pearl. The Backdoor to Ricky. The Old Bull to you.'

I said, 'What about the Chickering grand?'

'Mine,' she said.

I said, 'Why you? You don't even play.'

'Because Desert Star's mine,' she said. 'And everything in it.'

I said, 'Are you sure? Have you seen it written down?'

'Signed and sealed,' she said. 'Know why?'

I said, 'Because he came to his senses. Realised how much he owed to me.'

'No, Cled,' she said. 'Because it's going to be his memorial. To his gracious lifestyle. It's going to be a display of all his beautiful costumes. The suit that gave him visions. His light bulb cape. His lapis shirt studs.'

That were never paid for.

I said, 'What, people tramping through? And where are we supposed to live?'

'Where we are now,' she said. 'So I'll be on hand. To keep everything perfect. To make sure people remember him the way he really was.'

I said to Dilys, 'Did you know you were getting the place in Malibu?'

'Yes,' she said.

I said, 'Did Pearl know what she was getting?'

'Yes,' she said.

I said, 'So how come nobody told me?'

Hazel said, 'Because Sel didn't like people knowing his business. And you've got a mouth like the Mersey Tunnel.'

We didn't hear from Liquorish for a few days. Then he phoned.

I said, 'I'm not talking about wills. There's nothing to say.'

Hazel had written it on a pad for me next to the telephone, what I had to tell him.

'No, Cled, no,' he said. 'That's all in the hands of lawyers. But I wanted you to know we have breaking news. We have ourselves a love child. A twenty-six-year-old catering operative from Wilmington, Delaware. The mother's dead, of course, and the girl'll disappear when it comes to taking a blood test, but I predict she'll be the first of many. And stuff like this is gonna keep that Starlight name shining for years to come. Maybe I should get her on the *Craig Vertue Show*. Stay well, Cled. Don't you just love this shit?'

290

After the ball is over
After the break of morn
After the dancers' leaving
After the stars are gone
Many a heart is aching, if you could read them all
Many the hopes that vanished
After the ball.

HARRIS